# Houses On The Borderland

# Houses On The Borderland

### Edited by
### David A. Sutton

British Fantasy Society

British Fantasy Society

First published in Great Britain by *The British Fantasy Society*
2008
5 Greenbank, Barnt Green
Birmingham B45 8DH
www.britishfantasysociety.org

First Edition
**ISBN 095386818-4**

# Contents

# Introduction
## By
## David A. Sutton

William Hope Hodgson's *The House on the Borderland* provided the inspiration for me to edit this anthology of novellas. The book made a lasting impression on me when I first read it in the sixties and my mind was opening to the wonders of genre writing. H. P. Lovecraft summarised one plot strand in his essay 'Supernatural Horror in Literature': "Perhaps the greatest of all of Mr. Hodgson's works — tells of a lonely and evilly regarded house in Ireland which forms the focus for hideous otherworld forces and sustains a siege of blasphemous hybrid anomalies from a hidden abyss below". But as the story progresses Hodgson surprises the reader by taking his narrator on a cosmic journey to the end of the universe — a literary LSD trip that drips with melancholy atmosphere.

It is a marvellous tale of a house in a unique supernatural location. Others that still resonate include M. P. Shiel's *The House of Sounds*. The author's lavish prose and the evocative plot, set in a sepulchral brass and copper mansion chained over a thunderous cataract on a small island off Shetland, still rumbles its aura of strangeness and phantasmagoria down the years. And of course, that masterpiece of the modern ghost story, *The*

*Haunting of Hill House*. Shirley Jackson's terrifying mansion is the pinnacle of houses on the borderland. In her introduction to the Raven edition of *The Masterpieces of Shirley Jackson*, Donna Tartt tells us that Hill House exists, in the town of North Bennington, Vermont, where Jackson lived. Tartt likens the location to the Merry Maidens stone circle in Cornwall, a power node, "where unknown energies of natural and supernatural origin have for some reason converged". Paul Devereux (*Earth Lights Revelation*; *Spirit Roads*) talks about these places as sources for tectonic plasma and earthquake energies — spooklights and ball lightning the physical manifestation of subtle humours that affect the minds of the sensitive. Tartt continues, "And there was a strange — *pressure* is the only word for it — in the atmosphere which even the Indians native to the place were said to have recognised and feared". Whatever the reasons for the hauntings, these houses, as in Nigel Kneale's Taskerlands House in *The Stone Tape*, seem to have recorded malevolence and the otherworldly in their damp and ancient stones.

In selecting the stories for this volume, I have chosen a wide variety of buildings on the borderland. Another Jackson, a minor character in this case, sets the scene in David A. Riley's *The Worst of All Possible Places*. He is an unwilling public servant, but quite blunt, if unsuccessful, in trying to put off his prospective tenant. The Overlook Hotel meets sixties council tower block in this interface between our world and another, or between the disgraced teacher and his love affair with spirits of another kind. Furthest from such grimy architecture is *The Listeners* by Samantha Lee. Inspired by the de la Mare poem, the author weaves a beguiling fantasy story. Houses in the midst of the wildwood such as this exist in that subliminal world just beyond our childhood memories, or in fairy tales and their larger-than-life characters.

A School House could be a euphemism for another kind of institution. In *The School House*, Simon Bestwick's troubled asylum orderly meets one of his contemporaries from his school days. His subsequent journey into the mind of the new patient, and into his own suppressed schoolboy memories, is both nightmarish and painfully horrific. In *The House on the Western Border*, Gary Fry takes us west to the isle of Anglesey and an idyllic new start for a divorced mother and her daughter in an old house by the sea. Unfortunately past evil and the contemporary mores of our consumer society collide in this creepy tale of modern avarice and ancient greed.

Allen Ashley's slant on borderland houses, in *Today We Were Astronauts*, is an isolated lighthouse in Scotland. Set in the near future during the progression of an apocalyptic plague, this moving story explores its characters in extremis while the disused lighthouse entwines its own eerie spell around them. A hut in the snowbound steppe is the setting for Paul Finch's *The Retreat*. Taking place during the retreat from Stalingrad, the story centres around a group of frostbitten German soldiers trying to survive attacks from crack Russian troops and the weird, very weird log cabin where they take refuge.

A seaside home, a school, a fantasy castle, a lighthouse, a wooden hut, a run-down tower block — all are tainted by an abnormal atmosphere. Be wary of what's beyond the entranceway. For we have six dwellings eager to molest the human spirit at its lowest ebb, its most vulnerable time. *Welcome...* please step across the threshold...

David A. Sutton
Birmingham, July 2007

# Today We Were Astronauts

## By
## Allen Ashley

**ALLEN ASHLEY** is the author of the critically acclaimed novel *The Planet Suite* (TTA Press, 1997); two short story collections *Somnambulists* (Elastic Press, 2004) and *Urban Fantastic* (Crowswing, 2006); plus one book of non-fiction *The Days of the Dodo* (Dodo London Press, 2006). As editor of *The Elastic Book Of Numbers* (Elastic Press, 2005) he received the 2006 British Fantasy Society award for 'Best Anthology'. Current projects include editing another anthology *Subtle Edens* (for Elastic Press) and a collection of collaborations with Andrew Hook entitled *Slow Motion Wars* (due late 2007 from Screaming Dreams Press). He lives in London and is a regular fixture at BFS functions. "This story," Allen says, "is a conflation of a very old idea and a much more recent musing. I hope 'Astronauts' qualifies as being in that venerable British SF tradition of catastrophe stories, cosy or otherwise. Don't tell anyone, but I haven't always been the hugest fan of haunted houses... But a lighthouse on a windswept cliff? Now you're talking!"

ALMOST THE FIRST thing Harold did when the wind eased a little was to dispose of Evans. This had to be undertaken at night when David was asleep, or at least safely locked away from all ills inside his bedroom on the first floor of Macaverty Head lighthouse. Sprightly and focused throughout the horrendous journey here, Evans had succumbed suddenly to the effects of the Moon Plague. Harold had seen so much death these past months and had been unable to shield his young son from the horror that had gripped the country. Even so, small mercies and all that…

Evans had driven the armoured truck, second in line behind Harold's emergency supply lorry. His shotgun was occasionally visible poking out of a concealed slot in the darkened, strengthened windows. He was their eyes in the rear, dealing with any lingering resistance to their progress, their mission to maintain and preserve an outpost of the old order. Harold was sure David could hear the gunfire above the groan of the engine but still played a straight bat to all enquiries.

"Daddy, what happened to those men in the road?"

"We had to leave them behind, son. They, uh, someone will be along to help them in a day or two."

A division of labour: Harold, you keep on driving with your kid and your slowly sickening wife beside you, just make sure you get us there. Evans — no, Leslie, let's humanise him with a Christian name — you do the dirty work out of sight except in the grubby wing mirror.

And now after two frantic days setting up and securing this research outpost, Jennifer also was fading fast in the cloying, warm fug of her quarters, with a drip in her arm helping to temporarily preserve her existence, though not much of a life. And Leslie Evans had so abruptly slumped from the constitution of an ox to the condition of a carcass.

Dragged over the scrubby grass of the headland to the very edge of the recently rain-lashed cliff.

"I'm sorry I can't offer you a decent burial, my friend," Harold muttered over his exhaustion. "The sea will have to do."

With a final effort, Harold manoeuvred his colleague's body

so that the head and shoulders were dangling over a precipice. Mindful of his own safety, he pushed the corpse's legs through an arc that caused the late Leslie Evans to teeter and then plunge into tonight's wild water. Harold muttered a quick prayer half-remembered from some TV drama or other.

The Moon Plague had reportedly killed everybody within a six to ten mile radius. It was just exhaustion and fancy that had Harold imagining he could hear a choir carried on the wind as he consigned his dead companion's bones and flesh to their wild, grey grave.

*

The Mind Blocks were chattering, going over the same old ground. What was their purpose? They never seemed to have anything new to offer.

And I'm charged with maintaining the wittering existence of these arrogant brain patterns, Harold mused. I'm just the night watchman or the zookeeper.

— Suppose we caused a disaster that could have been averted. Humankind has become so powerful that, with a little foresight and willingness, we can prevent disasters almost as easily as we can cause them. Except we didn't really know what sort of disaster we were causing.

— Suppose they called a war and nobody came? My late father told me that everyone used to wear that slogan on a badge or a T-shirt when he was a young man. These days we have several ways of running wars which don't involve calling a multitude of young men to come and sacrifice their lives for the greater glory. We can arrange for all the killing to be done by remote.

— Suppose you thought you were harming the world in one way and were prepared for that but the damage you and your notional enemy actually caused caught you off guard and somewhat under-prepared.

— Notional enemy? The fighting, the aggression, the

brainwashing, the exertion of control, the land grabs — we're all much of a muchness in this.

— And yet, and yet… there was still time to make some plans, to preserve some of the what and the who of our culture and leave a cadre of brave fools to stand guard.

— The fallacy of this is that a disaster, any disaster, punctures the prevailing order and the wound never properly heals. Yes we can all start again but why would those who'd stayed outside, away from the bunkers and the sealed laboratories, allow the useless leaders to waltz back in and say thanks guys, we'll take over again now? The little Indian kid sewing clothes for a pound a week; the tea or coffee picker being ripped off by the multi-national companies; the illegal immigrant gypsy whore selling her body for a takeaway meal and a flop in a broom cupboard — all the wretched and deprived are going to have some radical ideas about the new world order, the *next* world order even. Behead the king! Guillotine the aristocrats! Vive le revolution! Bring on the next dictatorship!

\*

David had broken his thoughtful silence to yell, "It's a lighthouse! It's really a lighthouse!"

The adults smiled at his excitement. Macaverty Head didn't quite match up to the red and white barber pole storybook vision; rather its grey painted stone solidity stood as a reassuring standard against an uncertain sky. The outbuildings were slightly battered but fixable, useable.

Once the generator had coughed into life, they had begun an exploration of the interior with its mix of spiral staircases, access ladders and general paucity of windows for such a lofty building. David had rediscovered his childish joie de vivre at the prospect of staying in such a romantic habitation. Harold admired the boy's ability to compartmentalise, forget… maybe. Jennifer helped with what little she could manage; Evans attended to the electrics, the unloading and the transferring of the clone copies of the Mind Blocks into the main drive. Let these saved brain patterns recommence their pondering upon the purpose of life, the nature of the damaged universe and possible courses to combat and overcome — perhaps even cure — the dreadful disease.

After nightfall, with everyone safely quartered and as comfortable as could be expected, Harold had risen and made his way to the outdoor platform at the very top of the tower, braving the rising breeze next to the dormant, unlit giant bulb that had once warned sailors and attracted suicidal lovers. It was natural to fancy that one could feel a few ghosts in a location that had previously housed a laird's folly and a long since de-consecrated monastery. Macaverty Head had always meant something and now it was to be an outpost of knowledge, research, preservation — linked to the remains of the civilised world through the fraying strands of the World Wide Web.

The place held a dual history of being at once a beacon of hope but also a flame to the moths. Its bright beam had warned ships away from the rocks but the modern shallow hulled vessels plied their trade elsewhere these past decades. The light had called to the community in times of stress. The smugglers had used the old tower as a landmark and braved the stones and squalls and sharp precipices in order to unload their counterfeit and their booty. Harold had heard a tall fable that at one time there had been a lynching near here and the local priest or priestess was hung from the light itself. He or she had been the leader of an outlawed Moon cult.

The Moon and the lighthouse — both calling, both misused or disused, both attractive and attracting. Both leading to death.

\*

It's too obviously tempting to see a lighthouse as a phallic symbol: Man's firm, upright seeding of the headland. So, maybe as much as it's a beacon of hope spreading its illumination all around with a metronomic pass, it's also a brave attempt to use a stone

15

finger to point the way to heaven. An *optical* Tower of Babel.

Save our souls from shipwrecks. Warn us of the killing rocks. Become the focal point of our small, disparate community. Serve as a sanctuary.

Time moves on and buildings change their function or fall into disuse. Memories fade but legends linger. The winds batter this tall monument to ingenious construction and the will to ensure survival.

But we do not place our lighthouses in busy streets, shrouded by coal-fired power stations, shops and high rise blocks. Before the building comes the need. Not everywhere has the requirement; not everywhere has the resonance. Upon this bleak cliff, there was previously a cairn and prior to that a sacred place marked by even the earliest mapmakers.

Preceding humankind and its warped spirituality, the tectonic plates drifted and the mountains rose and fell. In a climate even warmer than our own, the plesiosaurs gambolled in the waves and cared not for the rocky outcrops and granite hazards hanging above their fishing grounds.

Yet this was always an area... a locale... a power node.

*

Harold knew this was just the latest in a series of "manly" talks with his son, none of which he'd either expected or desired. But the world and its thin patterning of human civilisation had changed so much since the onset of the Moon Plague that the "Be strong, be brave, be a survivor" mantra had become a nightly event.

He had cooked the last of their fresh food in pans over a couple of Primus stoves and set a cartoon with zany antics and uplifting music playing on a computer in the background.

"Daddy, has Mr Evans left us?"

"Yes, he... had some other business to attend to, David."

"He was nice. He was going to help me with my numbers and stuff... like Mummy used to."

"Yes, it's going to be hard with just the three of us, especially while Mummy has to sleep. Listen, David, you can play in the rooms I said but you really mustn't touch anything if I say you mustn't. Deal?"

"Mummy's going to die, isn't she?"

Dissolving now, needing comforting arms, calm words, reassurance and promises... white lies...

"She's going to be asleep for a little while. We must be gentle with her. I'm still hoping a doctor will reach us soon. She'll hold on till then."

As he wiped the boy's tears with a disposable tissue, Harold felt overwhelmed again by the changed responsibilities. Just a couple of years ago he'd stood at the apparent apex of his life: his son David cute and wide-eyed in his fresh school uniform; his wife Jennifer healthy and beautiful, about to resume her career in pharmaceuticals; his own promotion and raised security clearance bringing greater remuneration and the opportunity of seeking a bigger house with an enclosed back garden and lockable garage and other middle class aspirations for the nuclear family...

David pulled away from him suddenly.

"Daddy, I can hear the angels! They're coming for Mummy!"

He muted the PC, strained his ears in search of the heavenly chorus, began flicking switches and swooshing the infrared mouse.

"David, stop emoting! It's just some radio interference. Some show to cheer people up. Look, if you're worried, go and sit with Mummy for a while. But be very still and quiet."

The boy scampered away from his half-finished meal to his more than half-departed parent. Harold cleared up in a desultory fashion. He'd heard the ghostly choir too.

*

Harold's Notebook:
Macaverty Head is new to both David and my delicate, dying darling Jennifer.

17

The place was once a lighthouse — a single glance from a hundred yards away would confirm that — but it hasn't been active in that capacity for many, many years. Along with its sturdy outbuildings, it is the last house standing on this remote headland. There has been some subsidence over the decades but the tides have turned the other way now. I holidayed here when I was a kid. Something about character building in the bleak North wind; or else, we couldn't afford the Algarve or even Majorca that year.

I remember my father going the half a mile or more inland to the pub, which is now just rubble; and mother buying overpriced packets of tea bags and slightly stale cakes from the general store attached to the post office. All gone now in the climactic disruption. The previous occupant – Nic, Vic, the handwriting is barely legible – left a florid notice saying that for a time you could watch the angry waves spit and snarl salty saliva over the debris. Now the rise and fall of the tide is so uncertain.

So the sea's a bit troubled? Big deal! He won't have seen the real effects of the Moon Plague, the pandemic wiping out swathes of humans and higher mammals across the globe. The Judgement from Space punishing us for two million years of wrongs.

My wife is so much sicker than me, even with the occasional good spells. Why the hell are we entrusted with this preservation job? We've all of us come here to die.

\*

The latest emails had spoken of Congealed Clouds bringing a new strain of the Moon Plague to rain down its abhorrence upon the last people. If Harold, David and Jennifer didn't venture out for a few days... weeks... years, would they be safe?

But two of them were outside playing what the boy called "Pine Ears", although the father was actually checking the security of this haven. Automated in the nineteen fifties, decommissioned in the nineties, declared an off-limits government installation at the century's turn, Macaverty Head had seen a brief spell of hectic activity – fence erection, CCTV placement, stockpiles of fuel and food – about a year before the global disaster. Had someone high up known what was going to happen and already made contingency plans to preserve Western culture at this and other far outposts?

From ground level, the lighthouse was like an accusing finger pointing at the sky declaring, "That's where all your trouble comes from." Visible for miles distant, it drew locals and visitors alike with the power of a magnet amidst iron filings. A rogue German aeroplane had fired at its stone façade during the Second World War. Macaverty Head was not to be so chipped and dissed: the pilot crashed into a thicket below the headland and was left hanging from his harness by the friendly farmhands.

This once luminous minaret called all manner of people, like a Statue of Liberty without the stylised torch or the hopeful aura.

It stood on the site of a shocking massacre hundreds of years ago. Less a beacon and more a memorial marker. You could put the place in the hands of the Coastguard and Fisheries, the Ministry of Defence or the Coalition for Continued Survival… no matter. Macaverty Head the building, Macaverty Head the location had too much history, too much resonant and accumulated power to be overly affected by Man's squabbles.

Come inside and be protected from harm in this blunt instrument against the combined affray of meteorology and errant technology.

Enter at your own risk.

*

"Daddy, I want to go home."

"David, we can't go home, you know that."

"But I hate this place. It's cold and spooky."

"It's a lighthouse, Davie. Thick stone keeps the wind out. I think it's quite warm."

"There's ghosts and Jesus and stuff, Dad."

"What do you mean? Have you actually seen anything, heard anything?"

The young blue eyes were welling up, cheeks reddening. Harold realised he was being too hard on the boy. He spread his arms, welcomed the kid for a manly hug. He was surprised David could even remember home — by which he surely meant their old townhouse with its half lawn, half patio round the back where the sun sometimes shone. When the effects of the lunar damage and the subsequent Moon Plague were first suspected, Harold had been called into the initial safety of the government compound with the concession of being able to bring "spouse or equivalent and closest next of kin." As the unlucky "outsiders" died in their droves, the ruling cartel had made a policy shift to disperse resources and survival stations on the basis that, with more outposts, statistical chances of survival were much higher. He had volunteered for this lonely, crumb of hope mission for the simple reason that Jennifer had already contracted the disease even though she was a few days away from visible signs. Better to take their chances in the wilds of the North East Coast than be separated by the enforced segregation of quarantine laws.

"When I was a kid," Harold whispered, "we had a few difficult months when my father was out of work. We had to leave somewhere I really loved. I had a favourite apple tree. The apples were sour, what few the tree ever produced, but I had a rope and a swing and I could play pirates on sunny days. I never got over leaving. But I'd rather have you and Mummy. Shall we go and say hello to her? Very quietly."

"OK, Daddy. But can we play pirates later?"

*

Harold's Notebook:
I've set David the task of recording his day as a lasting record from a young and innocent perspective. If only I could apply such qualities to my own existence.

At school, despite my high grades in science, I'd always wanted to be a historian. From about the age of fourteen, I blagged my way onto local walks and river cruises, helping out with the commentary, the anecdotes and the provision of tea. The course was set. But I got side-tracked after a confusing series of university entrance interviews and found myself involved in what came to be known as the *Mind Block* programme. "We're going to tablet knowledge so that the great minds live on and keep creating even after the body dies," was the professor's summation. It sounded like some crazed cross between *Frankenstein* and Philip K. Dick but they were offering me a bursary that would keep even a drink-sodden student clear of debt. I was in… for good.

Technology was racing ahead and I became a minor player as brain patterns and thought processes were imprinted onto modified chips. Eventually we could transfer the whole consciousness, people's essences, their souls, if you like. Sitting here with their voices and random thoughts threatening a power surge from the generators at any moment, I can't quite decide whether their combined wisdom is truly at work to save and reclaim our great civilisation or if I'm simply in charge of a decaying, schizophrenic library of the electronic cerebellum.

Each memory module contains lives and speaks to me just the same way as, in ancient times, a god might have spoken from the bush or the pulpit; or a ghost from the very walls. Yesterday's superstition becomes tomorrow's science.

\*

Jennifer had rallied slightly and was awake briefly.

"It's just the final ray of sunshine before the slide into the dark," she whispered.

"Don't say that. You're strong. You're going to pull through."

"I'm not, Harold, and you know it. This is my chance to say a proper goodbye. Where's David?"

"Doing some lessons on the computer. Geography, I think."

"He won't need it. We've come to this haunted lighthouse to die, all three of us. Four of us, I mean. Where's Evans?"

"He… uh, he had to leave us."

She gripped his cold hand with all the strength she could muster. "We can't survive much longer. Soon it will be just you and David and the ghosts of shipwrecked sailors. God, what have we come to! We should do something romantic like make a suicide pact."

"Don't talk like that, darling. Whatever happens to either or both of us, we must do what we can to give Davie a chance. Now, is there anything you need?"

She managed a hollow laugh and for a moment he glimpsed again the goddess he'd first spoken to at the Graduate Careers conference more than a decade earlier. Green eyes, oval face framed by soft brown hair, warm and welcoming nature and altruistic heart. Now her eyes were all-washed-out white and she could hardly raise her hand —

"You've done a brilliant job with the IV drip, H. I can't get to the toilet. I need a bedpan and then... if you fix me up with a catheter, will you ever fancy me again?"

"I'll adore you in this life and throughout the next."

"You big soft teddy bear." Her lips brushed his forehead. They were dry like brittle leaves. "Let me see David," she whispered.

\*

David's diary:
Daddy wants me to keep this diary for something he calls "posterity". I don't no what it meant so I looked it up. Something about the future or your bottom. I think he means the future.

Daddy has to work. I no that. But I don't see him all day till tea time. Can't he have a day off or some ink?

And Mummy just lies their. I no she's ill but I wish she would talk or something. I don't think she's getting better even tho she's been their days. Daddy says the — hang on, look it up — journey made her tired. But she could be getting better now.

I'm cold. I'm hungry. Not starvers but bored with same old tin food and not even coke or tango. I'm bored. I try to do the sums and the reading off the computer and then go and play and pretend. Daddy dusent mind if I make a mess in the bedroom or the play room and thas cool. But I miss my firends, I mean friends.

I no he reads this. But as Johnny says, "Wos the worst that can happen?"

*

"O Lord, my shepherd,
   Protecteth me.
   Within thy bosom
   Thy warm, round stones,
   My hearth, my prison."

It was no spiritual he'd ever heard but seemed somehow pertinent to the persecution and siege. He could no longer pass it off as stray radio waves. The ghostly choir was louder every night. He could even discern whole lines of lyrics. The tune haunted him through the day: music to whistle while you work. Where would it all end? How much louder, how much more prevalent, how *present* would the voices become?

He re-programmed part of the brain tray to deal with the issue. How do you exorcise ghosts in the twenty-first century? How come there's still a necessity in these days of science and technology?

— Give them what they need to be at rest.

How am I supposed to know?

— Ward them off with spells, incantations or lengthy quotes from the Good Book.

They are the ones quoting the Bible!

— Break the bread of the holy sacrament, sprinkle it around the dwelling along with copious draughts of holy water.

We've barely got enough to drink; we're not even washing ourselves or our clothes. There's nothing holy about what little water we have left.

And sometimes, with the wind harmonising their heavenly hymn, he believed they were actually singing, "*Harold*, my shepherd."

*

David was having a major sulk, a succession of "why?" and "why not?" enquiries posed with the childish whine of a spoilt brat. When could he eat fresh food and bananas, when could he get attention rather than being on his own all day? He wanted to see his friends at school, he wanted to quit doing sums and reading, he wanted to jump on Mummy's bed. Christ, son, we all wanted those things! Harold was torn between the desire to be comforting and the need to maintain discipline and order. Survival was surely about self-control. Die tomorrow from indulgence today.

He locked David temporarily in the boat hut. There were some biscuits and water bottles in there and he could piss in a pot if he needed to, just stay out of my hair, I've got work to do that doesn't involve your tantrums.

The sky this morning was pale blue in all directions and Harold could appreciate the stark beauty of Macaverty Head and its surroundings. Early records had the place as a religious retreat until the community had been swept off the face of the Earth one desperate, stormy night. Today the sea still wasn't behaving itself but otherwise he was catapulted back to his own childhood memory of holidaying in the nearby camp site and taking invigorating walks up the slope to admire the view amidst the alternate encumbrances of sea-spray wind or sun-called midges. His parents had been the "outdoor types" until the Moon Plague did for them along with ninety-nine percent of the rest of humanity. How strange the way the past repeats and influences or interferes with the present.

So here he was back again on an ill thought through desperate mission that even Odysseus might find uninviting.

All was quiet back at the boat shed. Let David stew for a little longer, he had work to do. The greater good above personal indulgence. Always. Perhaps.

\*

Harold's Notebook:
It's a difficult balance to strike: I have to ensure David's safety and well being but I can't be with him every waking moment or else I'd

never get my tasks completed. And the world would… Well, part of me doesn't care too much about the world, what had it done for me and my offspring?

There are plenty of educational programs for him to complete, projects for him to research. Even at a similar, tender age, I had been very independent and self-motivated and my son has inherited that part of my character. From his mother — or maybe from Granddad, a moderately successful playwright and theatre director, the talent having skipped a generation — comes a lively interest in the internal life, a capacity for make-believe. He knows where he is allowed to go and what he is allowed to do; beyond that, the lighthouse and outbuildings are his mental playground. In the absence of other primary school age children, his only real option is to invent and pretend. Occasionally, I partake; mostly I leave him to it.

I should offer him more, guide him as only a father can. But we'd been through that intense male bonding business just to get here. We need to re-establish our own characters a little.

And one day, maybe very soon or at best only in the medium term, I will succumb to the after-effects of the Moon Plague and David will have to do what he can entirely on his own. Perhaps on his own not just on this bleak headland but within the whole area… the country… the world.

I've muted the response screens and I'm going to take a walk down to the locked stores, seek out a treat to take to the boy. I wonder what he's been studying or playing at this morning.

*

Every old building, every ancient human habitation has its ghostly presence and the Macaverty Head lighthouse is no different to the Tower of London or St John Ignatius' Abbey.

Ah, the lighthouse at Macaverty Head. A warning and guide through the rocks and rubble where a medieval village met its fate beneath the angry waves of the riled sea. That outcrop there is believed to be the remains of the church spire. The manor house lays scattered into wayward rubble. We lost a whole segment of cliff and half a dozen permanent habitations during that two-day storm. Lean-tos, encampments and their poverty stricken inhabitants, too, all gone, washed away, mourned, half-forgotten.

For a while there was only a blazing beacon here on the hilltop to warn away passing ships from the curse of Macaverty Head and its rock-strewn narrows. A campaign underpinned by a mixture of fiery sermons, misplaced guilt and local taxation raised the funds for a blinking cylinder to stand as both warning and memorial. Heady days of yore before the lighthouse was fully automated; then decommissioned. The whole area being declared off the beaten, wave tossed track for anything more important than a couple of local, semi-legal fishing boats.

Celebrate its surreptitious history: For a time, its very obviousness and cautioning aspect meant that it called to those somewhat outside the law. Lovers met on the perilous rocks beneath its gaze. Pray it's a dry night, Morag. Aye, with barely a breeze, Hamish, and we shall meet yonder where our parents can find us not.

Beneath its gaze, small-time smugglers unloaded their booty and counterfeit goods, daring Excise Men to negotiate the deadly waters in pursuit. Speculative maps of the best channels through the killing sea changed hands for good coinage in the local tavern.

There was many a slip 'twixt land and ship: Errant suitors who missed this and every remaining rendezvous with fair maid. Bringers of booty and treasure who misjudged the distances in the flickering floodlight and went down with their punctured craft.

It's not just the gulls and gannets who cry from beyond the almost bare granite face visible to the rain-lashed east. Listen carefully and you'll hear human cries of woe in the subtext: those who set off and never arrived, those who arrived on the outcrop but not in the hale and healthy condition necessary for continuance of life. Those who simply disappeared below the wrathful water. Their spirits haunt this building. Their memory lingers, however misty. They don't expect redemption or demand fearful attention; they simply remind visitors and residents that they are still there, though they would certainly have chosen not to be, never to be.

*

David's diary:
I know Daddy is busy with all his work and things. I'm trying to be a good boy and stay out of his way. He gives me stuff like school work and some of it's easy but some of it I need to ask him but I can't go and get him coz he needs to work.

He's told me I can sit with Mummy. He said he trusts me to be very good and quiet. I love Mummy so much but she's been ill for so many times and I sit with her and tell her stuff but she don't talk back and then I don't know what to tell her now. So it's quite quiet. Have I got them spellings right? My friend Johnny used to mix them up and teacher used to shake her head and make her brown hair go all floppy.

I miss Miss Humble and Johnny and Ashraf and Leroy and Mohammed and all my other friends. I often say that they are here and I talk to them and we play some games. Sometimes we just play that it's school and I do my lessons — the ones Daddy gave me, not Miss Humble's — and then it's playtime and I tell Ashraf he's on it or we stand around the climbing frame or play football with a tennis ball.

I can kick the ball against the wall and kick it back about a hundred times without missing. And it's hard with no friends there really. And in my big coat coz it's windy and a bit rainy.

And maybe Daddy will play with me tomorrow.

*

The alarms had been tripped. Harold set them to "Mute", swivelled the joystick, panning through the camera settings. The intruder had parked a 4 X 4 with blacked-out windows down by the five-bar gate cutting off the approach road. Perhaps spotting the camera activity, the driver stepped out of the vehicle and stood in full view. Harold nodded to himself, checked that David was safely engaged with his schoolwork, grabbed his rifle and set off to greet the visitor.

Up close, the man bore slight signs of the Moon Plague malaise. His naturally fair skin seemed a little too ghostly pale; standing up clearly tired him and he was already leaning wearily against his powerful car.

"Victor Trenchant," the newcomer stated, passing across his ID card for Harold to swipe with his pen scanner. "Vic, to my friends. Although they're… not here now."

"Why have you come?"

"I was here before. Didn't you see my notes?"

"You reclaiming possession?"

"Nah. Not yet, anyhow. Just a courtesy call. The government — or what's left of it — has to be seen to be doing something."

Harold frowned, answered, "I've posted everything I've got online, emailed all the answers the brains offer."

"People — survivors and hangers-on — don't trust technology much these days."

"Science is the only thing that will bring us the answer."

Victor shrugged then replied, "Knowledge is a double-edged sword. Or a bipartite apple."

"Sure, or Eve gave Adam the wrong fruit from the fig tree. You'd better come in. I've got tinned meat, beans, soup… Have you got any fresh food with you?"

"I can't help you there, mate. No one's got the long-term commitment to plant and nurture anything anymore. We'll soon be out of stores and oil across the globe. It'll be like a Biblical famine. Are you on your own here, Harold?"

"No… my wife's quite unwell but there's my son, David. He's eight years old. He seems to be immune at the moment."

"Lucky boy! You must be really proud."

"I am. But I'm shit scared, too, that one day soon he'll have to get by on his own. Anyhow, let's get up to the house. David could do with the stimulation of another person to talk to. If he doesn't get too shy."

*

"There's no milk, of course," Harold stated.

"That's OK, I've always taken my coffee black," Victor replied.

Harold blew on his heated drink. "It's so strange to be back here, what, twenty five years or so since I visited as a kid. I remember my grandfather telling me ghost stories about this place."

"Sure, the siege of the heretics of Christ. Biggest crime story ever in these parts. Guaranteed to spook the tourists. If only ancient tragedies were all we had on our plate."

Harold placed his mug down on the sideboard, asked, "What did you see on the way, Vic?"

"Dead people. Loose sheep. Vehicles all over the place. Not a single living soul."

"We're never going to get it back, are we?" Victor didn't reply. Harold continued, "Do you want some dried fruit or nuts? Vitamin tablets?"

Victor strode over to the porthole shaped window. "Sometimes I think I'll just take a whole bottle of happy pills and let it all go. But we've got to keep going. That's what Man does. Besides, you've got your son to think about."

"And Jennifer."

Victor wouldn't catch his eye. "Sure, your wife as well," he muttered, "proper little Garden of Eden. I'd better not stay too long or I'll be the snake in the garden of Macaverty Head." Then, with sudden intensity, "I'm sure you can hold on here in this windswept outpost, Harold. A lighthouse was always a beacon of hope. Even a disused one."

*

Evening. Victor cleaned his hands fastidiously with a disposable airline wipe. "Thanks for the grub," he muttered. "By the way, I've reconfigured David's educational programs. There's a whole load of Web-based material still available."

"I thought it had mostly crashed," Harold answered.

"No: there's a lot that's in stasis. Never updated but still accessible."

"He was quite a solitary boy even before the Moon Plague hit. He's going through a real fantasy play phase. I join in when I can but it's exhausting. Pirates, astronauts and similar make-believe adventures."

"You're holding up well, Harold."

"Am I?" He sipped at his instant coffee — bitter, dark and lukewarm. "Davie's full of questions which I try to answer as truthfully as possible. But I feel like I'm preparing him to be the last man on Earth."

Victor slowly unwrapped a second picnic packet of long-life biscuits, dunked one in his drink and replied, "There are pockets of survivors here and there. One day they'll link up and forge a new society, so — why are you waving your hand like that?"

"Those voices again. The choristers. Can't you hear them?"

Victor pursed his lips, twitched an ear, shook his slightly shaggy head. "Nah. Not that I disbelieve you. Then again, in this wind with the climactic disruption and the Mind blocks chattering in the other room... well, one might hear almost anything."

Harold picked up the two mugs and stood them in the sink. He would wash them when he could spare the water. "I thought you might be coming to tell me to go out and find fit survivors of child-bearing age and start up a new colony here," he stated.

"Very John Wyndham," Victor commented. "That may be my next task. I just follow the orders from on high."

Harold wiped his hands on his already grubby trousers and said, "That's all I've been doing, too. That booster shot they gave me, though, it's only warding off the symptoms. It's not a cure. Me, you... we're both starting to succumb. Evans has gone already and

Jennifer is... very sick... close to the end. We're not really in any fit state to start a new Garden of Eden."

"Maybe not. Still, there's always David. He seems to be in rude health. Let's pray he stays that way."

Harold nodded, whispered, "That's what keeps me going, pal."

\*

Morning. Victor was getting ready to go. He shook hands with Harold and muttered something about going off to do the Law's work.

"Let's hope we can maintain the rule of law," Harold concurred. "That's the only thing holding society together."

Victor gave him a beatific look, zipped up his jacket then mussed David's hair in an affectionate way. He smiled and said, "Look after the boy. He's the hope for the future. Kids like David will save Humankind."

"Don't put so much pressure on the poor lad," Harold answered. "We're just trying to survive till the summer."

"Have some faith — in yourself and others," Victor commented as he unlocked his armoured car.

The wind was gentler today and last night's pounding rain had ceased. The father and son stood awhile watching the deserter. Soon even the speck of his vehicle was no longer discernible in the distance. Even at this habitually bleak time of year there should have been more than the handful of scraggly sheep grazing on the scrubby hill; there should have been gannets and gulls circling raucously in the grey sky. Three years ago, migrating birds had brought a brief outbreak of bird flu; people had volleyed back something much worse. So now, Mother Nature offered only a weak sun pushing at the drab clouds and the damaged Moon hanging in the east — diurnal and accusing.

Harold took the kid indoors and began the morning search for symptoms. Anything silvery, unnaturally shiny or hinting of leprosy, eczema or related conditions about the skin, any milkiness around the eyes... David was clear but not clean. Harold himself had the disease at a vestigial level and tried not to peer too closely in the mirror. Keep up the pretence and you might just fool yourself into thinking that, since the antibiotic booster the General had administered back in Edinburgh, you were slowly recovering like one in a thousand, one in ten thousand, one in a million…

"We need to wash today, Davie boy. Can't have you becoming too crusty and full of scabies. I'm sure there's enough rain collected in the water butt."

"Daddy, I hate baths."

"That's because I've let you go too long without a good soak, sonny boy. We'll stand you up and use a flannel — you won't get too wet."

"Then will you play pirates or astronauts with me?"

"Sure, for an hour or so. Deal?"

"Deal."

\*

Where were all the psychoanalysts and the therapists in the world when you finally needed them? Where had all the overpaid shrinks gone? Gone to Moon Plague, every one.

Jesting aside, it was clear to Harold that even if he were just about keeping his shit together, the long-term effects on young David were likely to be catastrophic and would manifest at some point in the future. That which remained of such a suspicious prospect. He wished he could spend more time with the boy, indulge in the age-old father and son male bonding rituals, ground him in the necessary mind set for long-term survival. But his tasks here at Macaverty Head meant he had to leave the youngster to his own devices for much of the day.

If only Jennifer hadn't become so sick. Between the pair of them they could have protected David against every sling and arrow, every virus and psychosis. But she lay still in the locked third bedroom of the annex, a sleeping beauty not a Mrs Rochester, and, worry upon worry, Harold wished he and David could simply spend all day by her bedside; and hope and pray for her eventual recovery.

They were in the kitchen area with its bare boards and rain-lashed windows. At least they closed securely and, if you put on an extra jumper, you didn't feel the cold too much. Harold was reluctant to try and light the wood stove in this part of the complex. Therefore, it was a cold supper this evening: vitamin tablets, dry long-life crisp bread, bottled water and... sardines.

"I've taken the bones out, David, but chew the fish carefully just in case. It's Sunday tomorrow — maybe we'll treat ourselves to salmon, eh?"

"I like sardines, Daddy."

"Even the tomato sauce? You're a good lad. What did you play this afternoon?"

"Arty — er, Arctic explorering. Me and Jacko had to hide from a polar bear. You mustn't kill them, they ain't many left."

"That's true... sadly." Harold wiped ketchup from his lips, pulled a tiny white bone out from between his teeth.

"Daddy?"

"Yeah?"

"I heard the church singing again. Do you think...?"

"Now, David, I've told you that ghosts are just stories... like you and your polar bear."

"But..."

"Listen, David, I'm running so much electronic equipment inside the lighthouse that I'm bound to pick up old radio signals and all sorts of interference. You probably heard some BBC broadcast that's been bouncing around the ether for a couple of years. All right?"

"OK, but I knew what they were singing."

"You must have heard the song at school. Mr James probably played it in assembly. Everyone knows a few hymns and spirituals and the like."

With that sudden change of focus peculiar to the under-nines, David asked, "Daddy, is there any tinned custard?"

"All right, but it doesn't really go. Don't make yourself sick."

Whatever you do…

\*

David's diary:

Today we were astronauts. Daddy used some old car board boxes and we painted the helmets. We stuck an old rapping off a packet over the face and it made every think go yellowish. It was so cool! We bounced around like we was on the moon. Before the moon got damage. I wanted to play this game for ages but Daddy was too busy but today he said ok and it was brill. I want to be a astronaut when I grow up and go out in space and on rockets and go moon and make it all better. I no I ull have to train and that and it ull be hard and take a few years but is what I want and Daddy says go for your dream.

So we bounced around and made re pears — no, that's repairs — to our space ship and our space station and we put on voices to be earth and… mission control, no red line for spelling mistakes now — and we saw the stars and rocks in space and dug up stuff on the moon and kept the whole game going for the ages. It's the best day I had hear and I didn't think about Mummy tell later when I went and toll her all about it. She didn't say nothing but I no she heard. I just wish we could all free play the game.

\*

"Daddy, I'm scared."

"There's nothing to be scared of, David."

Except the present. And the future. And the legacy of the recent past: Humankind's constant meddling with nature and the repercussions that this time were inescapable and possibly insurmountable. Man must have his toys and must be at liberty to deploy them, if not inside the hearth and home then out in the back yard of the lunar surface. We have shifted our satellite in its orbit: we have broken its pristine beauty and silvery sheen into rubble and a dust cloud clogging up our atmosphere with subtle poison. Some have suggested that certain unscrupulous governments and cartels used the coming of the cloud to unleash their own biological weapons against their hated neighbours and rivals. Likely true but unproven: the net result was the same as first thousands and then millions upon millions succumbed to the debilitating effects of the Moon Plague.

With the changed gravitational relationship came the environmental disasters: the European tsunami, the increased tectonic plate activity, the desert scorch across the temperate zones, the crop failures, the wobbling of Earth's axis, the religious crises, the breakdown... The truth is that we can never get back to how things were before and that if a few pockets of civilised people do manage to survive, the best we can hope for is to preserve a little of our knowledge and culture and hope that the rest may one day be re-discovered.

The Moon Plague has left the air unfit to breathe and the water not safe to drink but we had to do it anyway and hang the consequences. The future was the next five minutes or twenty-four hours. To greater or lesser degrees, we were all infected.

David, my boy, you have every right to be scared.

"Shall we play a game of something? Ludo, snakes and ladders, cards...?"

"I'd like that, Daddy. Bagsy I get the blue counters."

\*

How long since he had a bath or a shower? There was always the option of the water butt, which had collected plenty of recent rain, but the lack of proper sanitation facilities was yet another irritation grinding them down. He and David flushed the chemical toilet once, maybe twice a day. It was no way to live in the twenty-first century.

What was the use of his pathetic mission here? Running the Mind Blocks with the wisdom of the age and the great brains imprinted into digital code hadn't yet saved anybody from the ravages of the Moon Plague. And just how many humans were left to rebuild and repopulate this ravaged Earth anyhow? Maybe we should all make our peace with God / Nature / or the universe and admit that we messed up our short span and should never have been given so much leeway in the first place.

He had seen so much death and desperation. As much as a survivor of the Somme, the Black Death and the *Titanic* rolled into one. And just what psychological scarring must David be shielding with his invented games of imaginary adventures?

And then there were the voices echoing ghostly inside his head and around the walls... but not registering on any recording equipment or empirical basis.

"Our Lord, my light,

Through darkness unending,

In broken skies,

Thy beacon shining,

My faith unbending."

But he had no faith, no belief in anything other than simple survival from one twenty-four hours to the next.

\*

A flag is an affront. So says any self-determining nation that didn't plant that particular pole in that particular surface.

We came in peace for all mankind. But not all mankind is at peace, far from it and not all of mankind feels you have the right to represent them. An old target, the stylised conflict of the age of the space race, suddenly became a field of conflict, a ball of rock worth squabbling about, a significant goal again. If you can build rockets to wipe out your neighbours' towns, ports and bus stations, you can build rockets to shatter the dust bowls on poor Luna. The technology is largely the same, it's only a matter of scale.

A sudden boom in sales of telescopes, a sudden rash of nocturnal and diurnal sky watchers. Look, I can see the damage from here.

We couldn't quite bring ourselves to kill one another properly down here on Earth, so we played it out on the less than neutral ground of our ancient satellite, thinking we had suitably externalised all our anger and acquisitiveness and one-upmanship. Oh so wrong.

The reflective silver sphere was more than just a mirror for all our hopes, our aggression and our lunacy. All our religions and spiritual beliefs had taught us that whatever we do in this life will eventually come back to haunt us. So the Moon shall take her revenge for such mistreatment and we shall suffer her unpredictable wrath. Had we not been sufficiently warned by her twenty-eight day moods?

Unpredictable tides. A wobbling in *our* orbit. Chunks crashing towards us, testing the accuracy of our fabled missiles and the efficacy of our response. And worse — a disease, a malaise, not immediately explicable by modern medicine, but effective nonetheless. Revenge is sweet, revenge is cold. Space is not sweet but it is definitely cold. And increasingly empty. What lies above shall be mirrored below. And who shall survive the Moon Plague?

\*

"Goodbye, Jennifer."

No matter how inevitable a tragedy, it still rips at the heart. David would wonder why he couldn't gaze upon his mother's sickly, somnolent form before bedtime but Harold would make some facile excuse about tiredness or disarray. For now. Perhaps tomorrow they'd face the truth of the McClair family being reduced to the purely masculine. Then there was the question of what to do with her body. Perhaps he would seek a suitably giving patch of soil to demarcate as a final resting place. He would not be hurling Jenny over the cliff in a panic, like he'd done with Evans's corpse, nor would he attempt a do-it-yourself cremation. Doubtless, there were tools here to dig the sod.

He locked the door from the outside, kept David busy all evening with an impromptu English, maths and geography test. Geography? Some of the mountains and rivers might be unchanged but many of the capital cities were no more than concrete cemeteries.

The ghostly singing was back. The unquiet congregation who'd sought sanctuary within these very rounded walls only to become the victims of violent religious persecution. The locals had suppressed their story for a few decades but ultimately the murderous stain showed through all the coats of whitewash.

A lighthouse ought to be defendable. You had the traditional siege advantages of height and three hundred and sixty degrees vision. But the sect had pledged their allegiance to non-violence and a spirituality more akin to certain Eastern beliefs, with a concentration on sexual enlightenment, food deprivation and the occasional assistance of illicit roots and herbs. No wonder the local Protestants had so taken against them.

And yet all their songs were recognisably from the Christian tradition. He could see David's lips whispering along with some familiar phrase or other. Perhaps they would become accustomed to this eerie serenade.

Maybe the voices actually were angels, come to comfort and collect…

"OK, David, what's the longest river in the world?"

But the answer was surely the river of tears. Ready to flood and engulf at any moment.

*

It was another wild night with the restless sea smashing into the rocks on what passed for the beach. The wind had been incessant for almost the entirety of the past two days and the nocturnal sky was wild with clouds scudding against the cliffs and each other. Where they clashed, they sparked off electrical discharges — flashes of light, thuds of thunder, a localised warning of meteorological apocalypse. And again, Harold thought he could hear the hymns of the old religious sect who'd sought sanctuary here but been trapped in a deadly siege. The story told that they had no weapons other than their faith.

Their spirit apparently lingered on whilst their murderers lay in the crumbled graves of the decayed churchyard. What was left of it.

What are they trying to tell me? Are they even here or I am just conjuring up an expectation?

The CCTV cameras showed nothing. He consulted the Mind Blocks. With steadfast scientific bent, they ordered him to go out and check the equipment. In this weather?

But there was surely movement over there on the curve of the headland, apparitions gathering in the spectral evening poorly lit by occasional lightning and the reflected silver nuggets of a cracked moon.

They were coming to take him.

They were coming to save him.

They weren't coming at all, just Harold losing his grip.

\*

Harold had kept David with him for almost the whole day. Keep him occupied, don't mention Jennifer, somehow we'll get through the next few minutes, hours… days. Initially the boy had been fascinated by the array of drives and monitors running the encryption of the preserved brain patterns of so many scientists, artists and renaissance men. Their chatter and conjecture was supposed to help Harold, David and everyone else survive, keep in touch with the other outposts and pockets of humanity. But to Harold's jaded ears all they seemed to do was bemoan their lot or demand things from him that he couldn't give and that were entirely inappropriate. He'd taken to calling them *The Wailing Wall*. He'd lately kept the speakers mostly on mute.

For all the high hopes and the hands across the ether, his world was narrowing and, despite today's surprisingly clement weather, Harold felt he was losing touch with the world. He had a truckload of oil, generators, supplies of wood and the lighthouse itself despite being cold stone, was thick walled and insulated quite well against the stormy spells. There was dried food, tinned food, bottled water. Between them, he and David could hold out doing the government's work in this bleak, promised land till the summer at least. But then what?

"Daddy, what's 'without form and void'?"

"It means there was nothing at all, David. Why are you reading the Bible?"

"Mr Victor gave it to me."

He held his hand out gently and David reluctantly handed over the book. The print was a little dense for Harold's liking. Along with a few Greek myths and philosophical tracts, this tome was the root of Western culture and, even in his short time at school, David would have heard the odd quotation at Christmas and Easter. Even so…

"Listen, son, if you want to read about Jesus or Noah, we'll get something up on the computer with simpler language."

"Mr Victor said I should try and read the orig— proper version."

"He's not my boss and he's not your boss, Davie. And he's not here now."

\*

It was time to undertake the daily trudge to the scrubby patch of hedgerow that Harold had denoted as the outdoor latrine. The wind was ripping through his jacket and the granite-faced clouds were starting to empty their own bladders. Gazing back at the sixty-foot lighthouse and the battered buildings adjoining its southern side, he wondered how much longer they could sustain themselves in this bleak promised land. He'd heard the voices again last night yet there was surely no one else around for miles. Electronic interference, then? Or a stone-held memory of previous occupants of this hopeless bolt hole?

His watch told him it was early afternoon although it was hard to believe with such a louring sky and daylight with the quality of gloom. Whilst he waited for David to relieve himself, he performed a cursory examination of his wrists and forearms. He needed a long bath or shower, that was for sure, rather than a quick rub with airline style hand wipes. He couldn't determine any new signs of Moon Plague, no leprosic silvering of the skin, so that was a small mercy.

For now. During the early days following the unleashing of the disease everyone had carelessly or unknowingly breathed the tainted air and drank the unsafe water — and hang the consequences. The future became the next five minutes or twenty-four hours. It was highly likely that at some level, every single person was infected. Even David.

"I can't go, Daddy. Just a little wee-wee."

"OK, son. But we can't come out again today. It will be raining cats and dogs soon."

"I'd like that!" David beamed.

He shared a smile with the boy at the idiomatic image. Anything was conceivable in these post-apocalyptic days.

As they hurried back to the shelter of Macevrty Head, he briefly recalled a few books he'd read during a brief flirtation with science fiction as a student. The last man on Earth tales often dealt with the difficulty of obtaining decent food from the abandoned supermarkets but no one ever dealt with bowel issues. All that tinned or re-hydrated mush sloshing around, giving you debilitating stomach cramps…

And was he now the last *man* on Earth? Had Victor made it back to base? Was there really anybody at the other end of the satellite-relayed communications? Could you count the Mind Blocks as being truly alive?

He squeezed David's gloved hand and — to a muttered "Yuk!" and screwed up face like the remnant of the Moon — told the kid, "Raisins and prunes for you tomorrow morning, my boy."

\*

The Moon Plague had hit just as hard here as everywhere else. Human and animal corpses littered the roads and hedgerows. They'd driven as courteously and courageously as they could but even so had occasionally brushed an outstretched limb or appendage. After a while they no longer thought of them as the recently living but merely obstacles like building debris after an earthquake or arboreal hazards after a hurricane and flood.

"O Lord, our shepherd,

Bring life and resurrection."

Some thirty miles earlier, a lone supplicant had begged help, succour, rescue… but he was clearly close to the last throes of the space-borne disease and they drove on despite his clutching hands, the rocks he launched and the painful cries for help.

So where had all these survivors sprung from?

"Save us for heaven,

Through thy holy son."

Go away, I can't help you! You don't get me or David!

If you really exist, head inland and loot the abandoned supermarkets for supplies and shelter!

If you don't exist, get out of my head! I don't believe in ghosts, spirits, haunting, the whole supernatural caboodle!

Launching his voice from the lighthouse gantry: "I deny you!"

\*

A silvering of the skin.

The epidermis takes on a slightly luminous sheen before beginning to flake and dry.

Lethargy, oh lethargy!

Today I have no energy.

Some stronger spells as my appetite waxes but then inevitably wanes.

I want to return to the place I call home,

Orbit around Mother's solidity,

Reflect her glory with the shiny membrane that once lived and breathed,

But is now merely my shroud.

Lethargy, oh lethargy!

I'm robbed of all my energy.

No strength: I am broken though I hang on still.

My influence once strong but now uncertain

Give me no food,

No air,

No water
I want to rebel and blame those who brought me to this state,
But I barely have the strength to whimper.
Leave me to my protracted death
In peace.

\*

"O Lord, our shepherd"
The shepherds are all dead; the flock is running free.
"Salvation is at hand."
No, you are bringing death, destruction, the final nail in humanity's coffin.
"Through your holy son."
He's my boy, get away from him!

\*

Harold knelt down in front of the boy and mustered as much manly earnestness as he could.

"Listen, David, we are in a bit of danger but we've got to be strong. The voices you've heard — the hymns and suchlike — they belong to some people who want to take over the lighthouse and hurt us. They think they've found God but really it's just a new strain of the disease. Do you understand?" A mute nod. Deeply frightened eyes. "OK," Harold continued, "now if I tell you to throw some rocks at these people, I'm not asking you to be naughty. We have the right to protect ourselves. Always."

The inevitable question. Harold looked away for a few moments to compose a plausible response. At last:

"Mummy's still very ill, David. She'll stay locked in her room where no one can get to her. But we've got to fight... like pirates or astronauts. All right?"

\*

So while his attention had been on the daily domestic ritual of feeding and educating his precious son and on running and overseeing the Mind Block program that was going to preserve Humankind and reclaim the Earth — Yeah, right! — Harold had temporarily taken his eyes off the bigger picture. All the half-dead and dying survivors of the Moon Plague must have massed over the weeks in the nooks and crannies of the cliff top, the hardy trees and hedges dotting the incline, and the bolt holes of the wrecked and wind blasted buildings way down in the village.

David has hardly spoken during the preceding three days. Only mortal fear has loosened his lips now.

You consult the modern oracles but their Delphic vision is self-referential... obscured... patently useless.

How secure are your outbuildings? And the lighthouse itself?

Because you knew they were coming. You heard them all along. The singing, the chanting, the rejoicing.

The expectation of a better life.

*

"Daddy, they're outside!"

"Stay strong, David. Keep your place at the window. Keep your eyes open."

"Daddy, they're trying to get in."

"It's OK, son, everything's locked and bolted."

Just how many were there? Such a mass of bodies circling the lighthouse, giving him vertigo, making him feel like he was about to fall into their spectral morass, give up the battle... No! He must hold on.

"Daddy, they're singing a song I know from school. Can you hear it? Daddy, ghosts don't sing."

Misplaced anger flavoured with fear: "They can talk, for God's sake!"

And pass through walls?

*

Evening and this time they were massing with intent, ready to claim — or even reclaim — this ravaged scrap of land. He'd fired a couple of warning shots above their distant heads but to no avail. This rifle was a long-range weapon, slow to load, wayward at close quarters. And Harold had had his fill of killing in order to survive.

"Daddy?" David's whisper broke his doomed watch. "Daddy, you know when King Herod wanted to kill baby Jesus? Well, they ran away to Egypt."

"Egypt's a long way from here, son."

And there's not really anywhere left to run away to. The last inevitable stop is high up in Macaverty Head lighthouse. This is the end of the Earth.

The constant background of chanted spirituals must be getting to the boy, reawakening memories from school lessons and assemblies. But the female member of this holy family was already dead and even in the original story did anyone know or care what happened to Joseph the father and protector?

The enemy was approaching. He loosed off a brief volley of bullets, taking down at least two of the diseased disciples. They were running now, a multi-headed beast of united voices joined in a violent song of praise:

"Kill the unbeliever!

Restore to us

The Lord's pure order."

There was no further point holding this window position. The key battleground had shifted to the locked and barricaded front door of Macaverty Head.

\*

Punch a ghost and your hand might go right through their spectral ectoplasm.

Push, shove, hold fast to your Alamo.

Feel resistant bone and muscle. No phantoms, these, but flesh and blood. Disease-ridden in many instances, shining phosphorescent silver like the Moon of memory. But still strong enough to keep attacking, pressing up the spiral staircase into this last chance panic room on the second floor of the lighthouse. They were ragged adversaries, to be sure, and their faces and flesh carried the mark of the Moon Plague; but they showed no apparent weakness. And there were so many of them; however hard you fight, there seem to be too many of them.

Hands pinned Harold's arms painfully behind his back; a scything kick took his resistant legs out from under him and he fell awkwardly to his knees. Worse, two men and one woman had grabbed David. The boy was scared into silence, trying to catch his father's eye for the slightest flicker of hope.

Pandora's Box was dark and empty.

A trio of combatants abased themselves briefly, offering a wordless prayer, then created a space for the grand entrance of their leader.

Victor.

Thank God for that! He would sort out this tragic misunderstanding.

Victor threw back his ceremonial cape and proclaimed, "The judgement is at hand. The broken Moon looks on. Those who breathe, those who believe, shall follow the new creed."

"What is this mystical nonsense, Victor? People brought this damnation down upon ourselves."

"Be silent, heathen. Your function is over as, sadly, is the dead modern Madonna. But no matter, for it is written that the meek shall inherit the Earth. The survivors. The new people. We have come to claim the saviour whose rebirth has long been promised."

"Take me!" Harold screamed. "Just leave David alone!"

"We don't require you and the other assassins of scripture. Science has failed us; your science has brought us death. We don't need so-called empirical knowledge, we just need faith."

The last word echoed around the cramped stone walls. Some of the disciples began humming the nocturnal spiritual but Victor's raised right hand silenced them.

Through bruised lips, Harold answered, "Your religion exported slavery, death and disease across whole continents. Science is the only answer to the challenges of the present and the future."

Victor smiled. "We know our future, we are sure of salvation now. The boy child of the Virgin will grow and lead us all to Paradise."

Harold struggled against his captors, momentarily freeing one arm and attaining a half-standing position. "This is utter nonsense!" he yelled. "Jennifer was not a virgin; David was conceived normally. Your Holy Spirit is... just a fairy tale!"

Victor turned his attention towards the holy boy and said softly, "David you will grow up to be an astronaut and you will lead us to the Moon and to Heaven. Come away with us now. I shall mentor you until... it is time."

"Daddy, I don't want to go!"

"David, stay strong. I will rescue you. Even from beyond the grave, I'll come — "

The blow to the back of his head was brief, brutal and almost instantly fatal. As Harold slumped for the last time, he saw silver — behind his eyes; at the edges of his vision; on his afflicted hands, fingers and forearms...

The boy was encircled. Victor spoke again, "You must consider today as your coming of age. The mission begins now, David. Leave this shabby existence behind you, special one. Destiny awaits you."

As the ragtag band quit the lighthouse, their prophet gave whispered instructions to disconnect the generators and set fire to the ancient stone building. Even if Macaverty Head itself wasn't completely razed to the ground, the burnt out black tower itself would serve as warning and reminder enough to any recalcitrant heretics hereabouts.

The twittering electronic voices of the great thinkers who had brought Mankind to this parlous state would be silenced.

The wind would carry abroad only the mob's joyously renewed songs of praise as they sought their twisted, unattainable vision of Paradise.

# The Listeners

### By
### Samantha Lee

*'"Is anybody there?" said the traveller, knocking on the moonlit
door.'*
Walter de la Mare (1873 – 1956)

**SAMANTHA LEE** began writing travel articles while she was still
a professional performer. Her output is as diverse as it is prolific,
covering both fact and fiction and including novels in the sci-fi and
dark fantasy genres, self-development and exercise books, short
stories and articles, TV series and movie screenplays, literary
criticism and poetry. Of her sixteen books to date the last five feature
in Scholastic's best-selling imprint 'Point Horror'. A regular
columnist for *Work-out Magazine* for five years and *The Marbella
Times* and *Viva Espana* for three, she has had over two hundred
articles published worldwide. Seventy-seven of her short stories
have featured on radio and TV as well as in various best-selling
anthologies and popular magazines. Her work has been translated

into French, Dutch, Spanish, Swedish, German, Croatian and Chinese. Sam has taught creative writing workshops in libraries and at literary Festivals all over Britain and acted as Master of Ceremonies at Fantasycon 11. In the Year of Literature she was writer in residence during the 'Welcome to my Nightmare' weekend. She currently lives in the hills above Malaga City in southern Spain. On the evolution of her contribution to this anthology, Samantha says, "I've always been fascinated by the notion of houses taking on the 'spirit' of events which have occurred within their walls. Thus my contribution for *Houses on the Borderland* began as a conventional horror offering entitled 'Beneath the Stair'. Dead babies, Victorian sexual hypocrisy, unquiet spirits – the usual. But half way through, the plot simply dried up. Still to be written, it was clearly not this particular story's time. Then one morning, I woke with *The Listeners* in my head. The Walter de la Mare poem had been one of my favourites since I discovered it in *The Oxford Book of English Verse* aged ten. The mystery of who the traveller was, who was listening and why he had come back, having 'kept his word' had intrigued me since childhood. The title was just the kicking off point because I decided then and there that my house would not be in a place but in a time, a space divorced from the usual linear continuum. From there the old Celtic myths of fairy rings and nights as long as lifetimes just fell into place. As for horror - hard enough to grow old gracefully in small doses. To be suddenly overtaken by decrepitude in a single jolt, must surely be the stuff of which nightmares are made."

HE CAME UPON the house just as he was beginning to think that he was going to have to spend the night out of doors. The sense of unease left by the old man's story still hung about him like a miasma, a second skin clinging to his own like a leech, sucking away his normally pragmatic approach to life, overlaying it with a strange giddy anticipation of something half expected, still unknown.

The feeling had persisted all through the day, much though he'd tried to shake it off, and was, if anything, amplified by the sight of the mansion, appearing so suddenly among the foliage, rising from the surrounding swampy ground like a mirage in the middle of a desert. A cold dread grasped at his heart. A sensation at once of both terror and desire, though of, or for what he could not say. Just as he could not rid himself of the quite ridiculous notion that he had been here before, when he knew very well that this was the first time he had ever passed through this particular region.

He could not understand why the old man's story had so affected him. The ramblings of that half mad ancient, who had risen to confront him as he entered the tavern, had sent a thrill of horror, potent as snake venom, coursing through his veins. A failing life-force that could scarce sustain the stooped body, shone fierce from the milky grey orbs, as though some agent stronger than flesh was keeping the paper bones from crumbling, the wrinkled parchment skin from falling in flakes to the tavern floor.

The old man had been sitting in the snug close to the roaring fire, those same rheumy eyes devouring the dancing flames, absorbed in pictures only he could see. He was mumbling to himself, and had looked up with only a brief curiosity as the newly arrived stranger entered. But once fixed on him, his whole aspect had changed and he had started as if in disbelief, staggering to his feet, reaching out a clawed hand in supplication or warning or both. From the cracked lips drawn back over toothless gums had issued two words, soft and sibilant as a breeze passing, so low that the traveller had to strain his ears to catch their meaning.

'Don't go."

He had tottered forward then, plucking at the traveller's sleeve, repeating his imprecations over and over again, so that the raven-haired landlady had been forced to come around from behind her counter and lead him back to his seat.

"How many times have I told you not to annoy the customers?" she had admonished. "Sit there and don't move. Otherwise I shall have to put you out in the barn with the horses. And you wouldn't like that, would you?"

The old man struggled feebly but she held him still until he quieted.

"I want a drink," he said peevishly.

"And you shall have it," she promised. "But only if you stop making a nuisance of yourself."

The old man looked at her with something like loathing then, as though the effort had been altogether too much for him, he had collapsed back into the ingle nook and resumed his staring and his ruminating, darting only the occasional covert glance in the traveller's direction.

Satisfied, the landlady had sashayed back to her place behind the bar, swinging her hips. She aimed a plump finger at her temples and made small circling signs, rolling her dark eyes at the traveller, inclining her head towards the wizened figure.

"Don't mind him," she had said...then. "Ale?" pulling a frothing glass before the traveller even had a chance to nod his assent, plonking it on the counter, wiping her hands on her checked apron, favouring him her best professional smile.

"Who is he?" the traveller had asked, draining his tankard at a swallow, handing it back for a refill... "Your grandfather?"

"Certainly not," she said, scandalized. "He's wearing my grandfather's clothes right enough. But they're hanging on him. My grandfather was a stout man to the last. We're a stout family", she added with a wink, jiggling her dumpling breasts at him. "As you can see."

"Who is he then?" the traveller asked, eyeing the merchandise appreciatively while taking a gulp of his second pint.

"Just some old tramp. Arrived one night outside the door, rambling on, like now, about some house in the forest, about music and feasting and desolation and decay. Said he'd been here before. Said he'd kept his word and come back. Madness. Delusion. If he ever was here it must have been long before my time. I'd never seen him in my life. And I've been here these twenty years. Besides, there is no house in the forest. Leastways, not so as I know."

And yet here it was, a house, like the old man had described, gabled and turreted, the newly risen moon striking sparks off the mica, turning the dull grey walls to shining silver in the midnight light.

The traveller shivered. He could always pass on. The old man had said he must, if he came upon it, that he would stay at his peril, or the peril of his mortal soul. The traveller did not believe in such fancies, doubted that he believed in souls at all. But still the house had a hypnotic quality. It shimmered in the tricky half-light, its hard edges softening in and out of fluidity.

Now you see it. Now you don't.

From this middle-distance it looked as though it was deserted. Certainly no welcoming lantern shone from the mullioned windows, windows built narrow and deep from a time when archers would have used them to defend the occupants from marauding outlaws. Or fire-breathing dragons, he thought with an inward smile.

Apart from that, it was late; the in-dwellers were probably fast asleep in their beds. But even if he was out of luck and there were no in-dwellers, those thick granite walls would offer some shelter from the cold, not to mention safety from the were-wolves that some said still roamed this part of the country.

Curiosity overcame apprehension as the traveller approached, the clip-clop of his horse's hooves dulled by the thick moss carpeting of the forest floor. Idly, his thoughts drifted back again to the previous evening's lost comforts.

"You're very kind to have taken him in," he had said, turning his attention reluctantly away from the plump landlady's ample breasts towards the decrepit figure in the corner. "Most people would have sent him away."

"Perhaps" said his hostess. "But then I've always had a soft spot for stragglers and strays. And strangers," she added, pausing to let this thought sink in. "Besides he's only a harmless old creature. He sleeps by the fire, he doesn't eat enough to keep a bird alive, he's company of a sort when trade is low and nobody would leave a dog outside, especially on such a night as this."

It had been a filthy night to be sure. Horizontal rain and driving winds. The traveller had taken his drink and his loaded platter of bread and sausage over to the fire, glad to be out of the storm, seating himself close to the fierce glow of the coals, directly opposite to the old man. He had brought a small cup of ale for him and made to nod a greeting. But the gesture was wasted, for the emaciated ancient had fallen into a snuffling doze, giving the diner a chance to eat in peace and to observe his companion, unobserved.

He was a pathetic enough sight, mouth slack, chin nodding on the pigeon chest. A small trickle of saliva ran in a narrow rivulet down one of the deep wrinkles that criss-crossed his disenfranchised face.

The traveller judged him to be about ninety. A travesty. Hardly human. Hanging onto life by a thread. A wheezing sound, half snore, half death rattle, insinuated its way round a protruding tongue, which lolled from the secret cavern of his mouth like a small pink worm poking out of a hole.

"I suppose that it comes to us all," the traveller ruminated, tucking into his supper, listening to the howling wind and the rain slashing against the secured windows of the inn, glad that his horse was safely stabled and that both of them were in out of the inclement weather. Glad too that he had many more years of strong manhood ahead of him before he was reduced to a parody of humanity like the decrepit figure dozing opposite.

"If I ever live that long," he had thought wryly.

He was a mercenary, a soldier of fortune as it was laughingly known. For he had yet to make one. But he lived in hope. This time he was en route to join up with the Duke's army in the mountains, there to lend his sword-arm against whomsoever the great and the good had decided was currently the enemy. In his time the traveller had fought against the French, the Austrians, the Italians, the Russians and the Turk. He had no loyalties, worshipped no banner, believed in no cause. Just so long as the paymaster forked out the readies. He had killed many men and bedded many women since he had left his father's farm in the lowlands at the age of fifteen. But except for the first in each category, neither of the above had made any great impression on him.

"Better to die on my feet than end up like that old scarecrow," he had told himself. "Make the most of it while it lasts."

Which was why, after dinner, when the other guests had retired to their rooms and the locals had braved the storm to hurry back to hearth and home, he had accepted with alacrity the landlady's offer of company in his rented bed, his philosophy being that, even though she might never see forty again, one should never look a gift-horse in the mouth. A very practised mouth it had proved too, he thought with a grin, which had only added to the enjoyment of the occasion.

Yet before that turn of events the old man had woken and engaged him in conversation. If you could term it such, rambling and incoherent as it was. A monologue that invited neither question nor response. Merely a listening ear. And an open mind.

Because a very strange tale it proved to be, what could be made of it. The traveller had let it wash over and around him like the stories his mother had told him when he was little and couldn't go to sleep. Reading between the lines, piecing together the snippets that made sense, it told of something, which the old man claimed had happened to him in his youth. A series of weird events concerning a grey house hidden in the forest and a woman made from moonshine and a long long night of feasting and merrymaking and love, which he remembered in such detail that the traveller thought the rest of the poor old zombie's existence must have been boring in the extreme.

As he listened, being now mellowed by his fourth tankard of ale and having nothing better to do until he retired, the traveller, watching the cloudy eyes fill with emotion of half forgotten memory, felt some unexpected stirring of recognition in the mouldings of the ancient face so that at one point he felt prompted to interrupt the narrative...

"I feel I know you, grandfather," he said. "Have we met before, do you think? In some other place, at some other time? I have journeyed to many countries and I have the strange sensation that this is not the first time we have been in each other's company."

The old man had not answered the question but instead had leaned forward urgently, gnarled fingers scuttling out like crab-claws to clutch the traveller's knee. His hollow eyes had taken on a crafty gleam.

"You know me better than you think," he said before repeating the first thing he had said when the traveller had entered the room. Only this time it came out almost as a whisper...

"Don't go," adding, in a tone of deepest melancholy. "If you value your life. Don't go into that house."

"Whatever you say," the traveller had answered, gently removing the clutching hand. "But whatever, I must go somewhere. I cannot spend the rest of my life here."

"Can't you?" the old man had said, vaguely. "There are worse places." And then... "But who's to say? Who's to know? Maybe it was worth it after all?"

He had lain back then, obviously exhausted, and had closed his eyes, those eyes that seemed to be the only real living thing left about him, and two large tears had insinuated themselves from under the paper-thin lids and run down the grooves in his face to drop onto the frayed collar of his ragged jacket.

Something flashed in the firelight, a glint of metal hidden beneath the cloth. The traveller had leaned forward to see what it was.

But just then the landlady had called time and locked the tavern door and having seen the company off, had come over to make her smiling proposition to which he did not object, so that, for the next few hours at least he forgot all about the old man, and his strange story and his urgent warnings.

When he had come down to break his fast in the morning, the landlady having left him several hours previous to get, as she said, her beauty sleep, the traveller had found the ingle-nook empty. Raising his eyebrows in query, he had been answered with a sad shake of the head from which he deduced that the old man had told his mysterious tale about the enchanted house for the last time.

"There is no house in the forest," the landlady had said, wiping her eyes on her apron as the death wagon removed the shrouded bones to where they would be deposited in some forgotten communal grave. "It was all in his head. Poor old soul. For all his ramblings, I shall miss him."

The weather had worn itself out during the night and the sun shone bright from a newly clear sky that hung over the world cloudless and turquoise as a plover's egg. The traveller had put a comforting arm round the landlady's shoulder.

"He was a character right enough," he had said. "But don't fret. I never believed there was such a house. Though the way he spoke of it, *He* seemed convinced that it was true."

"Old man's fancies," sniffed the landlady. "No house. No beautiful women waiting. Except me, of course." She grinned, patting the traveller's thigh as he mounted. "Come back and see me if and when you're passing. Always a pleasure to have a young strong buck about the place."

Leaning down to kiss her, the traveller had promised that he would, adding that of course he wouldn't forget her. Both of which statements were a lie. She would fade into the back recesses of his memory, as had all the women he had lain with in taverns while passing through to this war or that. They were all much of a muchness when all was said and done, some more passionate than others, some less so. He enjoyed them as he would a good meal, to be savoured at the time. His digestion was excellent. But it was not his practise to suffer from heartburn.

"Beware strange houses," she had called, laughing as she waved him out of sight. "And remember, if you get lost, you can always come back here."

And here he was. Not lost exactly. But faced with a house, even though she had said there wasn't one. Even though the old man had said there was. He shook himself, crossly. What did the landlady know? Or the old man if it came to that? He had been riding since early morning with only a small stop around mid-day. He should be delighted, rather than concerned, to have come upon a house, any house, at this time of night, this far from civilization. The day having been so fine, the air had turned uncomfortably cold with the sun's setting. A dwelling of any sort, no matter how grey or uninviting, should at least offer shelter from the night's chill.

Throwing the reins over his mount's head, leaving it to begin to crop the thick turf of the clearing floor, the traveller slid from the saddle, strode to the great oak door, and knocked.

Nothing.

No sound.

No sound at all.

Not the croak of a frog from the nearby swamp. Not the scurry of a hedge-pig among the fern-fronds. Not even the slither of a snake shivering the grasses underfoot.

And no one looking down from the sill to ask who was there.

The deathly hush engulfed him like a fog. Suffocating.

The traveller shivered, fingering the silver amulet at his neck, given to him by his mother the day he'd gone off to the wars, designed to ward off the evil eye.

He recalled his mother now, his plump jolly mother with her floured hands and her fund of stories, crying as though her heart would break when he left. He had been embarrassed by her show of emotion, anxious to be off to seek his fortune away from the drudgery of the farm. She might be dead, for all he knew. He hoped not. She'd been a good mother. Even so he'd never been back, never seemed to get round to it.

But he'd never taken off the amulet. More than most, fighting men have their lucky charms and this one had stood him in good stead. A couple of scratches and a stiff knee was all he had to show for fifteen years of battles and bar-room brawls. Not that he was a coward. Far from it. He had been in the thick of it. Yet while men had dropped beside him felled by axes, blown apart by bullets and bombs, he had emerged virtually unscathed from every confrontation. He had lived to tell the tale.

Once again, he shivered, acknowledging to himself that he would rather be in the midst of battle now, the acrid smell of blood and guts in his nostrils, his ears assailed by the screams of wounded horses, the groans of the maimed and dying, than here, alone in this wild wood, with nothing but this unnatural, unwholesome silence for company.

Quickly, he touched the amulet to his lips then raised his gloved hand and knocked again.

"Is there anybody there?" he shouted, his voice rebounding back from the blank walls, amplified by the silence.

But his cries went unanswered. Inside the house nothing stirred. The windows remained unlighted, blind eyes in the grey façade. No inmate descended to the arched entrance, bleary-eyed from disturbed sleep, carrying a guttering candle, to invite him inside.

And yet the traveller had the uncomfortable feeling that he was being watched, that within those thick granite walls someone, or some thing was listening. So he banged with his fist once more and shouted, even louder this time… "Is there anyone there?" rattling the great iron ring of the door-knob, half in anger, half in rising panic, turning and twisting it in an attempt to open the heavy oak door.

A flash of inspiration struck him. Somewhere round the back, might there not be another door? Even if the building was deserted he might be able to gain entrance. It was worth a try. Even an empty house, cold and friendless though it might be, would afford some protection against the night's chill and the snakes and the wolves and the spiders and who knows what else that might be lurking in the undergrowth. Like the centipedes that could crawl into your ear to lay their eggs in the cavern of your skull, the young hatching inside your head to drive you mad.

Where had all this come from? It was just old wives' tales. He had never given credence to such nonsense, never been afraid of the dark. Even at his smallest and most vulnerable he had not needed a night-light by the side of his bed. Anyway, it wasn't dark. The moon was so bright it could almost have been day.

A magic night. A night for romance.

Thoughts of the landlady's warm body came back to him with a jolt. He should have taken up her offer of a few days extra 'on the house'. Nothing to lose but the occasional day's pay. The Duke wouldn't have known one way or the other. Just think, he could be in bed now, warm and snug, with a malleable woman beneath a feather-down spread and a good dinner under his belt. Instead of here, in this godforsaken forest, at dead of night, with nothing but his horse for company.

But what difference would it have made? He would only have been putting off the evil day. Would have had to face the forest sooner or later. In this case it was sooner, so he might as well get on with it.

He decided to make a circuit of the walls, on lookout for a servant's entrance. Or one of those secret trapdoors, coming up from the cellar, which these old houses sometimes had hidden in the undergrowth, as escape hatches against siege situations. It was worth a try.

Stepping carefully in case of animal traps, (the last thing he needed was a broken ankle), the full moon thankfully lighting his steps, he made his way carefully around the building, slashing at nettles with the blade of his bayonet, thrusting and poking and prodding. But although he did come upon another door, smaller than the one at the front but still thick and strong, it too was shut fast. Short of climbing the walls to try to break a window, there was nothing for it but to sleep in the open.

Grumbling, he set about gathering what bits of fallen wood he could round the clearing, building it into a small pyramid over a mound of leaves. But even though the fire took, it was a poor thing, the swamp air having left both the branches and the leaves slightly damp so that they produced scant heat and certainly not enough flame on which to cook anything. The most he could hope for was that the smell of kindling and the thin column of smoke rising from the pyre would keep the wild beasts at bay while he slept.

After dining frugally on some dried meat and the remains of the bread the landlady had given him that morning (he had eaten the rest of it with some apples and cheese at mid-day and had finished the wine, so now he only had tepid water to wash his supper down), he laid his groundsheet on the driest patch of grass he could find and, sliding the saddle from his horse to use as a pillow, settled down in the lee of the grey house to try to get some rest.

He was just nodding off when a bird flew up from the turret above his head, startling him awake again. An owl. It sailed off like a silver shadow to disappear among the deeper shadows of the trees.

And as he settled down again the bird brought to mind one of the stories that his mother, who had had a fund of them, had told him when he was small. One of her favourite tales of betrayal and revenge. So when he eventually fell asleep, it was to dream of a beautiful woman made of flowers who had been turned into an owl by the vengeful wizard who had created her. And all because she fell in love with someone else.

*

He woke to the sound of music and merriment. Somewhere a harp was playing, the golden notes filling the moonlit glade with fluid melody. Light was flooding from the windows and through the open door.

The big house had come alive in the night.

The traveller closed his eyes and pinched himself, thinking he must be dreaming. But when he opened them again it was all still there. The music. The light. Only now someone was standing silhouetted in the open doorway. A small, androgynous person dressed in green, with curly hair and pointed boots, who raised a hand to invite him in. And the traveller, joints creaking stiff from the dampness of the ground, rose unsteadily and followed him inside.

He found himself in a high-ceilinged entrance hall, tiled in black and white, and strewn with rugs. To the left a wide staircase, the banisters carved in symbolic shapes, rose to the upper floors. All around hung banners emblazoned with similar runes and hieroglyphs, while from the domed ceiling which went up several stories, was suspended a crystal chandelier which sent sparks of light swirling round the room like fireflies dancing.

Without a word, the small green person trotted across the checkerboard floor and, just before entering the arched door opposite, turned to beckon the traveller to follow.

Which he did.

But found, when he passed under the lintel that the little man, if man indeed he had been, was no-where to be seen. At the far end of the narrow tunnel a blaze of light beckoned, brighter than the sun, dazzling his eyes.

The traveller hesitated. But only for a moment. Curiosity got the better of caution. He wanted to – no, he HAD to - see what lay at the other end of the corridor.

Cloaked in wonder, led on by the roundel sound of the harp music, he moved down the tunnel, his feet sinking into a soft carpet woven in rainbow coloured silks. Flaming torches set in jewelled braziers lit his way and at one point he looked up to find the ceiling was not a proper ceiling at all but a curving canopy made from intertwining hawthorn branches, the thick white flowers hanging in heavy clumps above his head. Rich tapestries covered the walls. Tapestries depicting all kinds of mythical creatures, woven by fingers so deft that it seemed as though the figures were moving to the harp's rhythm. Unicorns and mermaids, salamanders and centaurs, nymphs and satyrs appeared to cavort and caress, each scene, as he passed, more erotically lascivious than the last. Here a bull headed man embraced a woman with feathered feet. There a girl with the features of a tigress lay spread-eagled on a riverbank, claws unsheathed, opening her furred arms to a shower of golden rain. The strange characters enveloped and intertwined each other, overlooked and encouraged by ancient Deities from the time before time. Pan with his pipes, Cernunnos, the horned one, Aphrodite rising from her shell and Dionysus, God of wine and Lord of the Dance.

On and on the gallery went, in a long straight line, which stretched down and away to eternity. The traveller felt he had been walking along it forever when it suddenly gave onto the source of the music and light and he found himself in a vast hall, set with long tables groaning with all kinds of rich comestibles and sweetmeats.

There were whole suckling pigs, lark's tongues in aspic, boar's heads, game pies and huge hams larded with honey and studded with cloves. Crystal bowls of wild raspberries vied to tempt the palate with silver basins of figs soaked in brandy or tiered stands of iced cakes smelling of ginger and bursting with plums, while from golden goblets rose the rich overpowering scent of mulled wine.

The traveller, who had dined so frugally, felt the saliva rise in his suddenly famished mouth.

On either side of each table rows of finely dressed lords and ladies sat on padded benches. A few of them turned briefly to inspect the new arrival with inquisitive but not unfriendly eyes, before returning their chatter and laughter.

The new arrival on the other hand continued to gaze around him, scarcely able to credit his senses.

In one corner on a tiny platform set opposite a roaring fireplace where scurrying scullions turned sizzling sheep and capons on spits of varying sizes, the harpist whose music had woken him in the first place sat playing her siren song. A young girl, no more than sixteen summers, but with that gift of genius that comes at birth rather than as the result of arduous study, she bent her head into the fretted strings, coaxing the music from her instrument with practised fingers.

The traveller moved towards her drawn by the sound, nodding his head in time to the music, humming to himself.

He was almost at the head of the hall when he noticed the woman.

And his breath caught in his throat.

She was seated on a raised dais covered with carpets dyed in various shades of purple, and lolled, half reclining, on a throne which appeared to be constructed entirely of peacock feathers.

She was undoubtedly the most beautiful woman he had ever seen.

She smiled as he stumbled to a halt, waving him forward and, mesmerised, he crossed the remaining few yards to stand, open mouthed, at her tiny slippered feet.

On closer inspection the throne proved to be a richly carved affair, enamelled in peacock colours. Peacocks themselves dominated the design, but so too did groupings of exotic fruits and flowers. Pineapples and pomegranates, heavy clusters of grapes, arrangements of peaches and apricots lay intertwined with sprays of lilies, bunches of marigolds, coruscating vine leaves and fleur-de-lys, the whole picked out with gold leaf.

As for the woman, if anything she was even more exquisite face to face than she had seemed from a distance. A diadem of diamonds glinted in her lustrous hair, holding the cascade of its red-gold shine back from a perfectly oval face. Her skin was like clotted cream, her lips the colour of rose-petals. Emeralds glinted in her shell-like ears and encircled her long, swan's throat, echoing the green of her wide-set eyes, almond shaped and fathomless as rock pools, fringed with lashes dark and glossy as butterfly wings. Her long slim fingers were ringed with emeralds too, the nails painted gold, while her diaphanous gown, tissue thin to emphasise each curve of her voluptuous body, seemed to have been woven from stardust and sparkled every time she moved.

The traveller stood transfixed, struck dumb by such beauty. In all his years, in all his wanderings and of all the women he had ever known, he had never seen anything that could even remotely compare to this incredible vision.

There followed a long silence, after which it was she who spoke first. Her voice was soft and sensual, like rustling leaves sighing in a summer wind.

"Welcome stranger," she said. "What brings you to my house?"

And the traveller, finding his tongue, stammered something about being lost, falling asleep, nonsense that seemed foolish even to his own ears.

But the woman seemed not to mind. She merely smiled once more, a heart-stopping smile revealing a row of perfectly even white teeth. Then she patted the mound of cushions that lay at her feet, inviting him to join her.

"Rest," she said. "You must be fatigued after your journey."

Immediately two little people, identical to the one who had first ushered him in, materialised as if from no-where to help him mount the dais, for his knees were trembling, and to arrange the cushions and rugs for his comfort.

"Bring wine for my guest," the woman said, waving them off.

Then leaning forward, her eyes locking onto his, she smiled again.

The traveller found that he could not turn his head away. Not that he wanted to. He could die happy, he thought, looking into this woman's face. She was everything he had ever dreamed about, everything he had ever wished for and desired. She was the sun and the moon and the stars all rolled into one. He felt he could drown in her hair.

"I am Morgana," she said. Her breath, warm on his cheek, smelled of cinnamon and spices. "And you? Who, if I may ask, am I to have the privilege of entertaining tonight?"

The traveller answered as he always answered, force of habit, a habit born of one of his mother's superstitious warnings.

Never let anybody know your name, she used to say. Names have real power. If you tell someone your name then *they* have power over *you*. Ridiculous, of course, but the advice had had its practical side. It had stood him in good stead, many a time, this not telling of his name. In war and street brawls and sometimes when he had fulfilled some small job of espionage or betrayed another man by lying with his wife, not telling his name had saved his hide. If they had no point of reference, then they couldn't point the finger at you. If they didn't know whom to hunt for, how could they find you?

It had been so long since he'd used his real name, he'd almost forgotten it himself. And so...

"Just a traveller," he answered.

64

The woman's eyes hardened slightly and she turned her head away.

He sensed her disapproval like a blow to the heart, so that when she turned back to favour him with her smile again, not insisting, merely changing the subject, he felt absurdly grateful. Like a child that has been forgiven some small infraction for which he has been dreading punishment.

"No matter," she said. "And what do you do, traveller, when you are not wandering in the woods?"

"I am a soldier."

"A soldier." She made it sound like the most important and glamorous profession on earth. "I have a particular fondness for soldiers. Here soldier..." and she took the brimming goblet from the page who had just brought it and pressed it into his hand. "Drink," she said. "The night is young and you and I have many things to talk about."

Transfixed by her emerald gaze, the traveller lifted the golden goblet to his lips and drank deep, draining the liquid to the very last drop. And as he lowered the cup, handing it back, she chuckled, a sound that was half triumph, half amusement.

"You have an appetite for strong drink, soldier," she said. "Let us see what other lusts we can satisfy."

A thrill of apprehension shivered the traveller's spine, though for the life of him, he couldn't imagine why. Here he was in a situation for which most men would give their eye teeth. One that he had longed for and dreamed of all his life. Wine, women and song. In abundance. And all free, gratis and for nothing.

He didn't know how long it would last but this time he was determined to make the most of it. This time he wouldn't make the same mistake he had made by turning down the landlady's offer the night previous.

A fleeting memory of the old man's warning face insinuated itself briefly into his mind but he shook it away. Time enough to think of darkness and death when his own time came.

He was alive, and healthy, and lusty and strong. And sitting beside him was the most desirable woman in the world.

Destiny had brought him to this place. Good fortune. Lady Luck.

What could possibly go wrong?

The drink was honey based, sweet and potent. He felt it running along his veins like fire, his eyes glazing as it reached his brain, so that he slid into a strange stupor somewhere between sleeping and waking. A paradise of the senses where every sensation was heightened and every thought took on the lucidity of genius.

The traveller had never learned to read, had never had the need for it, an X having sufficed whenever he collected his pay. This also served as another excuse for not having to reveal his name. But even though he could not decipher script, he had always listened with enjoyment to his mother's stories and to those of the bards who still haunted the market places, telling their tales for money thrown in a hat or, if there was no money around, for a hot meal or a place for the night. They were the news-gatherers who passed the notices of wars and rumours of wars from place to place, reaching the most outlying outposts, travelling on foot in all weathers to entertain and inform.

When he was young he had often thought of being a tale-teller. But he had lacked his mother's facility with words. Or her memory. So he had become a soldier instead.

And he had never regretted the decision.

It was from one of those self-same storytellers, bemoaning over a shared fire the demise of better times when a bard was celebrated and feted by kings, kept in luxury at court for the entertainment of the aristocracy, trotted out as a possession prized even more than the obligatory jester to impress visiting dignitaries, that the traveller discovered that some modern raconteurs were experimenting with laudanum and other drugs in an attempt to pierce through the veil of reality to encounter a new truth beneath.

Whatever the truth was.

Bypassing the traditional oral skills of memory for those of written texts, they were searching for alternative sources of inspiration. Distinct from the tried and true. Seeking the lodestone of creation in an opium pipe, in the hope of developing a fresh fund of fantastic stories, rather than relying on the conning and recycling of old legends and far-fetched romances.

The bard had been scathing in his opinions of this new-fangled search for a plot. Listening to his bitter invective, the traveller had thought privately that people with no imagination of their own invariably resisted change, always criticised those things of which they were most afraid. The writing of new material was obviously the writing on the wall for the ambulatory tale-teller. Books would take the place of word of mouth. Books that could be taken out and read as and when one wanted. Over and over again. So that those who owned them, and their immediate families, could provide their own entertainment on a winter's night and not be reliant on a passing storyteller to inject an occasional ray of magic into a hum-drum existence. Soon not only monks would have libraries. It was a profound thought. One which heralded the end of an era.

Still, the traveller had been sympathetic. Could afford to be. Such modern notions were no threat to him. He was thankful for the choice he had made, felt that fate had leant a hand in holding back his mother's way with words, giving him instead his father's brutality. The world had always needed soldiers. It always would.

But remembering the old bard, cursing into that faraway fire, he reflected that these new poets' experiments with opium poppies might well bring on revelations such as he was experiencing now. For it was as though he had sloughed off his skin and had been delivered of a great weight. As though he didn't exist. Or existed everywhere, his consciousness penetrating other layers of time and space where normal rules ceased to exist. Where if he wanted to, he could fly.

That was it, he thought dreamily, he existed in everything, everything in him, the whole encased in the silken strands of the vast web of time. Every deed ever done. Every thought ever thought. Every invention ever invented, was part of one vast universal mind, which knew no boundaries. A mind that was also part of him. Certainly his mind at this moment was alive with all kinds of esoteric ideas which, had he had the ability to write them down, might have produced something profoundly wise for the edification of his peers.

The secret of life, the universe and everything.

He was suddenly filled with the certainty that time keeping was merely another mechanical device invented by man in an attempt to harness the unknown. That time wasn't linear at all but relative to one's point in space and one's point of view. That in reality, there was only the eternal now. The single moment of clarity that he was experiencing and which he wanted never to end.

He wondered vaguely what drug was in his drink. It must be something pretty powerful to produce these unusual revelations. And sensations. Because every sense seemed heightened, the colours brighter, the sounds more acute, the scents more exotic, the tastes more intense, the feel of the cushions under his back soft as swansdown. He looked up at his beautiful companion and was about to ask her what made the drink so potent when she clapped her hands and his attention was diverted once again...

This time because the entertainment had begun.

First came a fire-eater, moving it seemed in a circle of flame which enveloped him like a second skin. It crawled up his legs, licking round his body as he swallowed red-hot coals and ran scarlet pokers along his arms and across his chest without leaving a mark.

Then came a tiny girl, hardly more than a child, wearing a sheath of transparent silk, who wound her body into such incredible shapes that one would have imagined her to be boneless.

Next a whip-thin individual who tapped his foot and played the fiddle with such dexterity that he had the whole hall up and dancing like dervishes.

The traveller felt his blood race with the music and would have liked to have joined them. But when the woman pointed him onto the floor he found that his limbs were like lead, and she had laughed, teasing him.

"I thought soldiers had a capacity for wine," she said.

"Not *this* wine," he had said, not at all offended at her jibe, contenting himself with drumming his fingers on the purple carpet and humming along with the tune, while the woman laced her fingers into his hair, massaging his scalp, loosening any tensions that remained there.

And in between performances and waking dreams, and sometimes during them, Morgana fed him with tiny tit-bits of delicious food, held the cup to his lips so that he could sip more of the opium wine, wiping his mouth with a gauze handkerchief, stroking his face, patting his cheeks. So that it was his thirst for her rather than the liquid, which intensified as the night wore on. It rose in him like a volcano smouldering just under the surface, threatening to explode.

At times, while the audience waited for the next performer to make an entrance, the traveller would fall into a doze again, to a continuing dream peopled by a macabre parade of fighting men curiously similar to himself. The rational part of his brain told him this must be his mind playing tricks on him. The parade of warriors must undoubtedly have been triggered by his hostess's assertion she had a particular fondness for soldiers. But the visions were so specific it almost seemed as though these fighters were all doppelgangers of him, alter egos from another time, another place.

The dreams disturbed him, filled him with underlying unease, because it was obvious that the protagonists were not happy. Like flies trapped in amber they struggled to escape. But from what? And although he knew them to be only figments of his drunken imagination, they also roused a raging jealousy in him. That this beautiful woman, with whom he was becoming momentarily more besotted, should sometime, somewhere, have entertained other travellers like himself, was something he could hardly bear to consider. Even though in his heart of hearts, he knew it to be true.

The dreams enveloped and surrounded him. He was at once the protagonist and the observer. The subject and the object of each scene. Here he was a roman centurion, there a Norse berserker who thought he had found Valhalla early. Another time he was a knight in full armour, or a herald, a standard bearer, a drummer boy, a field surgeon, a woad painted warrior, a charioteer. Foot soldiers and cavalrymen passed before his eyes. Officers and cannon fodder. Heroes and deserters. Many faces and the same face. His face. They shimmered in and out of his parallax view like marsh-wraithes.

To a man they seemed to be trying to tell him something, straining to catch his ear. But their phantom voices remained just out of hearing, echoes of echoes blown away by the winds of time, incapable of penetrating the wall of jollity and merriment that filled the feasting hall.

More and more acts were presented for the traveller's amusement. Jugglers and tumblers and stilt-walkers and clowns, each more entertaining than the last until finally, when he felt he could hardly keep his eyes from permanently closing, for it had been a long long night, the lights dimmed and the drums began and a beautiful dancer made her entrance.

She stood in a golden spotlight at the far end of the hall and as the opening chords of her accompaniment began, all sound died away and all eyes turned in her direction, for she was obviously to be the star of the show.

Slim and elegant, her body that mixture of fluidity and strength which is essential in dancers, she moved to the centre of the hall and stood very still, allowing the audience to get a good look at her and to settle themselves completely before she began. Her long golden hair fell in a shining sheet to well below the jewelled belt of her rainbow tunic. Her arms and feet were bare and shone like mother-of-pearl.

When she was sure that all attention was centred on her, the scullions even stopping the spits to silence, she began to move, slowly at first, with an incredible grace and ease on feet so light that she seemed to be floating rather than dancing.

Swirling and whirling on thistledown toes she played her audience like an instrument, holding them in her thrall, willing them not to look away.

It was a dance of pure seduction. She undulated, writhing, sinuous as a snake as one by one she cast aside the thin veils of her tunic, dropping them to the floor like discarded lovers. Salome before King Herod. Then as the last gossamer fragment fell and the music died away, she stood perfectly still, gleaming like an opal in the lamplight. The perfect naked jewel.

There was a moment of breath-held silence and then the applause broke out, raising the rafters of the great hall. A little dwarf ran forward to cover her with a feathered cloak as she acknowledged the ovation gravely before moving to the dais to make her obeisance to the peacock throne.

"I hope she doesn't ask for my head," the traveller thought.

But it was another question that reached his befuddled ears, as his companion turned her tawny head to whisper softly, suggestively into his ear.

"Does she please you, traveller?" she said. "Do you desire her? Would you like to possess her? You are my guest. She is my subject. It would be my pleasure to gift her to you. Tonight, while you are under my roof, I will grant you whatever your heart longs for. Anything. I will not deny you."

And looking up into the green eyes, the traveller said huskily – "Anything?"

"Anything" she said, stroking his forehead with her golden fingers. "Ask and it shall be given unto you."

And because his guard was down and because of the amount of honeyed wine he'd drunk in the past...how long...and because she was looking at him with something like desire in her own eyes, he took his courage in his hands and told her.

"I want you."

"Then you shall have me," she said, gathering him in her arms. "But first you must tell me your name. I cannot take a man to my bed if I do not even know his name."

The traveller wanted her to take him to her bed, had never wanted anything so much in his whole sorry existence. To overwhelm her. To devour her. To drown in the waterfall of her auburn hair. He wanted her more than his life. And to hell with the consequences.

Her rose-petal lips, moist with promise, were an inch from his own. The green eyes locked onto his. The curves of her body pressed against him offering ecstasy and abandon. He felt all the resolve draining out of him.

"Your name," she whispered and he, powerless to resist any longer told her...

"Miguel."

"Miguelllll," she purred, huskily, the last syllable hanging on her breath like a sigh.

Then she kissed him and the traveller felt a sensation that blotted out the world, a feeling so intense that it seemed as though she was sucking out the very core of his being. The warmth, the cinnamon smell of her overpowered him. And with the kiss, the music stopped and the hall and its occupants disappeared and he and the woman were alone, lying together on a vast bed draped with heavy hangings through which soft light filtered but dimly. A tactile cocoon where all the nerves were strung taut, where anything would be permitted, nothing sanctioned. Just the two lovers, safe and sheltered from prying eyes, joined together in the womb of the world.

He felt her hands move to the neck of his tunic. He knew this wasn't the first time she had seduced a man, but for the moment he couldn't care less, was happy, eager to let nature take its course. The dream, the soldiers, his mother's admonitions, the old man's warnings were totally forgotten as her gold tipped fingers began undoing the fastenings on his shirt. His pulse quickened. He could feel the beat of her heart against his chest. The sound of his own heart was loud in his ears. Travelling lower, her soft hands brushed against his silver amulet.

She squealed like a stuck pig, drawing back suddenly. And even though the light was behind her, tipping the red hair with flame, the traveller could see that her face had altered. The eyes were rounder, frog's eyes, lash-less and bulging, while her milk skin had taken on a sickly tinge of green.

"Traitor," she accused, the harsh voice as ugly as she had become. "Deceiver."

Then her tongue darted out from between narrowed lips in a mouth that began to spread out to each side of her reptilian head. A black tongue. Forked. And when she hissed, like the serpent that was her true self, her once cinnamon breath enveloped him in a stink of rotten-ness and decay.

Her clawed hands reached for his throat and the traveller felt himself falling, falling into a vortex of colour and sound, assailed by snatches of scenes where tapestried figures clutched and scratched at his face. Hideous masks opening toothless mouths to shriek silent reproaches at him, were drowned out by music discordant as the wailing of cats in the moonlight. A cacophony of shrieks and blasphemies, of nameless things that tweaked at his clothes and nipped at his skin, taunted and tortured him as he fell. Round and round he went, down and down, swirling, twirling, his own voice a long sustained wail of horror and loss, dropping at last into a well of blackness that had no bottom and knew no end.

*

When he woke it was morning, and he woke, not to music, but to the same oppressive silence that had greeted him the first time he'd rode into the clearing.

He was lying on bare ground, sharp stones pressing into his back. A weak morning light was filtering through the low clouds and there was a hint of frost in the air.

Of the house or its occupants, there was no sign.

Where the building had stood, grey and proud, turreted and gabled and seemingly solid as a rock, there was now nothing but a few stones, outlining what had been the perimeter walls. Scabby couch grass covered the area where the great hall had been. It stretched from one side to the other, ragged and uneven, rolling in curious humps, like dirty green waves. Humps the approximate length of a man. Row upon row of them.

It was on one of these mounds that the traveller had been sleeping.

His saddlebag lay alongside him, the leather weathered beyond recognition. But his horse was nowhere in sight. The only sign of life was a raven that stood like a messenger of doom close to his head. It shifted its weight from foot to foot, weighing him up with baleful yellow eyes.

The traveller sat up and shooed it away. He had always hated ravens, had seen enough of them, God knows, scavenging the fallen on the battlefields. They went for the eyes first.

The bird didn't move, rather it scuttled a little closer, so he shouted this time, his voice hoarse in the silence, flapping his arms and, when it still refused to move, finally picking up a stone and throwing it.

With an outraged caw, the bird rose on fustian wings to settle in one of the bare branches of the surrounding trees. The traveller followed its flight and was horrified to discovery a veritable army of the things, lined up in rows all around the clearing. Observing him like professional pallbearers. Or a silent roman crowd, seething with impatient bloodlust, eager for the Emperor to give the thumbs down to some fallen gladiator.

At least he assumed they were rooks. His eyes didn't seem to be working so well his morning. His vision was blurred and indistinct where he had always had perfect sight. He was the one with the reputation as a crack marksman, the one they always called for to snipe a particular target from a seemingly impossible distance. And he seldom missed. He couldn't have shot a duck in a fairground at this moment, he thought. He knuckled his eyes but the fuzziness remained. No doubt it would clear as the day wore on. He figured he must have been asleep for a long time. And the dream, realistic as it had been, still hung about him like a shroud.

He rolled over onto his hands and knees and shook himself like a dog to try to get the blood circulating in his veins. Then he stood up slowly. He felt weak as a kitten and his head ached with the mother of all hangovers. Tucking his hands into the sleeves of his tunic, now ragged and frayed, he looked around him. He was stiff as a board and all his bones ached.

The vista did nothing to elevate his mood. All around was

desolation and decay. Withered trees held stark branches up to the pitiless sky and to add to his misery, a light rain had begun to fall. He looked around for shelter but there was none. Hardly a stone of the house left standing. What had happened? Had there been an earthquake? What? His memory seemed to be failing along with his eyesight.

He reached out a tentative foot to brush aside some of the fallen leaves which covered the mound on which he'd slept. They crumbled away to expose a powdery soil desiccated and dry, infertile as desert sand from years of neglect. Something white shone from beneath the dirt and the traveller, thinking it might be a daisy trying to push its way through, prodded it with his toe.

The earth slithered away to either side of the mound, revealing, not a flower, but a grinning skull, the colour of old ivory.

The traveller stepped back with a cry of distaste. Now he knew what the curious humps represented. They were grave-mounds. He ran his eyes over the clearing, doing a lightning calculation. There must be at least fifty of them.

And he had been earmarked as number fifty-one.

Memory came back in a rush. Disjointed. Scrambled. It hadn't been a dream after all.

He suddenly remembered his mother's warnings about enchantments, about beautiful women and drugged drinks. Stories of the 'little people' and how they sustained themselves by devouring the souls of those whom they lured into their hideaways.

So why was he still alive?

He raised his hand to his throat. Of course. His mother's amulet. His mother's amulet had saved him. He raised the small silver crucifix to kiss it in gratitude. And in doing so, caught sight of his hands. They were old man's hands, gnarled and twisted, covered in age-spots, the veins standing out like cords, the knuckles swollen with arthritis.

He had been saved. But at what price?

There are fates worse than death.

The traveller stooped to pick up his saddlebag, rummaging in it to dig out the mirror in which he was wont to shave his whiskers on mornings when there was a regimental parade. The mirror, which had been new when he had left the tavern, was spotted now with age. Like his hands. And somewhere along the line it had cracked from one side to the other. But even with his dulled sight and in the distorted image that reflected back at him, he was aware that he no longer had whiskers to shave. Children and old people have no pubic hair. Very old people have no hair at all. We are born bald as eggs and if we live long enough we die that way.

But how long is long? How old is old? Ninety? A hundred?

This was an old, old face, this thing staring back at him. This death's head with the sunken eyes and the sunken cheeks and the toothless mouth and the hairless head.

His knees gave way and he collapsed back onto the hard ground, suddenly sick to his stomach. The sky spun above him in that whirligig circle usually brought on by a surfeit of strong drink. A circle echoed by the stand of trees that whirled in sympathy. A circle which hadn't been visible when the forest was in leaf but which was now painfully obvious, the blackened trunks in perfect symmetry, the rooks sinister sentinels of doom.

A stand of trees set in a perfect circle.

The classic fairy ring within which time stood still.

And his mother's voice came back to him yet again. Telling and retelling her tales of the magic hordes, of their Queen Mab, also known as Morgan La Fey, irresistibly beautiful, irredeemably evil. Warning him of the faerie time-slips. Of people trapped in the silken web of enchantment. One night of their time, equal to a hundred years of ours.

One tale in particular had always amused him, and he had asked for it again and again. The story of Rip Van Winkle, the fool who had fallen asleep on a fairy mound and had woken to be enticed into a great house that hung on the borderland between dreams and reality. Entertained to a sumptuous feast and treated like a king he had enjoyed all the pleasures of the flesh during one long night of revelry. But when he woke from his drugged slumber a hundred years had passed, and the world had changed and all his friends were dead and no one believed who he was or what had happened to him.

Well, who would believe such a fantastic story?

It was just a story after all. Wasn't it? Wasn't it?

But all good stories have a grain of truth in them. They may be the stuff of legend but they must have started somewhere. Related with variations round winter fires in many lands, the same tales had fascinated generations of listeners down the centuries.

Stories about beautiful women who are really harpies in disguise. About vanishing palaces, lurking on the cracks between time and space. Or hidden away while a curse runs its course. As in the tale of Sleeping Beauty whose castle lay camouflaged behind an impenetrable hedge of thorns until her Handsome Prince arrived to waken her with a kiss.

She was lucky. Her death sentence had been commuted by the good fairy at her christening, to the lesser sentence of a hundred year sleep.

That hundred years again.

And in the Sleeping Beauty's case, she had woken looking just as she had when she had pricked her finger on the spindle. Young and in her prime.

Hope surged and the traveller struggled up into a sitting position and looked into the mirror again, praying that his first glance had just been a horrible aberration created by the crack in the mirror. Then his heart sank. Because whichever way he turned his head, and to whichever angle he rotated the looking glass, the reflection remained the same. Staring out at him was the portrait of a decrepit old man, his years of youth and vitality behind him, in front nothing but death.

The traveller could not recognise anything of himself in that death's head.

Or could he?

"Time flows in circles within the faery ring. It goes round and round. It can't escape," his mother had said and then, seeing his disturbed child's face and to make sure that he didn't have nightmares, she had laughed, pinching his cheek, kissing him goodnight. "So stay away from the little people, Miguelito," she had said. "If they catch you, they take you away so far you end up meeting yourself coming back."

And finally the traveller realised why the face of the old man, reflected in the flames at the other side of the fireplace, had seemed so familiar.

Two evenings – and a lifetime ago.

# The School House

### By
### Simon Bestwick

**SIMON BESTWICK** was born in 1974, lives in the former Lancashire mining town of Swinton, and has published about fifty stories since 1997, most recently in the Ash-Tree Press anthology *At Ease With The Dead*. His story collection *A Hazy Shade Of Winter* was published by Ash-Tree Press in 2004 and the title story reprinted in *The Year's Best Fantasy And Horror*. Further fiction is forthcoming in *Triquorum,* and the anthologies *We Fade To Grey* and *Inferno*. In addition, he has written a surreal audio comedy, *Map & Steads,* for Salford's Dark Smile Productions (www.darksmile.co.uk.), now available on CD. In what little spare time remains to him, he cooks, goes hiking, drinks real ale and malt whisky, goes to gigs (folk and rock music) and attempts to assemble a personal website at www.geocities.com/sbestwick2002. Simon tells us that, "The genesis of this story was a large, rather Gothic-looking building I passed on a train journey one day. The title of the story popped into my head and I spent most of the following year, on and off, trying to do justice to it. The fiction of Thomas Ligotti, the films of David Lynch, and the desire to write the darkest, bleakest and most disturbing story possible fed into the process; the present editor's invitation to contribute to this anthology gave me that final necessary kick up the backside. And no, before anyone asks, my schooldays were *not* happy. That said, Drakemire is a fictional school and the characters in the story likewise. If *The School House* is about anything, it would be life's central injustice — how the shapes of our lives are most defined by the incidents that scar us, at the times in our lives when we are most defenceless."

I WAS ON A TRAIN, an express; I forget where from. It went straight through the station nearest the school. The neighbouring woods blurred by. When we passed the building itself, everything went into slow motion for a second. The playground was screened off from the railway tracks by a chain-link fence and nothing else. Beyond it was Drakemire.

Dozens of windows all caught the afternoon sunlight. Even then, I remember thinking they were like tiny eyes — faceted like an insect's, following us as we passed. A predator glimpsing prey, weighing the pros and cons of giving chase.

Mum poked me in the arm, smiled and said: "You're starting there next week."

I was eleven. I turned my head and watched it recede: waiting for its prey to come to it.

*

Noakes was struggling with the new patient, trying to pin him down. They fought in the shadow of a willow tree, just off the gravel driveway where Dr Petrie's car had stalled, its doors open. Petrie wasn't doing much to help, but then he rarely did. He just dithered, opening and closing his mouth.

Denholm ran in and helped Noakes pin the new patient down. Petrie snapped out of it, blinking, then knelt and gave the man an injection. The patient stopped struggling; the orderlies stood.

"What happened?" Denholm asked.

"Bloody nutjob," grunted Noakes.

"He'd been very compliant," Petrie protested. "Then as we came down the drive he just —"

"Flipped out," finished Noakes. He had a black eye already, and a fat lip too.

Petrie's hair was dishevelled; buttons were missing from his shirt. "He managed to get out of the car."

"The doors weren't *locked*?"

Petrie went red beneath his tan. "Thank you for your help, Mr Denholm. Now I'm sure you—"

"Danny?"

The patient was a thin, scruffy man in dreadlocks and dirty jeans. Not what you usually saw at The Pines. But somehow familiar. Reddish hair, blue eyes, thin-lipped mouth... "Danny?" the patient asked again. His speech was starting to slur. "Danny Denholm?"

"Yeah," he said. "That's... Grimshaw?" The man's eyes were closing. "Eddie Grimshaw?"

The last word trailed away and his head lolled to one side.

Petrie stared at Denholm. "You *know* him?"

"Sort of." Denholm shifted, uncomfortable. "We were at school together."

*

Petrie looked out of his office window, fastening a new shirt. Denholm read from a crumpled sheet of yellow A4:

"'The School House is like a mad doctor's lab. They've still got bits of me in jars. Pickled but alive. They got to me. I am scarred. I am scarred. Kids march in; adults march out. The bits that weren't required are cut away.'"

Denholm put it aside. On the back of a flyer for an anti-war demo he read:

"Dreamt about it again last night. Wandering through the halls. Echoes. Laughter. Shadows. Corridor on corridor. Labyrinth."

81

*The happiest days of your life*. Denholm put that aside too. Quickly. Before any more thoughts followed.

"Were you good friends?"

Denholm looked up. Petrie was facing him now; silver hair combed neat again, hands behind his back.

"We got on." Denholm looked down at the next piece, a drawing in charcoal and crayon. Mostly red crayon. "Not best mates or anything, even then. As for now, haven't seen him in…" he considered, "…ten years, easily."

"And you both attended," Petrie consulted his notes, "Drakemire Grammar School in Elderham?"

"Yeah." Denholm studied the drawing. The building was a black, spiky silhouette, gables like shark's teeth, windows filled in red, like wounds or eyes. The train track in the foreground was smeared red, bits of stick-people strewed all along it; the playground was a clean white space dotted with more stick-figures, mutilated ones with blank faces staring out of the page. The trees in the woods looked like deformed, skeletal hands. Denholm tried a laugh; it came out shaky. "Don't remember it looking like this."

"Probably didn't, to you," said Petrie, knotting his tie and trying to look wise. *Berk*, Denholm thought, and shifted in his chair. Petrie stroked his chin. "Any idea why he might hate the place so much?"

"Not off-hand." No one thing, just a few thousand petty cruelties built up over years. Denholm studied the drawing again. "Could be drugs."

"Mm. Something of a chemical bin, our Mr Grimshaw. Very foolish." Petrie shook his head, which Denholm thought was a bit rich coming from a man who couldn't medicate the patients fast enough. Didn't he know they called him 'Dr Feelgood' behind his back? "LSD, Ecstasy, cannabis… But even so, why fixate on this in particular?"

Denholm wondered why Petrie cared. Word among the staff was, he was a complete disaster as a doctor, but looked good and licked arse. So here he was: zookeeper to fucked-up rich kids. The Pines was, officially, a care home-cum-psychiatric hospital; in reality it was a place to keep these permanent embarrassments to Mummy and Daddy out of sight and mind. Take the money, lock them up, dope them up. A cushy number, on the whole. Maybe Petrie actually wanted to do his job for a change. "I dunno," he said finally. "Don't think he was particularly happy there, but…"

"Were you?"

Denholm shifted in his seat. That'd been a surprisingly sharp one for Petrie. "I'm not the one ended up in a mental institution, though, am I?"

"Well, actually…" Petrie gestured round, then sighed. "All right. I'll be honest here. Mr Grimshaw isn't an ordinary patient."

Denholm waited.

"His father's rich and influential, as you'd expect. However… he badly wants an heir to take over the family business, and Grimshaw's the only one he's got. If we could cure him, Grimshaw Senior would be very grateful. Follow me?"

"Well, yeah. But it's not exactly our usual thing, is it?"

"Grimshaw Senior doesn't agree. And he's the one with the money." Petrie settled back in his chair. "Grimshaw says he'll talk about what he did, but only to you."

"I'm not a trained psychotherapist—"

"You don't have to be. You were at Drakemire together; he says you'll understand. Just listen, and report back to me."

"Well…"

"Your salary will be reviewed immediately," Petrie added. "This is a great opportunity for us all."

Denholm thought of his rent and his bank balance, and after a moment, nodded.

\*

Except for the bored—looking woman at the counter, Denholm and Grimshaw were alone in the canteen. Grimshaw's hair had been cropped and he was wearing pyjamas and a dressing gown; most of the residents ended up looking that way. But his eyes were bright and alert; little or no medication, that meant. Good news if he was chatty; bad if he was violent.

Rain slid down the windows, made rippling patterns on the walls with the faint light from outside.

"So?" said Denholm at last.

Grimshaw shrugged.

"You were the one wanted to talk."

"Said I'd talk to you," Grimshaw said, "Didn't say I wanted to do it *now*."

Denholm waited. Grimshaw fidgeted, chewed his nails. They were bitten to the quick. He was trying to act like he didn't care, but he was frazzled and on edge.

"You wanna know why I did it?" Grimshaw looked at him. "Or why I ended up like this? Rich kid like me?" His eyebrows rose. "Yeah? Which?"

Denholm waited. Grimshaw drummed his fingers on the table.

"Come on, Danny. Lost your voice? What d'you wanna hear about?"

"What do you want to talk about?"

Grimshaw slapped the tabletop. "I don't wanna talk about fuck-all! I was happy in my room!"

They glared at each other. "All right," Denholm said at last. "The school."

Grimshaw snorted. "That fucking place."

"You seem to have a real downer on it."

"Don't you?"

"I'm not in here for setting light to the place."

Grimshaw snorted again; this time it was almost a laugh. "Not telling me you never thought of it? Are you? Not telling me you were *happy* there? Fucking all right place if you were some cunt like Joe Kearney or Mark Thwaites, but people like us? *Real* people? Fuck that."

"Real people?"

"Like us." Grimshaw chewed another nail. "They brainwash you there," he said at last. "Tell you what to think."

"Come on, Eddie."

"I'm telling you. It *shapes* you. Make you into a 'good citizen'. And if you don't fit... if you *can't*... remember Martin Berry?"

"Yes." Martin Berry. Hounded and bullied constantly for his voice and girlish looks. Martin Berry hanged himself in a copse near his parents' house.

Grimshaw's voice was rising. "Not telling me you weren't like him or me, are you? Think you're more like Kearney, Thwaites? Those wankers? Are you?"

"I'm not like you." It seemed vitally important, suddenly, to deny that.

"No? Why aren't you a doctor, then? If a gormless cunt like Petrie can make it any muppet can. You're— what? An orderly here?"

Denholm kept his voice level with an effort. "We're not talking about me."

"Aren't we?"

"We're talking about you."

"Same thing."

"You're saying you're me?"

"Course not. But your story's my story."

"Don't be silly, Eddie."

"Shouldn't you be calling me Mr Grimshaw?"

"I looked at that folder of your stuff," Denholm said at last. Casually. He saw Grimshaw's face tighten, grow guarded. "Those scribblings of yours."

"That's private." Grimshaw spoke through his teeth.

Denholm had read them all in Petrie's office. "You keep saying in them you're scarred," he said. "Or mutilated. Same stuff keeps coming up in your sketches. Mutilation. Surgery." He recalled one sketch: three teachers in surgical gowns, wielding scalpels. And on the operating table, a boy's carcass, flayed and mutilated. Gowns flecked with dark gore.

Grimshaw smirked, but he was twitching. "It's a *metaphor*, Danny. If you could see the kids' minds, it's what *they'd* look like.

85

The *real* truth about that place." His fingers came to his mouth again. "How they made us *conform*. If I could just get *back*..." He gnawed his nails once more, and began shaking his head side to side.

"Yes?" No answer. "What, Eddie? What if you could get back?"

But Grimshaw just kept shaking his head, on and on, and Denholm could get no answer out of him. Not till he got up to leave.

"We're all still here, you know," Grimshaw said, folding his hands on the tabletop. Blood welled from the edge of a fingernail, where he'd bitten down too far.

"What?"

"All of us. Even Kearney and Thwaites. You never leave."

"What are you on about?"

"We're all still here. Here in the School House."

"This isn't Drakemire, Eddie."

The look on Grimshaw's face was almost pitying. "No?"

\*

I didn't recognise the corridor at first. After a moment, when I registered the walls, the trophies, the paintings, the photographs and the notice boards, I realised it was Drakemire.

It was dark, it was night. The place was almost silent, but not quite; there was a far-off soundtrack of background noise. Some of it was just creaks and rustles and dripping sounds, the kind you'd get in any big old building, but the others were different, I could hear scraping sounds and ticking noises, stuff like that. Made me think of machines, clocks and knife-grinders. Later on, I heard someone giggling, but when I looked around there was nobody there.

Another time I saw a shadow move, but I didn't go to chase it. I just kept walking. I didn't know what I was doing there

(*You've always been here. Always, and still are.*)

but I just kept walking. I knew I wasn't there to explore. I had a purpose. But I didn't know what. There was the me in the dream, knew why I was there, but the real me didn't. Does that make sense?

I crossed over a covered walkway at one point. I remember that. I remembered the walkway, it led into the bit of the building where the music rooms were. They were the only classrooms in that section. The rest was taken up with the staff room and different teachers' offices.

The walkway overlooked the playground, crossed it. Looking to my left, I saw it extending back to end at the tennis courts, the woods emerging behind them. To my right, I saw the other, leading up to the wire mesh fence overlooking the train-track. Suddenly, it was daytime.

A train was rushing past. It didn't stop. It didn't end. There was no start or finish to it, just an endless rattling metal blur that turned the countryside beyond it into a sequence from some grainy old animation film, the kind they might've made in Czechoslovakia around 1974.

The playground was full of boys. Thirty? Forty? Fifty of them? All standing still, arms at their sides, their backs to me, watching it go by. The train just kept on rattling past. I saw their hair and clothing flicker and flutter in the breeze off it, but they didn't move.

Then, suddenly, they all turned round and looked up at me.

But I was too quick for them. Ha. I spun around and bolted back the way I'd come. I didn't see them. I was too quick. I didn't see their faces. I didn't see them.

Well, no more than a glimpse.

Not quite quick enough then...

I stopped running and got to a classroom door. A wooden door, painted that sickly, institutional green you get in schools and prisons. And hospitals and police stations. And here at the Pines, come to think of it. A long glass panel in it, narrow and vertical. That frosted safety glass. You know the kind, with the wire mesh embedded in it. It was still daytime. Through the door I saw a tall blurred shape.

I pushed the door open and it was night again.

The only light in the classroom was the orange glow from streetlamps, seeping through. A teacher stood beside the desk. His head was bowed, and his upper body tilted slightly sideways towards me.

The boys were all sat at their desks, faces pillowed on their folded arms. Hair in *identical* pudding-basin cuts. Even the shade didn't vary, as far as I could tell in the half-light.

I walked up to the teacher and nudged his shoulder. He rocked slightly but otherwise didn't move.

Outside, the streetlights winked out. Birds began twittering. As the room began to lighten, I noticed each boy seemed to have a kind of metal brace strapped to his back. Each brace was fixed to a mechanism at the base of each chair.

Above me, there was a fast ticking sound. I straightened up as the fluorescent strip lighting in the ceiling blinked and flickered on.

There were other noises then, from the teacher. Clicks and whirrs and more ticking sounds. When I turned to look at him, he was straightening up. Remember, I said he'd been sort of tilted towards me.

It was like a machine. A clockwork toy, like Julie Andrews in *Chitty Chitty Bang Bang*. And then his head came up. His eyes were fixed and open. He blinked twice. His eyelids clicked each time.

There was another click and then a whirr as his head swivelled towards me. I recognised his face now. It was Mr Spanton, the Maths master. Slightly too-long hair and a beard. The boys had called him 'Jesus' behind his back.

He looked at me, face blank. Then his eyelids clicked as he blinked again. I don't know how long he stared, but then his eyelids clicked once more and his head swivelled back to face the class. The boys still lay face down on their desks. The surfaces of the desks looked different. Something on them, dried, crusted.

With a whirr, Mr Spanton's hands came up, stopped. Then he clapped them together.

I woke up a second later. Just not quite fast enough.

The mechanisms on the chairs had all been triggered when he clapped. And the braces on the boys' backs snapped upright, sprang them all into a sitting position.

I woke up then, but I'd seen. I'd seen their faces.

Only, they didn't have any. Some of them had had the eyes taken out. Some hadn't.

What got to me, what really got to me was…

Were they still alive?

*

Dr Petrie tapped his pen on the desktop. His smile looked forced.

"Very… interesting." he said at last. "Now, if we could—"

"Doctor… look, all I want to know is, does it, could it mean anything?"

"Mean?" Petrie managed to look impatient and mocking all at once. "What could it possibly *mean*?"

"The dream, Doctor. It's so like Grimshaw's drawings…"

Petrie sighed. "Ah. I see. Frankly I'm surprised."

"Eh?"

"His problem's schizophrenia, not chickenpox." The families of patients seemed to find Petrie's smooth baritone reassuring, to Denholm it was just oily. "A shared delusion — *folie a deux* — can develop between two closely linked people, but that hardly sounds like you and Grimshaw. Does it?"

"No, Doctor."

"Grimshaw's psychotic. In the circumstances, I'd be surprised if you *hadn't* had the odd nightmare." Dr Petrie leant back in his chair, making a steeple of his fingers. "But I'd've thought your new salary'd be ample compensation. Of course," (the voice grew oilier still) "I can't compel you to work with Grimshaw. But I do think you should consider the patient's welfare… *and,* with this particular patient, that of the home and its staff."

Petrie raised an eyebrow. His list of achievements had grown: looking good, licking arse *and* making veiled threats. Denholm nodded.

"Splendid. Now," Petrie donned his reading glasses and made a show of studying some papers on his desk, "it's looking like a nice day out there. I think a turn about the grounds'd do Grimshaw a power of good. What about you?"

*

"Think you're the dog's bollocks now, don't you?" said Noakes.

"What?" Denholm turned from the drinks machine, looked at him.

Noakes leant forward. He was balding on top and stank of sweat. On top of that, Denholm had known dogs with sweeter breath. "Too good for the rest of us, that it?"

Privately, Denholm had positioned Noakes several rungs below him on any evolutionary scale within five minutes of meeting him, but hadn't said so. If he called him a *Homo erectus,* Noakes would probably ask if Denholm was calling him a puff. "No," Denholm protested. "Look, it's not my fault, Geoff. I just went to school with the guy. *He* asked for *me*. Not like I could say no, really, is it?"

Noakes grunted. "Yeah, well. Just remember, it goes tits up with him, it's bad news for all of us. We lose out, cos way I hear it we're all looking at a good pay rise if we sort him out. All right? So just think on."

"No pressure or anything, then," Denholm muttered to the retreating back.

"What?"

Denholm held up placating hands. "Nothing."

*

One thing about The Pines: you couldn't deny the grounds of the place were nice. That was how they'd been designed. The building had been an old nineteenth century asylum, back in the days of 'moral treatment'. Closed down in the early eighties, bought up in the early nineties and put to a variant on the original purpose.

The stretch of path Denholm and Grimshaw were on led through woodland. A couple of large ponds were nearby. One was in sight as they rounded a bend; half a dozen mallards burst into the air, quacking loudly, wings beating.

Grimshaw leant on the safety railings. "Know what an oubliette is?" he said.

"No." Denholm did, but Grimshaw hadn't said a word since Denholm's suggested the walk. If he wanted to talk, let him. *Think on.*

"It was like a little cell. More of a pit, actually. You'd stand in it. They'd put you in one when they wanted shut of you. Just drowning in your own shit as it filled up. Down in the dungeon... It's from the French. *Oublier*, to forget. Where you'd put someone you wanted to forget about."

He was silent after that, looking out across the pond. Finally Denholm decided to prod him a little. "And?"

Grimshaw stared at him, shook his head. "*Duh.* That's what this place is, isn't it? Haven't you clocked that?"

"Don't see anyone drowning in their own shit, Eddie."

Grimshaw sighed, shook his head, then turned away, shoulders hunched, arms wrapped around himself. "You're so *literal-minded*, Danny," he said, licking his cracked lips over and over. "*Up here.* That's where it's all going on. That's where they're drowning. Doped up like cattle. Battery hens."

"What?"

"Food supply. For Drakemire, Danny. Don't you get *anything*?"

*Back on that again*, groaned Denholm to himself. Out loud he said, "Right."

"Fucking patronise me." Grimshaw glared. Denholm looked away. Grimshaw stared into the pond again. "How much do you know," he said, "about what I did?"

Denholm shrugged. "You went back to Drakemire and tried to set it on fire."

"Tried? Burned the fucker to the ground."

"That's a bit of an exaggeration, Eddie."

"You reckon? Oh, I know, it's still standing, just about, but they're not rebuilding it. Cost more than it's worth. A hundred years in the brain-fucking business, and now Drakemire's gonna close down."

"Good for you."

"Is it fuck. Not for either of us."

"What you on about?"

"Do you still not get it?" Grimshaw's voice was rising. "Drakemire's *alive*. We were its food. Toys too. Played with us. Remember all the little pecking orders there?" He began tearing at his nails with his teeth. "All the little hierarchies? The kids we picked on, picking on each other? Like a pyramid? A few at the top, a few more on each layer below, till you've got the mass at the bottom, crushed flat. That was *so clever*. Worked loads of different ways, like, one, a food chain. The small fry, you let the bigger ones eat them so they're nice and fat for you. Then when the kids come out, they're used to living like that. Preying on other kids, or being preyed on. That's what I mean, see? Training. The pyramid keeps itself in place, the structure. And of course, number three, we were all turning on each other instead of the structure, the school, the fucking teachers. Well, even the teachers were tools." Grimshaw broke off and sniggered. "Some of them were *right* tools, eh Danny? Eh?" He laughed then snorted at Denholm's half-hearted grin. "Fuck off then. But they were just tools, to make it all happen. Every boy ever went there had his head fucked with by that place. There's still a part of *it* in *them*. All I did was kill the body. The soul's still there. Ever see a hermit crab been got out of its shell? It's looking for a new home."

"What are you —" *on about*, Denholm was going to say, but stopped in time. "What do you mean?"

Grimshaw snorted, rolled his eyes. Two of his fingertips were bloody. "School. Prison. Nut-hatch. Places like this, for rich kids. How many of us do you think there are? Fucked in the head? It's bringing us back here. Feeding off us. It's going to make itself whole, get strong again. And then…"

"What?"

Grimshaw looked across the lake. "That'll do it for today," he said. "I fancy a walk. Be on my own."

He turned to go. "Oh," he said, and took a folded piece of paper from his pocket. "Present," he said, and walked off.

Denholm watched him go. In a moment he'd go after him. Keep an eye... he unfolded the paper.

It was a classroom. The teacher looked out of the picture at Denholm. He had longish hair for a teacher, and a beard. The boys sat at their desks. Some of them had eyes; some didn't. But all their faces were red blurs. And they were grinning.

\*

"I really don't see what relevance—"

"Look at the *picture*, Doctor." Denholm spread it out on the desk. "*Look* at it."

With a sigh, Petrie spared it a glance, grimaced and shrugged. "So?"

"Doctor, the dream I had last night."

"Oh..." Petrie snorted, waved a dismissive hand. "That again?"

"*Look* at it. The drawing. That image... it's exactly what I dreamt last night. And no, I didn't say anything about it to Grimshaw. He bothers me enough without telling him stuff like that."

Dr Petrie sighed. "Coincidence."

"Coincidence? Look at it. Even the teacher in the picture — it's Mr Spanton."

"Oh for goodness sake. It hardly looks like anyone."

"Long hair, a beard. There was only one teacher at Drakemire like that."

Petrie looked at him. "What are you trying to say, Mr Denholm?"

"I..." he tailed off.

Petrie spoke slowly and gently. "Do you believe Grimshaw's

claims that the school is alive?"

"Of course not."

"Is Mr Grimshaw telepathic? Does he read minds, share dreams?"

"No."

"Very well, then. And so what *are* you trying to imply?"

"I…" The wind went out of Denholm. He had nothing to say, but that doesn't take away either anger or humiliation. "I don't know, Doctor," he finally said through his teeth. "I'm just concerned here. And I'd like to be taken seriously."

"I do, Mr Denholm. You're doing important work. I recognise it's not easy. And I know some of your colleagues are putting you under pressure." Petrie put on an earnest expression that made Denholm want to throw up. "But we have to try and help Grimshaw, Mr Denholm."

"Yes."

"Good. Don't worry. Have a little faith. It's not as if I haven't done this before…" He broke off.

"Sorry?"

"Nothing relevant, Mr Denholm. Before you joined us. I'd just like to clear up a few details."

"Which ones?"

"Your conversation with Grimshaw yesterday. A couple of names— Kearney and Thwaites?"

Denholm nodded. "Joe Kearney… he was one of the top athletes in the school. Won a lot of prizes. Not a very nice guy off the sports field, or on it, come to that," he added, remembering a couple of Kearney's tackles on the football pitch. "Very photogenic, though. Last I heard, he joined the Army. Officer training."

"I see." Petrie made a note. "And Grimshaw?"

"Hated his guts. Kearney used to knock him about all the time. Wasn't just him, I mean, he picked on loads of kids. Teachers tended to look the other way because he was one of the star players. Credit to the school and all of that."

"Mm. And the other one—?"

"Mark Thwaites was the Head Boy in our year. Studying Law. He's with a big City firm now, I think."

"Another one Grimshaw didn't like?"

"Yeah." How did you explain it? There was the elite, the ones who stood out from the herd. And then there was everyone else. Like Martin Berry. There'd been rumours about Martin Berry. That there'd been more to it than bullying. Worse. But what?

"Mr Denholm?"

He blinked. Petrie was looking at him. "Is there anything else you'd like to discuss?"

"No. Thanks, Doctor."

*

The first thing I remember from the dream is a noise. There's only blackness but there's a sound.

The sound is some kind of machinery or a boiler. Yes, a boiler, a slow, rhythmic rumbling noise. But there's something else. Another sound, woven into it. *Two* sounds, in fact. A sort of low noise, grunting, like someone running hard, or doing push-ups. And then there's the other sound. High pitched. Whimpering. A squeak. It sounded like pain. But it reminded of the noise someone makes when they're being fucked, too. You can't always tell.

That's what it sounded like, but it sounded so like a part of the rhythm of the boiler, of the machine, I couldn't be sure.

Then I was looking out through the inside of one of the common rooms at the Pines. It was an overcast day and it was going to rain, I could feel it coming on. Standing outside on the lawn was a man in some kind of military uniform. RAF? Naval? Army? I don't know. I can't tell. I'm no expert. He had his back to me but I knew it was Kearney.

I ran across the lawn. "Joe. Joe!"

I don't know why I was shouting his first name. We'd never been on those terms. The age gap, for one thing, and that of status. And the issue of hatred on my side, contempt on his. But I shouted it as I ran up to him.

He wheeled around and slapped me across the face. His left eye was missing. In its place was a hole that went through to the back of his head. Through it I could see a train rushing and rushing and rushing past without end, behind a chain-link fence. He had a pencil moustache now, and blood was running from his eye socket down his face into his mouth, filling it up, bubbling on his lips. He kept having to spit it out.

"Don't fucking give me orders." His voice was shriller, younger. Bubbles of bloody spittle popped on his lips.

"Yeah, you little shit." I was shoved from the side. "What do you think you're doing ordering him around?"

"Yeah, he's better than you," said another voice.

"Dr Petrie said to — "

"Shut up!" Someone else slapped my face now. Thwaites. It was Mark Thwaites. He was in his school uniform. So was Kearney, now, and so was I. The top of Thwaites' head was missing, and it looked like bits had been taken out of his brain. A metal rim surrounded the wound.

Others were moving in. All kids from school.

"Danny?" I heard a voice from behind me. I knew whose it was. Martin Berry's. High and soft. "Danny, aren't you going to tell them? Danny?"

"Shut up, you queer bastard," said Kearney, looking over my shoulder. "Fuck off out of it."

"But — "

"Fuck off!" they shouted in chorus, and Martin let out a thin scared cry and I heard his bare feet running away. I was actually afraid. I didn't want to have to see his face.

We were in the playground. We were in the school playground. Kearney and Thwaites and their half-dozen or so mates were all grown-ups again now, dressed in their grown-up clothes, and closing in. Retreating, I had to move between row on row of boys standing motionless, staring out towards the train-tracks. I didn't look at their faces. I would not look at their faces.

"Where are you going?" Kearney bubbled through his bloody lips.

"Yeah, little shit. Where you going?" Thwaites.

"Where you think you're going?" Another man, laughing. He was very fat, and his mouth was split from its corners to his ears. A frame clamped to his head held his slit cheeks back from the bones, gums and teeth with an arrangement of steel hooks. He shouldn't have been able to talk clearly, but he did.

All the others were similarly mutilated or modified. They were spreading out, moving towards me.

I broke into a stumbling backwards run. A burst of metallic laughter rang out of them. Something in it made me stop. Their eyes gleamed. Their teeth were sharp. I thought of beaters on a hunt, herding the prey towards the guns, and turned around.

The school house had gone charcoal black. The windows glowed red; they were eyes. The big double entrance doors swung open. A stench like Noakes' breath gusted out. The doors were lined with teeth.

A bell shrilled.

"Dinner time!" shouted Kearney and I heard them run towards me from behind.

I broke into a run, weaving between the boys in the playground

———

*lacuna*

— weaving through tree-trunks in the woodland beside the school; the scene shifted, changed, in an eye blink. Behind me was a crashing through the woods, a shout of "tally-ho!" A horn blared.

I ran on. The sounds receded. I fell against a tree-trunk, gasped for breath. Heard murmured conversation and went still. It stopped.

I moved forward, reached a clearing. The clearing was bare except for a single tree in its centre. Martin Berry hung from it. He was naked from the waist down. His back was to me. There was blood and excrement on his legs. He began to rotate, slowly, on the rope, towards me.

Standing all around him, in a circle, were Kearney and Thwaites and three or four others. They were staring up at him. They were boys, in their school uniforms. I blinked, and they were men, in City suits and Army uniforms. They just stood and stared up at Martin's body. Kearney was smiling slightly, as you might at a blue sky in May when the weather is fine and your mood is good. The sky overhead was grey and overcast. With a hiss, rain began to spot the ground. They didn't react, just looked up at Martin. I remained still, tried not to breathe.

Martin's body rotated on the rope, swivelling around to face me. His hairless prick was erect; Kearney held his hips and sucked it. Martin's face was swollen and blue-black: his tongue, thick and swollen, bulged out through his teeth. His eyes were open and half out of their sockets. With a click, the eyelids blinked. Martin's arm rose and his finger pointed at me.

They all spun round and looked my way. Kearney wiped blood and sperm from his mouth and smiled.

I turned and ran down the school corridor. Behind me feet thundered on the floor. A voice shouted, deep, male, a master. You mustn't run in the corridors. But I had Kearney and the rest after me. I ran all the quicker.

Through a doorway, up a stair. Into a cupboard. Out the other side (Narnia). A room. A ceiling panel. Loft space. The roof.

Onto it, picking my way across —

"Den-holm!"

"Yoo-hoo!"

The shouts came from the playground below me.

I looked down. They were all stood there. Kearney, Thwaites and the rest, in their adult guises. Mutilated. The rows of boys in the playground faced outwards towards the fence and the endlessly rushing train. I could see further from here than ever before, but still saw neither end nor beginning to train or track, but as I watched they all swivelled around as one to face the school with a slithering sound of shoe leather on asphalt. I thought of moving parts in a machine.

Moving parts. Cogs. Mechanisms. Cycles. Circuits. The second hand completes the minute, the minute hand completes the hour, the hour hand tells off the day. And what then?

With a metallic clash-clack, like the bolt of a rifle snapping back, the boys in the playground looked up as if some steel brace had guided their heads, turning flayed faces up towards me.

I felt gears shifting, cogs turning, pistons moving, beneath the roof, under my feet. In the walls and attic space, basement and boiler room —

"Danny?"

Martin Berry stood next to me, naked. He opened his arms and puckered up for a kiss.

Laughter and jeers from behind. A chant: "Gayboy, gayboy."

Martin's eyes fell out and his jawbone dropped away.

"Gayboy, gayboy."

Gears and clockwork turned in the holes in his face. He fell apart, rained in cogs and laughter on the playground.

The roof shifted underfoot. Teachers stood around me, black gowns flapping from their shoulders. Spanton. Harkley, the English master, Liverton, the Music master. The Geography teacher, Burnslow, and Wildermoor, the History master.

I turned and saw the Headmaster. Mr Martinson. His eyelids clicked as he blinked. All their eyelids clicked as they blinked.

The roof tilted, dropping away and folding flat. The playground rushed up, the ground opening to reveal a pit lined with blades.

Or were they teeth?

*

That was when I woke up screaming. No surprises there.

I felt sick. But I thought I'd be ok. Until I realised.

Realised I'd forgotten something, a lot of something's. Realising just how much I'd forgotten about one person in particular, for a start.

It'd been shifting and stirring in me, ever since I'd encountered you. You mentioned him on the first day, the second, rather. Our first conversation, in the canteen. That was the first little bit of loose scree that goes sliding, dislodging more, which dislodges more, till the whole mountainside falls, crashing down.

You did it deliberately, Grimshaw, you bastard. You did it deliberately. Didn't you?

(Yes.)

Just so I'd remember.

(Remember what?)

Remember him.

(Remember who?)

You won't leave it alone, will you, you bastard? All right. All right. I'll speak his name, although you already know. Martin.

\*

I was never one of the golden boys. When I first came to Drakemire, back when I was eleven, fresh out of primary school, I thought I might be. It was a fresh start. A new beginning.

Primary school hadn't been much fun. But here was a new chance, a fresh start. A chance to be something else. Some*one* else.

That's what I thought at the time. But I was only a kid. I know, I know. How naïve can you get?

When do they pick you? When's your destiny set in stone? Mediocrity or excellence? Favoured or fucked? I have no idea. Was there ever a choice? Could I ever have done anything differently, that would've changed the course and direction? And would I if I could?

No answer, and it's all irrelevant now in any case.

I remember that first day. All the new boys. Out there in the playground, waiting for the teachers to come and show us in. First day. Nervous.

I thought, I'll make a good impression. I stepped forward and started talking.

"Hi. I'm Daniel…"

I tried to introduce myself to the others. Set myself up as a spokesman. A leader. Ridiculous in retrospect. Life story. Chapter and verse. They all just stared. Their faces said it all: YOU TWAT.

Signed, sealed and delivered.

Maybe it wouldn't've made any difference. Maybe I would have been marked anyway.

They don't mark you, though. That's the thing about a place like Drakemire. It's not a comprehensive, where it's free. And it's not a boarding school where no one ever sees your face back home. It's fee-paying. It's like a factory, only instead of being paid to march in through those gates, your folks pay for you to be degraded. Beat that for sheer irony.

You wake up in the morning. You lie in bed, listening to the house coming to life around you. Distant traffic on the main road. Plates and dishes rattling in the kitchen. The radio on. Waiting till the last moment when you have to get up. A stone dread taking shape already in your stomach, growing in your belly like an oyster in a pearl. A speck of gravel, a pebble, a rock, a boulder. You can barely choke your breakfast down.

"What's wrong, Daniel?"

"Nothing, Mum."

"Are you sure?"

"Yes!"

"God! All right. You're like a bear with a sore head."

*Leave me alone*, you think, *leave me alone*.

You can't tell her anything, you see. One, because you'll never make it sound as bad as it is. But two, even if you could, what'll happen? She'll ring the school up. And the worst offenders'll get pulled in, get a bollocking. And they'll lay off for a bit. For about five minutes. And then it'll come back worse than ever, with a new taunt added to the rest: *Mummy's Boy*.

No. Not that. Never again. You will not. You can't tell your parents, because at best you'll get lectures on 'controlling yourself', or not reacting. Ignore them and they'll go away. But they won't. They won't. Not unless the whole school's empty. They cluster around and they keep up until you crack. Their speciality is the kind of grief you won't be marked by. It's like one of the documentaries you see on *Wildlife On One*. Only when the leopard gets the gazelle or whatever, it's over, done, finished.

101

Kaput. A bit of pain as the claws rip through the flesh, but that's over soon enough. Here they catch you, they maul you, rip you apart. Shove you around. Dead legs, dead arms, a knee in the groin. Punches tipped with a single, extended knuckle that numbs you with the agony they bring. And the names. The whisper in your ear, the shouted insult. Hauled by handfuls of your hair. You can't take any more. You can't. You can't. But you have to. There is no choice.

This is your day:

Out, the front door. Walk into town. Through the town centre and out again, to the edge of the leafy suburbs, where the school house is.

Off the main road, a driveway. A sign. *Drakemire Boys' Grammar School. Est. 1907.*

Up the driveway. Trees shed leaves in autumn. Approaching from behind. The rattle of passing trains gets louder as you near the playground.

And now you've got to wait till they open the doors to the school. In the corridors, in the classrooms, you're easy prey, but out here in the playground, it's worse. You're anybody's mark. At least in the classroom, you can pinpoint the position of the enemy fast enough. In the playground, it's shifting. You need insect eyes, with 360-degree vision, to keep track of the predators. Insect eyes, like the school.

What'll it be? Volleyed insults? Hair pulling by the big Irish kid doesn't call his day started unless he's got your hair out at all angles? Or nick your schoolbag and sling it around, maybe go through it to see what they can find? Or shove you bully to bullyboy like a human fucking pinball?

There's more, but you get the idea.

Before and between lessons, there's the whispered insults, the snapped rubber bands, the dead-arms when you're not looking, your eyes out for another danger, or talking to a friend. If you can be said to have any. This is the worst. Friends don't always stand by you. In a pinch, there are so many, almost all, who'll turn away, or worse, take the piss out of you, join in. When you need a rock, it's subsided treacherously back into the deep, and you find only the sea. To defend you is to be lumbered with you as a burden, as your protector, if they're lucky, if they're big and if they're strong. If not, they're meat for the beast too.

During the lesson, you're afraid of getting a question. Afraid of getting one right, for all the cries and hisses of 'teacher's pet' and allegations of sexual slavery on your part to the teachers.

The breaks and the lunch-hour, turfed back out into the playground, the killing ground, the killing fields. The plain and the veldt, the rainforest and the tundra, the desert and the bush. The predator's ground.

If you're lucky, you can find your way to the library at lunchtime. If no one follows you in, to hound you even then. They can get you even in that place, sit at the table you've found and whisper more obscenities, insults, kicking you under the table, probing the shell for weak spots till you can bear no more.

Is it any wonder you fantasise some days about walking into school with a gun? That you daydream of the smirks becoming wide-eyed moans of terror, just before bullets smash faces that tormented you into pulp and gaping holes?

When, years later, you read of high-school massacres, like Columbine, you will be horrified and you will be disgusted.

But you will understand.

And then the afternoon. The final mercy of the exodus from school. The journey home, walking down side streets. Looking over your shoulder, waiting for the pack to fall on you. Sometimes they do; sometimes they don't. But they always *could*.

The other hard bit is that the list of enemies is never quite the same. Someone who made your life a living hell yesterday or last week is nice to you today. Why? You can't even begin to tell. It's like trying to divine the weather from chicken entrails. What's agony and the death of the soul to you, a passionate hatred, is just a way of passing the time for them. A pastime, a lark. They go home and forget about it, come in some days and can't be arsed, or think leave it a bit, let the damaged parts grow back (except they never will). It's hard to sustain an undying hatred when some days they do nothing to earn it. The list is never quite the same.

You go home and you do your homework. Watch a little telly. Maybe go out, or probably not because you never know which enemy's out there. Stay home; home is your refuge. Home is sanctuary. You do your best to hide from Mum and Dad any sign of what you went through today. Present a reasonably happy, normal face to the world, all the while screaming inside.

And so to bed.

And tomorrow you will suffer it again.

*

That was how it went. I can say, without exaggeration, that I probably had it worse than almost anyone in my year. There were others got it bad to some degree — like Grimshaw — but I probably had it the worst.

All except for one.

Martin Berry, like I said, had the worst branding any pupil at a private all boys' school can have.

Big, pale blue, long lashed eyes; wavy hair, a girlish mouth, a soft, high-pitched voice: he was effeminate.

In a place like that, no tag is more feared than that of homosexuality.

Puff, gaylord, gayboy, shitstabber, arse-bandit, shirtlifter, bender, queer, faggot, uphill gardener, bumhole engineer... etc. The list goes on. I was fat, but I could do something about it. (Although not easily, because comfort eating was how I dealt with things.) What was Martin gonna do? Plastic surgery? Unlikely.

For all that, we didn't move in the same circles, didn't become friends until quite late in the game, fourth or fifth year. Martin was adamant he was going on to Sixth Form College; my parents wanted me to take A-Levels at Drakemire. In the end, they lost. For the first time, at the end of the fifth year, I made a decision, an adult decision, and saw it through. I did my A-Levels at the

South Trafford College, among a very different mix of kids. Some of them were even girls, a species unknown on the planet Drakemire. One of them was called Dawn Finnegan, who I had my first proper snog with and went out with for a while.

But that was to come. What did I know about girls? There weren't any at Drakemire. It was all boys. And I didn't get out enough to meet any others at evenings or weekends. It's another story, and a happier one. Or as much of happiness as I was ever likely to know after what'd happened.

There's a received wisdom in our society that you can rise above anything; conquer your past, cut loose. That it doesn't have to shape you if you don't want it to, if you don't let it. That it's all your choice.

It isn't true.

In fact, it's a lie, and a cruel one at that. Some events are a cicatrice, a branding; permanent scars. Like you were saying, Grimshaw; like a mutilation. You were right. Pieces of us are still back in Drakemire. In the School House. We look unmarked, normal, whole, but if people could see our souls they'd run screaming from the sight.

If you're Jewish or Muslim and they circumcise you, does your foreskin grow back? Does it fuck. Your cock's shaped like that for good. No really bad side effects from that. But female circumcision, on the other hand... I saw the results of that once, as a hospital orderly, and I'll never bloody forget it. Not your fault, something you had no control over. But you're still marked by it for life. Not fair, but it's true.

You try to avoid self-pity. You do whatever you must in order to survive. You erect your defences. You carry on with a life, however circumscribed by previous damage. You forget stuff, if you have to; you pack it up and seal it away. Never doubt that it can happen. Haven't you ever thought of something and recalled an event that happened years ago but you just haven't thought of in all that time? *Good Lord, I'd completely forgotten about that.* That's all it is. Your memory's like a room of shelves, full of floppy disks. Some of them are dusty and you haven't looked what's on them or years. As you go on, some get damaged by fire or flood or just old age and you can't read any or much of what's on there.

And some, if you're sensible, you drop down the back of the shelving or kick under them, so they can't be found, the files retrieved, even by accident.

But you, Grimshaw, you turned the lights on in that dusty room, didn't you? you got me thinking, looking, probing. Where's that disk, the Drakemire disk, the Martin Berry one, I know it was round here somewhere, never knowing there was a damn good reason I hadn't been able to find it, couldn't remember what was there.

You let yourself, *make* yourself forget, if you have to. Till you're old and strong and distant enough to replay the old files. And deal with them

Or not.

*

And so.

It was lunchtime. A rainy April lunchtime. Not so rainy that we were all in the classrooms. A spattery sort of day. Odd, isolated showers. Light. Not enough to keep us in, but enough to make the library overcrowded. That would've scared me once. But not now, not anymore. I had another place to go.

Out in the corridors. No home and no roots, no shelter and no refuge. Prey. I would've been, right up until the middle of last year, my fourth at Drakemire. But not now.

Because by then I knew Martin Berry. I knew where he went.

I'd always been brought up to be a man's man. You didn't run away, you went back and fought the good fight. And, obviously, got your arse kicked. When I was at sixth form college, I started working out and dieting, shifting the spare tyre cos I'd heard Dawn Finnegan say I'd be all right looking if I lost that weight. She was talking to Sara Woods and Nell Laine at the time, and she didn't know I'd heard, but I did. You could see the results within a fortnight. A couple of weeks after that, we were going out, Dawn and I. Didn't last that long, just two or three months, but it was a start. Gave me that boost. And I kept working out, not just for the girls but for the confidence, the power. I'd realised I could be strong. Swore I'd never be a victim again. Hard to believe, when I'm restraining a violent patient that I used to be that fat kid everyone taunts.

But you're never far from your roots. And right then, in any case, I was a long way from a leaner physique and Dawn Finnegan.

Anyway, Martin, never brought up that way, had had more sense. He'd known he couldn't fight it. So he ran. And hid. If he hadn't, he'd have made his appointment with a tree and a rope a lot earlier.

So he found places to hide. And as we became friends, he trusted me enough to share them.

We got called the usual names, of course, for hanging around together. Bummer, bender, queerboy... see the earlier list. But there were two of us now. Martin was used to hearing it; I'd heard it myself already, because like I said, it's the ultimate insult in a place like that.

I ducked through corridors, down the stairs. Now it got tricky.

Martin'd shown me the way. I broke across a narrow courtyard to the annexe by the school caretaker's quarters; he was a sour, vicious man, who'd once hit me across the face for no good reason except simple dislike of my 'squeaky little voice'. So there was an added pleasure in sticking it to him. As it were.

There was a door, to the part of the building with the Head's office in it. Near it, just below ground level, was a recessed window. With a last look round, I slipped down into the gap, cracked the window open — it was always ajar, the frame long warped — and clambered through

The corridor I landed in was next to the boiler room. I moved away from it, although the low chugging hum of the boiler followed me, filling the air. There was extra space in that basement area, you see. Mostly used for storage, though it was rarely used now even for that. No one, not even the caretaker, usually went there.

The perfect place for me and Martin to hide. He'd found it by accident; on the run from the bullypack (Kearney, Thwaites) he'd rushed into the courtyard and found it deserted. Seconds before they'd arrived, he'd spotted the grimy, barely visible window and slipped down against it. Nearly killed himself when it gave and swung wide. Thinking fast, he'd dropped down into the corridor and found his little sanctuary.

Which now he shared with me.

I slipped down the corridor. There were three storage rooms, the third of which was all but empty. A few tailor's dummies (god knew why they'd had them), a couple of wooden crates and cardboard boxes, a small, chunky old wooden table. Nothing else.

Martin and I would hide down there, talk in whispers, swap books and comics, packed lunches and cans of pop. A den, a hideaway, a secret location. What all boys dream of...

First off all I could hear, as I approached, was the thrum of the boiler.

As I reached the door, I heard something else. Two other sounds, woven into it like a backbeat round a melody. Or vice versa. The boiler was the backbeat. The low, repetitive grunting, the bass line. The thin, high whimpering, the rhythm guitar or the synth.

I pushed the door slightly open, knowing something was wrong but not what, or how much.

The door opened and I saw... I saw but I didn't understand, couldn't comprehend it, couldn't believe I was seeing Martin Berry, stripped naked, gagged with his underpants, wrists bound with his tie, his and someone else's belt securing each ankle to a leg of the small, stumpy wooden table. Whimpering through the gag while Joe Kearney, trousers round his ankles, belt-less — I noted, as it sank in, that'd be what was securing Martin's other leg — grunting, clutching his hips with hooked fingers that seemed to be trying to rip away handfuls of flesh, his own hips pumping away with a brutal rhythm.

I saw it, but I didn't believe it till Mark Thwaites grabbed my collar and pulled me through the doorway, kicking at my ankles as I went so I hit the floor.

I let out a cry and Thwaites landed on me, pinning me on my back. "Fucking shut it you queer bastard."

He held a Swiss Army knife to my eye, the blade almost touching it. Totally banned in school of course, but hey, Mark Thwaites was the kind of boy who'd become a Head Boy one day. He grinned down at me; all the while I heard Kearney's grunts, Martin's cries, the boiler's thrum.

Kearney finished with a snarled cry that sounded more pain than pleasure, or maybe it was triumph. Thwaites climbed off me, handed the knife to him.

Thwaites moved towards Martin, unfastening his trousers. Martin's bare back, sweatily gleaming, heaved with desperate breath. His ribs showed. There was blood on his legs. I smelt shit. The whiff of that, rectal mucus and sperm, particularly strong off Kearney's undone flies.

He was looking at me with a sort of smile on his face, his hand in my hair. Not pulling, almost caressing. That was more frightening, in fact. Partly because the possibility of the pain was almost worse than the thing itself, but also because it made me think he might want to fuck me too.

Thankfully he didn't. Of course, he'd spent himself already. But partly it was because I wasn't Martin. That was why they really hated him, of course. He was the nearest thing they had there to a woman, and embodied all they couldn't stand. Or acknowledge in themselves.

Anything in a school like that, if it's not *male*, if it's not rage and domination or braying pack lust, or at least dressed up as it, isn't allowed. Porno mags are OK, cos it's just bodies and holes. Tits, cunts, arses. *Phwooar. I'd shag that, fuck it to death. Fuck her brains out.* Sex and violence. Raw lust is fine. But anything else, any of the emotions that go with it… Oh no.

Perhaps that was why they so hated Martin, went after him with a viciousness that eclipsed anything I'd been through. Nothing but sex misspelled. It'd never occurred to me there might be more complicated emotions than mere rage or cruelty involved in their treatment of Martin. That there might be other things presenting as rage as well. A desire they couldn't acknowledge or admit to, building to a peak and vented as rage; making this scene not impossible, but inevitable.

Kearney sat me back against the wall, knife to my throat and hand in my hair, my choice of views, his face or Thwaites pounding into Martin until he too spent his load. He let out the same grunted roar Kearney had, then slumped over Martin's back, panting, hoarsely.

"Oi," called Kearney. "Stop cuddling the queer boy. Come on."

Thwaites stood, pulling his trousers up, doing up his belt. Sauntering back, he thwacked Martin's arse. "Liked that, didn't you, puffter?"

They looked down at me. "What're we gonna do with fat boy, there?"

Kearney laughed. "*I* know."

\*

"Go on, fat boy, give your girlfriend a cuddle."

"Stop covering yourself up. Go on, kissy kissy."

The Polaroid flashed.

Got the picture?

I was naked. So was Martin. They made us pretend to fuck. And they took pictures. Blackmail, to shut us up. And then they went, leaving me and Martin naked and alone, still in the last embrace they'd made us pose for. For a moment it was real, for a moment I was hard. But then I pulled away, scrabbled for my clothes, dressed frantically, whimpering. Afraid someone else might come in.

"Danny?"

I didn't listen, didn't look.

"Danny?" Martin's voice cracked.

110

I knotted my tie, laced my shoes, beat as much dust as I could off my blazer and put it back on.

"Danny?"

I turned around. He lay on his stomach, the only position didn't hurt him, most likely. His skin was girl-smooth, girl-soft. I'd got a hard-on, pretending to fuck him. Kearney and Thwaites hadn't seen, thank god. There was still blood on him. He looked

—

— beautiful.

"Danny?" His face, streaked with tears and fright.

"Put your clothes on for fuck sake," I said.

I went straight out. Didn't wait for him, couldn't look.

"Danny?"

*

We said nothing. Thwaites and Kearney had the pictures; the only ones there was any evidence of queerness on the part of was us. If I'd thought clearly I would have seen maybe they had more to lose, what'd they been doing taking them? But then again, maybe not. My dad was relentlessly homophobic; pictures like that would've sent him mad. He'd have thought *some nasty little peeping tom snapped that*, but the sight of his son and heir doing... that... no. It'd've been too much.

I said nothing, to my family or anyone else. After all, I'd only been humiliated. Again. A new and horrible kind, yes, and a new and horrible threat, but still, in essence, nothing I wasn't used to.

As for Martin? Well, how often does sexual violence go unreported out of shame? He was a teenage boy, probably uncertain of his sexuality and made to feel, no doubt, responsible, by dint of his girly looks, his lack of *manliness*. Whatever *that* is. If it's being a Joe Kearney or a Mark Thwaites, sign me up for a Pride march here and now.

But that wasn't what killed Martin. Oh, it put the rope around his neck and him up the tree in the first place, but it wasn't what pushed him off the branch to choke and strangle slowly. (Maybe he'd hoped a quick leap'd break his neck. It didn't.)

No. It wasn't Joseph Kearney or Mark Thwaites that finally killed Martin Berry. That was me.

In the weeks that followed the rape, I cut him dead. We didn't hang out at lunchtimes anymore. We never went back, it goes without saying, to the basement room.

Martin would try to talk to me; I'd answer in clipped monosyllables that made conversation impossible. He'd try to walk down the drive with me after school. I'd walk away, fast. He'd try sitting next to me, on the bus or at dinner; I'd switch seats, or even get off the bus and walk home.

And then he did the unforgivable. He touched me.

We were walking down the drive, no one else in sight; I'd made sure I was first out, ahead of the rest, and he'd done the same. We walked together, me trying to outpace him, Martin trying to keep up.

At last, determined I wasn't going to avoid the issue, he caught my arm to turn me to face him. "Danny, we've got to — "

"*Get away from me you fucking queer.*" I didn't shout. It was worse than that. Even to me my own voice sounded strangled and inhuman. Unnatural and distorted. What Martin must have made of it, how it'd sounded to him, I can't imagine. Or what must've seen in my face.

Hatred, I expect. At the very least. All the rage and hate and venom and humiliation and shame, not just for the basement room but for five fucking years in Drakemire, boiled up and found a focus. A scapegoat. Kearney, Thwaites: out of bounds, invulnerable, protected by popularity, power and status as well as simple blackmail. So I'd focussed on the powerless one. All the stuff I couldn't deal with, processed into something simple, like rage. Dressed up like it, like a queen in drag. Just like them.

Just like them.

He stumbled back, almost fell. I knew what I'd said was wrong. Soon as I said it, I knew. But it was too late to take it back, and I couldn't say anything that might salvage the friendship. I had to throw it off. Reject him utterly. *I can't deal with this.*

"Leave me alone," I heard myself say in a flat, dead voice sounding years older than mine. "Just leave me alone."

I turned away from his white, stricken, face and walked down the drive. May was just beginning. Spring in the air. Sunlight. This time he didn't call after me.

Two days later, he was dead.

\*

I went to the funeral. A few boys from Drakemire attended. Thwaites and Kearney among them. I didn't see either of them come near me, but when I got home I found a Polaroid in my blazer pocket. It showed me and Martin, embracing, sat with our legs entwined, eyes closed, mouths brushing together in a kiss. It wasn't the worst one, not by a long chalk.

I tore it into shreds, kept the shreds well, *well* hidden till one evening when my parents were out and I could burn them to ashes. I opened all the windows to let out the smell. Mum asked if I'd taken up smoking.

Somehow, I passed my GCSEs. Shit grades but I passed. Teachers couldn't understand. I'd always been a good student. They were enough for sixth form college, though, and there I applied myself. Buried myself in work, and in girls, like Dawn Finnegan. Blanked out what'd happened. Martin Berry? Lad I was at school with. Got picked on a lot. Killed himself. Didn't know him well.

And I forgot. Until now.

\*

*The happiest days of your life.* That's what they say about school, isn't it? I think of that phrase every time I read about some school kid topping him or herself because of some gang of halfwits making their lives a living hell at school. I wonder how much that stupid lie contributed to their decision to end it all.

I wonder if it went through Martin's mind as he awkwardly straddled the tree branch, making one end of the rope fast to it, shaping the other into a noose. If all he saw, looping the noose around his neck, was an endless vista of life of more the same: predation and cruelty, intolerance, scapegoating, and betrayal. Always betrayal.

And I wonder, as he let himself fall sideways, if he smiled to think he was cheating such a fate of its prey.

And how long it took him to realise he was wrong.

\*

Crossing the lawn. Up the gravel driveway. Get out. A day off. Go into town. Coffee. A pub. Just away from here for five fucking minutes. Martin's face everywhere. Go. Get out. Out of Drakemire. No. Out of the Pines.

"Oi."

The iron gates, up ahead, closed. Walking faster.

"Oi!"

Coming from the gates, to intercept: Noakes. He blocks off the exit. "Think you're going?"

"Out."

"Oh, you think so, do you?"

"Clear off, Noakes. It's a free country."

Try sidestepping him; Noakes moves to block. "You're not going anywh..." He stops. Stares down. "What. The. Fuck?"

Flies undone? No. Zipped. Look up. Noakes's face wide-eyed, ashen.

Look back down. Hands. Hands are red, drying brown. Tacky. Darkness clotted under the nails. Trousers, shirt, stained too. Noakes didn't notice at first?

Look back up at Noakes. Noakes takes a step back.

A shout. Turn and look. Petrie's running across the lawn. The look on his face. He's never looked like that before. Agitated? No. Terrified.

Dr Feelgood's running, black bag of goodies in his hand. And he's not alone. Two, three other orderlies with him. The big ones.

Suddenly the need for a pint is physical, beyond tobacco cravings or hunger pangs. Time to go. Turn and run, skirt Noakes, get out the gate.

Turning back to run, but it's too late. Noakes's fist drives forward; behind it, his face, equal part rage and fright.

(Noakes? Afraid?)

Explosion: *blam.* White light. Back, flying back. Sky: blue. Sun: flash white. Ground: hard impact. Grass: green. Grass: crushed, smell of.

Dizzy. Try to rise. Fall back. Noakes's face above, joined by the other orderlies'. Petrie's face joining them. Dr Feelgood's mouth moving slow and slurred, underwater sounds.

Hands grabbing arms and legs, one orderly to each limb. Petrie holds up a needle. An arc of squirted liquid glitters on the tip. Petrie leaning forward.

A sting.

Thickness, rushing. Darkening skies. Fast falls the eventide —
And black.

*

The basement of The Pines contains a dozen soundproofed rooms with padded walls for patients who've become violent or otherwise out of hand. It's in one of those that Denholm wakes up.

He's lying on a cot. He tries to sit up. Can't. There are leather straps across his chest. Wrists. Ankles. He can't move. He strains. No. Helpless. What he always vowed not to be. Never to be, again.

He shouts. He screams. He makes threats. He makes demands. No answer.

What the fuck. *What. The. Fuck?* That's what Noakes said before decking him. What *is* this? He's an employee. Not a fucking patient. All he tried to do was leave, got out, and they acted like he'd —

Denholm looks down. His hands are still stained. It's a brownish colour now it's dried.

His clothes, but his clothes aren't stained.

But...

That's because these aren't his clothes. He's wearing a white smock. His feet are bare. A white smock. A *patients'* smock.

*The fuck?*

What's that on my hands? What is... what happened?

Lacuna. There is a lacuna. A hole, a gap. He can remember the nightmare. The nauseating rush as what happened to Martin Berry came back. He ran to the bathroom. Vomited. Copiously. And then...

Then what?

Shower. Warmth. Heat. Dressing. Lacing shoes.

(Like in the basement room, afterwards. Martin's poor pathetic voice bleating, pleading, behind him.)

And, and, and... what then?

*Grimshaw.*

What about him?

Something about Grimshaw. Looking for him. But... What had he?

There's a panel in the door. It opens. Framed in it: Noakes's piggy eyes.

"You sick fuck."

"What?" Denholm heaves at the straps. "The fuck are you calling *me* that for? You're the — "

"I've never seen anything like that, you cunt. I thought I'd... god, you twisted bastard."

"Mr Noakes."

Noakes flinches.

"Let's try to keep this professional, shall we?"

Noakes moves away, mumbling. Denholm hears:

"...should never have let him out..."

Petrie's face framed in the gap. "Daniel. How are we feeling now?"

*Daniel, all of a sudden?*

"Don't know about you, but I'm feeling fine." Denholm tries to sound casual about it all. Like it's all a joke. "Let me up and I'll show you how good I feel." He sees Petrie flinch, curses himself. "I mean, do a couple of laps around the lawn or something."

"I don't think that would be appropriate," says Petrie.

"Come on, Doctor. All I did was try and go into town. Get a pint. Haven't been off this place for..."

For how long? He suddenly realises he can't remember. His quarters are in the building. Well, that's a bargain, isn't it, accommodation included with the job?

...Only, does any other orderly actually live at the Pines? Noakes or the others? He... he doesn't think so.

*Why just me?*

*When did I last leave the building?*

"I'm afraid you did rather more than that, Daniel," Petrie says. "Don't you remember anything?"

"No. Not since this morning. Since..."

"Yes?"

"Nothing. Nightmare."

"Nightmare. About what?"

"Nothing."

"Must have been about *something*, Daniel. Don't you recall *any* details?"

Noakes: *Grimshaw... never seen anything like it...*

The one thought on his mind on waking:

*Grimshaw.*

"What happened, Doctor?"

Petrie looks at him, into him, and says: "Grimshaw's dead, Daniel. You..." He can't say more about it. "Some sort of frenzy. A fugue state. That's why you can't remember."

"But... why? That can't be. I've never... Nothing like this."

Petrie is refusing to meet his eyes.

"What?"

No answer.

"This is a set-up, isn't it?" Denholm begins to buck and thrash against the straps. "Fucking set-up!"

"Daniel, calm down! This isn't help — "

"One of your fucking inbred hooray-henry inmates did it, didn't they? You've shot me up — "

"You'll injure yourself — "

" — so I can't remember and now you're gonna fit me up for it!"

Denholm roars. In this moment, Drakemire and the Pines blur together, really *are* one in his head. The rage: all-encompassing. Petrie is Noakes is Thwaites is Kearney is Martin is Grimshaw is...

The strap securing his right arm breaks. Petrie's face is white, mouth agape.

An ankle strap breaks; Denholm reaches for the strap on his left arm. Petrie snaps out of the spell, wheels away from the door.

"Mr Noakes!"

Denholm's left arm snaps free. Bloodied, frenzied, his hands fly to the strap on his chest.

"*Mr Noakes!*"

A thunder of feet, and the door bursts open.

*

Trains rattling. Patterns of light flickering on the wall, from the train windows at night? Like a projector film, only there's no picture, just flickers and scrawls dancing in the milky light. There was a film called *Mothlight*: a director dusted the film with powdered fragments of moth wing. Looked a little like this.

Suddenly order leaps out of the chaos: the scrawled patterns form jagged, spiky letters on the wall:

DELAPSUS RESURGAM.

Quivering as in a high wind, and then, as in a high wind, torn away and gone. The light flickers. Goes black.

Whimpering. The light flares on again. The room, no longer empty.

Kearney, blood running from the hole that was his eye. Thwaites, his opened and segmented brain. Martin Berry naked at the bedside, reaching out. His fingers, gently stroking, are cold.

Grimshaw there too. His eyes are gone. His lips too. Bitten off by the look. He tries to speak, but it's not easy. A hole where his throat used to be.

"Almost done." Who speaks? Doesn't sound like Grimshaw. Doesn't sound like any of them. "Almost done."

Flickering sounds. More figures standing in the room. Teachers. Heads bowed.

Clockwork turning. Heads rise. Eyelids click. Spanton, Harkley, Barnslow, Wilderman... Martinson.

Creaking and groaning as of huge gears. Moving parts. Mechanisms. Cogs. Cycles. Circuits. Second hand, minutes, hours. Beyond that?

All looking, expectant. Martin smiling, unfastening the chest strap. The smile knowing, tender. Whimper with fright, if others see...

And the room is empty but for Martin. He leans forward. A kiss. Then the leather strap breaks and —

The thunder of the train, deafening. The strobe of its passage, and Martin's face rises from the kiss black and bloated, as he was found.

A scream and —

\*

Denholm sat up, gulping air. What time was it?

Birds were twittering. Must be morning, then.

But...

But the confinement room was below ground and soundproofed. You can't hear birdsong down there.

But...

But this wasn't the confinement room. He looked around. These were his quarters. The windows open. Curtains shifting in the breeze.

Nightmare. Must have been.

So why is there still dried blood on your hands?

Is there? He looks. Nothing. He breathes out in relief. Sits up in bed. Naked. The sheets stink. What time is it?

He looks at his bedside clock. Blinks. Stares. 10:17. Way, way past his start time. Someone should've been banging on the door by now.

Clock must be wrong. What time?

He pulls back the bedside curtains, gazes out. The sun is high. The lawn deserted.

Except for a body, spread-eagled there. A patient, he thinks, but can't be sure. The clothes are dark with blood. The grass around the body, too.

This isn't right. Shouldn't someone be called? The police or whoever?

Denholm looks down. From the bottom of his field of vision, protruding into view past the edge of the sill, he sees an outflung arm.

He scrambles out of bed, dresses. Scrambles into the bathroom.

What. The. Fuck?

There is blood in the sink, blood on the floor, blood in the bath, blood handprints on the tiled walls. A bundle of blood-sodden cloth. He refuses to look to see if it used to be a smock.

Breath coming fast. Hitching. Denholm heads back into the bedroom. Pulls on his socks.

Shoes, where're my —

And he sees them, lying by the door, one on its side. The soles, still glistening, clotted black. A fly weaves a lazy dance above it.

In through the door, staining the carpet, dark footprints, dried brown on the pinkish, faded carpet.

*Oh fuck. Oh fuck.*

Breath hitching. What happened? Holes. Gaps. *Lacunae.* What happened? All this, so much, gone down the fucking hole, gone. What happened? Happened to Grimshaw? Was he in the confinement room? The nightmare with Martin, Kearney, the rest, was that just a nightmare? What about walking across the lawn, what about Noakes decking him?

He touches his jaw. It hurts. Feels bruised.

No. I didn't kill Grimshaw. I didn't kill anybody.

(Then why is there blood in the bathroom? On the shoes? Those hand and fingerprints in blood on the bathroom walls, if they were tested, whose would they be?)

They've doped me up. Made blanks in my memory. Told me I did it. This whole thing with Grimshaw was fucked from the word go. Stank. It's a fit-up. Set me up to take the blame for something someone else did — it has to be that — has to be —

Have to get out. Find somebody. Get clear. Get clean. He pulls on the shoes, bloody though they are. His fingers are dirtied by the bloodied laces but he doesn't care.

Have to get out have to get out.

He pushes open the bedroom door and —

\*

The sound of a distant party. Night. The lights off.

I followed the sounds, alone, abandoned. The corridors seemed longer, more winding, then ever they'd been when I first was there.

A distant rattling: I looked out of the window (I was on the covered walkway) and saw the train still hurtling endlessly past the School House. Light flickering from the windows. Shadowy half-shapes, from behind the glass, pressing hands to it, pawing at it.

The boys still standing in the playground, watching, their long shadows flying back, splaying out from them towards the building.

The sounds carry from up ahead. The teachers' block.

I pushed the door open to it. Down the spiral staircase to the ground floor. Which way? The door to the Assembly Hall again; flayed-faced boys stood in serried ranks. Braces on their necks. A clack, and the heads snapped towards me. I turned away.

Right up ahead. The Head's office. The sounds coming through the orange-painted door. A deep breath, then forward and —

Instead of the Head's office, a large drawing room. An extended table. Bottles of wine; half-emptied glasses. Cleared plates. Bones on a platter. No head or limbs but the ribcage huge. Human?

Kearney has a thighbone. Breaks it with his teeth and sucks out the marrow. Blood from his missing eye runs down the splintered femur.

Music. There's music. Echoing tinnily. Elgar's *Pomp and Circumstance*. Other boys. The table extends into infinity, row on unending row of Old Boys, going back down the decades. Every few places along the table stands a teacher.

"Hello, Denholm." Thwaites. He raises a glass. "A toast, one and all! To Denholm! Arse-bandit extraordinaire!"

Laughter.

The tabletop's strewn with Polaroids of me and Martin. They're clapping slowly, mockingly.

"The man who tried to end Drakemire," says Kearney.

"But in our end is our beginning," says Thwaites.

Laughter. Gaping mouths, teeth. The laughter so loud, the reverberating *Pomp and Circumstance* march growing ever louder with it, I clasp my hands over my ears, screwing my eyes shut and —

Silence.

I open my eyes.

The dining room's empty. The table covered in dust. A rat scuttles through the cobwebbed ribcage of the main course, its own ribs showing through thinning pelt, in vain search of some remaining morsel.

Square shapes, just visible beneath the dust. I pick one up; dust sifts away from it. Another photograph. Martin and me. Faded. I let it fall.

On the bare, peeling wall, two words daubed in long-dried blood or shit:

DELAPSUS RESURGAM.

I blink.

The words are still there, but the room's changed. The Headmaster's office, at Drakemire. But dusty like the dining room was. Photographs on the desk, beneath the dust. Except one faded picture, picked up and dropped again.

I look down. I'm wearing my school uniform. My hands are the small pudgy hands of my child-self. How long have I been standing here, waiting for the Headmaster's judgement?

*We're all still there*, Grimshaw says.

A sofa, a leather sofa, is also in the office, slashed and ripped apart. The carpet pulled up, the floorboards bare. Tangles of bare wiring hanging from the ceiling and the walls. Wallpaper hanging down like dead skin.

The window is grimy and cracked but I go to it anyway. It overlooks the lawn of the Pines. Two bodies. The ones I glimpsed from my bedroom window before. A bird sings.

I hear the thwack of willow on leather, the gentle patter of applause. Cricket. The English game.

I go back to the Headmaster's desk. I leaf through the pictures of Martin and me, and pick the one I like the best. I feel like I should cry but no tears will seem to come.

"Can I go now, sir?" I ask.

*

The canteen is silent as Denholm goes in.

Half the windows are broken. All of the strip lights are gone; several of the ceiling panels have collapsed. The floor is filthy, crusted with rotten leaves, twigs, discarded beer cans. There's the remains of a crude fire in a corner. The remains of a small bird or animal skitter from his feet as his foot catches them.

No one has been in here for a long, long time.

He looks out of the window and sees two skeletons on the lawn.

He goes back to the counter. Behind it lies another skeletal shape. A few pieces of remaining skin, dried to parchment. Jawbone yawning in a scream. Skull split, by the cleaver lying on the countertop. Blood dried brown on walls and floor.

Denholm looks down and sees blood on his hands again.

The menu board is the kind where dishes and prices are spelled out in individual plastic letters. All these lie scattered on the floor with the dead, except those spelling out the two words:

*Delapsus Resurgam.*

Denholm turns and leaves by the main canteen door.

*

I stand in the trees at the edge of the cricket field.

Twenty-seven years old, tired and close to weeping.

Unshaven and grimy, in soiled corduroy trousers, t-shirt, sweater, and long coat. Matted hair and a beard.

Not a man whose life has gone well.

I am Daniel Denholm; two weeks ago I was thrown out of my last digs. In arrears with the rent, and into the bargain kept screaming in the night and waking up the neighbours. Landlord gave me my marching orders. Nothing much to take with me except medication. And the gun in the right hand pocket of my coat.

I bought it in more affluent times, as opposed to effluent ones, like these, ha-ha. It's always travelled with me.

Why did I buy a gun? For no reason I could easily explain. Just a vast, unruly dread. The sense of living in a constant state of threat. As I lived day after day at Drakemire.

I never left. God help me, in all-important respects, I realise, I never left. I tried to put it behind me, to forget. No. Never. I'm still there. Still the prey.

I know that now.

That is why I bought the gun. For defence. I thought at the time.

But, of course, a good offence is the best defence.

In my coat's other pocket is a half-bottle of the cheapest

whisky I could find. I uncap it and take a long swallow. Gulp it. Let it burn down.

Let it all burn down.

Applause. The sun is going down. Beyond the games fields, Drakemire rises.

The distant rattle of a train.

The drugs. Legal and otherwise. All useless. None of it screened out the secrets I couldn't tell. Martin. The basement room. Kearney. Thwaites.

All the dreams, of Martin...

No exit.

Lived rough. Begged and borrowed and stole, half-starved. But made it back across the country, to Drakemire. Love and hate, their pull's obsessive force makes them almost identical. Found out what I needed to know.

Thwaites is up to bat, waiting. Kearney is walking away. The devil's home on leave.

*Are you going to do this?* I know it's only me asking this, but it still sounds like Martin Berry.

"Yes," I say. "Fuck it."

I take the Browning automatic, ex-Army issue, from my coat pocket; pull back the slide. Take off the safety. Pocket it again. Inspect the whisky bottle. Only a couple of mouthfuls left.

Fuck it.

I drain the bottle, throw it aside. Step out of the trees and walk towards the cricket pitch, the Old Boys XI versus the Upper Sixth.

Kearney sees me. *Scruffy oik, looks like a tramp, storming purposefully on. Probably on drugs.* I doubt he recognises me. He moves to intercept.

"What do — "

He gets no further. I take out the Browning, cock it and point it in his face.

Army officer or not, he goes white. Well, you don't expect it here. Northern Ireland or the Balkans or Iraq, maybe, but not here, off duty, at your old school. Not here, to die like this.

His mouth opens. I think of Martin and me and shove the Browning in there and pull the trigger.

The shot changes everything. We are — I am — noticed. Hazed blood haloes out from Kearney's head as he pitches backwards. Wet and copper-tasting, it kisses my face. There are screams. I walk towards the pitch.

Some scatter. Some are rooted. One of the latter is Thwaites, who stands frozen by the stumps, mouth agape. A wet stain spreads down his trouser leg. He turns to run.

I shoot him in the back three times. He falls flat. I walk to him. I fire one in the air to scatter more people. I stand over Thwaites.

"Danny Denholm," I say. He can't move — a bullet must have hit his spine — but his head is turned to the side, one eye visible. It weaves around, focuses on me. "Remember me?" I ask. "Or Martin Berry? I'm sure you remember Martin Berry."

I screw the barrel of the Browning into his temple. His eye screws shut. A high, whining scream escapes his mouth.

I pull the trigger.

As I straighten up, wiping blood off my face, one of the Upper Sixth Formers becomes a hero. Snatching up a fallen cricket bat, he leaps in close and cracks me soundly in the head with it.

Lights out

Lights out

Lights out.

*

Dr Petrie is at his desk, but for once and indeed now for all time the good Doctor has nothing to say.

He lolls back in his chair, mouth agape, shocked death should spoil his careful plans for, well, everything. Not to mention his expensive shirt. A long cut runs down him sternum to groin, opening him up. Blood drips from the chair onto the floor. Flies buzz, even with the curtains drawn and windows shut.

Denholm hears none of this. He has the D drawer of the filing cabinet open, pulling patient records out, letting them drop.

*Have a little faith*, Petrie said. *It's not as if I haven't done this before.*

DENHOLM, DANIEL.

Denholm goes still. At last he takes out the file and opens it.

\*

A room in the infirmary at The Pines. Strapped into a chair. Petrie. Nervous. Face beaded with sweat. Shining a penlight.

"Watch the light, Daniel. Just follow it with your eyes."

The penlight moving back and forth, back and forth.

"You're feeling sleepy, Daniel."

Side to side. Side to side.

"By the count of three you will be asleep, but you will still be able to hear me. One..."

Kearney and Thwaites standing behind the doctor, bleeding from their wounds.

"Two..."

Thwaites and Kearney, gone.

"Three."

Unable to move, staring straight ahead. Petrie looking off to the side. "He's under."

Grimshaw coming into view. Suited, hair short. "Carry on."

Petrie licking his lips.

"You know what you need to do, Doctor. You've been told."

"Yes, yes. Just nervous. With what he did..."

"He'll be perfectly safe. A model employee. Won't you, Daniel? Now carry on."

Petrie licking his lips. "Daniel? Nod if you can hear me."

Nodding as commanded, unable to do otherwise.

"Daniel, you've been remembering things that didn't happen. You need to forget about them, for your own good. And you need to remember other things. The things that really *did* happen. Firstly..."

Grimshaw, hands folded, smiling. Lips moving in a whisper:

"*Delapsus resurgam.*"

*

"'This sore combat lasted for above half a day, even till *Christian* was almost quite spent; for you must know that *Christian*, by reason of his wounds, must needs grow weaker and weaker...'"

I put my file back in the cabinet. Will I get into trouble? I close the drawer and leave the Headmaster's office.

"'Then *Apollyon*, espying his opportunity, began to gather up close to *Christian*, and wrestling with him, gave him a dreadful fall; and with that *Christian's* sword flew out of his hand...'"

It's coming from the Assembly Hall. I go in.

Thwaites is standing at the Headmaster's lectern, reading.

"'...Then said *Apollyon*, I am sure of thee now. And with that he had almost pressed him to death, so that *Christian* began to despair of life...'"

Above him is a huge representation of the school crest. Below that, the school motto:

*Delapsus Resurgam.*

"'...but as God would have it, while *Apollyon* was fetching of his last blow, thereby to make a full end of this good man, *Christian* nimbly stretched out his hand for his sword, and caught it, saying, *Rejoice not against me, O mine enemy; when I fall I shall arise.*'"

Thwaites snaps the book shut and smiles at me. "*Delapsus resurgam*: when I fall, I shall rise again."

*

Striding towards Grimshaw. Grimshaw sat at one of the tables on the lawn at the Pines, reading. Grimshaw looking up, seeing. Rising, smiling. Says: "In my end is my beginning."

*lacuna*

Eyeless, no lips, no throat: Grimshaw lying in the blood-

rusted grass. The head turning. Bloody lips moving:
  "*Delapsus resurgam.*"

\*

Denholm goes to the infirmary.

Grimshaw is laid out on a table there. Denholm pulls back the sheet. It's as he was told. No eyes. No lips either.

"Was this part of the plan for you too?" He asks. "Bastard."

He empties the last of the petrol into the torn, gaping face and throws the can aside.

\*

Noakes is lying in the hallway outside Grimshaw's room. He's been struck with an axe, repeatedly. *Did I do that?* I wonder detachedly. *Where did I get the axe from?* Then I shrug. It doesn't matter, really. Nothing matters anymore.

I push open the door of Grimshaw's room and sit on the bed. In the distance, the roaring of the flames grows louder.

The door opens again but I don't look round.

"It's nearly over," says Kearney.

I ignore him and look at the walls. Grimshaw stuck press clippings on it.

BLOODBATH AT SCHOOL CRICKET MATCH, 3 DEAD. Hero schoolboy prevents worse tragedy.

*EX-PUPIL TELLS OF SEXUAL ABUSE.* A blurred, bad photo of me.

*'CRICKET KILLER' COMMITTED...* I look down, stop reading when I see *Dr Stephen Petrie.*

I look at the next two clippings: *THE DEATH OF DRAKEMIRE. SCANDAL-HIT SCHOOL TO CLOSE.*

*FIRE AT HORROR SCHOOL.*

I feel, hear, the turning of cogs, the grinding of mechanisms, circuits almost completed. The flames have reached the corridor outside. It's starting to get hot in here. "How have I helped you?"

"See for yourself."

I turn. Kearney is gone.

I look back at the wall, and so are the clippings. But two new ones are there:

*MYSTERY CARE HOME FIRE: DOZENS FEARED DEAD.*

I stop when I see 'The Pines'.

*SCHOOL CELEBRATES CENTENARY.*

I stop when I see 'Drakemire'.

The roaring of the flames is deafening. The room smells of smoke. I open the curtains. Below, in the playground, the boys stand, flayed faces turned towards the passing train.

"Danny?"

I turn. Martin stands naked in the doorway.

"Come with me. Quickly."

I hesitate.

"Danny."

Smoke is creeping up through the floorboards. Martin takes my hand and leads me through the door.

The corridors of Drakemire are dark and endless, but cool after the heat of the room. Martin draws me out into the courtyard, leads me to the basement.

We slip past the thundering boiler. I assume we're going to the basement room, but the corridor goes on, becomes a tunnel of sorts.

As we go, I see more tunnels, half-filled with discarded tailor's mannequins, just like the basement room had. Some of the dummies are naked and sexless, others wholly or partially clothed. Some are partly dismantled, missing an arm, broken in half at the waist. Wherever there's such a break, the limb or torso ends in a surface of smooth, pinkish plastic, from which a thick metal rod, threaded like a screw, protrudes. One of the dummies has Mr Spanton's face. Their eyes move; I can hear the clicking of the lids, like the rustling of undergrowth in the panic flight of small creatures, as I pass.

"Jesus!"

I almost fall over it. It creeps on the stumps where its hands and knees should be. No hair; no face. The mouth and eyelids sewn up; nose and ears gone, the skin sutured. The featureless head angles towards me, seeing me somehow despite the lack of means.

"What is it?" I whisper.

Martin tugs my hand. "Come on."

The tunnel extends. Some kind of firelight illuminates it; I can't tell where from.

"Here."

We've reached a room. A stained floor. A table with straps. On a stand beside it, rusty scalpels.

Scuttling sounds.

"Come on."

The room is long. The walls are lined with shelves. Each labelled. A boy's name. They contain organs, limbs, parts of faces.

I see half a face in one jar. As I lean close, the eye opens. The lips move.

"Here." Martin points. An eyeball and some organs in a jar marked J KEARNEY. "Here." A skullcap of scalp and bone, fragments of pulsating brain: M THWAITES. "Here." A face, Martin's face, in a jar: M BERRY.

You don't want to look at him, but you can't stop yourself. His eye sockets are empty, but he sees you. Takes your arm. Points.

As you turn your head to look, you see Martin's eyes open in the jar and follow you.

In the jar beside Martin's, you see various things, but can't put a name to them, because all you really see is the label: D DENHOLM.

You turn, but you are alone. Martin is gone. You stare at the jar. You stumble away. Blundering between the shelves, looking for a way out...

You find a side tunnel.

Whimpering with relief, you stagger down it.

You stop and look back. Behind you is a dead end.

You turn away. Move down the tunnel. Vision is flawed; what's wrong? You try to whisper reassurance to yourself but something is wrong with your speech.

Round the corner and something faces you. It is naked. There are holes in its body where organs have been taken out. It has no lips. Below the upper mandible is only a hole tapering into the throat and neck, rimmed with gristle or bone, edged with teeth. One eye remains; the other is gone, the socket fused, skin stitched crudely shut. The nose is a hole. Most of the skin is gone from the other side of the face; the surviving eye stands immobile and lidless.

You look at it a long time; at last you understand. But you do not believe, until you reach out and touch the mirror's grimy glass.

The mirror breaks and falls, becomes dust and less than dust. The firelight is going. With a groan of turning cogs, the tunnel roof sinks low. You drop to all fours, and as the light dies, you run. And all you hear is the scuttling of those like you, and from far above, the endless rumbling of a train. It is the closest sound to comfort you will hear.

# The House on the Western Border

### By
### Gary Fry

**GARY FRY** has a PhD in psychology, though his first love is literature. He's had around sixty short stories published all around the world, and his first collection The Impelled and Other Head Trips (Crowswing Books) was released in 2006, with an introduction by Ramsey Campbell, in which Gary was described as "a master". His second book is a collection of cosmic horror entitled World Wide Web and Other Lovecraftian Upgrades (Humdrumming; introduction by Mark Morris), and his third a collection called Sanity and Other Delusions: Tales of Psychological Horror (PS Publishing; introduction by Stephen Volk). Gary also runs Gray Friar Press, and amid his publishing schedule, is currently working on several novels and more stories. Feel free to visit him here: http:// www.grayfriarpress.com/gary-fry/index.html. Gary says, "The idea for *The House on the Western Border* came from my thinking about how I could, as it were, socialise the traditional haunted house theme – often my way of writing fiction. I'd been working as an academic researcher and was interviewing in Holyhead, Anglesey when it occurred to me that the town's location might serve a double purpose: 'Western' meaning its geographical position on the island, as well as its former status as a key port in the West's dominance of global commerce. Coupling this with an interest in how right-thinking individuals can nevertheless be addicted to irrepressible consumerism, the tale burst forth with a flood of ghostly imagery. And those *things* that appear at the end of the piece – if they're not real, then they ought to be..."


"MUMMY, IT WANTS ME!"

This comment from her daughter had been enough to make Charlotte buy the house after only one viewing. Melissa was only five and sometimes got her words in the wrong order, but the enthusiasm in her eyes upon looking at the stocky detached on the west coast of Anglesey had put a lump in Charlotte's throat, had caused her to make a spontaneous decision quite against her usual uncertain judgement.

They were on their way now. The hatchback rattled a little at higher speeds on the motorway from Yorkshire – too many bloody businessmen charging from one rotten deal to another, no doubt – so Charlotte stuck to the slow lane, using the additional time to think about her divorce settlement.

Out of court, Jeremy had promised enough to pay the mortgage and a decent allowance – of course he had: after his sordid little affair at the office, even a solicitor outside of his considerable tax bracket would have taken him apart. But Charlotte wasn't unreasonable. Yes, she'd been angry, but she always tried to see the best in people. The fact that he'd blamed her excessive shopping bills for his straying, despite the fact that she'd had little else to occupy her while he globetrot, was now forgiven: not forgotten, though. She'd developed at least this little wisdom from her failed marriage.

"Mummy, will there be lots of new friends to meet in Hang Hell Sea?"

Charlotte chuckled at Melissa's mispronunciation, even though the words had sounded sinister somehow, as if portentous... But she shoved aside such thoughts; she was obviously just a tad anxious, the kind of feelings which always accompanied such a major move.

"Where's Helen?" she asked, alluding to her daughter's imaginary friend, whom Melissa had invoked in noisy Bradford. It wasn't as if she'd known many other children around their secluded house in the city: what would be the difference between starting school there and in the Welsh island's capital of Llangefni?

"She couldn't come," Melissa replied, looking rather sullen in the rear-view mirror. "Her nasty Daddy said so. Are we nearly there yet?"

Charlotte wasn't at all concerned about her daughter's recourse to imagination; why, she'd invented people herself as a child. She thought this was simply nature's way of helping youngsters work through complicated experience. God, it was hard enough as an adult! Maybe what Charlotte needed was an ideal partner, yet short of conjuring one out of the ether, she didn't imagine she'd have any luck there in the near future. Never mind. Despite her loneliness lately, she'd always been resourceful. She must be so now.

"Not far to go!" she called over her shoulder, steering off an A-road and onto a long winding lane, which soon led to a coastline in front of a tiny village cut into a hillside. "Look at the beach, Melissa! You could build sandcastles every day!"

The thought of such property under threat from the elements contributed to Charlotte's growing sense of disquiet, but again she ignored these intuitions (if indeed there *were* such) and suddenly plunged the car into a tunnel.

Darkness slipped over them like a presence of danger, and once she'd throttled out of the other side, the world felt large and threatening. It was early autumn; the trees in the roadside were black, bony and naked. Nevertheless, when Charlotte hit the Menai Strait Bridge, she forced herself to be optimistic. They were both cutting ties with the grubby social world. The island would provide a cloistered, happy existence; she simply *knew* it.

Suddenly the radio she had on – hitherto playing relaxing instrumental music – started broadcasting a news report involving a suspected terrorist attack in a major city; the name "Al-Qaeda" was mentioned – but Charlotte switched off the unit before more could be mentioned. Her daughter tried unsuccessfully to pronounce what little she'd heard – "Al...ka...da..." – but that was all; there was no need to worry, and without doing so, Charlotte accelerated on.

Anglesey was somewhat barren, yet charming. Charlotte's Sat-Nav system led her to a sequence of deserted roundabouts, and then bypassed the administrative centre of Llangefni (which would be the place they'd visit for shopping and Melissa's school, and maybe even a part-time job if Charlotte fancied it, once she'd settled) to make for the west coast.

She'd spotted the property online. A private sale cutting out agents and the like had suited both parties, and the bank, taking a single look at Jeremy's annual income, had said yes immediately. The previous owner hadn't lived there (he was in fact based in London, running a property-development business), but had had the place whitewashed, the better for newcomers to stamp their mark upon it, however they desired. And Charlotte was eager to do so.

She wasn't an irresponsible shopper, but she'd always liked nice things. Okay, so there were millions starving in the world, and even countless folk on the breadline in the UK, but Charlotte had rarely been able to help herself when buying. She donated cash regularly to many charities, was a vegetarian, had taught Melissa not to be racist (quite a burning issue in their formerly native Bradford). So she was allowed at least *one* vice, wasn't she?

Charlotte was simply determined to make a fresh start furnishings-wise, and also to exact a little petty revenge on her ex-husband... But all that could wait till later. The removal company had promised to have their existing stuff delivered yesterday. Apparently, the one neighbour within walking distance had been entrusted with a key to let the guys she'd hired inside, to place her basic goods – two beds, a TV, a number of kitchen mod cons, and a few other sticks of functional furniture – in appropriate places. Everything was set for their arrival.

The Sat-Nav didn't recognise the lane along which a vivid memory of their previous visit prompted Charlotte to turn. She switched off the unit, telling herself that there *wasn't* a cruel, gathering wind interfering with reception in the area. There was a telephone connection in the property, and she had a wireless Internet account, so it wasn't as if they'd ever be stranded here...

Goodness, she was putting the frighteners on herself before they'd even reached the building!

And then they *had*.

Charlotte had been just about to announce the news to Melissa when the words were snatched from her. The house's severe gables had reared over the crest of a slight curve of rich land, like the prow of a ship seeking mysterious faraway territory... Indeed, with the sea behind it, currently choppy and swirling, this interpretation was even harder to resist. But then the hatchback ascended the slope and when it promptly trundled along a steady plateau, the property stabilised: solid, imperious, shadow-laden.

If there *was* any movement about its considerable bearing, it would be only inside.

\*

Charlotte quashed her mounting fretfulness at once. The glass in the windows which dominated the building's implacable façade had reflected the cloud in their wake, yet *only* this. There was no removal van in the broad, weed-patched driveway, neither any sign of the neighbour who'd been asked to pass on the key to her. The building must be empty.

Now that this was decided, Charlotte felt a little impatient. Men letting her down *again*, she thought, though she knew the accusation was unfair. They weren't *all* bad, and she mustn't become one of those embittered women who poison their daughter's minds against the male of the species.

Instead of dwelling on the past, Charlotte removed her seatbelt, was delighted to realise that she needn't slip the Sat-Nav off its stand and into her handbag (there would be no kids out stealing around *here*), and then twisted to glance at Melissa. The girl was sitting pertly on the backseat, her gaze fixed beyond her mother – on the house.

"Well, we've arrived," Charlotte announced, brushing a lapsed trestle of hair from her daughter's forehead with fingertips which quivered with – *excitement*, surely; anything else would be absurd. Then Charlotte added, "Do you still like it?"

Melissa suddenly caught her stare, and seemed to adjust her focus a moment, as if she'd just been jerked out of a trance of sorts…or a heavy, dream-burdened sleep. "I told you before, Mummy," she said at last, smiling a carefree smile. "It wants me. It *wants* me!"

Instantly she darted to the left and clattered against one of the rear doors. It arced open with a creak of hinges, mimicking the brief moment of panic which had assailed Charlotte's mind in response to the girl's comment.

*It wants me.* Hadn't she corrected her daughter's use of words the first time she'd uttered this phrase? Generally Melissa required only a single instruction to avoid making the same linguistic gaffe again, yet on this occasion that hadn't helped. Had she therefore *meant* what she'd said? The possibility was far too bizarre to entertain…

However, Charlotte found herself doing so as she climbed outside, stretched her legs and her back to alleviate the muscular tension of the long drive, and then slowly strode across to Melissa, who'd taken to performing an impromptu dance in the sketchy shadows of the property. It was five o'clock, close to sunset. The atmosphere in the region appeared too dense, too busy.

Charlotte glanced away from the house, at several shrubs and bushes that approximately demarcated the plot she'd purchased so recklessly. Beyond this cluster of vegetation, which the breeze now rustled with pernicious sentience, were miles and miles of nothingness: just faded green hills, a few electrical pylons, and a house further along the coast. The edge of the land looked severe; paths over this lip led down to the tide-wrinkled beach they'd surveyed during their first trip. They could explore this border more thoroughly another time – tomorrow, later in the week, the rest of their joyful lives... Yes, she *must* remain positive; this would be such a good place for them both.

Just then, Charlotte felt eyes upon her. Of course it was only her daughter, soliciting her prompt attention. Charlotte turned, using a smile to conceal the treachery of her tired, aging mind.

"Mummy, can we go in?"

"Of course! You don't think we travelled all this way to stand in the cold, do you?"

Melissa giggled. "Silly!" she said, the way she had sometimes when Jeremy had teased her with a good-natured joke – but there was little to be gained thinking that way.

Charlotte stooped to hug the girl, and as she did so, she shifted her head to view the house.

There were two storeys, the windows on this side giving on to a lounge and a dining room. Round the back was a large kitchen, and upstairs a bathroom and three bedrooms, while higher still, there was an attic: this latter was the only chamber Charlotte hadn't accessed during her viewing last month. A young chap with a slightly nervous demeanour – the owner's son, apparently, who'd happened to be in the area on business – had shown her around. Recently rewired, central-heated, the plumbing all sound...how could she have resisted? The surveys had come back clean, and the deeds had been sent to the bank from her solicitor (also Jeremy's) the previous week. It was amazing how plenty of money guaranteed such expediency.

Nevertheless, Charlotte didn't wish to dwell upon the rotten issues of finance and contracts and other related horrors. Instead

139

she wanted to think about the future that this place would offer her and her daughter. It was the isolation which had really attracted her: the modern world – yes, she could admit it – scared her. Her husband's huge deals and worldwide contacts had made her feel out of her depths. She was a simple girl from North Yorkshire, fundamentally a private person. A secret part of her was actually glad about what had happened in her marriage, though she'd rationalised this ostensibly ignoble sensation by considering Melissa. Charlotte hadn't wanted the girl to grow up in such a corrupt, frightening lifestyle, and that's what Jeremy's position at *OK Ideas* – the country's (if not Europe's) leading furniture outlet – had seemed to threaten. Look at what it had done to *him*, after all: working-class-lad-made-good, hard working and trustworthy, a talent for persuasion...in more ways than one now.

Charlotte shuddered, and then blinked. She looked anew at the house.

And that was when she saw the figure.

It was little more than a silhouette, possibly engendered by a fault in one of the lower panes. If there *was* someone inside, the reflection of branches in the untended front garden was merging with this image. It resembled a person made of bone and sinew – not stitched together properly, whether by flesh (an unthinkable prospect which almost caused Charlotte to cover Melissa's eyes) or clothing...

Then the shape vanished entirely as her daughter suddenly spoke.

"Man coming," she said, and the shudder which immediately assailed Charlotte's spine must have been a consequence of the sharp gust of wind that had just whipped around them both.

Charlotte broke their cuddle, stepped back a pace, and was relieved to notice that Melissa was staring *away* from the property. The girl couldn't have seen what Charlotte thought she'd seen. It had just been a trick of the damaged glass, hadn't it? Yes, of course it had.

Shrugging off these thoughts, she tracked the angle of her

daughter's gaze.

A man was indeed approaching. He was about Charlotte's height, yet somewhat stocky; he had on a pair of slack trousers and was huddled inside a great overcoat, as if he knew how nippy it could grow in the district, and therefore had much to teach them. As he drew closer, Charlotte noticed that he had short, greying hair, perched atop a craggy face sporting frameless spectacles. He appeared scholarly, friendly.

Despite the fact that she wasn't wearing a jacket, a little of her former unease fled her as the guy slowed to halt a yard in front of her and Melissa. However, Charlotte kept hold of the girl, pretending she was actually protecting her from the keening breeze.

"Good day!" exclaimed the newcomer, a broad grin lending his avuncular expression even more warmth. "I believe you're the Chappells – I was told to expect you."

In fact Charlotte had reverted to her maiden name – Fleece – but there was no reason to reveal this now. Melissa was still using her Dad's surname, and why not? Jeremy would play a major part in her life, whatever the distance now between them.

"Hi there," Charlotte said after only a small pause, during which she'd managed to reorganise her uppity mind. "And I guess you must be the neighbour who has our key?"

"I am indeed! Keith Morris, at your service." Suddenly he stooped, wafting both of his closed fists in front of Melissa. "Hey, now you look like a clever young lady! So tell me: which hand is holding the key to your...your magical new home?"

Charlotte had detected the hesitation in the man's comment, and wondered what it had betokened. Still, she was able to ignore this concern for the moment as her daughter wriggled free of her grip and then went to choose.

After a few seconds of pondering, Melissa eventually clapped the chap's right hand, which soon swivelled and unfurled...to reveal a set of bronze-coloured keys on a featureless fob.

"Hurrah!" said Keith, passing the keys to the girl by way of an impromptu prize, and then leaning back to address her mother. "A superstitious man might read more into that than is in fact there, but a dullard old researcher such as myself is thinking luck, intuition, innate smartness..."

Just then, there was *definitely* a movement inside the property, but when Charlotte glanced that way, she saw only an upstairs curtain twitching, presumably in response to the wind feeling at the pane.

She hastily switched her attention to the man.

"Thanks for this, Mr. Morris," she explained, and although a small part of her wished to be alone with Melissa on this momentous occasion, another significant part realised that it would be rude to rush away: the fellow had braved the cold to help them out, after all. Charlotte added, "Melissa, why don't you go and unlock the door? I'll be there in a short while."

"Yippee!" cried the girl, and offered the man the kind of confident, beautiful smile she ordinarily reserved for very close friends or family: her surviving grandparents, for instance, who'd pledged a visit later in the month.

"Please call me Keith," said the man, once Melissa was out of earshot. "I dare say we're going to be seeing more of each other, yes?"

Although his bearing didn't appear lecherous (this initial interpretation on Charlotte's part was obviously only perceptual residue from Jeremy's recent misdemeanour), his words had borne enough ambiguity to render her uncertain. She didn't desire romantic complications – at least, none so soon. Therefore, rather tongue-tied, she replied, "Yes, perhaps you and your...your wife and family might call in for a drink once we're settled."

Keith didn't take his eyes off her as he answered. "Oh, just me at home. Aye, just me."

He was pointing to the property Charlotte had spotted earlier: a smaller house further along the coast, currently enshrouded in mist and the declining daylight. She didn't really think his behaviour was actually the most obvious come-on she'd ever experienced – for one thing, the fellow must be in his late-forties; she was only thirty-three. No, he was simply stating facts: those he'd hinted at when revealing his profession about a minute ago.

Charlotte was about to go on – quite what she intended to add, she couldn't be certain – when Keith resumed.

"Yeah, I must say I was surprised when I heard that the old place had been sold. It's been vacant for about a decade. And such a curious way of going about it…" He seemed to hesitate, as if troubled, and then – that warm smile re-emerging – he looked at the house, which Melissa was still trying to prise open. "Still, what do I know? When I moved here, dinosaurs still…still roamed the earth!"

The comment had obviously been intended as a joke, yet Charlotte had been sharp enough, or highly wrought from recent stress, to detect another of those slight breaks in his monologue. She was intrigued, but it wasn't the time to enquire about this now. It was getting darker; there was much to do before a much needed early night.

"Mr. Mor…sorry, Keith. I wonder if you'll excuse me. I'm exhausted from the journey down here, and I have a few things to sort out."

"Oh, not at all! You must certainly do so."

"But I was about to say…"

"And your delightful daughter will naturally want something to eat."

"Yes, she will: burgers and chips, no doubt." That was another reason why the location had attracted Charlotte: no fast food restaurants; she might soon convince Melissa that vegetarianism wasn't as 'yukky' as she'd always claimed back in the city. But just now, Charlotte had to get on without offending Keith. Today was Wednesday – they'd be free at the weekend. Then she said, "Why don't you pop in for a drink on Saturday evening – about seven? I'd love to hear about the district: what to seek out, what to…to avoid, et cetera."

Her own hesitation had elicited a strange look on the man's face: it reminded her of her ex-husband's when he'd nervously broken his terrible news about what he'd been up to lately… But Charlotte was surely being oversensitive. Indeed, Keith soon accepted the invitation with some gusto, and then bidding her good luck rather than goodbye – a verbal curiosity which might be specific to the island – he fled rather hurriedly.

Charlotte watched him stroll away, still slightly puzzled; but a moment later she headed for the house.

Melissa had finally succeeded in turning a heavy key in a solid lock. The door stirred open, as if someone was inside...and summoning them forth.

*It wants me*, her daughter had said, and suddenly all Charlotte could picture in the chaos of her mind was Keith Morris's expression before his somewhat hasty departure.

*

The next few hours proved to be anticlimactic. Charlotte had been looking forward to this moment – moving in to their new home! – for weeks now, ever since the final documents had been signed, and the arrangements made for flitting. But the facts, as usual, had proved deceptive.

After an impromptu meal derived from several tins they'd unpacked (along with a number of other necessary items: crockery, cutlery, toiletries), she and Melissa were so tired that it was an effort to look around the house again with the refreshed eyes of ownership.

Her daughter claimed the smallest of the three bedrooms – the *cosiest*, she told one of her stuffed toys, which nodded resolutely with an instructive finger at its neck. Meanwhile, Charlotte examined the largest with a species of complicated dismay. She'd requested the double bed from the visitors' room in their Bradford house, and now here it was: too big, too cold, too clean. Indeed, her experience at present felt antiseptic, as if they were intruding on someone else's life, as if they shouldn't be here at all...

Charlotte soon managed to quell this mental rebellion with a few neat gins from the box of spirits that had been among the first things on her list of essentials. She made Melissa a mug of hot chocolate, and once the moon had risen full and white in a cloud-slashed sky, she closed all the makeshift curtains (she'd certainly replace everything the previous owner had left, including the bland wallpaper) and went to tuck the girl into bed.

"You okay?" Charlotte asked, feeling a tad guilty about everything that had happened, even though the only error she'd arguably committed was choosing a property so far away from Yorkshire. Nevertheless, Melissa's forlorn gaze caused her to experience every unpleasant moment of these misgivings.

"I hope they'll be some nice children to be friends with," the girl said, the words somehow slipping undistorted through a large yawn. Then she closed her mouth, though only for a second. Turning over, as if the act was a deliberate affront, she finished, "I miss Daddy."

*Yes, but darling, we've discussed all this, haven't we? How* he *was to blame, and why* I *had to get away...*

But what was the use? Melissa was probably already asleep, just as kids were somehow able to do whatever the circumstances. And it was certainly wrong to take out on her what Charlotte ought to reserve for Jeremy.

He was a *bastard*. Charlotte backed out of the bedroom, snicking shut the door. She'd already locked up downstairs, so there was nothing now to keep her from her planned early night. Only a noise from the ground floor prevented her from stepping reluctantly into the master bedroom, and she quickly descended: after all she'd been through lately, she wasn't scared of much any more.

There was of course nothing – *nobody* – in the dining room or the kitchen. So Charlotte returned to the lounge, where her unfinished drink appeared considerably less full than she believed she'd left it. She must have supped more than she'd thought! Perhaps this had resulted in some kind of weird auditory hallucination...

Oh, *whatever*. She stooped to the glass, found its rim colder than it surely ought to be, and then drained the contents. The fiery liquid burned her throat. She twisted to review the remainder of the room. Her laptop computer was positioned on a desk which the removal men had stationed behind the door. Yes, she'd have some fun with that tomorrow, and no mistake!

She made tipsily for the stairwell, refusing to grant the apparition that appeared in the peripheries of her gaze, beyond the jaws of the lightless kitchen, so much as a thought, let alone a glance. Then she stamped up the steps, each riser alcoholically reconfigured in turn as her husband's skull and that of his floozy, her husband's skull and that of his floozy… But she was being cruel, even if they both deserved more than she'd hitherto dealt them. Charlotte wasn't a violent person: she'd never do anyone any intentional harm; she wouldn't be able to bear the guilt.

Thus thinking, she washed and changed, in advance of climbing under her indifferently chilly sheets. After retreating from the bathroom she'd poked her head around the door of Melissa's room, and had been reassured to find her daughter sound asleep.

As Charlotte closed her eyes, she couldn't help wishing that there was someone here to do the same for her…and it was surely only this nebulous thought before drifting off which had her imagining a man standing at the threshold of her own room, just watching and watching with an indeterminable expression on his shadow-heavy face.

\*

She was awakened by a rough hand at her shoulder. At first Charlotte thought it was Jeremy, probably expecting a little morning nookie, but then as sleep fled her mind like general contentment had recently, she realised that those days were now gone. She opened her eyes and at once squinted in the wan sunlight falling through cheap, functional curtains.

"Mummy, I had a dream!" Melissa was saying. She'd already dressed, and was looking both forlorn and excited, as if her mood today might run either way. "I had a dream that we visited the best shop in the world and that it was right here, in Hang Hell Sea! Can we find it? Can we go in the car and look?"

" 'Morning, d-dear," Charlotte replied, her words compromised by her usual sluggish wakefulness. "Er, give me a few minutes, will you?"

"But, *Mummy*."

By now, Charlotte had managed to sit up, and would have appreciated a cup of tea if her daughter had been old enough to use the kettle. Her ex-husband had often greeted her on a morning with one... But she thrust aside these thoughts, the better to marshal her current situation.

"Okay, okay, we'll go later."

"*When* later?"

"Once I've...once I've done a few things around the house. We only moved in yesterday!"

"Boring! Boring, boring, boring..."

"*Melissa*." A renewed sense of guilt suddenly assaulted Charlotte; she still hadn't woken up properly. However, she managed to reply, "Hey, why don't you go outside and play? How many little girls get to live at the seaside? You should be...be grateful!"

Melissa pulled a face, but Charlotte realised with some relief that she hadn't taken the earlier mild admonishment personally. Indeed, the girl then smiled, and added, "Okay. I could go on the beach and build a sandcastle, couldn't I?"

And she was halfway to the doorway before Charlotte was able to call, "Be careful near the sea! If the tide's in, don't go too far!"

"I won't, Mummy! Bye!"

"Bye."

Once Charlotte had washed and changed, she was able to reflect to some purpose on several vague impressions running around her mind. She'd already booted up her laptop and removed her staff discount card from her purse by the time she questioned the double standards she seemed to be practising. On the one hand, she was eager to save her daughter from the worst excesses of consumerism – she'd seen how it affected youngsters, how it rendered their lives empty and meaningless. On the other hand, however, here *she* was, about to go online and spend a fortune at Jeremy's expense.

Amid the confusion and rancour of the divorce, her ex-husband had obviously forgotten to cancel Charlotte's account with *OK Ideas*. And this would permit her act of trivial vengeance. She clicked on the link from her Favourites column, and then started browsing the many pages of stylish fittings and furniture. She couldn't stop herself from amassing a heady list of objects, and even when she proceeded to the checkout to add her new address to the data saved on her hard drive, she requested the expensive option of Next-Day Delivery.

It was as if someone was behind her, encouraging her hand to carry out such ignoble deeds... But when she foolishly swivelled to glance, there was nothing in the lounge but a gentle breeze slipping through the window she'd opened earlier to let in a little unpolluted air. She hadn't done that often in Bradford, and this was another way in which she was saving Melissa from the grubby modern world.

Nevertheless, once she'd completed the order for a dining suite, chairs, a coffee table, a sofa, curtains, and more, Charlotte couldn't avoid pondering upon the hypocrisy of having done so. She'd tried to justify this latest act of heavy spending by claiming that she was doing it to punish Jeremy, yet if she was truly honest with herself, she knew she wouldn't have done anything different if she'd still been married to him – even if he hadn't had an affair.

However hard she struggled to protect her daughter from such a lifestyle, might Melissa absorb this behaviour by osmosis? Indeed, hadn't the girl woken this morning after a dream about a *shop*?

Just then, Charlotte heard footsteps in the hall passage. Quickly, she shut down the website and accessed another at random – a news report containing headline stories about the tumultuous Middle East and the terrible living conditions in other foreign places. Then, feeling even more uneasy about what she'd just done, she glanced up at the doorway, expecting her daughter to round the frame at any moment.

But no one came.

Charlotte frowned, closed down the computer, and soon stood to stroll for the hallway. Then she looked up and down it: there was no one there at all.

She shivered a little, shutting out nebulous recollections of certain events the previous evening. It must be the booze she'd imbibed before sleep which was playing merry buggery with her psyche.

She shook her head and advanced to the kitchen to make some light lunch.

\*

That afternoon, Charlotte drove them both to Llangefni.

Melissa had washed off the sand she'd been digging up all morning, and seemed mercifully unconcerned about what the sea would do to whatever she'd built on the beach. If she could be this dismissive of possessions, of commodities, there might be hope for her yet...

Nevertheless, as soon as they reached the small town at the heart of the island, Melissa started looking around, her eyes almost circular in the hope of spotting (Charlotte knew this expression well) her beloved *Toys R Us*.

In fact, on her reconnaissance mission to Anglesey, Charlotte had been keen to ensure that no such chain stores had branches here. There was a *Tesco*, of course, and less intimidating outlets of a few other nationwide companies. But on the whole, the shops were independent businesses, each offering goods too idiosyncratic to attract the common consumer. This had appealed to Charlotte a great deal.

Once she'd parked up beside a narrow river, Charlotte led Melissa into a small network of roads occupied by only a modest number of milling pedestrians. They both exchanged smiles with people who must live in the vicinity. Melissa, with her blond hair tied back in a cute ponytail, attracted several wistful grins from a number of elderly folk, who constituted the majority of the shoppers. Charlotte knew the population of the island had a high average age, yet she'd also checked that couples with kids lived here, too. Indeed, there were many such families. This was a good balance, Charlotte believed: not enough youngsters to lead to peer pressure and anti-social group mentalities, and a solid bedrock of tradition and respect for time-honoured ways. It was perfect.

They soon found a craft-shop selling handmade dolls, and Melissa was so charmed by a tall, stocky, rough-looking chap – possibly inspired by the sailors whom Charlotte had been told frequented Holyhead a few miles south of their new home – that she wanted it immediately. Charlotte felt a little embarrassed by her daughter's demands, and in order to shut her up under the (surely unintentionally) critical gaze of the store's vendor, she used her last £10 note to buy the product, and then exited the building at once.

"There! Happy now?" she asked the girl, who carried the bag so carefully that it might contain a lifetime of joy.

"Yes. *Yes*," Melissa replied, and she'd reminded Charlotte so much of Jeremy – principally after he'd had his wicked weekly way with her – that she felt simultaneously like crying and screaming. But she managed to withhold these mixed emotions, and soon moved on, the better to preclude any further unrest.

She needed to go to the bank. By now, her ex-husband's direct debit would have been paid into her account, and she must remove a sum in order to buy a few essentials – food, drink, some medication – before returning home.

*Home.* As Charlotte advanced into *Barclays*, a temporarily contented Melissa in tow, this thought felt good. She rolled it around her mind a while: *home*. Their *new* home... How lovely! Maybe all it would take was a short period of time to settle there.

Encouraged by such ruminations, she stepped across to join a short queue.

An old lady was soon the only person ahead of them. After a few minutes, this woman (responding to a rustle of Melissa's bag as the girl checked inside before issuing a renewed girlish coo of appreciation) turned to greet them, smiling thinly, yet appearing hesitant to speak. Eventually, however, she said something which wasn't in English, and which made Charlotte scowl involuntarily, while Melissa only chuckled.

"I'm sorry?" Charlotte replied, and suddenly realised that they'd been addressed in Welsh. "Oh, I beg your pardon. We…we don't speak that language."

Of course Charlotte had heard stereotypical rumours about racist attitudes held by the Welsh with regard to the English, yet she knew that these were largely ridiculous. She'd hitherto found the residents nothing short of charming and welcoming. Nevertheless, on this occasion, they might have hit upon a rare somebody who actually offered substance to the cliché. In any case, there was no chance to discover, since then the lady was summoned by a teller, and then Charlotte was, too – by the person in the booth beside the old woman's.

She went at once.

"Hi, may I draw two hundred pounds from this account, please?"

"Certainly, madam," said the young chap (he was really rather attractive, though far too young for Charlotte) who received her Visa card and proceeded to process the request. Then he added, "I haven't seen you around before. I know most people in the area – it's a small community. Are you just visiting?"

"No, we've – that is, my daughter and I – we've just moved here: from Yorkshire. Anglesey's a beautiful place."

The young man smiled, switching his gaze to Melissa, who'd suddenly grown shy and had immediately glanced away. "Splendid," he added. "I know you'll love it here. Tell me," – as he spoke, he had her sign a printed slip, in advance of counting her cash twice – "whereabouts are you living?"

"It's a detached property on the west coast, not far from…" If she got the pronunciation right, she might placate the possibly anti-

English woman beside her. "...from Llanfaethlu." Charlotte hesitated and then, for perhaps for the first time, spoke the name of her home aloud. "It's called Crossley House."

Nothing could have prepared her for the vehement response these words elicited.

Suddenly the old lady beside her was stuffing her handbag with a few notes she'd been dealt through the glass partition. Then she retreated swiftly, demonstrating an agility which almost certainly belied her advanced age.

Charlotte twisted to watch her go, intuitively holding Melissa to one side. When the old woman conceded a single glance backwards, she appeared frightened rather than angry, and soon she was gone, out through the doorway and along the pavement at an undiminished speed.

When Charlotte turned back to gaze at both tellers in quick succession, they appeared identically nonplussed. But they were young, and neither had a Welsh accent.

What on earth did *that* imply?

\*

Once Charlotte had driven back to the house, she'd had enough time to think. The old lady in the bank couldn't have been retaliating in a racist manner to the news that more English people had moved to the island, since she'd only reacted with such bizarre behaviour to the *name* of their house...

Before climbing out of the car, Charlotte glanced at the building. There was of course no movement within, just that single pane of uneven glass reflecting the many storm clouds loitering overhead.

Melissa beat her to the entrance, an impromptu race which raised Charlotte's spirits. Luckily, her daughter seemed not to have perceived anything untoward in the strange episode that Charlotte was struggling to rationalise. So Charlotte unlocked the door and paced inside, watching as the girl rushed upstairs with her bag, presumably to add its decidedly masculine contents to her collection of dolls on a shelf the previous owner had thoughtfully screwed to the wall above her bed.

*The previous owner...* Now Charlotte considered this, she realised that she actually didn't know anything about the history of her property. Maybe Keith Morris might help there: he would visit the day after tomorrow, for an evening drink and a chat... Of course Charlotte could simply access the Internet and Google 'Crossley House'; indeed, she was about to do so when a tiny shudder scudded along the length of her spine, and she didn't know why. Perhaps the central heating, which she'd triggered that morning, needed adjusting. She advanced into the lounge, setting down the bags full of shopping she'd purchased at a supermarket just outside the town centre.

And then she froze on the spot.

Her computer was on again. She was certain she'd switched it off before leaving. But her homepage was on display, its neat row of favourite sites lined up to the left.

In any other circumstances, she could blame stress for causing her to forget to close down the machine – but then she realised something somewhat unsettling.

Even if she *had* left it running, the laptop possessed a power-saving device; every twenty minutes or so, the screen went blank while the hard drive snoozed.

And Charlotte and Melissa had been gone for several hours.

*

The following day, the delivery arrived at 11 a.m. Whatever negative comments anyone made about the firm – and many people had; the company had been severely criticised by a number of significant cultural commentators for various reasons – it was as good as its word vis-à-vis customers. (Unlike its staff in relation to their loved ones, Charlotte couldn't help reflect rather sourly.)

As the three men hauled all the goods into the house, Charlotte took Melissa for a walk to the beach, the better to gather her own thoughts, which were running in danger of overwhelming her.

"Mummy, I'm *really* bored," said her daughter, as she kicked up a spray of sand.

"Oh, for goodness sake, Melissa!" Charlotte hadn't been able to prevent this snappy reply. Indeed, she didn't relent as she continued. "Just wait until you're an adult, then you'll realise how...*golden* your childhood is. Believe me."

The girl shrugged, responding to her mother's rare disciplinary outburst with a naïvely wise silence. Then she skipped on ahead, slowing only once she'd reached the sea, which soon lapped around her sandals in lively puddles.

Charlotte reflected on her own youth, growing up relatively simply in North Yorkshire. However, in the early 'eighties as a teenager, she'd been seduced by Leeds and had moved there with a few friends, enjoying the nightlife and her burgeoning career as a hairstylist. Then she'd met Jeremy at a party, and he'd impressed her with his talk of corporate life and unqualified ambition. They'd married soon after, and Melissa had come along about five years later, during which time Charlotte had begun – only tacitly to start with – to consider what she'd left behind.

Being a grown-up hadn't proved to be all she'd imagined; it had borne responsibilities and demands which jarred against the idealism of her younger self. Even now, she retained residual traces of her uncorrupted outlook: it had been as if the world had been waiting for her, as if there was so much of it to explore... In truth, however, very little of this had come to pass. While her ex-husband had jetted around the globe, she'd quite literally been left holding the baby. He'd always promised her that once their daughter was older, they'd both be welcome to travel with him, visiting such wonderful places as South America, Africa and the Far East.

And then he'd done what he'd done with his P.A.

Charlotte now reflected on what he'd said during his confession: Was it serious? Yes, it was serious; I feel we married too young, darling; I hadn't really *found* myself; we've both grown in different ways; look, I *do* appreciate your loving nature, your caring attitude, but...but...well, it's not enough for me.

You don't *excite* me – I'm sorry, and all that.

She gazed out across the Irish Sea. Okay, so she *had* changed since their wedding, yet surely any decent person would applaud her concern for charities, for her fellow countrymen, and for a better world. Oh, but not Jeremy, apparently. He wanted thrilling sex, and all that money could buy. Actually, Charlotte did miss having a love life, and often wondered whether she'd been sublimating the surplus passion born of her ex's neglect of her into rampant buying...

*A tad patronising, that,* said a voice in her head, which had a female tone to combat the male one which had hitherto been addressing her. No, in fact Charlotte *knew* that she was inhabited by a commercial demon, one possibly indoctrinated during the Yuppy period in which she'd grown up. She'd been poisoned, simple as that, and although she wished to suck out the pernicious infection – as might some primitive person on a similar, though foreign shore – she knew that this disease was, as it were, carved into her bones. Even now, she could hear the delivery men filling her new home with stuff.

*Stuff.* The new God, and all the other clichés which never made a bit of difference to the average individual's spending habits. This was the very thing Charlotte could acknowledge that she was attempting to protect her daughter from.

Stuff.

Charlotte was as haunted as she'd begun to think Crossley House might be.

\*

There were no more strange episodes before Keith Morris came to visit – at any rate, Charlotte was too inebriated by the quixotic lure of her new goods to notice any. Melissa kept bothering her as she tried out each item in turn and then made plans on a sketchpad for the application of wallpaper and paint soonest. Eventually, Charlotte grew so exasperated by her daughter's interruptions that she tore off a handful of sheets of paper and thrust these upon the girl, along with a packet of crayons, telling her to go and draw something, that she *liked* drawing, and that she should be creative, for God's sake! Crying, Melissa rushed away to her bedroom, and Charlotte wasn't disturbed again. At last she could enjoy the fruits of her deception; she found herself relishing the expression on Jeremy's face, too, when he discovered just how much she'd run up his company account. And when, as the darkness grew thick at the windows, she heard *two* pairs of small feet rushing along the landing upstairs, Charlotte merely ascribed these to echoes caught in the old, old building's mysterious web.

*

"Mummy, I want you to meet Aka."
  "Who?"
  "Aka."
  "Who's Aka."?
  "She's my new friend and she's very hungry."
  Charlotte turned off the oven in which she'd been baking a few tasty morsels to enjoy for supper once their neighbour had arrived. She glanced at her daughter, and saw at once that she was quite alone. However, she was holding out a hand in the general direction of a space beside the new kitchen table – a space wide enough for another child. A few flies buzzed in this general area, though these had obviously just flitted from the carved, shiny wood, presumably attracted by the smells of food that now suffused the house.
  "Then you'd better serve her a meal before bedtime, hadn't you?" Charlotte eventually replied, despite a moment of unease during which she pondered again on whether imaginary friends were actually good for children. Still, Melissa would be starting school soon, and would surely make *real* pals. In the meanwhile, there was no harm in encouraging her powers of imagination: so few kids had any at all these days.
  "She wants to meet the nice man, too," the girl protested once

Charlotte had handed over a plate of Chinese and Indian nibbles, each piping hot. Charlotte was eager for her daughter to be asleep *before* Keith turned up; she wasn't certain why – perhaps because of what she planned to ask him about the property she'd bought so cheaply, and whose very name had clearly frightened the old lady in the bank on Thursday. Charlotte also recalled the episode involving the computer, and although she'd since deliberately avoided interpreting any other events as so creepily inexplicable, she'd already supped a few glasses of wine, the better that her enquiry later *would* be made.

"She can meet him another day," she said, and then shooed the girl and her imaginary friend upstairs. There was just a pocket of coolness where Melissa had claimed this person had originally been standing; the central heating couldn't have taken full grip of the building yet.

Her daughter moaned as she left, but at least now Charlotte believed that Melissa was no longer feeling alone, however temporary this state of affairs ought to remain.

Returning to her preparation, Charlotte tried to scrub her restless mind of too much foolish material, and poured herself another glass of red.

And that was when someone knocked at the front door.

Seven p.m. Bang on time. She reflected that her husband had rarely arrived home from work so soon, especially towards the end of their marriage... Nevertheless, Charlotte struggled to eliminate any possible connection between these two men as she hurried along the hallway to let her neighbour inside.

Annoyingly, the door seemed to stick a little before she managed to yank it open, and from the top of the flight of steps behind her she heard a satisfied giggle. Just Melissa, she decided; her daughter would tease her tomorrow about having had a man in the house. But there was nothing like *that* going on at all – at least not with someone so much older than Charlotte.

"Go to bed!" she called, and there was no response, so she turned to smile at the newcomer, the wine she'd already consumed perhaps lending her a look of excitement which she hadn't planned. Indeed, she attempted to control any such floozy-like demeanour as she said, "Please come in."

"Thank you. Thank you."

He'd brought a bottle of white, she noticed, and the sight put her even more on her guard. However, she mustn't suspect that he was as bad as Jeremy had proved to be – trying to ply her into bed whenever he could. Keith probably remained a bachelor through choice, his work his real passion in life, just as the house was becoming hers. She'd polished and tidied the property all day. It looked pristine, nearly glorious. She was settling in very well.

"Won't you come through?"

And this time he offered her only a single, "Thank you."

They chatted and laughed quite a lot together, principally because, Charlotte suspected, he was able to adapt his more experienced personality to hers rather than vice versa. But that didn't matter, did it? It was the man's role to play the pursuer...

By nine o'clock, Charlotte had drunk a full bottle of wine, and now Keith was proposing to open another, clearly enjoying himself, too. Nevertheless, Charlotte claimed that she must first check on Melissa, and somehow she managed to negotiate the swaying staircase, whose banister felt considerably less sturdy than it had up until now.

Her daughter was sound asleep, the doll she'd purchased yesterday looming above her: it was a facsimile of a chap of the old school with a job which warranted a good wage, as opposed to the huge amount Jeremy had been paid for only his natural charm and wiliness...

God, how she *hated* him: yes, deep down, beneath the façade she'd been maintaining for the sake of her girl and which had now been prised open by alcohol, Charlotte wanted to punish her ex-husband, or wished for him to be hurt, and...and *horribly...*

Just then, however, she noticed something she hadn't earlier: there was a fault on the new set of drawers she'd ordered from *OK Ideas*. One leg had developed a blotch of sorts, a dark patch against the stained surface. She'd selected this type of blackish wood throughout the property – it was elegant and robust, befitting the character of survivors, as both she and Melissa were. But now this was tainted.

Indeed, her daughter then stirred in her sleep, as if someone was trying to rouse her.

*Her imaginary friend – Aka, had she been called?*

Oh, that was so much bullshit! Charlotte even laughed a little as she paced back from the threshold, closing the door to shut out the sight of a bed-sheet rising independently of the girl: this was only Charlotte's drink-challenged perception, as was the image's audibly *swishing* accompaniment.

Without further hesitation, Charlotte strayed across to the bathroom, had a quick pee, and then went back downstairs to reassure her guest that she was indeed still alive.

*

"So...so who lived in this house before I, er, *we* arrived?"

At last she'd asked the question, though none too cleanly. Nevertheless, the booze had served its purpose; she might let up on the wine now in order to listen to Keith's answer.

Charlotte could admit that she was fearful of what she might learn; she'd already grown attached to the property, and would certainly be reluctant to leave even for an outlandish reason. However, she quelled the confusion which appeared to have formed a knot directly at the heart of her, and listened as her older friend started to talk.

"Well, I'm afraid I can't enlighten you about the company which sold the building to you: I understand the owner snapped it up via the Internet, whitewashing the place for a quick sale. Certainly nobody in the area would buy it, and that's why it's been vacant for so long... Oh yes, of course, I should explain."

He paused to take a fresh sip of his drink – he could clearly handle it with ease – and then resumed his narrative.

"These are all rumours, but I suppose someone will tell you

before long, so it might as well be me. The house...*Crossley* House is reputed to be haunted. It's got quite a reputation in Anglesey, silly stories passed around the aged folk who were once young here, when everything Welsh *was* Welsh and the English had yet to discover the property market. But that's all by the by. Basically, the story goes like this..."

Charlotte hadn't noticed before now, but the guy was actually English. Lord knows why she'd assumed he was a native of the island. In any case, she said nothing. The word 'haunted', however, had caused her to pour herself another glass of the third bottle they'd hitherto shared: the effect of the alcohol had numbed the effect of the tale...*so* far.

"It was built in about 1840," Keith went on. "I know all this because...well, because I'm a historian, emeritus professor, affiliated to Bangor University. Anyway, that's the embarrassing introductory stuff out of the way. Let me tell you what you probably ought to know."

"S-Sorry," Charlotte intervened, a trifle tipsily, "what's...what's emeri-, emeritus mean?"

"It means I get paid a great deal of money to do very little."

*Like Jeremy, then*, Charlotte thought, and instantly experienced a moment of profound disappointment...which she disowned at once.

Then the man continued.

"As I say, the house is an early-Victorian dwelling, constructed by a man who made an indisputable fortune exploiting...forgive me, *exploring* foreign countries, particularly with an eye to shipping their many resources to Britain. *Arthur Crossley* was the fellow's name, and quite a character he's understood to be, too."

Now she was *very* interested. "Why?" she asked, and the word resounded in the hollow kitchen like the cry of a bird over the coastline.

" 'Inveterate womaniser' is one phrase I've heard applied to the cad. 'Ruthless capitalist' is another. 'Deal breaker', 'Brutal employer', 'Racist pig' are yet more. You catch my drift?"

"He sounds p-perfect...perfectly horrid," Charlotte replied, before again swallowing a mouthful of such verbal interference. And she *did* believe what she'd just said; even sober, she would have done. "Tell me m-more."

Keith took another gulp of the wine. He looked somewhat uncomfortable, possibly because she was staring at him without blinking. He must surely know that she'd want to learn as much as possible about her property. Nevertheless, after far too long, he only said, "I don't want you having nightmares."

*And how do you propose to help me* not *have them?* But Charlotte merely shook her troubled head, and then nodded in order to prompt the rest.

"Okay, but please remember," Keith obliged, "this is all superstitious nonsense. You know how these things blow up out of all proportion. I'm sure a...an intelligent woman such as yourself doesn't need *me* to remind her of that."

At last she blinked: her way of lessening the impact of his compliment. This may well have been innocently intended, but it had felt nice all the same; she sensed a little of her former tautness lapse. She smiled – an authentic gesture. Then her new neighbour proceeded to relate what was left of his story.

"Right. Well, Arthur Crossley hardly needed to raise the funds to build the property, though you could argue that the cash *was* blood money. He'd been a pioneer in what we all know...or rather, what we all *should* know is the rape of the natural world, let alone those populations who ought to benefit from their own nation's produce. He was by no means alone in these operations – this was the industrial age, and many entrepreneurs struck out abroad in order to milk underdeveloped countries. But Crossley...he held *no* scruples about what he wanted to achieve, and by the time he'd moved here, he was at the top of his particularly terrible game. Need I provide detail?"

The question surprised Charlotte, who'd taken to thinking about the possible connection the original owner of her home might have with her ex-husband. But Jeremy was fey and cowardly; this other guy sounded like a monster incarnate. So without fully knowing why, she shook her head, and feigned a sceptical grin.

"That's fine, thanks," she said, actually rather glad that the history of the property was rather humdrum. Nevertheless, there was something else she must enquire about, and she did so at once. "But…but what about it being *haunted*?"

Keith smiled, and then shook his head. "Oh, that's just the rumoured stuff I was referring to. I suspect that the…the original owner possessed the kind of anti-social attitude which rendered him larger than life – indeed, *so* memorable in many of the worst ways that he seems to have lived on in such a small community even *after* his death. This seems to be a convincing anthropological explanation for the existence of…of ghosts."

"I see," said Charlotte, not entirely satisfied, yet being habitually polite. The guy seemed to have more to relate, though appeared palpably uncomfortable. She shouldn't push him. "I think I understand enough now."

"Good," Keith said, somewhat flatly, but then turned to grasp the nearly-drained bottle and pointed the neck at her glass with an implicit enquiry.

"Oh, n-not for me, thanks," she responded, attempting to master her slur. "I think I've h-had plenty!"

She giggled childishly, and this ungovernable outburst appeared to bring him to his senses, too.

"Yes, you're right. I guess I ought to be on my way. It's been nice. I hope you'll come to mine next – you *and* Melissa, of course."

Charlotte didn't know whether to feel appreciative that he'd included her daughter in his invitation, or mildly disappointed that he hadn't. In the event, she rose unsteadily to her feet, and then cleared the table of several half-empty plates from which they'd gobbled tasty bites earlier. With her back turned to him, she wasn't therefore able to view what he was suddenly expressing concern over.

"Oh dear," he said, "I'm afraid something hot has been placed upon your new tabletop."

She'd told him about the furniture after he'd arrived, and about the little nasty trick she'd played on her ex. However, mischievousness was now suddenly the last thing on her mind. She whirled unsteadily, and glanced at the table's surface at once.

A black blotch had appeared on the varnished wood, exactly like the one in Melissa's room: a darkish blur, an ineradicable smudge.

Charlotte sighed. She would have to call the suppliers – *OK* bloody *Ideas* – first thing in the morning.

Thrusting aside the disquiet caused by so many curious phenomena lately, she then showed her guest out. He passed her a calling card bearing his name, a list of lettered qualifications, and a telephone number – the latter making her feel as if there was something he hadn't told her, as if he was concerned for her in some ridiculous manner… But she merely added this to the tangle in her skull, and after waving goodbye, closed the door, locked up, switched out all the lights downstairs, and trudged up for bed.

She called in briefly to see Melissa sleeping alone beneath her sheets. *Ghost be-damned*, Charlotte thought, and ascribing far too much to the alcohol she'd imbibed that evening, she went through to her own room, stripped naked, and fell onto the mattress broad enough for two.

\*

Jeremy was watching on as the hands ran all over her body. Her ex-husband was standing at the threshold of her room – *her* room, in *her* house – and this, finally, was his punishment for cheating on her.

*Now you know what it feels like, buster,* she thought in her dreamlike way, as the rough fingers continued to fondle and caress her. These weren't the appendages of any spook; they were solid, fleshy, and definitely supported by a skeleton…

*Are you getting off on this, Jez?* Are *you?*

Her ex didn't move, just stared, and as the hands proceeded

163

to offer more intimate ministrations, Charlotte added: *Okay, so your wage is paying for this house, but it's* mine – *do you hear?* Mine.

Then she turned to address whoever was making her feel like a woman again, after too long acting prematurely middle-aged...but when she opened her eyes to gaze, there was no one there at all.

Just shadows flitting around a few more of her new items of furniture.

\*

Charlotte had a hangover when she awoke the following morning, and this might have been why she cried out so vehemently.

She'd seen a blackish figure, dodging across the space in front of the chest of drawers that she'd had delivered yesterday. Then she'd blinked away the pain from her sun-startled eyes, and had seen the movement for what it was: an illusion caused by her involuntarily head movement...coupled with the dark blemish which had now assailed *this* piece of furniture.

She got up at once to tug her dressing gown over her naked body, which now ached from all the wine she'd consumed last night. Immediately she paced across to the drawers.

The wood wasn't merely stained; it had developed a kind of fungus which was aspiring to a shape that it would be surely imprudent – certainly in her present condition – to decipher. This growth was bulbous and quite smooth, like an effigy in a primordial state of becoming. It caused her to shudder, and her usual trick of rationalisation hadn't allowed her to ascribe this response to the cold in the room: it wasn't a particularly chilly day, anyway. When she drew the curtains with hands clawed with anxiety, the sky was cloudless, a fragile blue.

Just then, her mind full of perplexity, Charlotte whirled and hurried through to her daughter's bedroom. If the girl had heard her Mummy yell, she might be nervous. Nevertheless, once Charlotte had prised open the door, she noticed that her daughter wasn't there. The new doll *was*, however, along with the girl's own set of drawers. Although the former was as faultless as it had been in the shop, the bulky item beside the vacated bed had also grown some of the unsightly mould.

"What on earth...?"

Still, Charlotte's first concern was for Melissa. She backed away and scurried down the steps, calling her daughter's name very loudly.

No reply.

Charlotte entered the lounge, the dining room, the kitchen: each room bore more of those putrid ruptures, her tables and chairs and other commodities marred forever.

However, only one thought presently cut through her tangled brain: *It wants me!* This had been her daughter's proclamation upon first visiting the dwelling. And suddenly all Charlotte could think about was what had happened since their arrival.

If the house *was* haunted, what did it want of her? Or was it rather a question of a *person* haunting the house – *Arthur Crossley*, the man Keith had discussed the previous evening?

But there was in fact a worse possibility. Maybe *it* or *he* didn't want Charlotte at all.

Maybe it/he wanted *Melissa*...

At once she charged for the front door, overruling an impression caused by the rapidity of her movement that an indistinct figure had reared up behind her, the better to prevent her from opening up. But then she'd managed to do so...and at what she saw, a merciful breath of relief swept through her.

Though not for long.

Yes, her daughter was playing innocently and safely in the front garden – yet she wasn't alone.

From this angle, with the sun streaming into Charlotte's sleep-heavy eyes, it appeared as if a *person* was lurking behind the girl, mimicking her movement as she played with toy characters fashioned only from fistfuls of grass. Charlotte's initial thought was to be thankful that Melissa was being resourceful, deriving pleasure from such simple creations. But then the shape had started swirling around her daughter, to such a confused degree that Charlotte called out immediately.

"*Hey, what are you d-doing?*"

Melissa turned promptly and smiled. Indeed, the presence around her diminished at once; it had been only her shadow, after all, smeared out of position in Charlotte's visual field by a trick of the daylight.

Nevertheless, her daughter's reply was less than reassuring.

"*Playing with Aka!*" she yelled back, and promptly resumed her contented game.

Charlotte was speechless for several seconds. Then words seemed to come to her unbidden, as if something or some*one* else had precipitated them. "*May I...may I meet Aka?*" she shouted, and instantly felt foolish, lest anyone passing by might overhear such a ridiculous request.

But the environs were deserted; of course they were – this had been their principal appeal.

Melissa appeared to think for a moment, her face cocked away from her Mummy. It must have been just the sound of a breeze which had Charlotte believing that she'd heard her daughter say something quickly. But *that* was ridiculous; there was no one with her at all.

At last, the girl cried back, "*She's shy. But...but I can draw a picture of her for you if you like.*"

Well, in the absence of anything more concrete, that would have to do. Charlotte had quite enough to worry about without adding Melissa's childish inventions to her burdens. However, she ought to support her daughter, to whatever degree it felt treacherous doing so.

"*Yes, that'd be good,*" Charlotte replied, and then added, "*Listen, I'm just going to do a few things in the house. Don't stray too far, will you? I'll make us breakfast soon.*"

"*Aka's hungry, Mummy* – very *hungry. Can you do something for her, too?*"

Would it harm to encourage her? Intuition said *no*. So Charlotte quickly answered, "*Sure, no problem. Food for three coming right up! I'll call you*...both *in once it's ready, okay?"* She paused a moment, before finishing, *"Maybe by then you'll have done that drawing of...of Aka, eh?"*

*"Yeah. I'll get her to pose. But she can't stand for too long. She's really weak as well."*

*"Er...okay."*

And when Charlotte went back inside the house, rather reluctantly closing the door in her wake (would she be safer inside alone, or outside with her possibly deluded girl?), she found that she was shaking.

*

She had to get a grip on herself. But how could she when she found that she had little choice but to examine several more of those frightening growths on her new furniture?

She started in the lounge

She stooped to one on the wooden frame of her armchair, though there were others on the sofa, the dressing table, and the bulky TV/video cabinet. But a close assessment of just this one would surely be sufficient to steady her quaking body, her accelerated heart rate.

It was bulbous and as dark as night. Although the surface of the protuberance was smooth, the shape of it resembled something like the kind of shrivelled head she'd seen in old films about colonialism. And further down, were there rudimentary limbs, and even a sort of skinny, elongated torso? The whole body – if it *was* that – was currently about a foot high.

Or maybe she was simply imagining this, ascribing a lucid interpretation to what was actually only a random mass of tumescent tissue.

Charlotte stood, reluctant to touch the thing. Then she turned to look at the others which had grown overnight in her home.

All bore the same grotesque resemblance to developing human forms...or perhaps each was in fact similarly ambiguous, and she was being stupidly overdramatic.

167

At any rate, whatever else was going on in this house, she realised that the company which had supplied the goods – her ex-husband's employer – was responsible for at least *these* travesties.

This thought gnawed at her head the way a primitive person might relish a bone, and once she'd switched on her laptop and sat in her seat, her hands were already manhandling the telephone, the better to read the telephone number she'd summoned onscreen and then rapidly dial.

Yes, it was a Sunday, yet such a huge enterprise as *OK Ideas* had staff available to receive complaints all week. Indeed, its branches opened every day; Jeremy had hardly ever been at home, another reason why Charlotte had passed her copious time alone by browsing through catalogues, feeding her addiction...

Someone had answered the call.

In response to a request for her customer account details, Charlotte told the male telephonist that she had a store discount card, and then tried to outline the nature of her problem. But what could she say? That all her furniture had started developing weird effigies – *little people*? They'd think her mad, or at any rate, a crank caller!

In the event, however, it proved not to matter because the employee soon delivered a devastating piece of news.

"I'm sorry, Mrs Chappell, but your account with us has recently been cancelled."

"*What?*" she asked, her mouth hanging open in much the same manner as all the figures' gaping faces, which were presumably still burgeoning on her faulty merchandise.

The man continued: "Yes, but I'm afraid I don't know why. The company's undergoing a number of major changes at the moment; it may well be a temporary thing. May I suggest you call back tomorrow and speak to one of our managers? None of them work weekends, unfortunately."

*Oh, Jeremy* had *when he'd been with* me; *but now that he's with* her, *they're probably enjoying a few days in Paris, aren't they? The devious bastards...*

Nevertheless, none of this would serve any real purpose at the moment. Charlotte hung up rather abruptly, and hastily rifled through her purse to find her mobile phone. She still had her ex-husband's private contact number, and she was now determined to use it, Paris be-damned! So he'd discovered what she'd been up to, had he, and had cancelled her account as a consequence? Well, Charlotte wouldn't let him get away with this *that* easily.

She pressed all the relevant buttons, and then as the pulse trilled on and on, she waited...and waited.

Finally, she received a reply: "*Sorry, please try again later. The phone you are trying to contact is switched off.*"

"*Fucker!*" Charlotte hissed, and that was when the front door arced open seemingly of its own volition.

It was only her daughter. And as she entered the room, Charlotte noticed that she was carrying a piece of paper.

Melissa must also have had some pencils and a pad with her in the garden, since she'd drawn a very loose and rough sketch of what must be her new imaginary friend: Aka.

At once Charlotte gasped at the sight.

Then she grabbed hold of the girl in order to steer her towards the hallway. Once she'd forced her to put on a coat, and had done the same herself, Charlotte said, "Come on. We're going out."

Her daughter looked spellbound.

*It wants me*, Charlotte heard deep in her mind.

But then Melissa asked, "Where are we going, Mummy?"

In fact Charlotte had been eager only for the girl not to see the deformations of the furniture in the lounge; she mustn't have spotted any of them on her way out this morning.

"You wanted to meet the nice man who came over last night, didn't you? Well, now's your chance."

"Are we going to his house?"

"Yes," said Charlotte, and brandishing the drawing – while simultaneously trying to suppress its *disquieting similarity* to the things which had sprung up lately in this strange, old house – she pushed her daughter outside, locked up, and started to walk

169

alongside her at quite a heady pace.

*

They both studied the sketch while Melissa played with Keith's kitten on the sitting room carpet.

The man had been delighted to see them standing on his step, and then very receptive after asking them inside. He'd made Charlotte and himself mugs of coffee, and offered the girl a carton of fruit juice whose top she'd pierced with a sturdy straw, just as she'd enjoyed doing at *McDonald's* when they'd visited regularly for tea as a family...

Charlotte tried to quell the ungovernable sections of her mind, the better to focus on this one thing.

The drawing.

The drawing whose subject looked almost exactly like the strange growths which had appeared all over her new furniture.

Nevertheless, she'd waited quite a while before revealing the sketch, engaging in trivial chitchat in order to marshal her unsteady body. But finally she'd deemed it prudent to get down to business.

"So...what do you reckon?" she asked the man after a few minutes of silence, during which he'd clearly been thinking about the drawing. Charlotte had kept her voice quiet, so that her daughter didn't overhear, but when she'd snuck a quick glance her way, she'd discovered that the girl was embroiled in getting the cat to paw at her fingers – a silly, enjoyable game which maybe too many kids these days took for granted.

At last Keith replied. "Hmm. It's certainly interesting." And he soon sat in front of his idling computer on a desk beside a large window.

It was now early afternoon, but even so, the sky was dimming. Perhaps a storm was on its way; this would certainly reflect the turmoil currently at large in Charlotte's skull. Still, she needed to remain focused if she thought she might get some help from her educated neighbour.

170

"Does it remind you of anything you've ever seen before? Oh, I don't know – in your research, or whatever?"

Keith continued to stare at the sketch, and then Charlotte did so again, despite her serious dislike of it.

It showed a sticklike girl, as black as a misanthrope's soul. Her arms and legs were little more than straight lines, thickly etched in heavy pencil, while her ribs were highly visible, as well a head as tenuous as something desperate and uppity perched on the brink of a terminal fall. She was either starving...or already dead. Indeed, she didn't look as if she could support even herself, let alone the loneliness of another, far luckier little girl.

But the most upsetting element was the face: although the eyes and nose were relatively predictable for someone of foreign origin – rather large and dark – the mouth was a travesty of normal human features. The lips were pulled back, away from large, sharp teeth.

Frankly, around the jaw, she looked like an animal in a person's body.

This aspect was not something Charlotte had noticed about the curious growths in her home, either because the figures hadn't yet developed sufficiently, or – a far more preferable conclusion – they were entirely unrelated to the girl.

Keith must be responding to the same weird facial expression, since he suddenly said, "There *is* something about this which...which puts me in mind of...*something.*"

He promptly relinquished the picture, the better to access his mouse and keyboard. He jostled the first to access Google, and then hacked at the second to summon a web page that he presumably believed might help.

Charlotte watched as her friend went about his impromptu research. It suddenly struck her that in this moment in need – the tail end of a sequence of events triggered by a sodding man – here was another arguably helping her to restore some faith in the gender. And surely Keith's motives were honourable; he was just being a helpful neighbour. She wondered why he lived alone, why *anyone* ended up living alone.

But then her treacherous brain, having lapsed into momentary respite, returned its attention to the present predicament.

Had Arthur Crossley had a wife? Or any *kids*? From the way Keith had described him, both possibilities seemed unlikely. In which case, what was he now after? Charlotte certainly had to admit that her home was – good God, it sounded idiotic even to *think* it – that her home was indeed haunted…yet by *what*? How did the corruption of her new goods figure in this whole business? And what of Melissa's imaginary friend, Aka – the girl in the drawing?

Was there indeed a connection between all of these individual parts?

Charlotte might be about to discover…

Nevertheless, when she dropped her gaze to the screen which Keith was presently indicating with a puzzled grumble and a limp forefinger, she failed to see what the significance was.

The monitor displayed a site dedicated to what appeared to be a primitive tribe in Brazil. A further click on a link clarified matters to some degree. There was now a sketch showing a thin entity every bit as malnourished and insidious-looking as her daughter's version. Yes, the posture of the child – if *child* it was – did resemble Melissa's picture: it possessed the same long, bony frame, a similar hunch of the shoulders, and an identically ovular face.

Most crucially, however, it had the same peeled-back lips, the same large, sharp teeth.

"I…I don't understand," Charlotte said, again keeping her volume low. "Do you think…there's a link here?"

"I've honestly no idea," Keith replied, and soon grinned broadly, presumably to break the palpable tension. "Hey, they give me a doctorate and a chair in history, and then a little project like this stumps me!"

But it wasn't a *little* project to her! Still, she mustn't let her recent experience of men interfere with her task. She said, "What do you know about these people?"

172

Keith glanced over one shoulder, obviously to make sure Melissa wasn't ear-wigging. What he had to say could be disturbing, and therefore Charlotte braced herself to receive this information by sitting on a stool beside the homeowner's.

Then he started to talk.

"They were called the Alkada tribe. The last remaining members died out in the late-Nineteenth Century, almost certainly as a consequence of Western imperialism..."

"Would this...would this involve *Arthur Crossley*?"

"I wouldn't be at all surprised. But let me tell you what I know." Keith gulped a mouthful of coffee, before going on. "The Alkada tribe was characterised by a very specific idiosyncrasy which separated it from many other tribes that occupied this region of the Amazon rain forest for several hundreds years. The Alkada tribe consisted primarily of, not to put too fine a point on it, *cannibals*...yet, with a twist."

Charlotte said nothing. Although at first she'd thought she'd heard the name of the tribe before – in a different context, somehow, maybe involving Melissa – she discovered that she couldn't think from where... So she simply stared at the man.

And Keith required no further encouragement. "The members somehow managed to solve – provided of course that *these* rumours are even half-true – they somehow managed to solve the perpetual crisis of food provision. In short, they were reputed to have summoned their ancestors back from the dead, the better to feast on their flesh. Zombies rose like fresh meat, and the Alkadaians ate heartily!"

"But that's *horrid*."

This had been from Melissa who'd strayed across to join in the conversation, having grown modern-child bored with the uncontrollable cat. She actually sounded a tad unsettled. Charlotte hugged her immediately, and then Keith pinched his lips together, clearly a gesture of humble apology.

"That's okay," Charlotte told her daughter. "What Mr. Morris was saying is just stories. None of it *really* happened?" She turned to the man. "*Did* it, Keith?"

The historian looked a little offended, as if his own tale was being pooh-poohed, while she'd insisted that hers be taken seriously. But he surely understood that she was merely attempting to protect the girl; having no children of his own might have made him insensitive to this necessity. In any case, he eventually answered, "No, no, just stories. Rather like the tales you'll hear about your new home. Rumours, gossip, hearsay – the world is full of that, and often far worse stuff!"

Well, she couldn't disagree with this final statement, but a certain friction had developed between them; perhaps it was time to leave. It was darker now: the day had flown by, as if supernaturally. Charlotte felt uneasy; she would have to make her excuses, while maintaining her habitual politeness.

"Thanks for your help, but I think we ought to be going. I still have so much to do to the...to the house."

Keith visibly relented; his scepticism had fallen from his demeanour, just as fear had infused hers. "Don't worry," he said directly to Charlotte, as if trying to cut Melissa out of the issue entirely. "I was just free-associating there. I'm sure there's nothing more than coincidence at work here. And that stuff about...about *Arthur Crossley* – " He'd mouthed the name, presumably so that the girl wouldn't hear anything else to worry about. " – it's all rubbish. In fact I can't believe we're actually having this conversation!"

So Keith didn't believe what she'd told him earlier, about the few spooky events which had occurred lately; he'd been humouring her all along...

It was Charlotte's turn to be offended. She stood to grab her daughter by the shoulders and then led her to the front door. "Bye, then," Charlotte said, and Melissa waved an automatic hand.

Keith had already terminated the connection to the esoteric website. When he stepped across to let them out, Charlotte couldn't help feeling that she wished he'd do more, that he'd take over entirely and sort out this problem like a *real* man should. But of course he owed them no such obligation; Jeremy had failed her, yet

Gary Fry

why should she expect anything better from someone she'd only just met?

Nevertheless, it had pained her to realise that she *did*. And it was a truth difficult to accept.

She must therefore return to the house which she was now even more convinced was haunted by somebody...or at least some*thing*.

\*

The old man's ugly, decaying face was staring out of an upstairs window – no, more specifically, *Charlotte's* bedroom window.

So he did want *her*, and not Melissa. Charlotte didn't know whether to feel flattered, relieved, frightened or confused. In less than four days in her new home, she'd become an emotional wreck. Why, she might even be *imagining* the image at the pane: now that she'd drawn closer, it had seemed to have dissipated, becoming only a composite of reflections – of bony treetops, scudding cloud, and other raw elements of the natural world...

At any rate, she managed to steer her daughter's gaze away from the house.

"Look at the bushes swaying in the breeze, Melissa! Don't they look pretty?"

It was all she'd been able to think of to divert the girl, but having asked the question, Charlotte found herself answering it in her head. Yes, the foliage in the area was very attractive; this *was* a magical place hidden away from the ravages of modern society. Indeed, she had to admit that she'd already fallen in love with the region, and that it would take more than a few strange episodes to make her forsake it.

Determinedly, she dragged her daughter towards the front entrance, overruling an impression that in the gloomy afternoon light there'd been a few dense shadows lurking in the undergrowth alongside the building. If these had shuffled with movement, then the sound was surely just an effect of the wind growing stronger, rifling the branches, causing blackish shapes to cavort thinly behind them...

175

"I want to play with Aka," said Melissa as Charlotte unlocked the heavy door and then pushed with haste. It hadn't resisted – its weight had in fact shifted forwards, as if keen to let them inside, to be either safe from whatever was now scrabbling outside the property...or in danger from whatever lurked within.

Charlotte *had* to ask the question; she wouldn't have been able to rest if she hadn't. "Where is...where *is* Aka?"

"She'll be in my bedroom, Mummy. Can I go up?"

Charlotte *hadn't* heard a run of footsteps rush across the landing at the head of the steps – that would surely have been just a whisper of the central heating system, which she'd programmed to come on at about this time: it was nearly four o'clock.

At least Melissa hadn't asked to go into the polluted lounge, but if those ruptures Charlotte had noticed on her furniture this morning had grown worse in there, perhaps the same had occurred upstairs...

Before answering her daughter, Charlotte crept into the lounge, her fingertips fumbling along the wall in search of the light-switch. When she found and pressed it, stark illumination flooded the house, undoubtedly scaring away *any* meddlesome spooks.

Indeed, it had actually done more than that.

As a patter of what sounded like feet shorn of more than clothing scurried somewhere nearby – they'd sounded muffled, as if coming from outside – Charlotte was amazed to notice that the shapes she'd spotted this morning, each leaning anxiously away from all the new wood in the building, had now disappeared.

And they'd left only painful wounds: scars which wouldn't heal.

\*

She spent much of the evening in her bedroom with the telly on loud, and when it turned nine p.m., she called Melissa into her bed and proposed that they sleep together. Her daughter agreed, though only after saying goodnight to someone in her own room

– possibly the doll Charlotte had bought her earlier in the week.

In any case, when they both huddled under the sheets like two little girls fearful of the night and whatever it might bring, Charlotte refused to turn off the TV until they were very drowsy. Indeed, Melissa was asleep and Charlotte almost so when she grappled for the remote-control unit and thumbed the 'off' button. It must have been a pernicious element of her nascent dream which had her believing that she'd heard a newscaster say the name, "*OK Ideas…*"

Soon, however, Charlotte *was* dreaming. She *must* be. How else to account for the fact that when she opened her eyes, she noticed that her daughter had gone from beside her, and that the house was decidedly altered? Now the interior was heady and sombre – this was the look of a Victorian dwelling; she'd admired such décor in period dramas on film…

And that was when the man stepped through the doorway.

He was either very old or emaciated by rot. There *was* meat on his bones, yet not enough to conceal them all. He staggered forwards, an unmistakeably lascivious grin cutting across the lower portion of his face, whose teeth were surely far too numerous to allow any lips shielding them. Then as several dark shapes reared in his wake, this man said, "*I want you – nay, I already* have *you – but by God* and *by proxy, I want the other…and I* shall *have her!*"

Then Charlotte awoke with a yell, and the bright, brilliant sunshine all around her immediately cut away a number of blackish figures which had been writhing all over the *other* she'd just witnessed…in a nightmare that she suddenly couldn't recall much about.

\*

Whatever had upset her overnight was diminished by the daylight. She had things to do, tasks to keep her busy and her mind occupied. The first involved calling Jeremy to see what on earth was going on with her customer account, and how soon he could get her furniture replaced.

As she hitched up her phone beside her PC, she decided that she wouldn't volunteer much detail. The goods were certainly unsightly enough to warrant replacement, and in any case, Melissa – who *had* been lying next to Charlotte in the bed upon awakening, safe with her Mummy – was currently playing in the lounge. Perhaps her imaginary friend had already served her purpose, and they were both now free of whatever strangeness had beset them lately.

But Charlotte mustn't think about any of that, and at once there was a good reason not to. Her telephone call had been answered. And the woman who'd spoken was her ex-husband's P.A. – the one he'd had an affair with, and whom he was still seeing as far as Charlotte knew.

"Hello, *OK Ideas*. Jeremy Chappell's office. How may I help you?"

She sounded anxious, as well she might! Maybe she'd been dreading a call from Charlotte for weeks, ever since her and Jeremy's duplicity had been revealed.

Charlotte mustn't let her usual niceness prevent her from dealing with the woman as she deserved. "Hello, it's *Miss* Fleece here," she said, deliberately using her maiden name as a form of subtle rebuke.

Indeed, it took the bitch a while to make the connection. And when she spoke again, her voice had lapsed even further into uneasiness. "Oh yes, of course. Er, I'm afraid Je – uh, I'm afraid Mr Chappell isn't available at the moment. May I...may I take a message?"

"If you tell him who it is, I'm sure he'll be willing to speak to *me*." This was a command as cold as the breeze hissing against the lounge's window. Had something just stirred out in the garden? But the more Charlotte – her mood on edge – glared that way, the less the dark shapes she'd thought she'd seen resembled anything other than shadows in the wakes of innumerable nodding bushes. She added hurriedly, "Listen, lady, let's just cut through the crap. Put him on. *Immediately*."

The P.A. grew silent, and now Melissa had responded to overhearing Charlotte's authoritative tone. But Charlotte wouldn't be deterred, even when the woman proved to be even more stubborn than she'd imagined.

"I'm really sorry, Miss Fleece, but he can't be disturbed. As you've probably heard already, the company has just suffered a major crisis. He's in a meeting with the M.D. as we speak. But I *will* tell him you called, *and* have him ring you back soonest."

The frustration elicited by this comment caused Charlotte to slam down her fist on one of the damaged items she'd ordered from the outfit. Then she recalled something vague which had been lingering at the back of her mind – something to do with what she'd learned recently on telly about *OK Ideas*, and how that related the P.A.'s comment about having 'heard already' – but this didn't eliminate the real source of her sudden fury: the way the woman had called her 'Miss Fleece'. Had there been a hint of triumph in the woman's voice, as if she'd got one up on the jilted wife? Or was this only paranoia on Charlotte's part?

Whatever the case, she suddenly said, "Right. Well, fuck you! Tell him I'm driving up there. And I'll want to see him as soon as I arrive. Goodbye!"

She hung up, feeling curiously stronger than she had lately. Her daughter was staring at her, presumably shocked after hearing the language she'd used. However, Charlotte didn't cease moving. She was now on a mission, and she would see it through to its bitter end.

"Come on, Melissa," she said. "We're going to see Daddy."

"*Daddy!*" replied the girl with an inexplicable and rather unsettling enthusiasm. However, she appeared to think for a moment, before adding, "But...but..."

Charlotte had already grabbed their coats from the hallway, had thrust her own on. "But...*what?*" she asked, holding out her daughter's.

And as Melissa got up to pace forwards to collect the jacket, she revealed what she desired obviously more than any petty treat: "Can Aka come, too? She'd be lonely here today on her own and nobody would feed her."

*

Charlotte had decided immediately to accede to her daughter's request, and they'd just left the north coast of Wales – an hour's frantic drive – when Melissa started talking to herself.

The last thing Charlotte needed now was to worry about the girl, yet what other response was appropriate when she'd heard her say, "I think my Mummy's cross with my Daddy. What are your Mummy and Daddy like? Are they as thin as you?"

Charlotte, who'd hogged the fast lane as frequently as she could, glanced at once into her rear-view mirror. It must have been the sunshine behind the car which had produced the illusion of a short, dark, scrawny figure seated beside her daughter. And Charlotte was about to gaze more rigorously when a horn blared in front of the hatchback, causing her to snap her head forwards.

The driver of a lorry – whose side brandished the name of a major international high street company – had steered and braked as Charlotte's vehicle had momentarily veered into the middle lane. He soon stuck a hand out of the window, and flipped up his middle finger. Then he barrelled on beyond them as Charlotte nervously squeezed the brakes.

"Careful, Mummy!" the girl said from the rear. "Aka isn't used to travelling like this – *not* where she comes from."

"Oh, will you *please* shut up about all this nonsense?"

Melissa slumped back in her chair, and when Charlotte checked the mirror again – this time, very briefly – there was nothing to the girl's left other than the stained fabric of one of the seats.

Eventually, a little of her anxiety having been allayed by her sudden outburst, Charlotte managed to speak. "I'm *sorry*, love. It's just that...that I'm trying to drive, and I can only do so safely without any distractions. Will you just keep quiet for a while? And will...*Aka*?"

Of course the other girl had yet to say anything at all, but that was because she didn't exist...did she?

In any case, Melissa soon replied sullenly: "Okay. We both will."

As Charlotte steered on, leaving one motorway for another which would lead them north to Bradford, she started to reflect seriously about what was going on in their lives just now.

Had Keith Morris been as dismissive of her experience as every other man she'd ever known in her life? Charlotte wasn't convinced about this, however; despite his sour response to her having called his stories about the Alkada tribe just fiction, she was sure she'd seen something in his eyes which suggested that he *hadn't* disbelieved the episodes she'd told him about. When she'd first met him, he'd been evasive about Crossley House, and had obviously wished to flee its vicinity as soon as he could. Additionally, his account about the original owner (whom Charlotte *hadn't* dreamed about; that horrid person she'd imagined overnight might have been anybody, or perhaps only her subconscious mind conjuring demons beyond her ken) had been fearful rather than sceptical, especially since he'd delivered it in the notorious man's former home...

But shouldn't she presently be thinking about Jeremy? About why she was driving 140 miles just to wipe the smirk off his stupid face? This act *wasn't* to flee Crossley House: the property was *hers* – the one thing she now possessed, and all she'd managed to salvage from the wreckage of her marriage. Everyone needed a foundation in life; she'd once had a man to provide that, but not any more. In fact her home had since come to serve that purpose...but *what* was it doing to her, and more crucially, to Melissa?

*It wants me!*

*I want you – nay, I already* have *you – but by God and* by proxy, *I want the other...and I* shall *have her!*

These recollections, nebulous and without a conscious source, came at Charlotte as she headed onto a slip road and joined the ring roads around Bradford. The brand new headquarters of *OK Ideas*, where her ex-husband worked, was situated in a modern suburb,

181

presumably unaffected by the consequences of its deeds: the poor employees it paid a pittance, and who might be tempted to become anti-social in order to make ends meet. At any rate, Charlotte told herself that she hadn't actually been thinking about ghosts from the past which lingered in old property...

Soon she pulled her vehicle into a car park, which was thankfully unattended by a security guard. She climbed out, and in her peripheral gaze, watched her daughter do the same, a black shape looming thinly behind her – her shadow of course, trailing in the mid-afternoon light.

When they reached the entrance and then a pristine reception area which Charlotte recalled from previous visits, she told the heavily made-up woman behind the desk that she had an appointment with Jeremy Chappell, that she knew where his office was, and that she would head up at once.

"Wait a moment, madam," called the woman, once Charlotte had led her wholly silent daughter (she must be still smarting from her Mummy's strictness during the journey) towards a set of double doors. "I'll need the three of you...er, sorry, the *two* of you – I thought I saw...oh, never mind. I'll need you both to complete a visitors' book: your names, car registration, time of arrival, and the purpose of your visit. It won't take long."

"No, neither will I," replied Charlotte, with unprecedented steel in her voice, and she swiftly turned to barge through the doorway and then mount a flight of steps, before ascending to all the offices on the first floor.

In fact she found Jeremy in a corridor, delivering rapid requests to his P.A. – to his *lover*.

As soon as Charlotte and Melissa stepped into view, this painted bitch, with her long legs and deep cleavage, made a hasty departure, while muttering, "I *told* you she was coming. Why didn't you believe me? This is *embarrassing*."

Then Charlotte rounded gamely on her ex-husband. He appeared flustered, though not necessarily as a direct consequence of her arrival.

"Charlotte, I'm sorry, I did mean to call you back, but – "

Suddenly a large man emerged from a room further along the plush stretch of corridor; he had chief-executive eyes, narrow and devious.

"Chappell," he bellowed, "I thought you were leaving for your flight? Get to it, man!"

"*Flight?* Where are you going?" Images of romantic Paris had stolen into Charlotte's head...and her forlorn heart.

But as the big guy thumped away, Jeremy didn't reveal anything. "Hello, darling," he said, stooping to their daughter, an act which almost brought a lump to Charlotte's throat. Oh, where *had* it all gone wrong?

Soon, having plucked Melissa from the floor (her shadow gleamed blackly on the polished tiles, as if keen to scurry away from its source), Jeremy turned back to Charlotte; he looked astonished. "You mean, you haven't heard?" he asked, with no less incredulity. "Where the hell have you been lately? It's been on the regional *and* national news."

"*What* has?" Charlotte simply glared at him. "I don't...I don't understand."

"God, I wish *I* was headed for somewhere as peaceful and out-of-the-way as Anglesey! I suppose I should ask whether you've settled in okay, but...well, what with the crisis, I'm just *so* busy. And I have to leave – *now*, as it happens."

"Where are you going, Daddy? Can *I* come?"

Charlotte was about to suggest what a ridiculous idea that was – she didn't want her daughter to spend a single minute with the tart who'd stolen their family contentment – when Jeremy did so on her behalf.

"Not this time, honey," he told the girl. "I'm going too far away." Soon he glanced at Charlotte. "Bit of a scandal, I'm afraid. The company's ostensibly been exposed by some vindictive journo. It's all nonsense...I think. Anyway, I'm just off to unearth a few facts."

The reason she'd come was to demand to have her customer account re-established (since that was all she had left at the moment), as well as requesting that her new furniture be replaced

183

as soon as possible.

However, in light of this turn of events, Charlotte only found herself repeating the question their daughter had asked a minute earlier. "But where are you going?"

"Brazil," Jeremy told her, and after a few more seconds to let this news sink in, he hurried away, his shadow barely keeping pace with him.

\*

"Aren't you going to talk to Aka, Melissa?"

"Aka left me. She might have seen some other black children when we drove out of Bradford, and decided they'd make better friends. There was a Pakistani man in Daddy's offices – did you see him? *I* did. Maybe Aka thought that he'd be her Daddy. It's hard not having a Daddy."

Charlotte had been trying to test her daughter, to see what she could discover about what was actually happening to them. The girl's response had, however, pitched her into even greater confusion and misery. All she knew at the moment was that she *must* return to their new home, the better to deal with whatever was going on there. All the pieces were falling slowly into place, and if she spoke first to Keith Morris about what she'd learned lately, then they might be able to handle it together.

Once they'd passed Manchester, Charlotte flicked on the radio. Perhaps there'd soon be a report about the scoop on *OK Ideas*. To see her ex-husband suffer a little had perversely made up for not having had chance to have a go at him herself, yet if the situation was dangerous over in Brazil, she would worry about him, and this was more than mere concern about Melissa losing her father. Charlotte actually still cared for Jeremy; maybe her house *knew* that, and was seeking to tear her and her daughter apart by prompting complex psychological processes quite beyond her appreciation.

As she hit the road which led on to the Menai Strait Bridge, Charlotte felt she might burst with all this speculation. Perhaps there was a simpler, rational explanation...

Nevertheless, that was when the music – an ethnic band performing very powerfully on unusual instruments – broke off, and the five o'clock news was broadcast.

The sky had descended onto the isle of Anglesey; Charlotte's headlamps couldn't quite cut enough white into the cloying density of it – it looked as if entities, black as the impending night, were ready to rear up against the passing vehicle, all bony and vengeful...

However, Charlotte suppressed these involuntarily fears, and then listened carefully to the reporter on her stereo.

Indeed, the *OK Ideas* story was the headline feature.

"*...human rights activists, working in conjunction with* The Guardian *newspaper, are claiming that the multi-million pound British company has, for several years, been using sweatshops in South America; this in addition to buying material from the region at an exploitative rate in order to maximise profits on their popular household products...*"

Charlotte suddenly switched off the radio. And exhaled a lengthy breath of realisation.

She *now* thought she understood; the riddle had been solved.

\*

"Be honest with me, Keith. Tell me you believe in *ghosts*."

He simply stared at her. He'd opened the door as soon as he'd heard the car pull up in front of his house, and now he stood on the threshold, shivering in the chill early evening. "You'd better come inside," he said, and stepped back to prompt her to enter. "I do hope you haven't left your delightful daughter alone in *that* house."

"No, she's asleep in my back seat. And that's why I'd rather just talk here, if it's okay." Charlotte was thankful that the girl had nodded off; this had allowed her to bypass their home, the better to come here without any tiresome enquiry as to why. In truth, Charlotte didn't have an answer...which was why she asked her neighbour again: "Well, *do* you believe in ghosts?"

"Honestly?"

"That's all I've ever asked from a man."

"Then yes, I do." He hesitated, though only for a moment; perhaps he felt the situation demanded brevity. "Especially in relation to *your* property."

Despite her habitual decency, Charlotte couldn't help but feel offended. This was her *home* he was referring to – *hers*. Not Jeremy's; not even Melissa's. Her *own*.

She could only conclude that her addiction to commodities was incredibly extreme. Indeed, quite intuitively, she quickly managed to defend the building. And she finished with a simple statement of facts.

"It's *not* the house: as you said, all that's just rumours. It's the *furniture* I had delivered – it comes from Brazil...probably from the area once occupied by the tribe you mentioned...whose...whose members must have cursed the trees from which the wood came, or...or something. Anyway, the property is *fine*, and now that the...the *things* have dropped off the items I bought, and that...that Aka has gone at last, along with *all the others* who must have developed with her, we're okay. We *are*. I have my home back. *Mine*."

"Charlotte, you're not thinking straight!"

She didn't want him to go on, to spoil things for her as men always had, but her innate reserve soon allowed him to. He drew a heavy breath before speaking.

"I can't say I was delighted to hear that you'd bought Crossley House, but I tried to do everything I could to make you welcome. I hadn't learnt about its reputation before *I* moved here, and since that time, I've seen plenty to convince me that – despite my rationalist occupation – it's *not a good place*.

"Anyway, since you were already here, I decided to do whatever I could to make your stay a safe one. I didn't wish to lie to you, but as matters soon grew out of control, I became fearful for you. And now I hear about this business with your ex-husband's company. It's *all* connected, don't you see,

Charlotte? The whole of it leads back to – "

"*No*. That's rubbish! Don't say it!"

But he did. " – to *Arthur Crossley*. Back to the Nineteenth Century when global exploitation grew rife. And it hasn't ceased since…indeed, it's become *worse*. Developing countries raped by exploiters of the natural world. Many, many nations' resources stolen for Western gain. Their peoples offered jobs and paid next to nothing – at any rate, no more than slaves might enjoy. *We're* responsible, you know: we who benefit from this system, while suppressing our knowledge of its existence. We're *all* in league with the very Devils who started it, who *continue* to operate it to their outrageous advantage!"

Charlotte was aghast; she felt embarrassed and angry, as if much knowledge that she'd already been aware of had risen inexorably to the surface of her consciousness at precisely the same time as she was striving to crush it down. This was her *weakness* – her fatal flaw: it was what Keith was alluding to presently. Perhaps he'd observed this propensity in her, and was only now expressing his anger about it. Indeed, how could he not have noticed after she'd bought so much *stuff* recently? He'd called on her and Melissa, had seen all their items, and had said nothing. He was obviously a sensitive man – a rare one among his breed.

God, she felt as if she wanted the earth to open up and devour her whole in its tender maw.

In the event, however, she couldn't overrule a lifetime of compulsion – this was an illness which had been pressed into her flesh by a culture obsessed by merchandise. So she merely replied, "But…but my *house*…"

Keith paced towards her; they were both suddenly separated only by inches. "*Don't* go back there, Charlotte. You certainly *mustn't* take your daughter."

*It wants me!*

But despite her recent memories, Charlotte found that she was in far too deep; her identity, already under severe erosion, could surely be preserved in only one way. And she shouldn't wait any longer, lest her resolve falter.

"I *have* to," she said, and then turned away from the man, the better to reach her vehicle in preparation for driving home. *Home.* "There's *nothing* there now. It's all gone. Hey, if anyone deserves punishment, it's not *me*. There's Jeremy for one – and I wonder whether *she'll* fly with him…"

"Charlotte! Come back! You can stay with me tonight!" The man paused, but soon added more: "Oh, I don't mean anything like *that*. We're not *all* like most of them – *men*, I mean. I'm principally thinking of – "

Perhaps he went on to name names, yet Charlotte would never know which. She'd climbed inside her car and shut the door. She discovered immediately that her daughter had been awakened by Keith's cries; in the rear-view mirror she looked half-hidden by a sinister assailant – by simple moon-thrown shadows.

"What's happening, Mummy? Where are we? Where are we going?"

Charlotte had started the engine midway through the girl's enquiry. "We're going home, Melissa," she said, and then dropped the clutch in order to steer her battered hatchback back along the lane to Crossley House.

\*

The building watched them arrive – of course it did; it was sentient, but it certainly wouldn't harm her…or her daughter.

Charlotte parked the hatchback in the driveway, thinking about the demons which had recently burgeoned inside her home. These were gone now – she simply knew it. Knew it as well as she cherished the property. Arthur Crossley wasn't the owner – no man was. *She* was. It was *her* house.

She instructed Melissa to get out of the car. At first the girl resisted, claiming to be scared, but when Charlotte developed the first hints of a bad temper, her daughter eventually exited and quickly huddled close to her Mummy.

"There's something in the hedge!" she cried, clapping a hasty palm over her eyes.

Charlotte looked to where Melissa had vaguely pointed, yet in the sallow moonlight bleaching the area with a spectral gloss, she saw nothing untoward. Indeed, if the shadows *had* been astir, as she'd initially suspected, it was only as a consequence of the sharp breeze which seemed to inhabit all this land on the coast almost perpetually. At any rate, she *hadn't* noticed a bright gleam of several items – like teeth.

"Don't be s-silly!" Charlotte said, and began to steer her daughter towards the entrance.

The property loomed over them, and it was surely just an illusion caused by the poor viewing conditions that made it appear to lean slightly in their direction, as if eager to have them inside, its belly hungry, wanting to feed...

Charlotte produced her key and unlocked the door. *Nothing here,* she kept on telling herself, *nothing here now.*

Then they stepped within.

\*

She'd been correct: the interior was deserted.

It was now very late. They should both turn in for bed.

After flicking on a few lights and closing all the curtains downstairs, Charlotte locked the door, plunged the lower floor into darkness, and then guided her daughter directly upstairs.

\*

"Want to sleep with you tonight, Mummy!"

They were in Melissa's bedroom. Charlotte had just changed the girl into her pyjamas, and was currently trying to press her into bed.

"You'll be *okay*," she told her daughter. Then she plucked the doll she'd bought her in Llangefni recently – another satisfying purchase of the kind that Charlotte could no longer

189

deny; yes, she *was* lost…but it was a *nice* lost. "Here, cuddle up to Sailor Sam."

Her daughter scowled, as if she now hated the figure; and then a small, persistent part of Charlotte sensed hope for the girl… But this was soon gone entirely as Melissa said, "*He* can't help. I want Aka. *She's* not here any more. Not fair."

Indeed, this news provided Charlotte with even more confidence about their home: it *was* empty, after all.

"Good girl," she said, and suddenly tossed the hard-working man into one corner of the room, before switching off her daughter's lamp and prepared to leave. "We ladies must stick together, eh?"

Then she sealed the girl inside, and soon went to her own bedroom, and its cold, empty bed.

A tiny grin surfaced on her hungry lips.

\*

The man entered her room after she'd been asleep for about an hour or so.

Charlotte knew this detail because when she'd opened her eyes, still feeling groggy, a nearby digital clock had brandished its hot, red figures: 12:00AM – midnight.

Her sluggish mind failed to appreciate the fact that she didn't own such a clock (although she knew where she might buy a good one, and at a fair price), or that it actually appeared to be located *above* her head… In any case, this didn't matter. The world was shadowy around her; she'd yet to full awaken.

And the man was moving closer.

This was of no consequence, either, since he was clearly just a passenger of the plane on which she'd discovered she was presently flying. And the newcomer? Why, Jeremy, of course! They were both on their way to Paris, weren't they? He'd never taken her there before, despite his huge wage and his globetrotting job.

She was *happy* – this was the crucial thing. Her marriage was

190

strong, their daughter was safe at home, and all was well in the life of Charlotte Fleece...

Except she wasn't called *Fleece* at all, was she?

Hadn't she in fact meant *Chapell*?

And that was when her dream (yes, none of this was *real*) pitched slowly into a nightmare, just as the plane was certainly about to do.

A darkish figure, its limbs little more than withered sticks, had vacated the chair Charlotte had certainly occupied. It was the one next to Jeremy's; the man even smiled at Charlotte as he proceeded to sit anew. However, before he could, he was forced to pace aside...to let past the black, shrivelled creature whose face bore far too many bones. It skipped like an impish child – a *girl* – along the aisle between so many other seats, and when it hit the cabin at the top, it promptly blundered through a doorway, prompting screams and then a sudden canting of the aircraft: the engines roared, while people all around Charlotte – including her (ex-)husband – yelled out, and that was when...

...she awoke, smothered in sweat.

The dream encased in a nightmare or maybe vice versa had ended. Now Charlotte was confronted with what was actually somewhat humdrum, yet greatly treasured: her house. Crossley House. The one thing she genuinely cherished in her new life.

"*That's good,*" said a figure standing in the doorway. His voice was an age-ravaged whisper; his comportment had little more to offer. "*I like the turn of your noodle, my dear. Oh yes, first you, and then...*" The entity – which moonlight spilling through the curtained window was slowly turning to flesh, even though its body had largely failed – pointed a loose, limp arm the way of Melissa's bedroom along the landing. "*...and then the* other."

This *couldn't* be Keith; he wouldn't speak in such a lapse manner; and Jeremy would be halfway to Brazil, wouldn't he?

So who *was* her visitor?

All Charlotte knew was that she was about to be seduced by someone who wanted something only a woman could grant him. She'd long ago understood this: how men accepted sexual favours in exchange for essential money, which women used to buy...to buy whatever *men* had put in their heads in the first place!

The insight came at her like plane falling from the sky. At once she felt resistant to the cheap ministrations of the person stealing towards her with tangible lust in its incomplete frame.

It *was* Jeremy, yet not really; but it *wasn't* Keith, not at all.

And it was just about to make its final move when Charlotte spotted a solid shape in its wake.

*Melissa?* No, she wouldn't have the courage, not so soon; Charlotte hadn't built up her daughter to overcome such seedy deceit, but before long she *would*: just as soon as Charlotte got herself free of this uncontrollable situation, she certainly would, she would, she would, she –

Suddenly several more of the creatures reared into view. They were all dark, almost black, and when they cocked what passed for their heads in ravenous manoeuvres, Charlotte noticed teeth, teeth, teeth – lots and lots of them, all immediately chomping down on the figure which had sought to assail Charlotte in her moment of foolish weakness.

They ate – nay, they *devoured*.

And soon, of the man who, among others, had started out the social process leading to these entities' tragic extinction, there was little more than feeble dust.

*

Charlotte got out of bed and without looking at the countless figures writhing upon what little remained of – yes, yes, it *was* – Arthur Crossley's corpse, she charged to the doorway, passing through it, and then turned to race along the landing, telling herself that she *hadn't* seen the shapes in her wake smiling, smiling, all those unshielded teeth dripping chunks of gore and bone. That interpretation might break her mind in a more terrible way than her house had attempted to do.

Indeed, she managed to suppress this impression, and crash

into her daughter's bedroom, rousing Melissa with both shaking hands. The girl stirred, glanced up, looked panicky; but she soon obeyed the silent communication from her Mummy: they must leave *now*, lest any of the...the *things* in the larger bedroom remained hungry!

A moment later, they were away, hardly dressed for the unforgiving night, but having little choice other than to unlock the front entrance before scrabbling over the threshold. If there *were* pursuing footfalls behind them, there wasn't enough to any of them to denote a substantial threat...yet Charlotte had seen what those creatures were capable of, hadn't she? They'd *summoned* the previous owner; and they'd demolished him.

As she and Melissa hurried for the car, a man suddenly reared up ahead of them, no more than a silhouette, though reassuring in demeanour: it was the slightly stooped, caring posture of Keith Morris. He'd obviously been watching all evening, certain that something would transpire. And now it had. He'd been right all along.

Nevertheless, Charlotte still couldn't completely eliminate her commitment to the house. Even though her neighbour took her in his arms, and then also hugged her daughter, Charlotte strove to seek excuses: she told herself that the entities had achieved their purpose; that they'd surely move on; that the ghost in the property had been exorcised by new ones; that presently the cosmos was in balance...

But Keith would have none of this.

"If the spooks only showed up *after* you had the furniture delivered," he said, looking on at the building with knowing eyes, "can you say for certain that you didn't detect any supernatural events *before* it arrived?"

Charlotte wanted to say no, yet doing so would involve lying – the very thing she hated most about men. At least her neighbour had been only economical with the truth; she should surely be the same in return.

She recalled the footsteps she'd heard in the hallway when no one had been there, as well as the episode with her computer. Then how *could* she argue against what Keith was suggesting?

In the event, therefore, she didn't.

And he went on.

"Members of the Alkada tribe are reputed to have summoned their victims, so how could Arthur Crossley have been around *in advance* of their visit?"

Now Charlotte gazed at the house, too. It was gloomy and sullen, its windows like disturbed eyes, its open doorway a ragged mouth. The brick frontage appeared shameless, as if the whole of it had been built without a single care in the world.

"It's a *bad place*, Charlotte," the man continued, covering Melissa's ears with his palms, in order to avoid upsetting her dreams in the future – indeed, *for* the future. "*OK Ideas* is a massive company: those cursed goods you bought would surely have also been placed in others' properties...yet have we heard of any more disturbances like this one? No! It's just *here*, I tell you." He paused anew, drew breath, and concluded: "Some houses are financed and constructed by evil hands. It doesn't matter about the nature of the ghosts – the fact is that they *exist*, and probably always will. Crossley House wasn't only haunted once, or twice; it's simply *haunted*...and it deserves no more than demolition."

Charlotte nodded, noticing that nothing had followed them outside. Perhaps the property was finally free of possession... What would Jeremy say if she told him that his mortgage payments would have to be upheld while she and her daughter sought alternative accommodation? There were *always* monetary matters to consider.

However, she then looked at Melissa, saw her still-innocent face glaring up between Keith's paternal hands, and she immediately realised that her ex-husband wouldn't have any such concerns any more: the poor bastard had in fact been killed by his modern lifestyle; Charlotte simply knew it.

The girl was all she had, and was also – she'd finally decided – all she *needed*; Charlotte would therefore protect her from everything which had threatened her own delicate state of mind.

She soon turned away from her new home, and even resisted Keith's comforts as she cried for her soul. She and her daughter would cope with this alone, and if any men were ever involved in their lives again, it would be on their *own* terms. None of them would ever *buy* Charlotte; quite simply, she wasn't for sale. Melissa never would be, either – Charlotte would guarantee that.

It was possibly all that the girl required as she grew older and older in a culture more polluted than Charlotte's heart had been...and was no longer.

# The Retreat

### By
### Paul Finch


An ex-police officer and journalist, **PAUL FINCH** is now a full-time TV and movie scriptwriter. He cut his literary teeth penning episodes of the popular British crime drama, The Bill, but he's no stranger to prose either. To date, he has had six books and nearly 300 stories and novellas published on both sides of the Atlantic, mostly in the horror and fantasy fields. His first collection, Aftershocks, won the British Fantasy Award for 2002, while his novel Cape Wrath was short-listed for the Bram Stoker Award that same year. He is currently working on three horror movies, including a big screen adaptation of Cape Wrath. Paul lives in Lancashire, northern England, with his wife Cathy and his two children, Eleanor and Harry. "The idea for *The Retreat* came to me during a dream inspired by a book of old folk-tales that I picked up in a shop in the Lake District. This was about two and a half years ago. It was January, and the following morning I took my dog for a walk through a bleak, snow-bound pine forest. As always, I had my trusty dictaphone with me, and was able to make copious notes. When I actually sat down to write the story early this year, it was so fully developed in my mind that it poured from my keyboard. The concept of an innocent old world being ruthlessly superseded by a hard-assed modern one has featured many times in my work, at first quite subconsciously. I guess it's because I don't like the notion (and know I'm not alone in that), that I usually portray this transition from one to the other as being fraught with unseen menace."

THEY SLEPT well inside the woodland house, for the first time in none of them knew how long. It hadn't been especially prepossessing when they'd first laid eyes on it: a rough and ready log-cabin, deep in frozen snow, icicles suspended from its stick-thatched eaves, its crude front door hanging open on a dark, leaf-strewn interior.

And with no windows.

No windows at all. Not even shuttered ones, not even slots cut for ventilation.

That hadn't made any sense to them. In fact, it had seemed ominous, but they hadn't been in a position to be choosey. So they'd entered uninvited. And now they were asleep here; Krebble and Getz on straw-covered trestles, Hauzmann and Brunner slumped to either side of a rock-built hearth, which was filled with soot and cinders and clearly hadn't been lit in many a month, though strangely it issued a kind of warmth.

In truth, the entire place was warm. Oddly warm, Hauzmann realised, as his thoughts descended through the dreamy luxuries of sleep. The biting chill of the Steppe didn't exist in here. Granted, they were still booted, gloved, buttoned up in layers of coats, swathed at head and neck in scarves and wrappers. Yet it wasn't thanks to that. They, and so many others like them, had worn this ragged garb for weeks now, yet frostbitten fingers had still snapped off, hypothermic hearts had still given out in vain efforts to pump hot blood through bodies as cold and stiff as cadavers.

That wasn't the case in here.

Despite the wailing wind outside, this place was warm to the point of being snug.

They'd questioned this on first entering, had demanded urgent answers of each other. But bone-numbing exhaustion had had the final say. So now at last they were asleep, and none of it mattered any more.

\*

Crossing the Kumskiy Bridge was the most difficult part of the breakout.

It was a serviceable structure, a concrete roadway laid eighty yards across legs of riveted steel. Not that it would normally be needed in winter, for sixty feet below it, the Mishkova, which for three-quarters of the year poured noisily down towards the Volga, lay beneath a layer of river-ice so dense that a coach and four could have ridden over it. On this occasion, of course, things were different. For countless miles, Russian troops had placed demolition charges on its gleaming white surface, shattering it so spectacularly that the river's black waters were flowing furiously again. With the bridge itself guarded, this particular stretch of the Mishkova, which lay thirty miles southeast of the hellish, fiery ruin that was the city of Stalingrad, was now almost impassable.

Yet desperate men can achieve astonishing things.

Delighted at the intelligence that Field Marshal von Paulus – commander of Germany's Sixth Army, which had been entrenched in the wretched city for two hundred days – had formally and unconditionally surrendered, the eight Russian soldiers were in relaxed mood. By the looks of them they were factory militia, wearing fur caps and fleeces over improvised uniforms; low-grade troops by regular Soviet standards. Yet even so they were at least as well equipped as their enemies, being garlanded with ammo-belts and carrying Thompson and PPSh submachine guns. Now they walked back and forth at the centre of the bridge, sharing cigarettes and congratulating each other. They weren't expecting the attack.

Hauzmann opened up first with his *Schmeisser*. He'd taken point in the bombed-out shell of a guardhouse on the east side of the bridge. The Russians had posted two men there, but both now lay with slit throats. Hauzmann's raking fire came as a fearful shock to their comrades. The ranking officer was struck in the head and went staggering bloodily and drunkenly to the nearest barrier, which he toppled over face-first. A second reached for his Thompson, but was hit squarely in the throat, and sank to his knees with hands clawing at an arcing ruby fountain.

Getz joined the assault. He opened fire with a *panzerfaust*, having scrambled his way down the snowy embankment to the very edge of the river. His missile ranged diagonally upwards on a streak of grey smoke, and detonated under the bridge's north barrier, where the bulk of the Russian militia had instinctively clustered. There was a loud *CRUMP*, then twisted metal and scorched concrete was flung everywhere. Another Russian fell screaming and burning to the frigid waters of the Mishkova. A fourth went twirling through the air, his midriff half-severed, sliced gizzards spinning like fleshy tentacles.

Brunner advanced onto the bridge itself. He lobbed a grenade, which a surviving Russian snatched up in order to throw back, only for it to explode in his hand, blowing him apart at the seams, eviscerating those clumped around him.

"Now!" Hauzmann roared.

He and the rest of the squad went forth to join Brunner, who'd continued the attack with an MG 42, which, with his usual ingenuity, he'd adapted to be portable. Only Seefeld held back. As a seventeen-year-old, his schooling in the combative world of the Hitler Youth was still fresh in his memory, but months of close-quarter battle in the seething Stalingrad pocket was enough to knock the stuffing out of even the hardiest youngster. These days he was near-catatonic, a stumbling wreck, the eyes glazed yet bulging in his grizzled, rat-thin face, his gait the stumbling shuffle of the *stalag* inmate rather than the quick, crisp drill of the *Wehrmacht*.

Getz appeared and pushed the youth. Seefeld tottered forward and tried to reload his rifle, but his bandaged fingers were too cramped with cold.

Getz darted leftwards to what remained of the north barrier. Hauzmann, Brunner and Krebble were against the other one, but were already half way across the bridge. Through a mist of grenade-smoke, a mass of mangled corpses emerged ahead of them. One Russian was still alive, though gouting blood from a shoulder that had partly cracked away from his torso. He leaned on the south barrier and squeezed off rounds from his *Tokarev*. Brunner was closest; he drew his *Luger* and shot the wounded man through the neck. Another live Russian was half-concealed among the dead. His left knee was a jagged stump, white bone sticking spear-like from it, but he was jabbering insanely and pointing with his PPSh, which he continued to trigger, even though its magazine was spent. Krebble tossed a grenade at him; it detonated in his crotch, smashing him backwards through the barrier, a mass of rags and smoking meat.

Hauzmann now dashed recklessly forward, his hobnails crunching the bloodied ice. Some of the Russians might be feigning death. That was entirely possible, and, just in case, Krebble and Brunner riddled their bodies with additional fire. But Hauzmann had to take the chance. His priority was the T34 parked on a riverside approach road just northwest of the bridge. The assault had so far been quick and clinical, and more than likely the T34's crew, having heard about Sixth Army's capitulation, would be drunk on cheap vodka or fuddled with the fumes of opium cigarettes. But some of them at least might still be able to respond. As Hauzmann reached the west end of the bridge, he saw the tank's turret turning slowly towards him. Breathless, he dropped to one knee, unslung the *panzerfaust* from his shoulder and fired.

The molten round struck the T34 on the side of its gun, buckling the huge barrel, then careened sideways and slammed full-on into its turret, which exploded upwards and back like the top of a beer bottle shaken to frenzy.

Hauzmann dashed forward again, crossing the road at a low angle. A machine-gun began to chatter from somewhere. It kicked up divots of snow at his heels, but made no contact, and he threw himself into the bushes on the west side. Now under cover, he started threshing his way forward towards the smouldering hulk. Behind him, Brunner had also reached the west end of the bridge. His MG 42 spat fire. Its 7.92mm calibre bullets shrieked as, one by one, they ricocheted from the tank's blistered shell.

It was all the distraction Hauzmann needed. He sprang up onto the T34's right-hand caterpillar track, and lobbed grenades into the smoking cavity of its interior. Three went down before he dived and rolled for cover. The first detonation blew the thirty two-ton vehicle around on its axis. The second and third rocked it over onto its side, oily smoke spurting like blood from its fractured joints.

Brunner came hurrying up the road. He'd paused only to rip a gore-stained sheepskin coat from one of the dead militia and now was pulling it on over his khaki fatigues. At the same time he was firing, sending burst after burst across the river towards its east shore, where more Russians had appeared in the cluttered ruins of the buildings. Krebble came pelting off the bridge as well, puffing clouds of breath as he charged headlong into the underbrush. Getz was last. Having further ground to cover, he ran a zigzag course, also shooting indiscriminately behind him.

But no – Getz wasn't the last.

Last was Seefeld.

The shell-shocked youngster had been so little use over the last few days that Hauzmann had all but forgotten him. The older man now watched dispassionately, barely wincing as Seefeld, who had just waded through the mass of mutilated flesh that had been the Russian guard-unit, was shot in the back of his legs. Lumps of bone and bloody cartilage burst like deaths-head flowers through the front of his trousers. Then his knees gave way – each in a different direction – and he fell sideways.

His normal expression of stupefaction transformed to one of horrific agony. Piercing shrieks split the air, but were quickly silenced by new volleys from the east shore. One shot struck the side of Seefeld's helmet, flipping it clean off his head. A second clove his right shoulder like an axe-blow. He howled all the more.

The air was thick with a variety of pungent stenches: cordite, burnt flesh, loosened bowels. A black smog drifted across the centre of the bridge. But even as Hauzmann stared at it, he saw figures emerging – squat, thickset, in glimmering white coveralls, with crossed skis on their backs.

Siberian Guards. Hardened fighters, and infamous vengeance-seekers.

Their submachine guns were lowered, even though Brunner had taken it on himself to give Seefeld covering fire. Streams of his slugs struck sparks from the twists of steel that remained of the bridge's north barrier, but the Siberians simply took cover behind it and advanced all the more eagerly. They wanted Seefeld alive.

"Kill him!" Hauzmann shouted.

Brunner looked round.

"Kill him!"

But Brunner, who had now ceased firing, could only shake his head and hold aloft his empty weapon. "I'm out."

"In that case move it! Quickly!"

Brunner nodded and retreated to the tree line. Hauzmann followed him.

Neither looked back.

Unfortunately the woodland soon thinned out, and all four Germans – the sole remnant of a company who when the campaign on the Volga began had numbered seventy men – were ploughing as fast as they could across open land. The wreckage of earlier fighting loomed around them, the frozen plain dotted with ammo crates and oil drums, with the burned carcasses of trucks and troop-carriers, the relics of artillery – everything from howitzers to anti-aircraft guns, all now broken and abandoned. And of course there were corpses, legions of corpses, most now skeletons in snow-covered rags. There was even a charred Tiger tank with its barrel bent upwards at a curious right angle, and a skeleton still in its tank-lieutenant uniform sitting upright in the hatch.

It all afforded cover of a sort. But it was no surprise, several moments later, when they heard fresh gunfire and the whining zip of bullets passing closely by. Krebble fell facedown, and at first Hauzmann thought he'd been hit and, somewhere inside, was grimly pleased that the only ardent Nazi in their group had finally paid a price for the *Fuhrer's* pride. But then Krebble was back on his feet and blundering forward, and Hauzmann supposed that this was a good thing too, because they'd need as much strength as they could muster in the coming days.

More trees were ranked ahead: deep and tangled, yet bare enough to show snowy trails meandering away into their depths.

"Keep going!" Hauzmann urged his men.

Not that he needed to. They were long past the stage where fatigue could slow them down. They were puppets now, mindless, jerking things of strained sinew and creaking bone. They kept going merely because they were automatons, because thought and desire and even physical pain no longer had meaning for them. All the same, Hauzmann was forced to duck when he was still ten yards short of the next tract of woodland and heard a shrill *SHRIEEEK* come hurtling up from behind.

Initially he imagined it was Seefeld, hundreds of yards away yet venting his agony as the Siberians tortured him. But then he recognised it for what it really was: an 82mm mortar shell.

He hurled himself to the snow, hands clamped to either side of his head.

The impact, which was very close by, was cacophonous, ear-numbing. A wave of searing heat gushed over him, and then a vast orange glare seemed to fill Franz Hauzmann's entire world...

*

Hauzmann's eyes snapped open, and the first thing he saw was a large fire in the middle of the hearth.

At first he was too groggy to realise what this meant. The fire was feeding off a stack of freshly cut logs, which crackled and spat noisily. Krebble, who had discarded his greatcoat and webbing, was kneeling in front of it, his face and hands glowing rosily as he offered them to the flames.

A second passed, then Hauzmann sat bolt upright. "Are you crazy? Damp that Goddamn fire down now!"

Krebble looked around, startled. His blonde hair was tousled, sweat-sodden. He quickly replaced his gold-rimmed spectacles. "Didn't *you* light it?"

Hauzmann jumped to his feet. "Of course I didn't!"

"But you were right next to it."

"I was asleep, you fucking idiot!" Hauzmann glanced to the far side of the hearth, where Brunner had been slumped: he wasn't there now. "Brunner? Where's Brunner?"

"Here," came a sleep-fuddled voice. "What's the trouble?"

"Did you light this fire?"

"No ... no I didn't."

Thanks to the blaze, much of the previously darkened interior was now visible. It was quite a surprise to see that Brunner had found himself an armchair – an odd-looking thing, crudely constructed from timber and leather.

"What are you doing over there?" Hauzmann said.

Brunner sat up. He too was pop-eyed with sleep, his face sallow, though clearly he'd found the chair comfortable; he'd removed his sheepskin and unzipped his khaki waterproof. Now he pushed his cap back, scratched his dirty brow. "I got too warm, so I moved."

"Too warm?"

After the last few months, those were two words that Hauzmann had never expected to hear used in the same sentence again.

Brunner nodded and smiled. "Suddenly I was very warm. I moved, I think."

Hauzmann turned back to Krebble. "Put it out."

"But there's no-one around."

"Half the Goddamn Red Army must be outside by now!"

Krebble shook his head "We walked for two whole days after crossing the Mishkova. We didn't see a single soul in all that time."

That wasn't strictly true. En route here, they trekked endlessly through snowbound forests, but some time during the second day came upon a scarecrow-like figure standing alongside a tree trunk. It was a fellow German, a motorcycle courier by the looks of his long leather coat and hanging goggles. He was ragged and rail-thin, and when they first encountered him, one of his arms was pointing southwest. Initially they were confused, but then they got closer and saw that his eyes were empty sockets. Evidently, birds had pecked them out, which meant that he'd been in this position – pointing, stone dead – for the last three months at least.

To many, such a sight would chill the blood, yet these men's blood was already chilled to the point where it barely flowed. Besides, eyeless holes in rotted faces, the rending sound of dead flesh as it's torn away from frozen wood, the brief stench of foetor as green, stagnant meat is exposed to the icy air – none of these things were unusual any more. They thus threw him down and searched his pockets and pouches thoroughly, only finding a single round for a *Luger* and a couple of grains of tobacco, but snatching them eagerly, like beggars grabbing at bones. Then they continued on their way, automatons again. The only difference was that now they were following the direction the corpse had been pointing in. None of them knew why, nor did they try to explain it.

By sheer instinct, they veered south-west, hobbling like hunted dogs between trees stunted and blasted by the tundra winds, wading through fresh snowdrifts that came at times to their knees, and then suddenly, as new flakes again filled the gunmetal sky, arriving at the house.

At *this* house.

"Put it out, Krebble!" Hauzmann barked. "That's an order."

Grudgingly, Krebble dashed his *Schmeisser's* butt into the burning logs, scattering them from the hearth onto what Hauzmann, to his immense surprise, now saw was not a beaten earth floor, or even naked boards, but a carpet. As Krebble stamped out the last few embers, darkness returned.

"So if none of us lit it," Brunner said, now fully awake, "who did?"

It took a moment for the implications of this to strike them, and then there was a mad rush as they went for their weapons. Getz, who still lay snoring on his trestle, was roughly shaken awake. He groaned and scratched at his lice. Hauzmann questioned him, demanded to know if he'd risen earlier and started a fire. Getz denied all knowledge.

"Check through there," Hauzmann said to Brunner.

There was a single arched doorway, minus a door, at the far side of the room. Brunner drew his *Luger* and hurried over there. He threw himself flat against the facing wall and glanced through. "Can't see anything."

Krebble opened the front door a little. The dimness retreated as pale, wintry light stabbed in.

"It's a passage," Brunner said. "Two or three rooms leading off it."

"Rooms?" Getz said, puzzled. On first arrival here, they'd thought this place nothing more than a woodland hut or lodge.

"Outside?" Hauzmann asked Krebble.

Krebble glanced around the front door, then shook his head. Hauzmann joined him. He stared out through the narrow gap, but saw only snow again. It plastered the trunks of the surrounding trees, and lay between them to a depth of several feet. Another fall while they'd slept had rendered its surface smooth and even. Their passage out of the woods was only vaguely identifiable – a groove-like dint, weaving erratically up to the door.

"Check those other rooms," Hauzmann said. "Unless there's another way out of here, whoever lit that fire is still inside."

Brunner nodded and, unsheathing his knife, slid silently into the darkness of the rear passage. Getz slotted a new clip into his *Schmeisser*, but he looked uneasy.

"What is this place, anyway?" he asked. "Why are there no windows?"

"When we first saw it," Krebble replied, "I thought, well ... a house of the dead."

They glanced at him.

Before the war, Krebble had attended Heidelburg University, where as well as stuffing his head with all sorts of National Socialist nonsense, he'd occasionally found time to assimilate facts about other cultures (*inferior* cultures it went without saying, the study of which served only as an aid to devise means by which to destroy them).

He tried to explain what he meant: "In ancient times, the Slavic peoples of the Steppe – the Uralic, the Tungusic. They were nomads, hunter-gatherers. They lived a primitive existence, but instead of burying their dead, they built wooden houses for them. Secure places with only one entrance. The idea was that bears could dig down into shallow graves, but they couldn't open doors to enter buildings. You must have heard this?"

"A house of the dead – with a carpet?" Hauzmann said. "With an armchair?"

"More than one armchair," Getz corrected him. "See."

Krebble opened the front door wider. More winter light penetrated, and now they saw that there were two armchairs rather than one. They faced each other from either side of the room. The trestles placed between them were not actually trestles but low tables – they looked like coffee tables; they were crudely made, yet polished to a fine finish. Hauzmann was certain there'd been straw on them when they'd first entered. Likewise, he thought there'd been a scattering of leaves on the floor, but now when he looked, all he saw was the carpet again. In truth, it was more of a rug in that it only occupied the central area, but it was rich and deep, and coloured with vivid inks; its central image was a Russian horseman, a Cossack by his garb, blowing on what looked like a ram's horn.

207

"This is no house of the dead," Hauzmann said. "It's a house of the living, and it looks as though someone's been living here quite recently."

"Look at this!" Getz added, crossing the room.

Beyond the armchairs, against the rear wall, there was a handsome sideboard. It had been cut from walnut or some other costly timber, and had then been carved intricately. Its legs were pillars of twisting vines, its cupboard doors depictions of fruit and flowers and frolicking beasts. In its top section, there was a row of drawers, each with a wolf's head knob-handle. Getz opened one of these, and picked out a handful of silver cutlery. Next he opened a cupboard; inside it there were metal goblets, porcelain plates.

Hauzmann now came over. He gazed up at the wall. Spaced about three feet apart, there were two picture-plaques. At first they'd looked like religious icons, but closer inspection revealed that the first, which had resembled an image of the Madonna and child, actually showed a fair-haired girl in peasant dress, feeding fragments of bread to a wooden doll wrapped in swathing bands. Likewise, the second, which had initially appeared to represent Saint George and the dragon, was in truth a young lad, again of peasant stock, climbing into a hole in the ground while a dragon looked on. It was difficult to tell, but both looked to be made from painted enamels, inlaid with silver and gold.

"A winter cabin?" Krebble suggested. "For a hunter or trapper?"

"So near the city?" Hauzmann replied. "And with all these riches?

At which point Brunner reappeared. Both his gun and knife were re-sheathed, but he seemed wildly excited. "You won't believe it. There's a kitchen! A full kitchen!"

Hauzmann and Getz followed him through, passing three closed doors – one to the left, two the right – and entered a spacious rear chamber, where, even in the darkness, for there were no windows in here either, they could distinguish a long, central table, several more cupboards and a huge, old-fashioned range of the sort found in the kitchens of Prussian country houses.

"Not only that," Brunner said, "there's a cold-room over here." He worked his way around the table, which had two stools to either side of it, and opened another door. Beyond that was a much smaller room. Brunner entered it, then re-emerged carrying two hams, which he threw down on the table. After this, he brought out a leg of mutton, two rabbits, a loaf and an armful of carrots and turnips.

"Can you believe this?" he said, delighted. "It's all just been left here. There're three game birds hanging back there as well. There's cereals and grain, a tub of cream, a pat of butter, a canister of milk – which is fresh. And there's a stack of fresh firewood, to light the range. It's all just been left here."

The others regarded the banquet in stunned silence. It was so long since they'd seen food like this, much less eaten it, that they couldn't remember when it had been. And it looked even better a moment later when Krebble joined them, now carrying an oil-lamp that he'd trimmed and lit.

"Where'd you get that?" Hauzmann asked.

"The mantel over the hearth."

"I never saw it."

"Did you look?" Krebble wondered, though he too was distracted by the sight of the food. The hollow cavity of his stomach groaned audibly.

Brunner now grabbed one of the hams and made to bite into it, only for Hauzmann's whipcrack voice to stop him: "Wait!"

The men glanced around.

"Denying us food as well as fire, Sergeant?" Krebble asked. "I mean all right, perhaps heat is more than we deserve, but at least we can eat, no?"

"We'll eat," Hauzmann said, "when we've secured this area. Private Brunner, you were instructed to reconnoitre these premises. Did you carry out that order?"

Brunner lowered the ham to the table. "I regret to report, Sergeant, that I did not. The downstairs is clear. But there's an upper floor too."

Hauzmann was perplexed. "An upper floor? I didn't see one

from the outside."

"There's a stair. That's all I can tell you. I haven't been up it yet."

"Show me."

Brunner led them out into the passage, then opened the door on the left-hand side. A narrow wooden stairway led up into blackness. Hauzmann turned to the two doors on the right. "What's in these?"

"Storage space," Brunner replied.

Hauzmann opened them. The first was a closet filled with brushes, brooms and such. The second was more like a wardrobe. Four heavy coats made from animal skins hung above four pairs of leather, fur-filled boots.

"We'll be snug enough when we walk out of here again," Krebble remarked.

Hauzmann turned back to the stair, then cocked his *Schmeisser*. "Brunner, there's no other way into or out of here?"

Not on the ground-level."

"Krebble, take the front door. Keep a watch on the woods. Brunner and Getz, you're coming upstairs with me."

They filed up, the stair so narrow they could only move one at a time. Despite their best efforts, their boots *clomped* on the dry woodwork. Hauzmann now had the lamp, and even though he'd lowered its flame a little, he had no option but to hold it out in front of him. Getz followed directly behind, the barrel of his *Schmeisser* resting on Hauzmann's shoulder.

On the upper floor, a passage led away into shadow, both to the left and right. Again Hauzmann was perplexed. When they'd first arrived here, the impression he'd had was of a snow-bound forest cabin, functional but very small. Of course he'd been half-dead with cold and fatigue, so he could have been mistaken – but he'd seen nothing at all to indicate extensive dimensions like these.

"I was wondering, Sergeant," Getz said. Oddly, considering the hardened soldier he'd become in previous months, his voice sounded nervous, shaky. "Could one of us have lit that fire? I

210

mean, in a stupor, sleep-walking?"

"We'll worry about that afterwards. Brunner, go left. Getz, come with me."

Hauzmann started along the right-hand stretch of passage. Warily, Getz went with him. Brunner's big form, shaggy in sheepskin, went the other way, vanishing into the darkness like a shadow, his knife and *Luger* again at the ready.

"Sergeant, I ..." Getz began.

"Quiet. Talk in a minute."

A door now stood to their left. Like everything else on this upper level, it was plain wood. There were no adornments up here, yet it was clean and dry, and this in itself was unusual. Throughout the invasion of Russia, they'd taken shelter in many shacks and barns, and even those still in use had been thick with dust and festooned with cobwebs: there was none of that here.

Getz went to one side of the door, while Hauzmann took the other. Both *Schmeissers* were cocked and levelled. They hadn't been taught this caution at basic training; they'd learned it the hard way, during months of bitter house-to-house fighting.

"Ready?" Hauzmann whispered.

Getz nodded nervously.

They kicked the door open and went in barrels first, both covering different quadrants of the small room. They needn't have worried; it was empty.

Its floor was of smooth boards, its walls of neatly cemented logs. Again, there were no windows; in fact there wasn't a chink of light from the outside, not a breath of wind. The craftsmanship in this place was astounding. Above, the ceiling was sloped, but where they might realistically have expected rotted lathes, loose rafters, the underside of the stick-thatch, it actually consisted of closely fitted oak shingles.

And there was something else in here, something that made it rather different.

The room had been painted white.

At first they thought this was a trick of the light, maybe a result of the reduced glow from the oil-lamp. But Hauzmann turned the flame up, and they saw that every part of the room – walls, floor, ceiling – had been thoroughly whitewashed. While this in itself was perhaps not strange, the fact that the room was completely empty, that there was nothing else in there at all, gave it a bleak, ghostly aura. They stood there for several moments, sniffing at the air: there was a slight musty smell, rather like a cage, or more accurately a stable. But this didn't linger.

Eventually they withdrew, and went on to another door, this one on the right-hand side. They took the same precautions before entering, though on this occasion they had to kick and batter the door before it broke open. The room on the other side was also empty and windowless, and smelled faintly sour. This one had been painted a brilliant red.

"What does this mean?" Getz asked. Again, his voice was querulous.

Hauzmann shrugged. "I don't know. Colour-coded bedrooms? Maybe this is some kind of novelty inn or hotel? A holiday lodge perhaps."

"This is Soviet Russia. They don't have holiday lodges or hotels. And even if they do, why hasn't it been flattened, ripped apart? Christ's sake, Hauzmann, every town or village west of the Don is a desolation, we've seen that for ourselves!"

"What do you want me to say?" Hauzmann hissed. "I don't know what it means, but in all probability it means nothing." He paused, then added: "Your nerves are frayed. I understand that. We're all in the same fucked-up state. But for Christ's sake get a grip on yourself. You're a soldier, not a fucking boy-scout."

Getz nodded and swallowed. By origin a farm-labourer from Silesia, even on first arrival at basic training he'd been something of a roughneck; a hardy soul, well built, used to the outdoor life. His travails in Sixth Army – battles at Liege and Namur in the Low Countries, and on the outskirts of Paris – had toughened him even more, so by the time of Barbarossa[1] and Stalingrad in particular, he'd become an excellent man to have in a tight corner. Yet for all that, despite the many excruciating horrors he'd both

---

[1]. The German plan to annihilate the Soviet Union

experienced and perpetrated, thanks to his rural upbringing he'd remained resolutely religious and even superstitious. He never saw the irony in wearing a crucifix alongside a swastika.

They proceeded along the passage. They were almost at the end of it, but now a third and final door appeared, this one on the left. Again they took care when going through. This one didn't need to be smashed open; it was unlocked. But it was the same tale of emptiness on the other side, the only difference being that this room was painted black.

"Surely the best of the lot," Getz said.

"Don't read anything into it," Hauzmann replied. "You know what a sombre sod Ivan can be."

"And no windows again. Why? Why the hell are there no Goddamn windows?"

"There're windows down here," came a third voice.

They turned. Brunner was in the doorway. He glanced around the black room, briefly fascinated, but then, in his simple, soldierly way, shook it from his mind.

"You want to come and see?" he asked.

They followed him down the passage, passing the stair, and a few yards further on, coming to two doors that faced each other from opposite sides. Clearly Brunner had investigated both. The first door stood open on another small room; again it was windowless, but it wasn't empty. What looked like four bed-frames were propped against its walls. There was no paint in here; everything had been left natural. The other door opened on a second stair, this one even narrower than the first, almost claustrophobically so, though half way up it they felt the cold winter air on their faces.

At the top was what looked like a watch-room. It was low-roofed and there was space for only two or three men to stand inside it. But the upper sections of all four of its walls were shutters with simple bolt-locks on them. Brunner had already opened the east and west, so they could now look out over the tops of the forest. Even then there wasn't a great deal visible; a cloying white mist had descended and was wreathed around the house. The immediate ranks of trees, leafless and ice-clad, were all that could be seen.

"There are *these* too," Brunner said. "Whatever they're actually for."

Two items were suspended from hooks, one on the pillar in the northwest corner, the other on the pillar in the southeast. The first looked like a frying pan without a handle, the other like a small mattock with a rounded head. They were beaten from tarnished metal. Compared to everything else here, they looked old, overly used.

"A mortar and pestle," Hauzmann said. "Kitchen utensils."

"So why are they in the watch-tower?" Brunner asked.

"Who knows, maybe…"

"God in Heaven!" Getz suddenly shouted.

He spun around, knocking the other two aside and raising his *Schmeisser* as though to fire overhead. Brunner and Hauzmann also went for their weapons – but a moment later they lowered them again. Getz was still staring upwards as though bewildered.

There was a notch in the woodwork, in the northeast corner of the ceiling. It was large, maybe the size of a man's two fists clasped together, and it had curious features: there was a slash-like fissure that resembled a pinched mouth. Below and above that were pointed protuberances, rather like a nose and chin. Slanted cracks might have been eyes. Along one side hung thread-like strands, similar to sticky, matted hair. It was horrible: wizened, twisted out of any normal proportion. Yet, for all the world – very fleetingly, when seen in the corner of your eye – it was a hag or crone, leering down.

Of course in reality it was just a notch, a simple and natural contortion in the wood.

Getz apologised: "It was like a face just appeared over the top of me. I suddenly felt I was being watched. I glanced round and up and … saw it. I panicked."

He continued to stare at the thing. Leading away from the notch, there were odd striations, water-marks or something: faint, wavering lines that tapered across the ceiling to the other side, though if you looked closely enough, they suggested that a human body, or at least a human outline, had somehow been impressed into the wood.

Getz took off his left glove. Only three fingers remained on the hand below, and one of these was black with cold. He ran them over the ceiling's surface.

"Has someone done this deliberately?" he wondered. "Did they sculpt it somehow?"

"What does it matter if they did?" Hauzmann asked.

Getz now realised that his comrades were watching him curiously. He shrugged and pulled his glove back on.

"Brunner, stay here and keep a look-out," Hauzmann said. "I'll have some food brought up."

Brunner nodded.

Hauzmann went down. Getz followed, but when they were on the landing of the first floor, the sergeant whirled around, grabbed the private by his lapels and slammed him back against the nearest wall. "What the devil are you playing at?"

Getz seemed unable to answer.

"I have three men left, and one of you is going fucking crazy? You think I need shit like that?"

Still Getz couldn't speak. Sweat glinted on his brow.

"Well … what's wrong with you?"

"I… I don't know."

Hauzmann stepped back. "Four weeks ago, Viktor, I watched you painstakingly shovel your best friend's intestines back inside him so he wouldn't have to look at them while he died."

Getz hung his head.

"At Voronezh, you took out four BT-7s one after another, while lying flat in the mud and letting them roll over you so you could attach limpet-mines to their bellies."

"That's war."

"Yes, war! Blood, bones, death, destruction unleashed on Earth! And now you're frightened of an eerie old house?"

Getz glanced up again. "That's just it. That's the perfect word. It's *eerie*."

"Private Getz, with all the real problems we have…"

"Who made that fire? If none of us, who?" Suddenly Getz was wild-eyed.

"Like you say, it probably *was* one of us…"

"Well where did we get the logs from, the kindling?"

"They'll be lying around here somewhere."

"Yes, but how did *we* find them? We'd only just come in from the cold. We were zombies, we didn't know where we were, we dropped where we stood."

Hauzmann moved impatiently towards the downward stair. "Enough of this crap!"

*"Sergeant Hauzmann!"*

There was such urgency in Getz's voice that Hauzmann glanced back.

"You forget my upbringing," Getz said. "I was born on the banks of the Oder. Before this war started, I lived my entire life in the foothills of the Carpathian Mountains. There are strange stories about these eastern forests. Old Russia is full of ancient myths …"

"Old Russia!" Hauzmann snapped. "Old Russia doesn't exist any more! Haven't you seen that? There's industrial wasteland where hunting parks used to be. Riverside factories pump out filth where once there were fishing villages. Most of the population are in faceless, concrete towns where the apartment houses are like stacks of matchboxes. They're crammed together like vermin, under orders not just to live their life but to *love* it … or face the rest of their days in the asylum or the gulag. That is Russia now."

"Oh yes," Getz said sarcastically. "You mean the Russia we've come to liberate?"

Hauzmann snorted and moved on to the top of the stair.

"Old Russia will strike back."

Hauzmann started down. "And why should it strike at us? Our desecrations are minimal compared to those inflicted by the Bolsheviks."

"Maybe it won't strike at us. Not yet."

"This is demented gibberish, Getz. I don't want to hear any more."

"You won't," Getz murmured, descending after him. "At least, not from me."

*

"So," Hauzmann said. "What exactly have we got?"

Getz scrubbed a hand through his hair. To take his mind off other things, he'd been given the task of making an inventory of their remaining ordnance.

He shrugged. "Specifically … three MP40 machine-pistols[2]. Approximately fifty to one hundred rounds each. Four light grenades and assorted side-arms."

"We're not going to be fighting the war much longer on that little lot," Krebble said from the hearth.

Hauzmann had permitted him to make another fire, but only a small one. On reflection, it didn't seem likely that one more smudge of smoke in the Russian sky would be much of a give-away. Not that it would even be noticeable in the heavy winter mist.

Hauzmann glanced around the cabin's living room. Weirdly, it seemed even more comfortable than it had done before. They'd now found a second lamp, which gave them extra light. This showed patterned fabrics on some of the walls – Hauzmann didn't remember seeing those when he'd first arrived – while the back of the front door appeared to have been lined with flax, no doubt intended as a draught-excluder. To the right of the hearth, there were shelves with dishes arranged on them. More icon-like paintings were visible; again they were gilded with gold and silver, and were the sort of things any passing troops – no matter what their political persuasion – would shove into their knapsacks as quick and portable wealth. Even in rural Germany this would be classed as living in style, but in Communist Russia it was quite staggering.

Krebble stood up and beat cinders from his hands. "Are we going

[2]. The official name for the *Schmeisser* submachine gun.

to eat now?"

The new fire was burning, its heat seeping through the room, though in truth they'd already removed many of their outer layers because the house itself, being well insulated, was pleasantly warm.

"Food, yes?" Krebble said again.

Hauzmann nodded, then took one of the lamps and led them through to the kitchen. He didn't know why, but suddenly he felt reluctant about this. When they got in there, the various consumables were still arrayed on the table, as Brunner had left them earlier.

"We'll eat," Hauzmann said. "But we should do it sparingly. None of this is ours."

Krebble glanced sidelong at him. "We've looted, raped and burned our way across half of Russia. Is this going to make much difference?"

"It may."

"Why do you say that?"

Hauzmann pondered as he walked around the table. "Think about it. For weeks we've been living off rat-meat, roots, crumbs of biscuits. For liquid we've swallowed handfuls of dirty snow. You think we should sit down and feast ourselves now ... on innards as wasted as ours? It'd probably be the death of us."

Getz sniggered. "That'd be amusing. The Bolsheviks' bullets don't kill us, their hospitality does."

"So we just take a little," Hauzmann added.

There was no real dispute. Krebble, though inclined to be argumentative, was enough of an intellectual to realise that his sergeant spoke the truth. A hefty, solid intake of food now would likely do them more harm than good. As such, he volunteered to cook a pottage for them – a light gruel made from turnips and carrots mashed with salt and butter. When they finally came to sample it, it was like ambrosia. Even before it was ready, the smell was so delicious they were ready to faint.

Shortly afterwards, Hauzmann put his coat and gloves back on, and took a bowl up to the tower-room, where Brunner was still on watch.

"That Nazi bastard Krebble has his uses," the sergeant said. "He even found some herbs, would you believe. This is seasoned to perfection."

Brunner took the bowl and ate gratefully. While he did, Hauzmann scanned the fog-bound woods. It was late afternoon and night would soon be falling. Night was generally to be welcomed on the Russian Steppe. It made you feel marginally more anonymous, slightly less of a target.

"Anything at all?" Hauzmann asked.

Brunner was scraping the bowl clean with his fingernails. "Nothing. Which is strange, wouldn't you say? I mean, we're only two days from the biggest city on the Volga ... yet there's nothing. It's like we're suddenly in another time, another place."

"It's Russia, isn't it. Goddamn Russia."

Hauzmann didn't need to elaborate. Any German soldier in that position would have understood what he meant. The sheer size of this country had presented the invading armies forging into it with a unique kind of problem. Quite simply, it was a landmass that went on forever. None of the vast range of geographic obstacles that it threw at you – the rivers, the mountains, the swamps – could dispirit you as much as the fact that there never seemed to be an end to the advance. Even in summer, the sun-baked plain had a near-hallucinogenic effect. You could see as far as possible in every direction, yet it mesmerised you, caused you to miss things that were right under your nose. The smoke of torched villages, the dust of the *panzer* vanguards as they stormed ahead, the eye-watering stench of roadside gallows laden with the corpses of Jews and commissars – none of these could induce the same feeling of melancholy that the pure enormity and emptiness of Russia could.

"It'll be dark soon," Brunner finally observed. "Are we moving then?"

"Where to?" Hauzmann asked.

"Back to our lines."

"Where are they, do we know? Do we know if we've even cleared the Russian lines yet?"

Brunner shrugged. "We can't stay here."

"Why not? At least we're not under fire while we're here."

"They'll come eventually."

"The question is," Hauzmann said, "do we really *want* to go back? If we make it, we'll be debriefed. We may even be accused of cowardice for retreating. Either way, they'll then rotate us straight into the front line again."

"We might get leave."

Hauzmann chuckled. "You think so?"

"It's not unknown."

"It will be from now on. You're a good soldier, Max. But you're no strategist. Think about this. With Sixth Army destroyed, we must have lost, what – eight-hundred-thousand men?"

"Easily," Brunner said.

"That's a whole quarter of our entire eastern forces. As it is, Ivan's coming at us like swarms of ants. You think anyone will be spared from the defence? They'll be calling up old men and boys next."

Brunner pondered on this, then said: "So we're just staying here?"

Hauzmann chuckled again. It was pointless trying to paint a bigger picture for Brunner. He'd long been one of the best men in the platoon, an iron-hard regular, who'd enlisted before the war having tired of his penniless existence in the slums of Hamburg. But in many ways he was like a mule. He'd endure any hardship without question, carry out any duty no matter how distasteful. Whatever the circumstances, he was content to simply follow orders and let his officers do the thinking and worrying.

"No, Max," Hauzmann said. "We're not just staying here, but we might as well rest while we can. Keep alert. Another hour, and I'll send Krebble up."

When Hauzmann went back downstairs, Krebble and Getz, having eaten better than they had done in months, were both asleep in the armchairs. Determined to stay awake a little, he wandered around the ornate room, still marvelling that such a place could have remained untouched in these frozen, war-ravaged wastes.

The paintings caught his attention again; the girl with the doll, the boy descending into the Earth at the apparent behest of a dragon. He looked at a couple of the others. The first showed a woodland cottage with a crimson flower prominent in its upper window, and perched on the roof, a bird with rainbow-coloured plumage. The second was of a scraggy, aged man – naked, yet armed with a curved sabre – seated on a small horse. Despite their odd subject matter, all were exquisite in their craftsmanship

As a youngster, Hauzmann had been taught to appreciate the arts. The son of two schoolteachers, he'd been brought up in a quiet suburb of Berlin, where the walls of their small, neat bungalow had been adorned with prints by Nolde and Kirchner. His father, a book-collector, had kept many classic editions on the shelves, while his mother had been a talented pianist; many an evening, there'd been polite soirees in the Hauzmann household.

Of course, that place no longer existed.

A British bombing-raid in September 1941 (which Hauzmann had learned about somewhat belatedly in March 1942), had flattened the house completely, killing both his parents outright. The same had happened to his own, more modest home in the city centre, several weeks later, though his wife Gretta, who was by then living in a shelter, had afterwards written to tell him that she was safe. Of course he'd received that final letter from home eight months ago. He didn't know whether Gretta was alive or dead now. Not that Hauzmann worried about things like this – not any more. Over the last few months, he and so many others like him, had suffered emotional tortures beyond the compass of any prior human experience, and if it had taught him anything it was that worrying about things wouldn't change their outcome. Worrying was one more way for a man to cause himself pain; and what was the point of that when there were so many other causes that he had no control over?

Eventually, deciding that enough time had passed, he replaced Brunner with Krebble. Brunner dropped into an armchair, where he immediately fell asleep and began to snore. Hauzmann settled himself down by the fire, kept his *Schmeisser* handy – though now, at last, he was daring to hope that he wouldn't need it – and placed a few more sticks of kindling on the dwindling flames. Shortly after that, he laid his head back and he too slept.

But he didn't sleep for long.

At first he assumed it was a dream: a loud knocking on the front door of the cabin. It was thunderous and prolonged.

He stirred, struggling against wakefulness, and eventually it stopped.

In that typical way of dreams, he knew the knocking hadn't been real, despite it disturbing him. But then it came again, and it persisted for longer this time – even after he'd opened his eyes.

He sat upright.

Abruptly, it ceased.

Startled, but still mildly dazed, he glanced around the room. Only a faint orange glow emitted from the hearth. The shapes of Brunner and Getz were still slumped in the armchairs. Both of them were now snoring, but only gently. A dream after all, then.

And the knocking came again.

Hauzmann leapt to his feet, *Schmeisser* at the ready. He wanted to shout the others, but for a moment his throat was too dry – which was probably a good thing, because if he alerted those inside, he might also alert whoever it was outside.

He moved on catlike feet to the door and listened, now hearing nothing. Was there someone out there listening back? He began to suspect that there was. But who the devil was it? Certainly not the owner of this place, as he'd just have walked in – the door wasn't locked after all. A friend perhaps, a relative? In which case, they too might walk in. But who'd travel abroad to pay visits in weather like this, and at such a time as this – with battles raging across a corpse-strewn landscape?

The word 'corpse' lingered in Hauzmann's thoughts. Because there was someone else, of course, who might be on the other side of that door. The only other person who knew there was anyone here. The person who'd shown them the way in fact – the motorcycle courier who'd been frozen to the tree.

The notion was ridiculous. But suddenly Hauzmann found himself wrinkling his nostrils. Despite the thick coat of flax on the door, there was a distinct odour – rather repulsive: of decay and corruption, of green, maggot-riddled meat.

Hardly believing what he was now thinking, he whispered: "Who goes there?"

Only silence responded.

Unable to take it any longer, Hauzmann pushed down the handle and yanked the door back. As it swung open, he raised his *Schmeisser* to shoulder-height.

But there was nobody outside, just an unbroken vista of snow. Even the tracks they'd made coming here were now obliterated. The milky light of dawn was spreading, but the nearest trees were still only vague, motionless shapes.

Hauzmann didn't allow himself to relax. Someone had definitely been here. The corpse of the motor cycle courier? But that was ludicrous. Where on Earth had such an idea sprung from? Yet, whoever it was, he'd heard them knock with his own ears – and on the Eastern Front you never disregarded the evidence of your own senses, not if you wanted to survive.

He risked poking his head out of the door. Nebulous mist-forms rolled and undulated on the far points of his vision. But nothing seemed to be out of the ordinary.

And that was when he heard the noises overhead: a scratching, a heavy scraping, as of clumsy, lumpen feet. Hauzmann looked sharply upwards. The noises persisted but seemed to be moving away from him – and ascending, as though climbing towards the top of the roof. Now they were *clumping*, almost *clopping*.

To his complete disbelief, he realised that he was listening to what sounded like hoof-beats.

*

When Hauzmann burst into the watch-room, Krebble was asleep. He'd brought a stool up for himself and was now slouched on it. Despite the bitter chill from the open shutters, his helmeted head was cocked to one side and he was breathing deeply and slowly.

"Krebble!" Hauzmann hissed. "Krebble!"

The sentry leapt awake. "What's happening!"

"Lower your voice. There's someone up here on the roof."

Both men leaned out on opposite sides of the tower, but saw only pristine snow sloping down into the icy haze. Several moments passed.

"I can't see anyone," Krebble finally said.

"You can't see the whole of the roof, that's why."

"I can't hear anyone either."

"Then shut up and listen."

More time passed, the moments becoming minutes. Soon, Hauzmann, who'd dashed up so quickly that he hadn't thought to put on his greatcoat, was shivering violently. He'd been nineteen months on the Steppe, and the harrowing cold of these winter nights was still unbearable to him.

"You didn't notice anything unusual?" he eventually asked. But then he answered his own question: "No, I don't suppose you did, damn your hide! Because you were asleep, weren't you! At your Goddamn, fucking post! You were fast asleep!"

"I ... I can't deny it."

"Don't even try. Anyway, we'll talk about that later. Keep quiet."

They listened again, but the silence remained unbroken.

"What was it you think you heard?" Krebble finally asked.

"I didn't *think* I heard anything. Someone or something knocked on the front door. Then it came up onto the roof."

"Some *thing*?"

"It sounded like ... what does it matter?" Hauzmann couldn't bring himself to admit that he thought he'd heard hooves, or that he'd imagined the unseen caller to be the dead motorcycle courier. "Whatever, it sounded as though it came up here."

"You probably just had a dream."

"It was no dream."

"I had a dream too." Fleetingly Krebble sounded vague, uncertain of his facts. He indicated the face-like knot in the wood of the ceiling. "About that thing. It was telling me stories. Fairy stories."

"What are you talking about?"

"It sang songs to me as well. Nursery songs." The young Nazi looked confused. "I think that's what put me to sleep."

Hauzmann regarded him long and hard. "Krebble, in the next ten seconds I'm going to do for you what all your friends in the Party never did for anyone else in the ten fucking years they've been running Germany into the ground: I'm going to give you a second chance. That means you're on sentry-watch from now until noon. I catch you sleeping again, I'll beat your fucking brains out. Am I clear?"

Krebble straightened up. He took his spectacles off and rubbed their lenses with his sleeve, something he always did when tense or angry.

On first arriving in the company, he'd been an impressive sight: tall, fair-haired, handsome. Even now, wearing a patched-up greatcoat, and underneath that a uniform stuffed with rags, he had an unusual air of authority for a private soldier. Despite being as dirty and unshaved as everyone else, though his face was grizzled and blotched with sores, his lips cracked from the cold, he still retained this air of superiority, which probably stemmed from the confidence he had in his Nazi Party connections. Of course, he wasn't the pontificating extremist he'd once been. As they'd advanced further and further into the maelstrom of the Eastern Front, putting an ever greater distance between themselves and home, fighting endless battles, their ranks steadily thinning, their supplies draining, the average German soldier had got used to the reality that he wasn't an Aryan superman and that the *untermenschen* he was fighting were a tireless, resilient foe, at least as mentally strong as he was and masters of their own arduous landscape. In the light of that, the word of Krebble, and others like him, had meant progressively less and less. Tolerance of his hard-line views had gradually changed to impatience and finally to open, fearless disrespect. By the time they'd actually entered Stalingrad, he'd become a marginal, isolated figure in the company.

However, he wasn't entirely divorced from his opinions. Not yet.

"Who are you, a man frightened of nightmares, to give orders to me?" he said.

Hauzmann, who'd been about to descend, turned slowly to face him. "What?"

Krebble sneered. "There was something knocking at the door, was there? And then it was on the roof. Some *thing*, Sergeant Hauzmann? And you call yourself a soldier of the Reich. No wonder we're retreating in such disorder."

"You little swine ..."

At which point the sergeant suddenly heard his name being called from below. It was Brunner and Getz. Both sounded frantic.

Hauzmann jabbed Krebble in the chest with a thick forefinger. "Stay at your post, Private. Leave it for one second and you're a dead man."

He hurried downstairs, but found neither Getz nor Brunner in the living area. He turned and went along the passage to the kitchen, which, when he got there, was basking in the glow of candles arrayed on the worktops. Getz and Brunner were standing in its doorway, still fuddled with sleep but agog at what they were seeing.

Hauzmann himself struggled to comprehend it.

The kitchen table had been laid for breakfast. Down its centre there was a row of silver platters. On the first there were rashers of fried bacon, on the second slices of blood-sausage, on the third half a dozen poached eggs swimming in melted butter. There was also a loaf cut into slices and two glass pitchers; one contained what looked like orange juice, the other fresh, creamy milk. In front of each stool there was a dish, a knife and fork and a bowl. A pan of oat-porridge simmered on the hotplate.

"What the hell is going on?" the sergeant said.

Getz merely grunted. He was gazing glassy-eyed at the feast.

"I woke up needing a piss," Brunner replied. "I came in here to find a pot. Instead, I found this."

It briefly occurred to Hauzmann that the time was shortly before six. Breakfast bells would be ringing in barrack halls throughout Germany just about now.

"But this isn't all," Brunner added. "After I pissed, I thought I'd smoke. You remember the tobacco we took from the motorcyclist? It was in my waterproof pocket. But I couldn't find the damn thing, so I looked for it. I finally found it in here."

He opened the wardrobe door. Inside it, as well as the fur-coats that had previously been there, their army greatcoats were suspended from hangers, alongside Brunner's khaki waterproof and the heavy sheepskin that he'd stolen from the Russian on the Kumskiy Bridge. All looked as though they had been laundered and pressed; there wasn't a spatter of blood nor a speck of dust in view. Incredibly, all rips and tears in them appeared to have been darned.

"Get your kit," Hauzmann said slowly. "All of you. It's time to leave."

"Shouldn't we eat first?" Brunner asked.

Hauzmann stared at him. "Are you mad? This food could be poisoned. In fact, it probably is. Can you think of any other reason why a Russian would want to provide something like this for the likes of us?"

For the first time ever Private Brunner looked unwilling to follow orders. He bit his lip, agonised, as he gazed again at the breakfast delights.

"We're moving out," Hauzmann said, and he dragged his greatcoat from the wardrobe and pulled it on.

"But we don't need to move out," Getz suddenly asserted. "Sergeant, we honestly don't."

"What are you talking about?"

A strange, almost dreamy smile appeared on Getz's face. "I think I know what's happening here. It's ..."

There was a sudden wild shout from upstairs. It was Krebble: "Hauzmann! Hauzmann!"

They went swiftly to the bottom of the staircase. Krebble was at the top.

"Ivan!" he hissed.

"How many?" Hauzmann asked.

"At least eight. Coming in from the northeast. Ski-troops."

"Fuck! ... Siberians. How far away?"

"Eighty, seventy yards. Closing fast."

"Back to your post," Hauzmann said. "Don't open fire unless I do it first. You two, quickly!" He raced through the house to the front door. "Brunner, you're coming outside with me. Getz, you stay here. You fire when you hear us fire. Not until."

Getz nodded, but still seemed distracted. He glanced behind him, taking in the luxuries of the once rough-and-ready living room. Linen cloths had now appeared on the coffee tables. A pile of fruit gleamed from a basket on the sideboard.

"Are you listening to me!" Hauzmann snapped.

That seemed to wake Getz. "Of course."

"As soon as we start shooting, you do too. Until then, stay concealed. I want them caught in the open out front, so Krebble has a good angle of fire down on them. Got it?"

Getz nodded again.

Hauzmann looked at Brunner. "You ready?"

As always, Brunner was.

They opened the door and stepped quickly outside, closing it behind them.

The mist was dissipating a little and morning light now filled the clearing. The snow surface was still crisp and level. Nothing moved in the bright, white tangle of the woods, though voices could be heard approaching.

"Doesn't sound like they're expecting trouble," Brunner whispered.

"It doesn't matter. Over there." Hauzmann pointed to the southeast corner of the building, setting off himself towards a clump of brush on the west side. "We catch them in a four-way crossfire. Make every bullet count."

Moments later, they'd concealed themselves. Brunner had vanished from sight completely. Hauzmann, though he'd fallen to his belly, felt more exposed. No matter how deeply he inserted himself into the snow, he was only hidden by leafless twigs, and his field-grey would be visible to close scrutiny. He drew his bayonet and quickly tried to dig himself in deeper. Of course, this wouldn't stop the Russians from spotting the tracks he'd left behind as he'd come over here from the front door. His main hope was that the sight of the cabin would surprise them, and that they wouldn't initially look for anything else. If so, a few seconds was all he'd need.

The voices were now much closer. There was laughter, open discussion; as Brunner had said, they clearly weren't expecting anything. The muscles began to knot between Hauzmann's shoulder blades. His finger crooked hard on the trigger of his *Schmeisser*.

He glanced again towards the cabin. The exterior was still as crude and functional as it had been before: logs and thatch, with little indication that it contained so many home-comforts. At the apex of the roof there was a raised section, almost like a small belfry; the watchtower of course. Thankfully Krebble had had the sense to close all the shutters, thus masking its true purpose. The dwelling looked innocent enough, though with luck it would still startle the Siberians.

They now came into view, emerging one after another onto the open snow. There weren't eight of them, as Krebble had thought, but ten. And as always with this tough, hard-bitten breed, they were squat, broad-shouldered men, clad entirely in white. As well as their heavy backpacks, also camouflaged with white, each one of them carried a Thompson submachine gun.

Hauzmann cursed under his breath.

The American-made Thompsons had first appeared en masse in Soviet hands during the second phase of the fighting in Stalingrad, when Sixth Army, having cut its way through the central part of the city to the western river bank, had suddenly found itself surrounded. Easy to use, quick to reload, highly reliable, the Thompsons had more than played their part in tipping the balance. No doubt each Siberian would have three or four of those circular, one-hundred-round magazines in his pack. As if that wasn't bad enough, one of them was wearing what looked like a tank of fuel; it was a flame-thrower.

Hauzmann gazed along the barrel of his *Schmeisser* as all ten Siberians skied into view. However, instead of stopping-dead and appraising the cabin, they now formed a communal circle. To his surprise, he saw their officer break out a bottle of vodka and a packet of cigarettes, and hand them around. None of them spared a glance for the house, which possibly meant that they'd known about it beforehand, though if so it was strange that they hadn't already looted it or weren't looting it now. Whichever, they were so preoccupied with their cigarettes and alcohol that they didn't even react to Hauzmann's fresh tracks.

He looked quickly across to the southeast. Brunner, whose only firearm at present was a *Luger*, had stepped partly into sight and was taking careful aim with it.

Hauzmann glanced back at the Siberians. Now was the time. They stood in a huddle, and were completely unsuspecting. A single fusillade would account for them all.

But there was something wrong here – it was too easy.

He stared backwards over his shoulder. Did they have flanking guards maybe? Was there a support unit close by? That was the only explanation for their complacent attitude.

But even so, though they were idling about, laughing loudly, getting drunk for Christ's sake, any second now at least one of them would surely spot his tracks.

Yet still some sixth sense restrained Hauzmann.

Maybe they were bad soldiers and would move on without noticing?

That would be the best outcome of all, because then they wouldn't be missed and no one else would come looking for them.

The more he watched, the more it seemed as if the Siberians *were* getting ready to leave. He saw their officer slip the vodka bottle back into a pouch at his hip. The others were now throwing away their cigarette stubs, forming up again behind him.

That was when Krebble opened up from the watchtower.

There was a thundering chatter of fire, then snow was spurting up all around the Siberians. Immediately two sagged to their knees, crimson chunks torn off them

In the same instant, Getz, who'd clearly been waiting on a hair-trigger, yanked open the door of the cabin and leaped into view, his *Schmeisser* blazing.

Hauzmann rose up and began shooting, training his sights on the disoriented mass of men, working it across them as he spewed bullets. From the southeast corner, Brunner started squeezing off deadly accurate pistol-shots.

The ski-troop was being hit from all sides simultaneously. Another two dropped, twitching as they were repeatedly struck. Their officer was hit in the head and then the stomach, then in the chest and in the head again. The flame-thrower man tried to run, but because he was still in his skis, he tripped and fell. When he scrambled back to his feet, he was facing the southeast corner – Brunner put a single round straight through his forehead.

The rest of them were now taking evasive action. A couple had thrown themselves full length, and were returning fire. It was haphazard, untargeted, but a stream of lead slashed through the undergrowth above Hauzmann's head, showering him with frosted splinters. He rolled to one side, again trying to burrow into the snow. Hurriedly, he reloaded before firing again.

Already, only five Siberians were left. One had kicked off his skis, thrown away his pack and was running wildly towards the trees. Brunner took a careful pot-shot at him – his aim was true. The Siberian was hit through the right arm and right side, the slug exiting his lower belly in a deluge of blood and fecal matter. But as he fell, he swung around, and with the Thompson in his left hand, fired off the entire magazine. A line of bullets cross-stitched the front of the cabin.

And they cross-stitched Brunner as well.

The big private tottered where he was for a moment, then his knees buckled and he flopped backwards, his boot-soles still planted in the snow.

Hauzmann swore aloud. He drew a grenade from his belt and

lobbed it into the midst of the remaining Siberians. One grabbed at it, but fumbled it with his padded glove. It detonated. There was a flash and a *CRUMP*, and the entire group, both dead and alive, were flung twisting and turning through the air. The two who'd been lying down and had thus survived the blast, jumped to their feet and raced towards the cover of the woods. Hauzmann dashed into the open, still with half a magazine left. They were already weaving their way in among the trees, but were still in range, and whatever happened, they couldn't be allowed to escape.

He knelt, took aim, pumped his trigger.

And the wretched thing jammed.

There was another burst of fire from the roof. It kicked up plumes of snow in the Siberians' wake, but failed to hit home. But Krebble, who had a better view of the battlefield than anyone else, merely had to adjust his position and fire again. This time, the one on the right was hit in the back of the head, from which a mass of bone and brain visibly blew outwards. The other one, in a desperate attempt to veer away, slipped and fell. Getz charged out of the house, ran sideways to get a better angle on him, then dropped to one knee and fired through the timber. The Siberian was struck first across the throat. His head jerked backwards, and red froth burst from his mouth. Then it was his ribs and belly, which were simply blown apart.

He dropped forward like a stone, and lay face down in the snow.

Hauzmann lurched across the open space, grabbed up a Thompson and sprayed the pile of corpses. Many had already lost limbs or heads, or had simply burst asunder, disgorging their entrails in glimmering, butcher-yard heaps. But it was a chance you never took. He emptied the Thompson, then threw it down and continued across towards Brunner, who still lay unmoving.

He too was past repair.

His eyes were glazed, his yellow teeth showing through a rigid snarl. There was a hole in his midriff the size of a man's fist. For several yards around him, the snow had turned the colour of claret. Getz then came rushing up. He stopped when he saw the body of their comrade, though he didn't look especially horrified or even upset.

"He's in a better place now," was all he could say.

Hauzmann snorted. "Right at this minute, Private Getz, that could be anywhere else in the universe."

"Sergeant Hauzmann, there's something you should know."

"I'm all ears."

"If you're thinking of leaving this place, we don't need to." Getz was now smiling – weirdly, almost triumphantly. "Don't you see what's happening? We're completely safe here."

Hauzmann bent and scooped up Brunner's *Luger*, then turned and walked towards the front door of the cabin. "We might have been safe for a little longer, Viktor. If our fanatical friend upstairs hadn't decided to leapfrog the chain of command."

He entered the living room, stalked straight across it and started up the stairs.

"But we're safe," Getz jabbered, scurrying after him. "We don't have to leave."

"Get your kit ready," Hauzmann said. "And grab yourself a Thompson as well. In fact, grab yourself a couple. And go through those Ruskie survival-packs. There'll be plenty we can use."

At the top of the stair, he turned down the left-hand passage. He was vaguely aware that Getz was still following him, still talking, but now Hauzmann was focused entirely on the door ahead, the one that led up to the watchtower. And then Krebble suddenly appeared from it, *Schmeisser* in hand. Hauzmann stopped dead.

"Did we get them all?" Krebble asked. He looked pleased, exhilarated.

There was a taut silence, and then, very slowly, Hauzmann said: "You God-damn fool. Didn't I tell you to wait until my signal?"

In the typical manner of a man stressed by battle, Krebble's mood quickly turned. "What the fuck are you talking about? If it hadn't been for me, those sons of bitches would have escaped!"

"If it hadn't been for you, *we* could escape!" Hauzmann

retorted. "But now it'll be ten times more difficult. They'll send search-parties."

"If those Siberians were on a forest patrol, it could be days, weeks even, before they're expected to check in. We'll be long gone from here."

"You disobeyed a direct order, Krebble. You will now place yourself under arrest, and when we return to battalion I'm going to see that you get court-martialed!"

"Look, there's no need for this," Getz chipped in. "We're safe now."

Hauzmann glanced irritably at him. "What the hell are you rabbiting about? I gave *you* an order as well."

"Look at this, look ..." Getz said, and he kicked open the door opposite the foot of the tower-stair.

On the other side, the room that previously had contained only empty bed-frames propped against the wall, was now resplendent. Lush fabrics, emblazoned with Slavonic imagery of woods and beasts, covered the walls. There was a rug on the floor, and to one side a chest of drawers, from the top of which another oil-lamp emitted warm, cozy light. Its most impressive feature however, were the beds – three, not four as they'd first thought – now placed side-by-side, and fully made up with mattresses, plump cushions and rich eiderdowns.

They regarded the room with astonished silence, before Hauzmann finally turned and faced Krebble again. "You've been busy, haven't you!"

Krebble looked astonished. "I'm not responsible for this!"

"I suppose you're not responsible for cooking breakfast as well."

"What the devil are you talking about?"

"It *had* to be you. Last night, during your watch."

Again, Getz tried to intervene. "Sergeant Hauzmann, it's nothing to do with Private Krebble ..."

"The hell it isn't! Last night, I heard noises upstairs. I thought it was someone on the roof, but clearly it was *him*. He was up to something. And now we know what."

Getz shook his head. "He didn't have time to cook us breakfast as well, did he!"

"That's debatable," Hauzmann said. "He was awake for hours while we were all asleep." He rounded again on Krebble. "What is it, Willie? Were you trying to win the lads over for the Party? Were you showing them the lifestyle they could become accustomed to if they fought this war to win rather than simply to survive?"

Krebble shook his head. "You're unhinged Sergeant Hauzmann. I think I'm relieving you of command."

"And I think you're not!" Hauzmann took a step back and pointed the *Luger* square at Krebble's chest. "Getz, disarm him."

"There's no need for any of this," Getz said tiredly.

"Do as I damn well say! Disarm him!"

Getz shrugged and turned to Krebble. "I'm sorry ..."

Krebble handed over his *Schmeisser*, but he continued to glare at Hauzmann. "It hardly matters, Viktor. So long as you understand that what you see before you here is the entire reason why we're losing this war ... is the embodiment of disloyalty and defeatism, is a man who would hand our mothers, sisters and daughters to the barbarian hordes on a plate rather than get his own hands dirty."

"I wonder why they didn't let you in the SS, Krebble?" Hauzmann countered. "You look the part, you sound the part, you clearly believe the part. I wonder what it was?"

"You know what it was. My father was a political dissident."

"Oh yes, I forgot." Hauzmann laughed. "Mind you, we've only got your word for that, haven't we? As your father died ten years ago and none of us knew him, there's no way to prove it. You know what I think the real story is – you're mentally unstable. You may strike a pose as the perfect Teutonic warrior, you may adhere strictly to the required thinking ... but if secretly your brain's a scrambled egg, you're a likelier candidate for Hadamar[3] than for Bad Tolz[4].     The SS have to be pure to the

[1] A clinic in western Germany, where the 'biologically unfit' were disposed of.
[2] A training school for officers in the SS.

core, isn't that right? They have to be strong and healthy in every respect. And you Krebble ... well, you're clearly as mad as a hatter. Have you got designs on this place, is that what it is? Is it going to be your reward for the role you played in the great ideological war? Is it going to be your personal piece of *lebensraum,* as promised to you in *Mein Kampf?*"

"I hope you're listening to this treason, Getz," Krebble said.

"I'm not listening to either of you," Getz replied, sounding exasperated. "Because neither of you are listening to me!"

He shouted those final words, and, surprised, they glanced round at him.

"Must I spell it out for you," he said. "They didn't *see* this place, quite evidently. The Siberian troops – they didn't see it. It was hidden to them. And only one building I know of is selective about those it allows to see it."

"Getz?" Hauzmann said.

"Baba Yaga's hut."

"Baba ... what?"

"You must have heard of her," Getz said. "The woodland witch. An old Russian goddess, worshipped by the Slavs before they became Christians."

"Private Getz ..."

But Getz was becoming more and more animated. "This is her house. Don't you see? Everything points to it. The hospitality – she always shows hospitality to those who dare enter. And incidentally, it's a hospitality that *must* be accepted, or else a grave insult will be taken."

"Private Getz ..."

"The whole place is run by invisible servants. You must have heard this story? I mean Baba Yaga's a hideous hag, but she's still the queen of the forest. Look, those bedrooms back along the passage. They house three other servants of hers – three riders, a white one, a black one and a red one. Didn't we smell horse-sweat in there, Sergeant?"

"Private Getz, for Christ's sake!"

"The white one rises as dawn," Getz said. "The black as nightfall

– the caller in the early hours this morning, that will have been him returning. And as for the red one – his room was the one we had to break into, remember that? That's because he represents the sun and there is little for him to do at this time of year. But seeing as we freed him – well, today will probably be a beautiful day."

He treated his two comrades to another broad smile.

"The truth only dawned on me slowly," he added. "But surely you can see it for yourselves now? All we need do is stay here, accept Baba Yaga's hospitality and the war will pass us by."

There was a moment of silence as he awaited their response.

Finally, Krebble turned back to Hauzmann. "So what are you going to do now, Sergeant? Now you head a company of *two* madmen. Are we both responsible for constructing this Germanic nirvana in the heart of the taiga?"

"There's nothing Germanic about it!" Getz insisted, now sounding angry. "Look at this place – the simple rusticity of it, the furnishing, the carvings on the woodwork. It's Russian through and through. But it's old Russia, *real* Russia."

"Go to the watch-tower," Hauzmann told him. "Keep your eyes peeled."

"Sergeant, I ..."

"Just follow the fucking order, Private Getz!"

Sullenly, Getz handed Krebble's *Schmeisser* to Hauzmann, then unshouldered his own and retreated up the stair. But as he went up, he warned them: "Don't refuse the hospitality of this house. Do that and you'll anger its mistress. And above all, don't criticise the service."

"Okay," Krebble reassured him. "We won't criticise the service."

"You demand answers of her servants, and you'll enrage her to the point where she'll kill us all," Getz said. And then he was gone.

Krebble turned to Hauzmann again. "Still think it was me?"

"I ... I may have been hasty," Hauzmann admitted. "After all, you were asleep too, even though you shouldn't have been! Maybe you didn't have as much time for mischief as I thought." Reluctantly, he lowered the *Luger*. "But I still don't trust you."

"Until Ivan shows up. Given the standard of the rest of your unit, I suspect you'll have no choice but to trust me then. Of course, by then it could be too late."

Resignedly, Hauzmann handed the *Schmeisser* back.

Krebble took it and cocked it. "So what do we do now?"

"Gather what ordnance we can from outside." Hauzmann turned and led the way downstairs. "In particular, I want that flame-thrower."

They passed through the living room, which looked even more sumptuous than it had before. There were now cushions on the easy chairs. Painted figurines sat to either side of the fruit-bowl.

Krebble shook his head, baffled "Where do you suppose he found all this stuff?"

"Who knows? Probably a couple of trunks in the closet."

Outside, the mist had fully dispersed to reveal a clear blue sky. It was still bitingly cold, but the sun now glistened on a pristine white landscape. With the frozen woods in such close proximity, it was reminiscent of a Christmas card. Except for the open ground in front of the cabin, where the corpses lay scattered and trampled, crimson snow extended for yards in every direction. With Soviet aviation now granted free-range overhead, it wouldn't take a particularly eagle-eyed pilot to note this mass of isolated carnage.

"We should cover all this up," Hauzmann said.

Krebble agreed, but first they looted the bodies, collecting not just the Thompsons, but ammunition belts, grenades and even land mines. In the Siberians' backpacks they found tins of salted beef and pork, packets of powered soup, chocolate, matches, tinted goggles, trenching-tools, extra blankets and small medical kits. They acquired as much of this as they could carry, then stripped off several sets of white coveralls – those that weren't too torn or drenched with blood. Hauzmann took charge of the flame-thrower, hoisting it onto his back, then fastening its harness at his waist. After this, they dragged the bodies into the cover of the trees, then kicked fresh snow over the blood and char.

Once back indoors, they assessed the haul.

"We won't want for equipment," Krebble said. "Though we shouldn't try to take too much. More than anything on this journey, we'll need food. We should leave plenty of space for that."

Hauzmann shook his head. "The soup packets, the salt meat. That'll do us."

Krebble stared at him. "Why? There's a kitchen-full back there – quality stuff. And it's just waiting for us to help ourselves."

He walked down the passage, but at the far end halted at the sight of the breakfast that had been prepared for them. In addition to everything else, a large coffeepot now sat bubbling on the stove.

"I see what you mean about someone being busy," he said. "Getz has surpassed himself."

"I still think we should leave it," Hauzmann replied.

Krebble started opening pouches on his webbing. "Still worried our guts will reject it? Sorry, that's a risk I'm prepared to run."

He took a swig of milk, then commenced wrapping bundles of sausage and bacon in napkins.

"Damn it, Krebble!" Hauzmann shouted. "Don't you ever listen!"

"And what exactly am I doing wrong this time, Sergeant?"

"Haven't you had enough of this! Taking things that aren't yours?"

Krebble looked stunned. "Are you serious?"

Hauzmann rubbed his tired brow. "Where are the owners of all this? On a work-detail somewhere? Dead in a communal grave? Or hiding in the forest, waiting until we've gone? I suspect the latter, given the state of this place."

"What does it matter?"

"Aren't you sick of it? This murder, this endless pillage."

Krebble shrugged. "That's what we're here for, in case you'd forgotten. *All* of us, whether you happen to be a Party member or not."

Hauzmann shook his head. "It's not what *I'm* here for. I mean yes, I share your dislike of the Bolsheviks. But this isn't them.

239

Like Getz said, this is different, this is old Russia."

Krebble snorted. "Getz also said that we should accept this hospitality. And I for one intend to, because I'm sick to death of being so hungry that I can feel my backbone through my stomach."

He began stuffing his pockets and pouches.

Hauzmann watched worriedly. "Accepting hospitality means sitting here and dining like guests. Not bagging it all and running away like a bunch of thieves."

Krebble laughed aloud. "Thieves is what we are, Sergeant. Old Russia, new Russia – what difference does it make? They didn't invite us here. We kicked our way in and we're taking what we want."

There was a thundering *CRASH* from somewhere to the front of the house.

Both men dashed back down the passage into the living room, where they slid to an astounded halt. At first glance nothing had changed; everything was where it should be.

Except for the front door.

Which was no longer there.

Bare logs had replaced it, fitted tightly together. The flaxen coat that had kept out drafts had also vanished.

So it wasn't just the door; it was the entire doorway – it had simply gone.

"This is a trick," Krebble said.

Hauzmann raced forward. He slammed his hands against the logs, but they didn't budge an inch. He began feeling with his fingers around the areas where the edges of the door should be, but found nothing. There was no sign a door had ever been there.

"How is this possible?" Krebble asked.

Hauzmann shook his head and backed away.

"Getz hasn't done this as well!"

"No," Hauzmann agreed. "Getz hasn't done this."

"Then who? *Who?*"

"Probably the same person who's been waiting on us hand and foot."

"You said it wasn't Getz ..."

"It isn't Getz! How the hell could Getz be responsible for this!"

*"Who are you?"* Krebble howled, spinning around. He unleashed a volley of shots across the room, shattering its furnishings. "Where are you? Come out, you cowardly bastards, so we can see you! Stop hiding and meet us face to face!"

In response, there was a sharp but prolonged splintering of wood from somewhere upstairs, immediately accompanied by a gargling screech.

"Getz?" Hauzmann said. He looked at the ceiling. *"Getz!"*

The screech went on – horrible, agonised. They wanted to rush up and help, but something now held them back. A few seconds later they heard the sound of stumbling feet on the landing above. Warily, they moved to the passage – just in time to see Getz come staggering down the stairs, at the bottom of which he sank to his knees.

His face and throat were gory ruins. It was as though someone with talons had been at him. His nose was missing, both eyes hung from their sockets on strands. One ear and most of his scalp had been wrenched off, leaving bare, cranial bone. He tried to speak, but blood was pulsing from his throat via three gruesomely deep slashes.

He reached weakly towards his comrades, then stiffened and toppled forward. He slid face-first down the opposing wall, at the foot of which he lay perfectly still.

Hauzmann and Krebble were at first too astonished to speak, or to register the continued sound of tearing, twisting of wood upstairs. Only when it actually ceased – abruptly, as if a switch had been thrown – did they actually come round. They glanced at each other, then up the staircase. The top of it was still dark, but now they could hear another pair of feet approaching it, and then coming down. There was an eerie smell: sap or resin, the mulch of leaves, woodland compost, and suddenly a figure was visible, descending steadily through the dimness: it was thin and spindly, yet hunched, with straggling, filthy locks and terrible raptor claws that were clenched and dripping.

Hauzmann shoved Krebble aside, took aim with the flame-thrower and sent a *whooshing* blast of fire up the staircase. The figure was entirely engulfed. It stood rigid yet quivering, a black outline on hellish orange. Shouting, Hauzmann let loose a second blast, which roared up the narrow passage, filling it from wall to wall and floor to ceiling, entirely immersing the thing that stood there. Now Krebble joined the attack. He emptied his magazine at it, then hurled two grenades up, one after another. Frantically, the two soldiers scrambled through into the living room, where they dived for cover.

The grenades discharged simultaneously; furious explosions, the contained volume of which was ear deadening. Furniture was flung over and smashed. Smoke, dust and wood-splinters gusted through the entire downstairs and filled it with a choking cloud, which took several minutes to settle.

Eventually Krebble looked up. He laughed and coughed at the same time: "That did it. That did it all right."

And then something else happened.

There was a deep rumble and the entire house began to shake.

"Good Christ!" Hauzmann said. "A barrage!"

The floorboards started shuddering violently, as though to an earthquake, and then suddenly they tilted upright. Both men went hurtling sideways amid a sliding mass of broken furniture. The next thing, they were being tipped the other way and fell entirely across the house again, a second tide of flotsam flowing alongside them. Thunderous detonations could now be heard on all sides. The cabin had clearly been blown from its foundations; it felt as though the entire structure was flying through the air. It rocked, tossed, tilted yet again. Soon the furniture was reduced to matchwood, yet the building itself remained intact. At any moment the rolling, shouting men anticipated a direct hit, expected the ceiling to come down on them in a glare of flame and steel. But that never happened.

Instead, the ordeal went on and on, seemingly without end.

They lay huddled, hands around their heads, despite being

thrown back and forth, up and down, now in a chaos of debris that was lit only by the fiery glow of the stair-passage. But still no flattening impact fell; there was no final, crushing blow to pulverize them into the very earth they'd raped and despoiled.

And then, with equal swiftness, it all stopped.

There was an alarming stillness, a deafening silence. The men glanced up from under the wreckage that half-buried them. There was a long, low *creeeak*, and the cabin teetered – precariously, as though perched on the edge of a cliff.

They glanced at each other, white-faced.

And the whole thing tilted over again, far more terrifyingly than at any time before.

They tumbled forward, yelling, grabbing at anything they could, caroming off each other. A bright light flooded upwards as a trapdoor swung open beneath them.

Though of course it wasn't a trapdoor, it was the front door.

They dropped clean through it, fell maybe four or five feet through the air, and then were in snow; soft, deep snow, which was white and clean and unblemished, instead of black and cratered, as they'd imagined.

They jumped desperately to their feet, knowing that only immediate flight could save them. Yet initially there was no obvious direction to fly in. They'd expected to see what remained of the forest: smashed timber, burning branches, uprooted trunks – yet there were no trees, living or dead, anywhere near them.

What there was, however, was the charred relic of a Tiger tank with its barrel bent upwards at a curious right angle and a skeleton perched on the top.

And directly in front of that, there was Private Seefeld.

Who'd been stripped naked and nailed Christ-like to two planks set up as a cross.

Needless to say, he was dead. He'd been dead for some time. His wounds were deep, gangrenous fissures now covered in frost. His face was grimacing clay, his eyes lustreless orbs. A single red-green icicle hung several inches from his left nostril.

At first Hauzmann was too perplexed to be appalled by this

vision. But then a hand was clamped to his shoulder. He turned, and now he *did* see trees, though they were some way distant. Krebble was pointing at them, or rather at the log cabin receding through their top-most branches, tilting and jerking as though walking on gigantic legs.

"T-tell me you see that," Krebble stammered. "Hauzmann, tell me you see that!"

"I see it," Hauzmann confirmed. "But do you think *they* do?"

Krebble glanced around. Beyond the burned-out tank and the crucified boy, he now noted regimented lines of grey, triangular tents, out of which figures were issuing like ants: figures in brown uniforms, wearing quilted jackets and fur hats; figures armed with all types of weapons from hunting rifles to submachine guns.

"You see it?" Krebble shouted at them, continuing to point, the sheer improbability of what he'd just witnessed making him oblivious to reality. "You must see that!"

"Krebble, it's pointless," Hauzmann said quietly.

On all sides, Russian voices muttered incredulous curses.

"Idiot Communist scum!" Krebble screamed. "For once in your worthless lives, don't miss what's right under your noses!"

They didn't.

# The Worst Of All Possible Places

## By
## David A. Riley

**DAVID A. RILEY** began writing horror stories while still at school and made his first professional sale to the *Pan Book of Horror Stories* in 1969. The story, published in 1970, was chosen by John Pelan for inclusion in *The Century's Best Horror Fiction*, a two volume collection with one story published during each year of the 20th Century (1901-2000) as the most notable story of that year. This anthology is published in 2007 by Cemetery Dance. In the late sixties and early seventies, as well as writing other stories, including the title story of *The Satyr's Head and Other Tales of Terror*, he had a number of articles published in David Sutton's prestigious fanzine, *Shadow*, with pieces on Franz Kafka and William Morris. His first collection of short stories, *The Lurkers in the Abyss*, is due to be published by John Pelan's Midnight House in hardback later this year. He recently had stories published in *Alone on the Darkside* (ROC Books, USA) and *When Graveyards Yawn* (Crowswing Books, UK) and has a novelette due to be serialised in *Dark Wisdom* magazine in the

USA. In 1995, together with his wife, Linden, he published a professional science fiction/fantasy magazine called *Beyond*, which ran for three issues, with covers by Martin McKenna, David A. Hardy and Les Edwards and stories and articles by some of the biggest names in the genre: Karl Wagner, Ramsey Campbell, Simon Clark, Stephen Laws, Stephen Gallagher, John Brunner, Kim Newman, David A. Sutton, and others. He and his wife now run a bookshop in Oswaldtwistle, Lancashire, which has a large stock of fantasy, horror and science fiction, as well as more general topics. They recently bought some properties in Bulgaria and intend, within the next year or so, to alternate their time between living there during the summer and Britain during the winter. His daughter, Cassandra, recently graduated from the prestigious Mountview Academy of Theatre Arts in London and is now a professional actor. David Riley is a member of the *Horror Writers Association*. Dave reveals that, "A family member once spent a couple of years in the tower blocks near Queens Park Road in Blackburn that gave me the idea for this story. I helped to move his furniture there (and out when he left) and was amazed at some of the people who lived in the place, including dogs similar to – if an awful lot less demonic than – the ones in the story. Some of the events actually took place in them, including the chainsaw murder. They were, even without the help of the supernatural, nightmare places (there were three towers blocks clustered together, now demolished), and peopled with the kind of human wreckage I have used in the story. They needed little elaboration."

*1612*

THE MINISTER *looked around the tiny church. His followers were busy blockading the doors with everything they could put their hands on, from piles of books to the heavy, oaken pews,*

246

*but he knew they were doomed. The Sheriff's men were already on their way from Lancaster, and it would not be long now before they could add their weight to the forces Sir Roger de Lacey had already mustered outside against them.*

*They would not get him to the gaol at Lancaster to be hanged for witchcraft, the minister thought as he climbed the rough wooden steps that took him to the top of the church tower. He looked out into the valley below where the small village of Edgebottom glowed with lights. Already there must be over a hundred down there.*

*The minister knew what he and his handful of followers had to do. This sacred site was theirs. Long before the church was built here there had been a shrine. No more fitting, welcoming place was there in the whole of Lancashire for them to die as true followers of the ancient gods. Their blood would be their final sacrifice.*

*He drew a dagger from his belt, then opened the sleeve of his shirt so that his lower arm was bare. When he returned to the floor of the church every eye was on him.*

*"Brother and sisters," the minister called to them. "The time is upon us." With unhesitating speed he drew the blade of his dagger in a deep, straight line from his wrist upwards. Blood welled from the wound. And he watched with satisfaction as his supporters, heedless of the blows being battered on the doors, drew knives of their own.*

\*

Sticky heat played havoc with Bill Whitley's neck. Twice now he'd needed to probe a finger round the collar of his shirt, but to no avail, and he knew the real problem lay in the fact that it was just too tight. A couple of years ago it had fit perfectly. But too many beers and take-aways since his wife left him had added to his weight. Surreptitiously, he loosened the top button beneath his tie. The relief was immediate.

"Mr Jackson is ready to see you now," the receptionist

247

announced. Bill wondered if there was a note of scorn in her voice, as if she had seen him fiddling around like a miscreant schoolboy waiting outside the headmaster's office.

Self-consciously, he felt at the knot on his tie, tightened it a little in a forlorn effort to smarten his appearance, then strode down the short corridor in the council offices to the door at the end. He knocked, then opened it.

"Come in. Come in."

Bill felt like saying "I already am," but didn't.

Wearing a suit that looked far too expensive to wear for work, Jackson, short, slim and giving off an air of self satisfied complacency, was leant as far back as he could in the chair behind his desk. He watched while Bill, unavoidably prying a finger yet again beneath his collar, seated himself.

"I've studied your housing application as sympathetically as I can, Mr Whitley," Jackson said. "Unfortunately there is a severe housing shortage in Edgebottom at the moment. Last month alone we had to find places for over fifty asylum seekers."

Bill nodded. "Wasn't there something about that in *The Chronicle?*"

"Ah, *The Chronicle.*" The corners of Jackson's pert mouth had a minute hint of scorn. "Their articles were not very helpful. More misinformation than fact, I'm afraid."

Bill nodded sympathetically. He had no idea what the man was talking about. Although he did remember glancing over the headlines, he had paid little more attention than that. Since his divorce he had had no real interest in newspapers, other than as something to shuffle in front of him while he worked his way through the first few pints of the night. Thinking of which made him wish he had decided to go along with his first inclination to have a whisky before his appointment at the housing office. It was too late now, but his fingers felt twitchy as the council official gazed at him.

"Things are getting desperate," Bill explained.

"You have somewhere to stay at the moment, though, haven't you?"

248

"A friend's putting me up on a bed settee in his living room. Not ideal. Tracey—that's his wife – she's had enough of me living there. It's three weeks now."

"Your own house was repossessed?"

Bill nodded.

"After I lost my job at the school I couldn't keep up the repayments. It was bad enough before my divorce, even with my ex's wage to help out. We'd gone into it way over our heads, especially when interest rates started to rise. From the start we began to fall behind on our repayments. After what happened, the court case and all, when I had to rely on unemployment benefit - "

"You have been trying for a new job, though?"

Again, Bill nodded, though the truth was he had made little effort. After he lost his job at St Cuthbert's Secondary School, he'd been unable to apply for any more teaching posts, and he didn't seem fitted for much else. Ten years as a teacher had seen to that.

"There aren't any council flats available at the moment that would suit someone of your background," Jackson said.

"What about flats that wouldn't suit someone of my background? I really am desperate. Another few days and I might be out on the street anyway."

Jackson stared for a moment at his fingernails. "There are *some* flats available, of course. There always are. In *certain* blocks. But you really wouldn't want one of these. They wouldn't suit you at all."

"Why's that?"

"For a start off you aren't a crack head, Mr Whitley. You haven't done time for armed robbery or mugging. Or selling drugs."

"It's only a roof and four walls I'm after. I don't care who my neighbours are. If it's only a matter of a few weeks—"

"Or months. Perhaps longer," Jackson said. "I can't guarantee how long it will be before we could offer you anything better. There are other people higher up the list. Single parent families, for instance. You're unmarried, a man and have no dependants. Unfortunately for you, that places you pretty low on the scale of priorities."

"A few weeks. A few months. I can survive that." Bill tried to put as much emphasis as he could on the sheer desperation of his need. It was difficult to express just how bad the situation at Wayne's was becoming. How could he explain the exasperation Tracey felt at his presence in their home, especially when he returned the worse for drink after a night out, drowning his sorrows?

"I don't think you fully appreciate just how bad some of these tower blocks are," Jackson said. "They're not safe. Some of the people living in them are on medication. They're schizophrenic— or worse. Some of them are downright dangerous. Quite honestly, I think a lot of them would be better off in a controlled environment than in the community. I wouldn't normally say this, but with your background it's plain to me how difficult you would find it living amongst them."

"But I wouldn't be living amongst them for long," Bill insisted. "Just *temporarily*. Till something better turns up. That's all, isn't it?"

Jackson shook his head. "You really don't understand."

"But I do," Bill said. "I appreciate what you are saying, but I need somewhere soon. A place of my own, if only for a few weeks. While I'm there I can keep my head down. Avoid the neighbours, if necessary. I don't care. When you've somewhere better, I'll take it. Gladly, I'm sure. Till then, I mean it, anywhere, *anywhere at all*, will do."

And, for all that he really still didn't appreciate just how sincere Jackson's advice to him was, Bill was satisfied that his own assertions were justified. He could cope. He knew it. He was sure. After all, he'd managed to cope with all that had happened to him over the past twelve months. The court case for assault. The disgrace. His sacking. Having his face headlined on the front page of *The Chronicle*. "Teacher Found Guilty of Assaulting Pupil" – even though the boy concerned was a six-foot fifteen year old with a record for bullying other pupils. Even if Bill's mind had been obsessed with his own problems at the time and his head had been throbbing that day from a hangover a nearly full bottle of whisky had induced the night before – even if he had been more worried about his growing debts and his inability to keep up the repayments on his mortgage, or even remember half of the stuff he was supposed to be teaching that day, he could cope.

Jackson sighed. "I suppose it will be all right, so long as you know." He reluctantly picked up a sheet of paper. "There is a tenth floor flat we could offer you. It's in one of the tower blocks near Queen's Park Road. All of them are due for demolition next year, and all but one have already been emptied. One of them, Daisyfield

House, is a sort of holding post, where anyone we've not been able to re-house elsewhere has been put for the time being. You could certainly stay there for the next few months. There's nothing in the way of furnishings. After the last tenant was removed – or left, I should say," he corrected himself, " – we had to fumigate the place. Some of them leave things in a disgusting condition. What furniture there was had to be destroyed, carpets and all."

"I've a few sticks of furniture of my own stored away," Bill said. "Enough for a flat."

"You wouldn't want anything too good," Jackson said. "Chances are it'd be stolen. Security's important where you'll be staying. Keep your door locked whenever you can. I don't want to alarm you, but the incidence of burglary in Daisyfield House is higher than anywhere else in Edgebottom."

"I'm a careful man," Bill said. "Belt and braces. I'll make sure the place is secure, even if I have to go out and buy some additional locks myself."

"Which wouldn't," Jackson added, "be as frivolous an idea as you might think."

\*

"Thanks for your help, Wayne. I really appreciate it."

Bill stood by his friend's van, the back of which was loaded with most of his furniture – a bed, a couple of small armchairs, a table, a stool, a chest of drawers and a cardboard box filled with cutlery, pans, an electric kettle and a small TV, together with a couple of carrier bags of groceries he'd picked up from Asda.

The day had turned cold even for October, and the towering concrete blocks off Queen's Park Road loomed miserably before them against clouds that all but filled the sky. Set on the higher slopes of the broad, moorland valley within which Edgebottom had grown as a cotton town in the early decades of the Industrial Revolution, the winds here were notoriously fierce at the best of times.

"If I'd known how bloody cold it'd be I might have let you borrow the van and left you to come here on your own. I hope you've got some good heating up in that flat of yours. You'll need it." Wayne grimaced as a fresh gust swept over them. "Straight from Siberia, that," Wayne said, his teeth chattering.

"We'd better get on with it. The guy at the housing office said not to leave the van parked here too long."

"I know, I know. Otherwise one of those thieving bastards you've got as neighbours'll be away with it. Friggin' marvellous. I hope your ex realises what she's done to you."

"*I* don't," Bill said. "She'd be laughing her tits off if she could see any of this. Anyway, the sooner we start, the sooner we'll finish. Then I'll treat you to a pint or two at the Potter's."

The two men watched a pug-faced skinhead lurch from the direction of the flats, one hand stuffed in the pocket of his jeans. In the other he clenched a chain dog lead. An incredibly ugly pit bull terrier strained at the heels of his Doc Martins.

"Hey!" Wayne shouted. "Which of these is Daisyfield House?" From the ground they all looked equally derelict, with boarded up windows and entrance doors, as if they were all under siege, like some kind of modern day Rourke's Drift.

The skinhead paused and looked their way.

"You looking for Daisyfield House, mate?"

252

"That's right. My friend here's moving in."

The skinhead laughed. "You must be fuckin' desperate."

Wayne sighed. Bill could see the exasperation in his friend's face. "That's right."

Laughing again, the skinhead jerked his head at the block to his left. "The door's a bit stiff, but if you give it a good push you'll get in."

The two men strolled down the slight incline from the car park to the entrance. Paint had been sprayed all over the boarded up windows on the ground floor and the doors into the lobby. Bill had to give the doors a hefty shove, using most of his weight, and it seemed for a moment as if they had been nailed shut, till they suddenly creaked and gave way beneath him. When his eyes adjusted to the gloominess inside he thought at first that the lobby was empty. Then he realised that a large, overweight man with dark yet somehow piercing eyes, was stood by the lift. Dressed in a baggy, dark blue suit, he looked over at the two men as they stepped inside.

"You new here today?" the man asked in a loud, pompous voice.

Bill nodded. "That's right."

The man smiled. "I'm the caretaker. I've been waiting for you, Mr..." He hesitated as he regarded Bill with a slight look of concentration. Bill disliked the way he stared at him, as if he was some sort of a seedy stage hypnotist. Perhaps even the caretaker in a place like this had to be a bit creepy, he thought. "Mr Whitley, is it?" the man said finally, a condescending smile on his long, lugubrious face.

"That's right. William Anthony Whitley. Bill to my friends."

The caretaker strode forwards. There was a key in his hand, its palm the colour and texture of wet putty. "For your flat. Tenth floor. Number three."

\*

Even after eight pints in the Potter's Wheel and a large glass of whisky when he eventually stumbled back to his flat in the early

253

hours of the morning, Bill couldn't regard the sparsely furnished living room with anything other than a feeling of depression. Part of this could have been the dull forty-watt bulb he'd been provided with, which looked like cost-cutting gone mad to him, though he doubted he could spare the cash to buy a more powerful bulb in the near future. Besides, he reminded himself, this wasn't permanent. Only till the council had somewhere better for him. Or safer, he added. Outside on the corridor he could hear someone arguing. Only the occasional swear words rumbled through the walls with any kind of clarity.

Bill turned on the small TV he'd stood on a table by the central heating radiator, hoping to drown out the sound, then poured himself a second whisky. He had hardly taken a sip of it when someone began to pound on the wall from the flat next door. The thumps were so loud they could have been done with a hammer.

Shocked, Bill automatically turned down the volume on the TV. The thuds ceased at once, though he thought he heard someone laugh, then swear vindictively to themselves in a high-pitched voice.

Bill took a deep swallow of his whisky, glad that Wayne hadn't come back with him. His friend would have been banging on the wall by now if he'd been here. And swearing too. But Bill had soon begun to realise that even Wayne, whose aggressive tendencies rose to a peak each Sunday morning when he played for the Potter's Wheel Eleven, was out of his league here. The few other tenants of Daisyfield House he had seen while they were carrying his furniture to the lift had soon confirmed the warnings about this place that the housing officer had given him. "Nutters and crack heads," was how Wayne had described them, when they'd eventually finished moving his stuff in and had driven off to the pub for a well-deserved pint. "No wonder the place is wrecked, especially that god-awful lift."

The lift had been more than an ordeal, reeking of urine and stale vomit, with violent graffiti daubed on every wall in various colours of felt tip pen and spray paints. "Probably used as a dog toilet," Wayne had suggested, after they had seen more tenants, in flagrant disregard of the council's no pets policy, taking short, squat, vicious-looking brutes either into the lift or off down the dark, concrete depths of the stairwell. "And what's that with all those friggin' pit bulls?" Wayne asked. "Is someone breeding the bloody things there?"

"Wouldn't surprise me," Bill said. "I don't suppose anyone from the council goes there to check."

"Not without a tactical armed squad from the police to back them up," Wayne retorted with a laugh that had a pitch of nervousness in it. "I'm bloody glad it's you, not me, that's moving into that shit hole, Bill. Makes me feel guilty seeing you move somewhere like that. Perhaps I should have a word with Tracey. I'm sure she'd understand if you came back for a while longer – at least till the council can fix you up with somewhere decent. If she took one look at that dump she'd agree."

Bill shook his head. "Honestly, Wayne, you've done more than enough already. I'll be all right. I'll only be there for a week or two. I can keep a low profile. Mind my own business."

"Put a chair behind your door. And watch your back," Wayne went on. He shivered melodramatically. "Anyway, mate, any problems – any problems at all – don't hesitate to call me. You know there's a bed settee available at a moment's notice if you need it."

As he sat in the dull silence of his flat at ten past one that night, Bill wondered whether he should have taken Wayne up on his offer.

*

The next day Bill woke up feeling cold and miserable. The central heating had gone off during the night and, despite fiddling with the controls for over an hour, he hadn't been able to start it again. Added to that, the large window in the living room rattled from the winds that wailed around the flats at these heights. An icy draft blew in from one edge of its metal frame, which he knew he would have to seal at some time, perhaps with tape.

Bill rubbed his hands together in an effort to generate some warmth, then bustled into the kitchen to prepare himself a mug of coffee. Asda's cheapest, Farm Store variety, since he couldn't afford anything better these days, topped with several drops of whisky to improve the taste. Cuddling the mug in his hands like a small, well-loved pet, Bill rambled aimlessly about his flat. As he looked morosely at the lack of comfort he decided that it could do with some rugs or at least some patches of carpet to cover the floor tiles, which were an ugly utilitarian grey, pockmarked with cigarette burns and dark, greasy, mouldy-looking stains. With only a few oddments of furniture, the place looked bleak, unloved and uncomfortable.

Dispirited, he topped up his coffee with some more whisky. The mixture seemed to be working well. And already he was beginning to feel less depressed than when he got up. Even the dark grey clouds that filled the sky for as far as he could see didn't seem quite so grim anymore. Tots of whisky and the minimal effort required in watching daytime TV were all that held him together most of the time these days. He would have gone for a walk, but the idea of using the lift was far from appealing, not with a hangover still playing havoc with his stomach, while the stairs were too much of an effort, even going down. Besides, the smell inside the stairwell was only marginally better than the lift. The drafts inside it helped to lessen the odours a little, but it would take more than those to clear them completely. Nor had he liked what he'd seen of the cack-handed drawings scrawled all over its concrete walls. Besides disturbingly graphic, crude depictions of copulation, there were other, even cruder scenes of violence, invariably splashed with daubs of red.

Having seen what some of the tenants of Daisyfield House had done to the place, Bill could understand why the council had decided to demolish these buildings. They didn't provide homes. They had become nothing more than gathering grounds for deviants, die-hard junkies and sick-minded psychopaths. And he was glad that he wouldn't have to live here for long.

Without warning, there was a sudden series of high-pitched, maniacal cackles next door. From the same flat, he realised, where someone had hammered against the wall last night. A few seconds later these were joined by low, bestial grunts.

Automatically, Bill reached for the whisky. He poured some into his empty mug. Gulping it down in one swallow, he wondered if he should hammer on the wall in retaliation, but he was far from certain how this might affect his neighbour. He didn't even know who lived there yet. Nor how many there were in that flat. What was it he had said to Wayne? Maintain a low profile? Keep his head down? And wait till the council could find somewhere better for him to live? Perhaps it would be better to stick to what he had said he would do. That would be the sensible thing to do. He drank some more whisky. But, as the cackling and grunts went on and on, with no sign of coming to an end, he began to feel angry. So angry, in fact, that, banging his mug on the table so hard he almost broke it, he stood up and, before he even realised what he was going to do next, he strode to the wall and slammed the edge of his fist as hard as he could against it. Twice, three times he hammered it again.

Almost instantly there was silence.

Amidst sudden qualms at what he had done, Bill unconsciously held his breath with expectation.

He did not have to wait for long.

Retaliation came with a furious, almost insane storm of blows that shook the wall. Shocked at the deafening, ongoing onslaught, he stumbled away from it, appalled at the anger he could sense in the blows. They scared and alarmed him. It was as if whoever was doing it wanted to break through the breezeblocks and plaster to get in here at him.

Bill reached for the whisky and tipped what was left in his mouth.

On an impulse he put the emptied bottle down and scooped up his coat from the back of the armchair, where he'd slung it last night. His keys rattled in one of its pockets. After making sure that he had his wallet, Bill went and unlocked the door. When he stepped out onto the corridor he could still hear the bangs and crashes, though muffled now. Confident that whoever was doing it would be unable to hear his door being shut, he locked it behind him, then hurried towards the lift.

Several minutes later he was still waiting for it to arrive, with no indication that it was even working. He had heard that the lifts in these flats were notoriously unreliable. Perhaps it had broken down. If it had, there was only one other way out. He glanced towards the stairwell and flinched. Ten flights was a long way to go, and his legs felt wobbly after what he'd drunk. But there was no other choice, unless he went back to his flat.

With an irritable grunt, Bill started towards the stairwell. He tried to ignore the graffiti on its walls and the rancid smells that filled it with a doughy, almost palpable miasma. Here and there, someone had scrawled what looked like runic symbols amongst the obscenities. There was the occasional five-pointed star and, in one spot, in between floors, a detailed crucifixion had been painted in red and black. A hideously crestfallen Christ-like figure was nailed upside down amidst highly stylised flames. Though crudely drawn, with no pretension at art, it was nevertheless powerfully effective and, if he had been at all religious, Bill was sure it would have affected him more. As a piece of blasphemy it was even disturbing to a long-time agnostic like him.

By the time he reached the entrance hall, Bill was short of breath and beginning to feel dizzy as he trudged past the used hypodermics that littered the floor amidst dog-ends, dog-dirt and broken bottles. He could scarcely believe the local council was still housing people here. It was as if they had abandoned the place. No wonder Jackson had done his best to dissuade him from moving here. Perhaps he should have listened to him.

Outside, Bill stood for a moment in the fresh air, breathing it in, though even when he'd walked some distance down Queen's Park Road he could still smell the cloying, lavatory-like smells of the stairwell.

Like the tower blocks, most of the streets around here were due for demolition, with lines of poor, working-class terraced houses, and barely a garden in sight. Most of them dated back to Victorian times. Many were boarded up, derelict now, with gaps in their roofs where slates had either blown off or collapsed inside. Downhill there was a gradual improvement, with the occasional shop, while, near to the junction with the main road, Bill spotted a pub. He checked his watch. It was just past eleven. With any luck, he thought, the place would be open. More than ever the prospect of a pint of beer, a pie and some crisps and some sane company appealed to him. Smiling, he quickened his pace.

An hour later, three pints down, Bill was on his mobile to Wayne.

"I'd love to help you," Wayne said. "I really would."

"You did say that the bed settee was still available to me," Bill added.

"I did. I did. And I really, really wish I could tell you to pack your bags and come round now, but Tracey's mother arrived today. She'll be with us for at least a week. You understand, don't you? I'd help if I could." Wayne took a deep breath, obviously embarrassed. "You've not even been there a full day yet. Surely it can't be that bad? I know it's not good, but how bad can it be?"

How could he explain it? Bill stared round the pub. It was so comfortable in here – plain and simple, homely even – that it was difficult to get his head round just how repulsive Daisyfield House was. How disturbed he felt there. Especially when he hadn't even met his neighbours yet. Even telling Wayne about the banging on his wall or the high-pitched laughter didn't seem credibly unnerving.

"Look," Wayne said, "we'll get together tonight. Have a few pints. Tracey won't mind. Give her a chance to have a natter with her mum. Gives me a chance to get out of the old bat's way. What do you say?"

Bill agreed straight away. After they had made their

arrangements, he rang off and reached for his beer, though he knew he would have to take it easy if he was going to have a session with Wayne tonight. He'd have one more pint, perhaps buy another meat and potato pie, then amble up the hill to Daisyfield House.

And hope that someone had got the lift working by the time he got back.

Whether it was the alcohol or tiredness, but the walk back several minutes later seemed longer and harder than it should have been. The day had grown gloomy and a mist was beginning to close in on the heights at the end of Queen's Park Road. By the time he reached the rundown streets which immediately surrounded the tower blocks, the mist had solidified into a dense fog. The temperature had dropped and Bill shivered beneath his coat as he hurried the last few yards to his own block of flats. He didn't like his obscured vision. Odd shapes seemed to loom through the fog. Figures which lurched onto the edge of his sight, then veered off again and disappeared before he could get a clear impression of them. Almost as if they were playing games with him. He pushed open the door into the flats, then pressed for the lift. To his relief the indicator light came on at the top. A few seconds later the steel doors opened.

A short man, stocky, with deep set eyes beneath a thick, woollen hat, was stood at the back of the lift, leant against the wall. His denim clothes looked old, careworn and grubby. From around the soles of his tatty-looking Nike trainers a dark puddle was starting to spread across the floor of the lift. Bill stared at it for a moment in disbelief, then looked again at the man's face. His expressionless, grey, almost vacuous face. There was no reaction in it. No movement. And at first Bill was puzzled. Was the man drunk, high on drugs or seriously ill? For a moment more Bill stared at him, waiting to see if he would make some effort to leave the lift. Instead he remained motionless, apart from the widening pool about his feet. Uncertain, Bill wondered whether to step into the lift, ignore the puddle of what he was sure was the man's urine, and press for the tenth floor. But there was something about his face that worried Bill. It was too still. Too pale.

As if he was dead.

No sooner had Bill thought this than the man began to shudder, pushed himself up off the wall, then staggered forwards. He stared at Bill, dull eyes vacuous like those of a drunk, before he pushed himself past to walk, stiff-legged, out of the lift.

\*

"I'm not exaggerating," Bill said, later that night in the Potter's Wheel. They'd had a few rounds by now and Bill was not bothered any more how foolish he sounded.

For his part, Wayne had begun to accept much of what his friend said to him with an open mind.

"It's a piss hole," Wayne said. "And that fellow just went on to prove it." He put down his half emptied pint of beer. The Potter's Wheel was busy tonight with a darts match between the home team and one from the Bell and Compasses, and he had to raise his voice to be heard. His face became serious for a moment. "You are taking care to keep a low profile, aren't you?"

"Of course I am," Bill said, "apart from banging on the wall when that idiot next door started to cackle like a maniac."

"Be careful, Bill. Some of those guys would be better off in an asylum. The rest aren't that much better. You remember that murder a year ago? The girl who killed her boyfriend with a friggin' chainsaw while he was asleep in bed? That was in those flats."

"Wasn't she an out and out pot head? Off her head on drugs?"

"Which doesn't make it any less real. For all you know you might even be in the same flat. There was another block there that was even worse. They shut that one down after some idiot cult got a grip on a group of people living in it. Ended with some kind of mass suicide. A dozen or so of the mad fuckers, from what my wife told me before I came out. She remembers shit like that, God bless her. Not like you and me, who've only got time for the sports pages."

Bill drank some more of his beer, thought about what Wayne had said, then shook his head. "The only problem I have is that nutter next door. *Eek eek eek*," he imitated badly. "I know some of them are dangerous. Which is why I want to get out of there as soon as I can."

"And why I feel guilty about not being able to put you up till you can get somewhere better," Wayne admitted

Bill shrugged. "It's my fault. I should have listened to that guy at the housing office. He tried to warn me." He gazed at his beer for a moment, lost in thought. "You know, that bugger in the lift really put the wind up me. I watched him go across the lobby towards the doors. The way he walked you'd have sworn he was an extra from a George Romero zombie flick. If I'd been anywhere else I'd have cracked up laughing. As it was, I couldn't wait for the lift doors to shut."

"Even with his piss all over the floor?"

Bill shook his head. "If it was piss," he said. "It didn't look all that much like piss really. Not when I looked at it. Of course, there was no way I could tell from the smell. It stinks like a friggin' toilet anyway."

"Too fucking true," Wayne added.

"And I can't say I was particularly keen on looking too closely at the stuff. Though I had to keep my eye on it. I didn't want any of it touching my shoes."

"What makes you think it wasn't piss?"

"It didn't look right, somehow. Too dark. Though that could have been the dirty floor."

"Perhaps something got spilt in the lift and your yobbo friend stepped into it, too doped up to notice."

"Though it was still spreading while he was stood in it. And I'd swear some of it had dribbled down the legs of his jeans."

Wayne shook his head. "I don't know what to say. Perhaps you should see if you can get the council to re-house you somewhere else. Tell them you've been threatened."

But Bill was unsure. "That might get the police involved. I don't fancy that." Not after his conviction last year. There were too many unresolved grudges amongst some of the police who'd been involved, especially after his suspended sentence.

When they left the Potter's Wheel an hour or so later, Wayne's taxi dropped Bill off at the end of Queen's Park Road. As the car sped off, leaving a wake of mist in the frosty air, Bill stared for a moment at the imposing bulk of the tower block ahead of him. Few lights showed in any of its windows, and it loomed like a huge, black monolith. Even one of the supposedly empty blocks had more lights on than Daisyfield House, making it look, by contrast, even grimmer.

Bill hurried the last few yards to the lift. This time, though, there was no response when he pressed the button. Bill felt his stomach sink as he realised that he would have to climb the ten flights of stairs to his flat

In desperation he went to the caretaker's office, but the door was locked and no one answered his knocks. Not that he really expected anyone to be here at this time of night. Finally convinced that he had no other choice, Bill trudged towards the stairwell. His legs felt heavy. And he knew that the amount he'd drunk in the Potter's Wheel had not prepared him for a climb like this.

Despite this, though, he managed to make it past the first two floors without too much trouble. Head down, eyes fixed on the steps ahead of him, he even avoided having to look at most of the drawings and other graffiti that covered the walls. By the third flight, though, his gasps were starting to hurt his chest. Too many fags and too much beer, he thought to himself between wincing at the pains that razored his ribcage. Hauling himself, one step at a time, he grasped on tight to the banister rail for leverage.

After five flights, though, he had to rest. He couldn't go any further till he'd caught his breath. A half flight more and he was sure he would have a heart attack.

Wheezing badly, Bill let himself slump onto the concrete steps. He no longer cared how filthy they were, though he could feel their icy coldness strike through his clothes and deep into his buttocks.

Fewer of the wall lights were working here and the place was sometimes so gloomy he could barely see the stairs ahead of him. Then he would come to an area that was so brilliantly lit that, however much he tried to resist looking at them, the graffiti would almost leap out at him from the walls. Bill stared at the agonised expressions on their crudely drawn faces. Someone up here was seriously disturbed. At this level there were other figures too, large and lumpy, round-headed shapes with obscure faces. These, somehow, were even more repulsive than the rest.

As he rested, slumped against the steps, Bill heard something move on the floor above. It sounded as if someone was dragging a heavy sack.

With a grunt of effort, Bill forced himself to his feet. He knew he couldn't rest for long or his muscles would start to stiffen up. They were aching already.

Eight steps later and, finally, he reached the next floor. He glanced at the closed doors into the corridor to his left. Through the wire-mesh and glass security panels, he could see someone halfway along it, bent almost double. Perhaps that was who he'd heard, he thought. Bill squinted through the panel, with its odd distortions, puzzled and beginning to feel concerned at what he could make out. Perhaps the figure wasn't moving at all, only one of its arms? As he approached the glass for a clearer view, his breath caught in his throat. He stopped, took an involuntary step back from the doors, glad they were shut, then narrowed his eyes. He was certain he'd glimpsed what looked like a knife in the figure's hand. It was long. And pointed. A kitchen knife. The kind he would have used for carving a joint.

He heard the knife strike whatever it was hitting with a meaty *chunk*.

Trembling, Bill hurried back to the stairs. Even with a stitch that almost doubled him up he managed to climb the next three floors before he was forced to stop once more. When he did, he almost collapsed on the steps in a sodden heap. Sweat stung his eyes, and he had to reach into his trouser pocket for a handkerchief to mop them with. If he had been cold before, he was roasting now. And exhausted. He stared through the gloom at the floor he'd just left, trying to control his breathing so that he could hear if there was anyone there. *If anyone had begun to follow him.* But nothing moved. Even though he could still make out the faint *chunk-chunk, chunk-chunk* from far away. Steady. Relentless. Machine-like. On and on and on.

Bill gulped. Again he forced himself to climb the stairs.

Only a few seconds later the stabbings stopped.

Or perhaps he'd climbed too far to hear them now?

Bill paused. He held his breath, certain he could hear something move. As if the doors onto one of the corridors below were being opened.

*And someone was coming out of them.*

Panicking, Bill pushed himself towards the next bend on the stairs where he wouldn't be visible from the floor below. Though why he felt the almost desperate need to conceal himself from whoever was down there, he wasn't sure. Irrational, he knew. But he couldn't ignore his gut instincts. And, despite his exhaustion, despite the red-hot pains in his chest, he forced himself to keep on going, till his feet were clear of the next bend in the stairs.

Only then did he stop.

Only then did he wonder how far he had to go till he reached his flat. By now he had lost count of how many flights of stairs he'd climbed. Was it nine or ten? Or even more? Had he passed his level?

Bill stumbled towards the doors onto the corridor. It looked like his, and he wondered if he could have finally made it. He fumbled in his pockets for the key to his flat. Already he could hear footsteps echoing up the stairwell. The outer doors swung shut behind him as he started to run towards his flat. Only then did he see one of the apartment doors ahead of him open. Light leapt across the corridor as a man looked round the doorway at him, perhaps disturbed by the sound of his feet. He was short and skinny, in an oversized combat jacket and jeans. His mouth opened wide in what looked like a protest, then Bill pushed him into the room.

"No!" the man managed to squawk as he tumbled over the tattered wreck of a settee behind him. "Get out of here!"

But Bill could already hear the doors at the end of the corridor open. He pushed the apartment door shut behind him and fastened its locks. Only when his back was pressed against it, did he look at the man he'd forced into the room.

"You can't barge in like this." The man's scrawny face was contorted with indignation and fear. His voice was a pathetic whine. Thin strands of hair hung over his face, though much of his scalp showed through on the crown of his head, pink and shiny.

Bill glanced around the flat. Apart from the settee, which looked like it had been salvaged from a refuse tip, with stains and tears on its old fashioned covers, there was no other furniture in the room. It was more like a squat than a rented flat. There weren't even any blinds or curtains at the window. Take-away cartons littered the floor amongst scattered bottles: White Lightning, sherry and non-generic bottles of vodka. All of them empty. On the seat of the settee Bill noticed an old tin box. Beside it lay a dessertspoon, heat-stained and grimy, with some kind of dark residue on it, and a heavy-looking hypodermic.

An alcoholic junkie, Bill thought to himself in disgust.

The man giggled in fear as Bill stared at him. Hearing the high-pitched sounds, Bill suddenly realised who he was.

"You banged on my wall," Bill said, unable to hide his disbelief.

"*What?*"

How often had he heard that self-righteous whine from horrible little brats at school? "Last night. When I turned on my TV. You banged on my wall, you fucking bastard. And again this morning."

As he looked at the man's perplexed eyes, Bill wondered whether he even remembered doing it.

Before Bill could say anymore, there was a loud scratching at the door behind him. The little man stifled a yelp, then crouched, cringing, behind the settee.

Bill turned and saw the door handle move. But the two locks, a solid Yale and a heavy bolt with a security chain attached to it, held firm. As he watched the door, Bill felt himself start to share his neighbour's fear. His throat felt dry and he could feel his bowels melt inside him. He'd be shitting himself in another few minutes, Bill realised, though he felt no humour at the idea. He moved away from the door as the furious scratching started again, so hard he could see the panels shake.

"What the hell is it?" Bill asked.

The little man shushed him to silence. His face trembled with agitation.

"*It'll hear*," he whispered tensely.

It seemed as if whoever was outside the flat had heard him, though, as the scratching paused, then started again even more fiercely than before, as if an enormous rodent was trying to claw its way through.

"What the fucking hell is it?" Bill asked.

"*Don't!* It'll know we're here."

"It knows we're here anyway," Bill said. "Whatever *it* is."

"*Not so loud!*" The little man held his hands up for emphasis, and Bill was surprised to see how violently he was shaking. "Move away from the door. *Please!*" In his agitation, he almost dragged Bill back across the room to the window.

"What do you know about whoever's out there?" Bill asked.

"Haven't you heard it? Night after night. Walking up and down the corridors."

"I've only been here since yesterday. I didn't see anything when I came back last night."

"You used the lift?"

Bill frowned. "It was working then."

"Not now?"

Bill shook his head. "I had to come up the stairs."

"Despite those warnings?"

"What warnings?"

"On the walls? Those warnings painted on the walls?"

"That bloody graffiti?"

The little man laughed contemptuously. It was laughter, though, that was edged with fear. "You were lucky, mate. Others haven't been. I heard one poor sod earlier tonight. Must've been new here, like you. Probably thought it was fuckin' squatters' paradise. Till he found out different."

"I'm not a squatter," Bill said.

The little man scoffed. "You're not telling me the council sent you here? If they did, they'd have sent you to Daisyfield House."

"What do you mean? This is Daisyfield House."

"Like bollocks it is. That's the one nearer the road. This fuckin' shit-hole's been condemned for months. No one lives here now except those of us who've broken in. That's why there's no maintenance on the lift. Now and then it works. But that's sheer luck. Surprised there's still any power. Shouldn't be, by rights." He peered at Bill. "You telling me you thought this dump was Daisyfield House?"

Bill remembered the skinhead who'd directed him here. *The door's a bit stiff, but if you give it a good push you'll get in.*

"That's rubbish," Bill said finally. "I was given my key by the caretaker."

"The caretaker? What fuckin' caretaker? There's not been a caretaker here since they decided to close the place down after what happened last year."

"There was one when I arrived," Bill insisted. "A tall man. Long faced. With piercing eyes. He had a rather nasty pallor."

The junkie shook his head.

"Someone's been having you on. They shut this place down after all those deaths."

"What deaths?"

"It was a suicide cult. Twelve of them topped themselves. Even their leader, some mad arse called Chambers. It was in all the papers."

Not for the first time, Bill regretted his inability to pay any real attention to the news these days. "It may well have been," he said, uncertainly. "If it was, I didn't read it. Anyway, you've got to be mistaken."

"If I am, it'd be a surprise to those of us who are squatting here."

"And what kind of people are they?" Bill asked.

"There aren't so many of us. It's only 'cause we've nowhere else to go. And we're careful. Keep ourselves to ourselves."

"Like hammering on my wall last night?" Bill said.

"That stuff will have made me," the little man said. He pointed at the syringe on the settee. "I go off my head sometimes."

Bill thought he was probably a bit "off his head" most of the time. He'd even managed to spook him over whoever was scratching at the door. Though Bill had to admit he had frightened himself in the stairwell even before he got here. Whoever was out there was probably just another drugged-up squatter. Though not necessarily harmless, he thought.

"Are you staying here all night?" the little man asked. He squirmed inside his oversized combat jacket like a skinny kid playing at soldiers in his father's clothes.

Bill hadn't thought about staying here, though he didn't feel like opening the door just yet. Whoever was out there was still clawing at it. Nor had he forgotten the knife he glimpsed earlier. If it was the same person he saw on that corridor, the only option he had was to wait till they'd gone. Either that, he thought, or phone the police. Bill reached in his pocket for his mobile phone. "Damn it," he grunted. The bloody thing had no signal...

"You can use the settee if you like."

Bill looked at it. The stained fabric was so filthy he would have been happier on the floor, except that the shag pile carpet looked even dirtier.

With what he'd drunk and the strain of climbing ten flights of stairs to get here, Bill was feeling exhausted already. Perhaps a few minutes rest would help to revive him? Shaking his head, he let himself slump on the settee, surprised that it was much more comfortable than it looked.

And, although he hardly trusted the junkie, Bill felt sure that if the little man did try anything stupid, he could handle him. He knew that part of this feeling of complacency was because of all the alcohol he'd drunk, that if he was sober he'd probably not take his eyes off the man. As it was he felt far too tired. Even with the non-stop scratching at the door, he began to relax, and it was all he could do to keep his eyes open.

Some time later—it could have been hours; it could have been a scant few minutes—he awoke with a jolt. Everything was in darkness, except for a thin beam of moonlight. He felt cold and stiff and he grunted with the effort to move his cramped-up legs. His mouth tasted of stale beer.

And for a moment he wondered where he was.

Then he started to recall what had happened since his return to the flats.

Alarmed by the disjointed memories that came back to him, Bill stared around the twilit room. There was silence now. Whoever had been scratching at the door had gone. And Bill grimaced as his memories of the evening became even clearer. Where was the junkie who lived here? Groaning, he pushed himself to his feet. Though there wasn't much light, there was enough to make things out, even the tin box and the hypodermic that had been abandoned near the window, monochromed by the moonlight.

Then he saw where the little man had fallen asleep on the floor, knees drawn up towards his chest. He was very still.

Disturbed, Bill stepped towards him, aware that the junkie's chest didn't seem to be moving. Cautiously, he knelt beside him, his kneecaps popping with twinges of pain, and gently tried to wake him. The shoulder beneath the damp material of his combat jacket felt unnaturally thin. And Bill felt nauseous touching it.

"Hey!" he whispered, as loudly as he dared. "Wake up!"

He pushed him again. This time harder. And the man's body, which was even lighter than it looked, began to roll over. Gasping for breath at the sudden shock of what he was looking at, Bill saw

David A. Riley

there was barely any flesh beneath the pale grey skin on the junkie's face. It was stretched and wrinkled and damp with mould. Dark holes stared at him from where the eyes should have been. With a hand to his mouth to stifle the almost automatic urge to vomit, Bill realised in horror that the man he was looking at must have been dead for months.

*Who the hell, then, did he speak to earlier?*

Repulsed and frightened, Bill stepped away from the body. He stared at the baggy combat jacket and the dirty, patched-up pair of jeans, through which the hard outlines of the man's skeletal legs could be clearly made out. He knew these clothes were exactly like those worn by the junkie. He even recognised the thin strands of hair hung over the ruined face. Everything about him, his size, his clothes, his hair, even the shape of his almost non-existent chin, was exactly the same. But how? Bill could not understand what he was looking at. It was insane. *Madness.* It just did not make sense. Unless he was starting to hallucinate. Perhaps too much alcohol. Or too much stress. Or the trauma of living in this place. But he knew he was desperately trying to rationalise things in an effort to make sense out of what had happened. What else could he do? Accept everything that appeared to have happened as reality? Accept that he had spoken to a man who'd been dead for God-knows how many months? Whose face was no more than skin and bones, whose only colour were the layers of mould that were growing on what was left of him?

For the first time in months Bill felt the shakes in his arms and legs. It had been so long a time since he'd had them last that he really thought he'd been cured. Now, more than ever, he felt convinced he'd been teetering on the edge of another breakdown for some time. Which was why he knew he should never have come to this place. It had been a mistake. He couldn't take it. Stumbling into the junkie's apartment and finding what was left of the man's body must have been enough to push him over the brink, that and all the alcohol he'd been poisoning himself with for the past few months.

Hands quivering, Bill reached inside his jacket for his mobile. He would have to let the police know what he'd found. He didn't dare do otherwise. He knew his fingerprints would be all over the flat. As these were already on record, if there was anything suspicious about the man's death, he didn't want the police to think he had had anything to do with it, even if the man had been dead long before he got here. But there was still no signal on his phone. Either the walls were too thick or there was something wrong with the nearest mast. Frustrated, Bill put it away. He'd have to try and ring them later. He could have tried going back downstairs to see if he could get a signal outside, but there was no way he was going to do that yet. He was too exhausted. And too fuckin' frazzled, he thought to himself with a desperate attempt at some sort of humour.

He unlocked the door to the corridor. It was time to get away from this flat and return to his own. God, he thought, he'd even had hallucinations that this wasn't Daisyfield House at all – as if he could place any credibility on what he thought he'd been told by someone who was already dead! Bill grimaced as he glanced at the body near the window. Later, when he'd had some sleep, he'd phone the police and let them know what he'd found, though he winced when he thought about all the inevitable questions they would badger him with. He would also make an appointment with his doctor. Perhaps he could prescribe some pills for him that would sort him out. Maybe even help get him out of this hellhole and somewhere safe. Somewhere where his mind could cure itself.

Though what he felt most in need of now was a glass of whisky.

He could almost feel it on his tongue already, burning away the aftertaste of last night's beers. Steadying his nerves.

Bill looked both ways down the corridor, then stepped out of the junkie's apartment. With less than a third of its lights still burning, the corridor was worryingly gloomy, with far too many shadows along it. They made him feel uneasy as he remembered some of the things his memories told him had happened earlier that night. Things that he was certain must have been his own imagination.

As he approached his apartment Bill wondered what time it was. His watch was useless. Its battery had run out weeks ago and he'd forgotten to replace it. Outside it was still so dark it could have been the middle of the night. Apart from the moon, everything was black. When he'd glanced out of the junkie's window he'd been unable to see a single street lamp, as if everything below was covered in fog.

A few strides took him to his door. He looked forward to tumbling into bed and a few hours sleep. Time in which to try to forget about the body next door – and all the other self-induced terrors he'd been frightening himself with tonight.

He'd hardly started to turn the key when he heard someone scream.

It was a woman's scream.

Full of fear.

And loathing.

And desperation.

*No, no, no, no, NO*, he thought. And for a moment he hesitated, key in hand, ready to ignore it. He'd had enough already. He was whacked. Exhausted. Ready for nothing more than to close his eyes and try to forget all the nightmares his over-exhausted mind had been frightening him with.

The woman screamed again, hysterically now, and he knew that he would have to do something, even if it was only to see what was going on.

Reluctantly, Bill pocketed his key and stumbled back towards the stairwell.

Now, more than ever, he felt the need for a glass of whisky. Sweat soaked his skin. It felt hot and rancid beneath his clothes, and he was sure he must stink.

At the doors into the stairwell he paused for a moment to catch his breath and steel his nerves. Then he pushed the doors open.

The screams were even clearer now.

"Hey!" Bill shouted in what he knew was a pathetic effort to scare whoever was making the woman scream. His voice cracked with tension. "What's going on?"

Grumbling to himself, Bill started to clatter down the stairs, making as much noise as he could. He was not a brave man, and he knew it was probably only a residue of the alcohol he'd drunk and remnants of adrenalin from all that had happened that were making him act even now. *That and not knowing what was down there, he thought.*

A memory flashed back of a half-seen figure with a knife in one hand.

*Chunk-chunk! Chunk-chunk!*

And Bill hoped to God that *that* was something his drink-addled mind had dreamt up for him. It hardly seemed credible he could have seen something like that even here.

Two floors down and the screaming suddenly stopped.

In the abrupt silence Bill's mouth felt dry. His heart pounded. And his hands began to shake once more.

"Bugger," he muttered to himself, sotto voce.

He had two choices now. Either turn back and try to forget what he'd heard or keep on going and see what was there? Bill dithered. His conscience told him that he had to keep going, that someone might need his help. On the other hand, whoever had made the woman scream might still be down there. He had seen enough of the kind of people who lived in this place not to wish to pit himself against them.

Bill took a few more steps down the stairs. Slowly, reluctantly, he approached the next bend, more alert than he'd been in years. His whole concentration was so focused on listening for sounds of movement or a glimpse of someone down the stairs that he was barely aware of the graffiti on the walls.

Hardly daring to breathe in case he made too much noise, Bill turned the next bend.

The pool of blood on the landing below was so large that at first Bill did not realise what it was. Uncomprehending, confused, he stared down at it. It almost filled the entire floor between the doors to the next row of apartments and the stairs. It had already spilled over the topmost step.

When he finally realised what it was, Bill threw himself back from the sight and gagged with nausea. He turned away from it, and for a moment he thought it had to be another hallucination, that there really wasn't anything there at all.

But when he looked again nothing had changed. Almost black in the twilight, the blood looked fresh. And there was so much of it. Pints upon pints of it. More than he had ever seen in his life.

His breath rasped through his chest in ragged gasps as he began to retreat up the stairs. He knew he had to call the police. Perhaps if he climbed to one of the higher levels he would get a signal on his mobile. Down here there was nothing more he could do – except risk meeting up with whoever had caused this bloodbath.

Before he had taken more than a couple of steps, the doors onto the corridor below began to open.

A shadow fell across the landing. Alarmed, Bill turned and began to retrace his steps up the stairs as fast as he could.

The shadow was large and lumpy.

And barely human.

One hand raised above its head, the shadowy fingers looked long and thin. In Bill's heightened nervousness they seemed far too long—and far too thin.

And even though he knew that the shadow could have been wildly distorted by the angle of the light behind it, he was too unnerved to wait and see any more.

Bill had only just turned the first bend in the stairs, his heart pounding hard enough to have alarmed him earlier with thoughts of coronaries, when he heard someone step onto the landing. He could hear their breathing: *their heavy, raucous, asthmatic breathing.*

At last he looked back.

An old man, a kitchen knife shakily clasped in a liver-spotted hand, was stood on the landing. There was so much fear on the old man's face that Bill immediately knew there was no threat in him, despite the knife. Dressed in a scruffy old woollen jumper and brown pants, he wore a shapeless pair of well-worn slippers, all of which added to his look of harmlessness.

The old man stared at Bill with glistening, pale pink eyes. Apparently unnoticed, the pool of blood almost touched the toes of his slippers.

"What's going on here?" The question came in a tremulous whisper.

And Bill wondered what an old man like this was doing here. If the housing office had serious doubts about sending Bill to this place, how many more doubts should there have been at letting a man in his seventies or eighties end up here? It didn't make any sense. For God's sake, he thought, this was a dumping ground for junkies and psychos and social dropouts, not feeble old geriatrics.

"I don't know what's been going on," Bill said. "I was going to try and get a signal on my mobile higher up the stairs. To call the police."

"Mobile?"

Hearing incomprehension in the old man's voice, Bill rummaged in his pocket for his four year old Nokia, though the man's face showed no more understanding even when he saw it.

"Mind that blood," Bill warned as the old man started to shuffle towards him for a clearer view of the phone, and for the first time appeared to see the blood on the landing. His response was a strangled grunt of horror. He stumbled backwards, at the same time waving the kitchen knife in front of him as if in some way that could ward the blood away from him.

Alarmed that the old man was going to hurt himself, Bill hurried down the stairs, circled the edge of the blood, and took hold of the man's free arm. He'd no sooner touched him, though, than the old man flung his other arm round. Bill saw the knife blade flash, reflecting light from the neon strips above, as it darted towards him. There was a burst of pain as the knife cut through his sleeve, and Bill realised, with a feeling of shock, that he had been stabbed. Instinctively, he lashed out. His fist glanced off the old man's face.

Then, reeling and dizzy from the pain in his arm, Bill snatched at the knife, wrenched it sideways, and felt it come free from the old man's grip.

"You fucking old bastard," Bill complained in disgust. Holding the knife in one hand, he started to back away from him, then turned and splashed and skidded across the blood towards the stairs.

Even as he grabbed at the banister rail for support, he sensed movement behind him. Something hard and sharp bounced off his shoulders. He squawked in surprise, tugged at the banister to get away from whatever had hit him, and started once more to climb the stairs. But whoever was behind him had not given up. And again something heavy crashed onto his shoulders. This time it caught. And Bill gasped at the pain as he wrenched himself free. Ready, though, he had the kitchen knife gripped in his fist. Bill glimpsed something tall and dark move behind him and jabbed out at it. The knife jarred as it hit something that gave beneath its sharpened point.

He saw the old man's face, distorted in pain, too close to his own.

Taller now, more menacing, with hands that reached towards him with splayed, long-nailed, nicotine-stained fingers, the old man grimaced with effort. Bill gasped, then stabbed him again. The knife hit hard into the old man's jumper. Sank deep into it. Blood instantly soaked its bobbled fibres.

Shocked at what he had done, Bill saw the old man clutch his chest, then collapse on his knees. The liverish wattles on his neck quivered as he looked up. His rheumy, almost blind-looking eyes were consumed with hatred as he stared at Bill. For a moment more he grasped at the knife wounds. Blood bubbled from his mouth, before he fell onto the landing.

Even as the old man hit the ground, Bill raced up the stairs, unable to believe that he had been forced to stab him. He stared in horror at the blood on the knife blade. With his criminal record, he knew he could never convince the police he'd had to do it. It was as if he was in a nightmare, in which events piled up on top of each other, each one worse than the last. How many times had he stabbed the man? Twice? Three times? More? He knew the police would never believe it was self-defence. If he had stabbed him once, maybe. But twice? *Three times?*

Bill knew he would have to get rid of the knife and any of his clothes that had the old man's blood on them. Anything that could link him to what had happened.

By the time he reached his own floor his eyes were burning with tears. He could barely breathe, and what breaths he took came in torturous wheezes. He knew he had reached the end of his tether. Physically and emotionally he couldn't take much more. All he could think of now was to get back to his room, where he would strip off his clothes, bundle them up with the knife, then take a long, hot shower to wash away every vestige of blood off his body. Come daylight he would go downstairs, get rid of anything that could incriminate him, and hope that that would be enough, that he could convince the police, if they came to ask him any questions, that he had had nothing to do with it.

As he approached his flat, Bill saw that the door to his neighbour's room was open, though he was sure he'd shut it behind him when he left.

Cautiously, he hid the knife in his coat pocket, then slowly moved towards the doorway. He could hear music.

Bill looked into his neighbour's apartment and was relieved to see that it still had the appearance of a squat, though now there was a small CD player on the windowsill; green lights oscillated across its display screen in tune to the music. Outside the large, curtainless window the night looked just as dark as before. The junkie, whose body Bill last remembered as a desiccated corpse, curled like a grotesque foetus beneath the window, sat cross-legged and breathing shallow, trance-like breaths near the CD player, while he stared across the room with vacant, drug-dazed eyes. His mouth hung loose, a dribble of saliva caught mid-drip on his glistening chin.

Relieved, but bewildered that the man wasn't dead, that he must have imagined the months old corpse, Bill hurried past before the junkie noticed him, then reached for his keys and let himself into his flat, certain now he was suffering from some sort of a nervous breakdown.

He wondered, sickly, just how much of what had happened was real.

Bill laid the knife on the kitchen table, its blade still slick with blood. Had he really used it to stab the old man? *If* there had ever been an old man. *If* he hadn't just been in his imagination or part of some crazy nightmare.

Unable to trust whatever he remembered anymore, Bill wondered if this was what it was like when someone began to lose his or her mind. He stared at his face in the mirror above the sink. In his reflection he looked old and haggard, with eyes that were desperate, blood-shot and full of fear. Sweat sheened his skin, which was grey and lifeless in the stark neon light.

Though it probably looked grey and lifeless in any light now, he thought to himself.

Bill opened a cabinet next to the sink, took out a bottle of whisky and poured himself a large measure in a plastic mug. He emptied it urgently, in a gulp that left his throat feeling raw.

He'd needed that.

He'd really, *really* needed that.

*Though he knew he would need much more than this before he could rest.*

Resignedly, his head beginning to ache already, he refilled the mug.

At some time during the next few hours he somehow managed to fall asleep. There was no more than an ashen hint of dawn through his living room window when he awoke, feeling stiff and sick. A migraine pulsed inside his head with agonising intensity. Hardly willing to open his eyes again, he rolled over on the settee he'd fallen asleep on, as disjointed memories from the night before came back to him.

There was a buzzing sound. It was this that had woken him, penetrating his sleep like a bad toothache.

Feeling fragile, every joint in his arms and legs aching so much he wanted to cry out at the pain, Bill placed his feet on the cold surface of the floor.

It was then that he realised that the buzzing sound was his doorbell.

Bill groaned. Who the hell could that be?

His mouth dehydrated like a sun dried sponge, he pushed himself off the sofa and walked, stiff-legged, to the door. He peered through the spyhole.

The distorted image of Wayne's face stared back at him through the fisheye lens. There was someone beside him, but Bill could only see part of a shoulder.

A woman's shoulder.

"My God, you look wrecked."

"Thanks, Wayne." Bill cast his friend a poor pretence at a smile as he stepped back, letting him in.

"I hope you don't mind that I've brought Tracey," Wayne said. "I thought she ought to see this place for herself—to see how bad it really is."

Bill waved them in. "Forgive the mess. I haven't had time to tidy up yet," he joked feebly, his head aching so much he found it hard to concentrate on what he was saying.

"Wayne told me how awful it was. But I didn't realise just how bloody awful till we got here," Tracey said sympathetically; her presence somehow helped to brighten up the room.

Bill glanced at them both. "Did you use the lift?"

"Too true we did. Can you see Tracey trailing up those stairs? All ten flights?" Wayne laughed, though Bill could see the concern in his eyes. "Been on the sauce already?" Wayne asked.

"What else is there in this bloody place?"

"I think I would have been tempted to join you," Tracey said with a broad, sympathetic smile. Which was a miracle for Tracey, who normally had an annoyingly puritanical attitude towards drink.

"Why did you decide to come so early?" Bill asked.

"Early?" Wayne glanced at his watch. "It's nearly noon. That's hardly early, even for a man of leisure like you."

Bill looked at his window. What hints of light he could make out through it were so dull it could have still been night. Wayne followed his look, and expressed surprise.

"How dirty are those bloody windows of yours?"

"Hardly dirty at all," Bill mumbled. He crossed the room, opened the door onto the small, concrete balcony. Even outside it was dark. What light there was didn't come from the sun but from a sliver of moon high in an otherwise pitch-black sky. When he looked down to where he should have been able to observe Queens Park Road there was nothing but darkness. Like before, no streetlights showed, as if there had been a power cut.

"What kind of a crazy, fucked up place is this?" Wayne asked.

Bill shuddered. "I don't think you and Tracey should have come here."

"Don't be ridiculous," Tracey said, but Bill could hear doubt in her voice, as she stared through the window, her brows furrowed with a look of perplexity. "There must be a heavy fog or something."

"There was no sign of fog when we got here," Wayne said. "Everything was clear."

"Then it must have closed in while we were in the lift."

Wayne snorted, though he too had begun to look worried. "You must be joking. We were only in it a few minutes. That wouldn't have been long enough."

"It must have been," Tracey insisted. "It's here now, isn't it?"

Wayne shrugged. "Of course it is."

Bill watched them argue with feelings of unreality. They too were being caught up in the sheer oddity of this place. Its lack of rules. Its bizarreness. Its bloody ridiculous lack of credibility.

"Hey," he interjected. "There's probably a completely logical explanation." Even as he said it the words sounded ridiculous. There was nothing logical about anything he remembered happening here since he arrived.

Bill returned to his living room.

"You should leave. Both of you," he said. "We all should."

"That's what I came here for," Wayne said. "That's why I brought Tracey. So she could see." He stopped, as if he realised just how much he had underestimated this place. He looked at Bill for help.

"I need some water," Tracey said suddenly, her face pale. "This is getting too much." She headed for the kitchen. Even as she moved Bill suddenly remembered the knife he'd left near the sink, but before he could forestall her Tracey had already gone. Her cry of disgust was immediate. "Wayne!"

Bill's friend glanced at him, almost reproachfully, as if to say "What the bloody hell have you done now?"—then followed his wife into the kitchen. His own response was just as blunt. "*Fuck!*"

Wayne stepped back into the living room, the knife held between his thumb and forefinger with a look of disgust. It looked even worse than Bill remembered. Most of the blood had dried into ugly, red-brown crusts. Even the hilt was caked with it.

"What the hell was this thing used for?" Wayne asked, accusingly.

Bill shook his head. "I don't know. I'm not sure." Which he knew was the truth.

"It looks to me like something you shouldn't have been able to forget," Wayne said.

Tracey appeared beside him, white faced and looking sick. "I think we should go."

Wayne looked again at the knife, then flung it to the floor.

"I don't know what's been going on here, Bill, but you need to sort yourself out. Unless things have already gone too far."

"What do you mean?"

Wayne shook his head. "I think you might know." He nudged the blood-caked knife with the toe of his trainers. "Where the hell has all this blood come from, Bill?"

"You wouldn't believe me. I don't even know if I believe what I remember happening here last night myself."

"Are you being serious or are you simply going off your head?" He looked as if he would have added "again" but had held back from doing so.

"Probably I am going off my head," Bill admitted.

"Perhaps we should get going now," Tracey suggested to her husband.

"You'll come with us?" Wayne asked. He was watching Bill doubtfully.

Bill nodded. "I hate this place. I don't ever want to come here again."

He could tell, looking at Tracey, that she was unsure if she wanted him to go with them or not. But what could she say? Stay in this dump while we desert you? Bill tried to smile reassuringly at her, but his face felt as if it was stuck in some bizarre sort of rictus.

It was then that Bill's sometimes dead, sometimes spaced-out junkie neighbour decided to burst out in a series of high-pitched, maniacal giggles that came through the wall as if it was no thicker than a sheet of paper.

Bill saw Tracey jump with alarm. Instinctively, she moved closer to her husband, who put an arm protectively over her shoulders.

Bill shrugged. "Par for the course in this sodding place."

Wayne grimaced. "I'll take your word for it, Bill."

But Bill's attempts at levity hardly mirrored his own anxiety. He could feel a subtle change in the atmosphere. Though far from warm earlier, the air felt icily cold. It had a chill that penetrated deep inside him. And he half expected to see the air before their faces mist whenever any of them spoke. With a suppressed shudder, Bill headed for the door. At the last second he felt an intense premonition of dread, even though he knew it was really no safer inside his flat. Whatever madness had taken a grip on this place was no weaker here, he was sure. With an instant's hesitation, he pulled the door open, perhaps harder than he had intentioned. The lights along the corridor flickered, as if ready to expire. Shadows juddered back and forth, especially at the far end, where the lights were weakest.

"Someone should have paid the electricity bill," Wayne muttered as he followed Bill. Hugging herself against the cold, Tracey stepped out close behind him.

As soon as he'd shut the door they headed towards the lift. Again Bill saw the door to his neighbour's apartment was open. Light from inside spilled out onto the corridor. The little man's ridiculous giggling sounded even louder now. And Bill hesitated at passing it, worried what he might see inside – and even more worried at how his neighbour would react if he saw them. But there were three of them now, and their numbers gave Bill a vague feeling of confidence. He looked at Wayne, whose frown seemed even darker now, then continued forwards.

Whatever he might have expected to see when he looked into his neighbour's flat, Bill was totally unprepared for the hunched-up, grey-faced creature crouched, open mouthed, beneath the dark window, giggling insanely. The junkie's face looked barely human. And Bill was sure, no matter how many drugs the man was on, that these could not account for the grotesque contortions on his face. His mouth was open far too wide for anyone whose jawbone hadn't been dislocated. Nor could drugs account for the jagged lines of teeth exposed between his lips like shards of broken pottery. While his outspread fingers looked impossibly long. And made Bill shudder as he recalled the claw-like hands that reached out for him last night.

Tracey could not restrain a squeal of fear when she looked in the room. The junkie's eyes peeled away from whatever dreams he had been gazing at to focus on her, red-rimmed and oily, with a look of decay.

Acting on instinct, Bill lunged into the room, grasped the door handle and, as the little man started to lurch forwards like some strange, ungainly beast, slammed the door in his face. There was a violent thud, then an infuriated scrabbling as sharp fingernails scratched at its panels.

"Keep going," Bill said. His voice was hoarse with tension. The scratching on the thin, wooden panels reminded him of those that had scared him last night. Which did nothing to lessen his feelings of dread, especially when he remembered talking to the man only hours ago.

David A. Riley

Must get out of here, Bill thought to himself. I must. *I must.*

Wayne jabbed at the button by the lift. But the indicator light above the door refused to respond and, even though it might have been working perfectly well a few minutes earlier when his friends got here, Bill knew the lift wouldn't come for them now.

"It's useless," he said. "We'll have to use the stairs."

Tracey stared towards the stairwell with a look of disgust. Even here they could smell it. And to Bill it seemed much worse than he remembered. Something new had been added to its usual odour of stale urine. A sour, coppery kind of smell. Like blood, he realised, as he remembered the massive pool he saw last night only a few floors below. He had begun to hope that that had been part of some bizarre hallucination, a drink-induced madness that didn't exist outside his mind. Unless, he realised, all of what was happening now was a part of that madness. That he was trapped inside it.

He felt sick and empty at the thought.

"We've no choice, have we? We'll have to use those fucking stairs," Wayne said. "Come on, love," he added to his wife. He gave her a reassuring hug, then headed for the stairwell. Bill wanted to warn them to take care, but Wayne was in too much of a hurry, taking the stairs two steps at a time. Tracey struggled to keep pace in her high-heeled boots and had to grasp the banister rail for support.

Bill trailed increasingly further behind them. His legs were still too stiff to attempt to keep up with his friends. Nor did he have the stamina now. It was not long before their footfalls began to fade into the distance as they disappeared into the depths of the building. And once more Bill felt as if he was alone in this place.

When Tracey screamed a few minutes later, he was not surprised. He had been dreading and fearing and expecting it. This place had far from finished with them yet. It would take more than a headlong dash down the stairs to get out of here.

Almost at once he heard Wayne shout something in anger,

285

but even with all the floors in between Bill could hear the fear in it too.

"God, no," Bill mumbled. He tried to run faster, though he knew that whatever was happening he would be too late to do anything about it.

Tracey screamed out again. This time Bill was certain it was the scream he had heard last night. Its pitch, its fear, its disgust, its horror were unmistakeable.

Deja *fucking* vu, he thought, trembling with fear. He didn't want to go down there. He knew that he couldn't stop whatever was happening to his friends. That all he could do was get himself killed as well.

Or worse.

Trembling, he stood in the stairwell, unable to make himself go any further. Next to him on the dirty concrete wall was the blasphemous painting of the upside down crucifixion he saw last night, with its stylised flames. A Christ dragged down into the depths of Hell. A fitting touch of spay-painted artwork for this place.

Impotent with fear, Bill could only listen to Tracey's screams and Wayne's increasingly more frantic shouts. Tears in his eyes, he gazed desperately along the wall to where there was another painting. This showed a bizarre version of the Last Supper, surrounded by a circle of ugly, squat-bodied dogs. All of the people in it wore modern day clothes. And each had huge, vertical cuts the length of their forearms, as if they had sliced themselves open to commit suicide. Blood spurted across an oblong banquet table. At the head of it, his arms cut like the rest, was the thirteenth figure, standing in a mimicry of Christ. His long, pale, staring face looked so much like that of the caretaker. He remembered what he'd been told about a suicide cult that established itself in one of these blocks. A cult that ended in a dozen deaths. Was this someone's crude depiction of what happened there? And had the caretaker somehow been involved in it?

A sound further up the stairs made him spin round in alarm.

286

The junkie was stood, looking down at him from the next bend in the stairs. The little man's face had reverted back to a semblance of normality. He looked concerned. And frightened.

"Go down there and he'll get you," he said in not much more than a whisper.

"Who will?"

"You know who. He runs this building."

"Chambers?" That was the name, Bill remembered now. The cultist who'd persuaded those others who had joined his group to end their lives.

The junkie snickered nervously. "Don't say it too loud. He'll hear you."

"Will you help save my friends?" Bill asked.

"And get both of us killed?"

Bill felt tempted to tell him he was almost certainly dead already, even if he didn't realise it. He remembered the desiccated face he'd seen in the junkie's flat last night, the little man's skeletal shell of a body curled up on the floor like a badly preserved Egyptian mummy.

"What would you suggest we did?" Bill asked. "I don't want to stay here."

"Do you think you have a choice anymore? It's *his* place now. *He* decides who goes or stays."

"But why? And how?"

The little man merely shook his head.

"I'm going back to my rooms. It's safer there." He paused as the screams and shouts from down the stairwell suddenly ceased. "There's not much time. You can come back with me. Or stay and face whatever's down there on your own."

Bill glanced into the gloom below. He felt sick at the silence. He felt sicker still when he realised that the silence was far from absolute. That he could hear something being dragged. And the *chunk-chunk, chunk-chunk* of a knife being stabbed into meat. Slowly, mechanically, on and on …

But it was the sound of footsteps coming up the stairs that jerked Bill into making a decision.

Hastily, he followed the junkie up the next few flights of stairs, the aches in his legs all but forgotten in his urgency to get away from whatever he could hear below.

As soon as they arrived back at the little man's flat, the junkie quickly locked the door, then offered Bill a seat on the sofa before going over to start rummaging furiously through some old newspapers scattered by the kitchen door. He brought one over. It was a tattered, year old copy of *The Edgebottom Evening Chronicle*. The headline read:

*Suicide Cult Claims 13 Lives*

Bill scanned the article beneath.

*"Moorend House at the troubled Queens Park Flats was cordoned off by police today after the discovery of thirteen bodies locked inside one of its apartments. A spokesman for the police refused to confirm reports that all of the deceased had cuts on their arms or whether the deaths are believed to have been the result of a mass suicide pact. There have been allegations that most of the dead were members of a religious cult founded by local businessman and entrepreneur Conrad Chambers. Chambers held a series of controversial meetings in Edgebottom earlier this year, which were condemned by most church leaders in the area because of the unorthodox beliefs expressed at them. All of the remaining residents in Moorend House have been rehoused elsewhere while police carry out their investigations."*

"That was here," the little man said.

"It says Moorend House." Bill said. "But I thought—"

"You thought wrong. Whoever sent you here had a vindictive sense of humour. Only dossers like me would choose to come here. And only then because we didn't know any better."

"But the caretaker?"

"Was Chambers. Hadn't you guessed that already?"

"Where you here when all that happened?" Bill asked.

The little man shrugged. It was a very Gallic shrug, though he probably didn't realise it. "I came here after the building was closed. I didn't realise what had happened. I don't come from around here. I didn't know any better. Otherwise I'd have never dared. That was months ago. I think. With all the shit I take I can't hardly remember most of the time. Time gets fuzzy. A few weeks. A few months. A few years. I don't fuckin' know."

Bill guessed that his uncertainty worried him. As well it should, Bill thought. Especially if anything of what he'd seen in this place was true. He still hoped much of it was just imagination. If it were, he wouldn't need to feel guilty about deserting his friends. Though he knew there was nothing he could have done, that if Wayne couldn't handle whatever was down there he would have been even more useless, this didn't help Bill feel any better about himself. After all, he thought remorsefully, they had come here to help him. And all he had done was turn tail and run as soon as things went wrong.

"What did Chambers hope to gain?" Bill asked.

Again the little man shrugged. "Perhaps he had no choice. Perhaps something already here made him. Used him. Like it's using us. Perhaps it's these fuckin' flats."

Bill stared at the junkie worriedly. Was he about to change again? Become that gibbering, grotesque creature that had bounded across this room only minutes ago?

"Don't you want to escape?" Bill asked, hoping to keep the man's mind concentrated. To stop him from becoming something else.

"Escape?" The little man laughed bitterly. "There's only one way to escape – and that doesn't work, not all of the time, believe me." He turned his head towards the small tin box by the window.

A sudden scratching at the door made both of them jolt.

The junkie struck a nicotine-stained finger to his lips. But Bill had no intention of making a sound anyway.

He heard Tracey's voice.

"Bill, let me in. *Please let me in.* I need help."

"Don't do it!" the junkie whispered urgently, a look of terror on his face. He reached out, grasped Bill's arm and added: "It's not her."

Bill irritably tugged his arm from the junkie's fingers. He half rose, undecided. He knew that it probably wasn't Tracey.

*He knew this.* After all that had happened he had learnt better than to take anything at face value here. The transformations of the man he was with had taught him that. He wasn't stupid. But the voice was so distinctively Tracey's. And she needed his help. Help which he couldn't keep holding back from her. Not after how he had deserted her and Wayne in the stairwell.

Bill backed away from the junkie, ignored his urgent hand signals to sit down again, and moved towards the door, half tempted to open it, despite what he feared to see outside.

He heard Tracey sob. She banged at the door. Urgently. Pleadingly.

"Bill, please help me. *Please!*"

Unable to ignore Tracey's pleas any longer, Bill grabbed the door handle. He sobbed in fear as he reached for the Yale lock and turned it. The junkie made a last minute attempt to pull him away, but Bill managed to shrug him off, then whipped the door open. Tracey fell onto him. Blood covered her clothes, and she looked as if she had been cut or ripped about the arms and shoulders. Her hands were drenched with so much blood it dripped from her fingertips.

"They've killed him," she stuttered as she clung on to Bill. "They tore him to pieces."

"Who did?" Bill felt his arms and legs start to shake again and he had an overwhelming need for alcohol. He could almost taste whisky on the tip of his tongue. "Who killed him, Tracey?" He pulled her into the room, then kicked the door shut behind him. The junkie hurriedly locked it again while Bill half carried, half guided Tracey to the settee. Trails of blood stained the floor behind her. And Bill knew she needed to be taken to hospital as soon as possible. Her face looked wretched. Stained with a mixture of tears and blood, her eyes stared into his with a look of hysteria and blind panic.

"There were dogs. Wild dogs. Horrible, ugly pit bulls, Bill. But worse. Much worse."

"Pit bulls?"

"I've seen them," the little man interjected. "They roam here sometimes. In packs," he added, with a shudder. "Nearly caught me once, the bastards did."

"Who owns them?"

The junkie laughed harshly. "If anything their owners are even worse. You must have seen 'em. Sometimes they look normal. Other times they look like they ought to be buried."

"There are a few people like that here," Bill said pointedly, though the junkie didn't seem to notice.

Bill returned to the door. He pressed one ear to it, though his heartbeats were pounding so loudly it was almost impossible to tell if anyone was moving out there. Even so, however frightened he might be, he knew they couldn't remain in the junkie's flat. It might offer them some sort of protection now, but it was no better than a prison. They had to be able to get out of here and out of the flats and back to the real world, he knew, at the same time wishing he had thought to bring a bottle of whisky with him. Or anything that would help to numb his fear.

"What are you going to do?" the junkie asked.

Bill looked at him.

"Have you any knives in your kitchen?"

"Knives?"

"You heard me. Knives. A hammer. Anything that could be used as a weapon. To defend ourselves with."

"I've nothing like that. All I've got is what you see in this room."

Bill gritted his teeth in exasperation. What else should he have expected from the pathetic little drug addict? He looked again at Tracey. She had begun to slump on the settee. The pools of blood beneath it were still growing, and he knew that she needed help as soon as possible if she was going to pull through. Her wounds looked bad, and her face looked even paler now.

Bill returned to the door. If only he knew what was out there. Even though he couldn't see anything through the spyhole, this meant nothing. Its area of visibility was too small. And he knew there could be anything beyond it. Anything at all.

"Don't," the junkie warned, but his voice held little hope that he could dissuade Bill, who had already, suddenly made up his mind. If he didn't act now his doubts and fears would build up again.

Bill grasped the door handle and suddenly turned it.

He stepped out onto the corridor so quickly the whole thing felt totally unreal. The door was violently tugged from his grasp and slammed behind him by the junkie, who just as quickly fastened its locks.

Bill's breath came rapidly as he stood on the corridor, relieved to see that it was empty, despite the sounds of movement from the stairwell. Ignoring these, he hurried to his flat. As soon as he was safely inside, he went to the kitchen where he gathered together a handful of the largest knives he could find amongst the odds and ends of cutlery he had brought with him. At least with something to defend himself with he could make an attempt at getting Tracey out of this place.

What else was there?

His eyes lit on a nearly full bottle of whisky laid on the floor by his bed. He had forgotten about it, though he knew he had reserves like this scattered all about his flat. He took a long, much needed swallow from it, then put the bottle in one of the pockets of his coat, along with most of the knives. He kept one of them, an old, well-sharpened carving knife, in his hand. Ten inches long, its blade was reassuringly heavy.

Bill returned to the corridor. There were still sounds of movement at the far end through the doors to the stairwell, where the lights flickered as if the electrical wiring was coming loose.

"Let me in," Bill whispered urgently as he knocked on the junkie's door.

There was no response. After a minute, Bill knocked again, louder this time.

"Hurry up, for God's sake!"

Still getting no answer, he tried the handle. And was surprised to find that the door wasn't even locked anymore.

Nervously, he stepped inside. The room was darker now, lit only by the moon. Even in the gloom he could see that Tracey was no longer sat on the settee. Instead, curled up on the carpet beneath the window, lay the junkie's corpse. His dried up face stared sightlessly at him.

Bill backed away from him. The room reeked overpoweringly of death and decay, of mustiness and drugs.

Bill choked back a whimper. How much of all this was real anymore?

His back to the edge of the door, he looked again down the corridor. He had to get out of here. He had no choice.

"But you have."

Bill froze. He recognised the voice, though he had only heard it once before.

He looked towards his flat. Stood in the same shapeless suit he was wearing before, the caretaker looked larger, more imposing than in the lobby. Bill disliked the bland intensity of his eyes.

"I want to leave here," Bill said.

"Of course you do."

Bill's hand tightened about the wooden hilt of the knife.

The caretaker's eyes glanced fleetingly at it, and Bill was sure there was a glimmer of something that might have been either amusement or contempt.

Or both.

Bill turned. He ran down the corridor to the doors at the end, slamming them open with the palms of his hands. One of the wall lights crackled loudly and there was a smell of burnt metal as it flickered, then died, making the area even gloomier than before. The lift doors were open. Inside stood the blank-faced man he'd seen before. Like before, a dark liquid trickled across the floor from about his trainers as he stared at Bill with eyes the colour of rotten eggs. Bill considered the knife in his hand, but somehow it no longer seemed adequate. He contemplated going in the lift with the man, but he knew there was no way he could make himself do that. Instead, he ran towards the stairwell. So far it looked empty. But there were too many sounds of movement below for him to have any illusions about it being empty for long.

The aches in his legs forgotten now, he ran down the stairs with more speed than he'd used in years. He knew this was something he could not sustain. Already his dizziness was getting worse and it was only the momentum of his descent that was keeping him on his feet most of the time. At each turn he had to cling onto the banister rail to stop himself from falling. With the knife in one hand, this was trickier each time he did it, especially when sweat made his palms slippery.

Four flights down and he saw the carnage.

Was this where Wayne had been attacked?

*If, he added to himself, his friend and Tracey had ever even come to this place.*

Panting heavily, he stared at the bloodied shreds of material scattered across the landing. It looked as if someone had not only been mauled by dogs but almost literally torn to pieces. Some of the piles of rags looked as if there might even be lumps of flesh hidden inside them.

Gagging with disgust, Bill hurried on past. The closer he got to the ground floor he knew there would be more chance to escape. There were still at least six more flights to go. Too many, he knew, to relax.

Tracey's voice halted him.

She was stood on the landing by the torn clothing. Leant against one wall, her own clothes were just as drenched in blood as when he last saw her.

"Where have you been? How did you get here?" He retraced the half dozen steps he'd taken.

"He won't let you go," Tracey said. "He wants you. The whole place wants you."

With a feeling of nausea, Bill knew that she couldn't be real. That she had never even been here today. Neither she nor Wayne. It had all been a trick.

Bill turned away from her and, ignoring whatever she called out to him, raced downstairs with even greater determination.

He started to count each floor he passed. But by the time he'd reached what should have been the ground floor, he was disturbed

David A. Riley

to see that it blatantly wasn't, that there were still more flights of stairs ahead of him. Could he have miscounted? That would have been easy enough given the circumstances. But, after two more flights and still no sign of the lobby, he knew there was something wrong. What windows he passed showed pitch-black emptiness outside, with no indication of how high he was. After two more floors, he knew he should have reached ground level. Yet still the stairwell continued downwards.

He looked up the stairs. There was someone there, just out of sight. Bill tightened his grip on the knife, though his legs felt weak from all the running he'd done. He reached one hand inside his coat for the bottle of whisky. Unscrewing its lid between his teeth, he spat it out onto the floor, then took a long, hard swallow.

He'd needed that.

He'd been too sober too long, he knew.

And, with a sigh, he took a longer drink.

"You are welcome here."

Conrad Chambers stepped into view. He whistled softly and Bill heard a mad scampering of feet from further down the stairwell.

Dogs' feet, he realised.

Bill listened to them with horror, then held the bottle above his head. Its contents spilled over him, drenching his hair. There had still been nearly two thirds of a litre in the bottle. It dripped down his coat, filling his nostrils with its heady smell of alcohol. He licked his lips.

Saving a large, last portion, he tipped the bottle to his mouth. He'd need it. He would need it more than he had ever needed it in his life.

"You are being foolish," Chambers said.

Bill looked away from him down the stairwell. He could hear them louder. Only seconds later the first of the ugly, deformed brutes looked round the bend in the stairwell at him, its overbite dripping strings of saliva.

His hands shaking, Bill felt inside his coat for his cigarette lighter. What he was going to do terrified him, but it was better than what he knew would happen if he did nothing.

He held the lighter for a moment before his whisky-drenched face as the dog pack started to climb towards him. Powered by button cell batteries, the lighter was exceptionally reliable. It had never failed yet.

But it failed him now.

Three times he tried it. Even a last minute frantic fourth attempt failed to solicit even so much as a spark from the thing.

Bill stared in panic as the grotesque pit bulls edged towards him. He heard Chambers' laugh of mockery. Then watched in horror as the pack surged forwards.

For a moment Bill tried to ward them off with the knife, but there were far too many. They overwhelmed him. Nor were they bothered by the wounds he was able to inflict on them. Almost instantly his wrist was seized between a pair of powerful jaws that remorselessly ground, then broke his bones between razor-sharp fangs and jagged molars the size of oysters. His flesh was shredded into tatters between them. Screaming in agony as the rest of the dog pack ripped and tore and bit at him, Bill tried to fight back. But it was a useless one-sided battle. Blood and flesh, cloth and bones, even the leather from his shoes were ripped and strewn about the stairs as he tried to scramble free. Half blinded by blood, Bill somehow managed to reach the landing, where he had wild hopes of escape through the doors into the corridor, but the powerfully muscled dogs relentlessly dragged him back to the floor. He felt helpless beneath their wild ferocity. A huge, black-faced brute, with pointed, chewed-up ears, transfixed its teeth into his shoulder. It shook him from side to side as if it was trying to rip the flesh from his bones. When he attempted to push himself to his feet, his hands, already missing several fingers, slipped on his blood, and he skidded beneath the dogs, which renewed their attack with even more vigour.

The pain and terror seemed to go on for hours when he finally heard the caretaker's high-pitched whistle. Growling deep inside their massive chests, the dogs reluctantly drew back from Bill, some of them chewing on scraps of flesh still gripped between their teeth.

David A. Riley

Through a haze Bill looked up from the ground as Chambers reached down for him. His grey, pulpy, dead man's fingers grasped hold of Bill's collar, and he felt himself being dragged along the floor towards the doors into the corridor. Neon lights flickered noisily overhead with sharp hisses and pops as he was hauled between them.

When he saw the knife in the caretaker's hand Bill knew that his ghastly visions were coming true. Unable to restrain himself, he shrieked for help. But his shouts and screams reverberated along the corridor, echoing and dimming through the endless depths of the stairwell unheard. Chambers, his body monstrously huge and all but shapeless in the growing darkness, loomed above Bill, the carving knife raised high above his head.

For the first few blows that rained down on him Bill's screams continued.

But not for long. And in their place came the *chunk-chunk, chunk-chunk* of a blade hitting meat.

On and on and on...

*

Twelve months later explosives were laid about the foundations of Moorend House. After years of scandal and endless debates in the council chambers, one of the area's last bastions of Sixties' architecture was about to be demolished. Notorious for years as a haven for drug dealers and addicts, suicides and murders, and more atrocities than most of the rest of Edgebottom had seen in over a century, there were few who would mourn its passing.

Larger crowds than expected had gathered for the spectacle, including newsmen and crews from most of the major broadcasters. There was even a well-known anchorman from BBC North West.

Feeling almost lowly amongst such exalted company as a mere photographer from *The Chronicle*, Paddy O'Shea panned the high-powered telescopic lens of his camera across the tower block. He whistled to himself contentedly, knowing that he was

297

going to get some genuinely dramatic, prize-winning shots today. For once the weather was absolutely bloody perfect. Just the right amount of light and shade, with loads of nice, artistic contrasts. Topping this, he had one of the best positions to view the event from, well above most of the others, on the slopes near the park.

Paddy smiled to himself as he concentrated on zeroing in for a few close ups of the building before it was destroyed.

Which was when something odd caught his eye.

"Two minutes to go," Des Chapel, the reporter who'd been sent to accompanying him, whispered unnecessarily in his ear as a siren began to sound its warning. And, although Paddy should have been readying himself now for a shot of the demolition, his fingers remained still. Almost mesmerised with incredulity, the photographer could not believe what he saw through the lens. Despite the dazzling bursts of sunlight that reflected off some of the windows he was sure there was someone inside the building. This was impossible, he knew. Or should have been. The police were supposed to have searched the flats to make sure they were empty, then sealed them up. Besides, no one in their right mind would want to sneak in there, not when it was about to be reduced to rubble.

Incredulous, Paddy tried to focus more clearly on the tenth floor windows. He could have sworn a thin-faced man with hollow eyes had looked out of one of them. Even more incredibly, there was another man too, he was sure. One window along. Plumper. Taller. Staring with a mournful, frightened expression on his face.

Finally convinced it was not just a trick of the light, Paddy started to shout a warning when the explosions began. Immediately the tall tower block gave a massive, almost slow-motion shrug, as if the whole monolithic building had turned in those instants into an ancient, weatherworn giant. Panic-stricken, birds took to the air in flocks all around the area, while a cloying mixture of brick dust, plaster and shattered concrete erupted across the slopes as the building began its collapse.

Paddy barely noticed any of this. Engrossed, he made his camera follow the window he was watching as it slid with increasing, devastating speed towards the earth, till it finally disappeared amongst the dust and debris that swelled to meet it, unable to take his eye off the face behind it.

Only after he had developed the last few pictures he snapped that day did he realise where he had seen the man before.

Bill Whitley had been on his way out of court two years ago, disgraced and jobless, having been found guilty of assaulting one of his pupils at the school he'd been teaching at. Paddy's photograph had dominated the front page of *The Chronicle* the following day.

How the hell did you end up there, Paddy wondered as he stared at the pictures he'd taken, *how the hell did you end up there?*